Let the story continue...

First published 2021

This book contains sexually explicit scenes and is not suitable for anyone under the age of 18 and may not be suitable for all adult readers.

Published under licence by Brown Dog Books and
The Self-Publishing Partnership Ltd, 10b Greenway Farm, Bath Rd,
Wick, nr. Bath BS30 5RL

www.selfpublishingpartnership.co.uk

ISBN printed book: 978-1-83952-380-9
ISBN e-book: 978-1-83952-381-6

Cover design by Kevin Rylands
Internal design by Andrew Easton

Printed and bound in the UK

This book is printed on FSC certified paper

FSC
www.fsc.org
MIX
Paper from responsible sources
FSC® C013604

Natalie
Enjoy :)
Nov 22

Let the story continue...

R DONALDSON

BROWN
DOG
BOOKS

This book is dedicated to my long-suffering husband,
'Mr International Man'
My best friend.

(For the record, get no ideas my love, it's fiction!)

My thanks go to Jo for giving me the self-belief
that I can do this.

Following *'Let the story begin'* we pick up with the whirlwind romance of Lottie Dean and her new husband Edward as they start their married life.

They continue to battle with emotional situations and demons from the past which have not yet been laid to rest. They suffer the stress and consequences of being strong willed professionals in a modern world. People can change the things they want, their desires and needs, their hopes, and their futures. Can money buy them everything for a perfect life and at times can they afford the cost?

'Let the story continue ...'

Chapter 1

The time went by so fast following their wedding that the winter was soon well under way. Christmas had been their first together and the first as a married couple. Their lives snowballed so fast that no sooner had they met, but they were engaged and married. Some may say this was all too fast.

For the first time Ed had asked that a staff Christmas party be organised for all the London-based employees, not just his own office, and more unusually it was to include their children and families too.

The fortnight before Christmas on the Sunday afternoon, the whole ground floor was booked at the Grosvenor with the ballroom hosting the main event including clowns, games, magicians, and a disco, all of which were aimed at entertaining the children, while their parents took advantage of the free bar. Father Christmas had a present for every little person as they left. Many people remarked on how Ed had laughed and smiled and tried to make it round to all the groups and all the tables, most of whom he had no idea who they were, what they did or what part of his company they worked for.

Many of his staff had only come to see what he looked like, as they had never met him face to face. Most of them could not believe that this was the same badass employer who many would never have approached even if they had been given the chance. They looked and admired him as he showed off his new wife, never leaving her side or even letting her walk without being touched or some form of personal contact made in some way. The whole event made the paper columns the next day and was almost viral on several twitter feeds as it happened live.

In a repeat performance a week later, the Saturday before Christmas, Lottie and Ed hosted a Christmas party for their own friends, families, and those of the many charities they supported. A slightly more formal occasion in dress, but the theme was for the children, nevertheless. Father Christmas did have gifts for the parents, but they had to bid for them in aid of the charities; it was a fundraiser, after all.

Lottie had been delighted to see Agnes and her family. Bella and her husband had also been invited. Sarah and Bob had arrived with their children. Scotty came along later after the bar had closed. Lottie found it hard to look at him without wanting to say something about the Tap and Tune, but a look from Ed was all she needed to keep this little bit of the truth from him once more. Todd had returned from America for Christmas but was due to return in the New Year for another month. Then he was coming back to the UK, but whether this was for good, he was still undecided.

Gramps had been overcome with joy when Father Christmas handed him a pre-arranged gift. It was a large canvas print of his whole family at race day, with a proud Simon sat on Gramps's knee behind the wheel of a fast, shiny red sports car. A smaller photo in a silver frame shaped like a racing car was given to Simon for his room. As the boy ran at Ed and hugged his legs, several of the guests stood in awe of the response of the CEO who picked him up and spun him round, laughing and tickling him before he was placed back on his feet, dizzy and wobbling.

'I'm not sure what has ever got into Edward, Mrs Dean, but I hope that you are taking some credit for this. He is the happiest we have ever seen him,' Mrs Barbara Taylor-John, one of the wealthy benefactors of Dean Charities, commented as they looked on. 'Edward had always been most kind-hearted with his money, but we have never seen such personal joy my dear.' The middle-aged woman was well-dressed and shone with diamonds and pearls, that for sure were the real thing. She smiled at Lottie, patting the back of her hand.

Lottie smiled at the group that they were both standing with. They were all fixed on her for a reply. She was not sure what to say and went a little red at the comment.

She had chosen a full-length, figure-hugging dark grey silk dress, with a heart-shaped neckline and full-length sleeve, instantly recognised by Bella as 'one of hers' when she had arrived. The single diamond choker at her neck, small stud earnings and her wedding jewellery were all that accompanied the ensemble. The cut of the dress had reassured those speculating on the need for them to marry as quickly as they had on the desert island a few months before; it was just that – speculation. The tone of which was noted in a tabloid newspaper report from the week before, this put aside by Lottie when she'd read it. Ed had been fuming, wanting to call the paper and sue, but Lottie had asked that nothing was said or done and to let it blow over.

Of course, she'd not forgotten what had happened to them both in the weeks after the wedding, but they had chatted about it more and both agreed that they had to try to move on.

Edward walked to his wife and put his hand around her shoulder. They smiled in unison at each other.

'Edward we were just talking about you,' Mrs Taylor-John remarked. 'You look remarkably at ease here, it is so good to see such a wonderful family event.'

'Christmas should be about giving, but also being with family,' he replied. 'On that note do you mind if I steal my wife, my mother has something to show her?' he asked, looking at Lottie who looked back at him, confused. She had spoken to his mother several times during the day and was not sure what she could want.

'What have I done?' Lottie asked as they started to move away from the group.

'Nothing, I just wanted to get you alone, Mrs Dean, it seems to have been ages.' He stopped and kissed her. She responded as the smell of his aftershave stimulated her senses. The strength of his arms and upper body embraced her and she felt him take her, gently brushing his tongue along her teeth. As he left her with her eyes still closed, he continued talking, 'Ages since I did that!'

'All of about half an hour.' Lottie smiled, still encased in the power of his arms, looking playfully at her watch.

'Too long!' he said, assaulting her lips again with his.

'Please you two, get a room!' Bob said as he walked past them to go to the bathroom. The spot they had stopped in was far from private, and they had turned more than just one head as they'd kissed. They both giggled like children who had been caught snogging for the first time.

'One is booked!' Ed smiled and raised his eyebrows at her in a suggestive way when Bob was out of earshot.

'No? Really?' Lottie said looking at him.

He did look totally hot in his black tie and white shirt, tight along his shoulders and chest line. She could see herself removing it at some point tonight and being able to kiss along the muscle line that lay beneath.

'Yes!' he whispered in her ear as he kissed her neck along the shiny diamond choker. 'Really.'

She lovingly slapped his shoulder and pushed him playfully back. 'You are incorrigible Mr Dean!'

He laughed. 'Well to be truthful, there are four rooms booked – there was last week too.' He paused, and Lottie waited for the rest of the reply. 'We thought that if any of the younger children needed changing, feeding or to sleep the nannies would have somewhere to go, and the parents could stay longer, but I'm sure if we wanted too,' he pulled her closer again, 'we could find an empty one!'

She giggled into his chest, thinking how sweet it was that he had thought of everything. Then she blushed, knowing what he was really thinking. She felt the warm glow between her legs at the thought of Edward's skin on hers. She took in a deep breath.

'Mr Dean?' Zoe interrupted them. 'I'm sorry, Mrs Dean. Lord Bennington is about to leave, I thought you would want to know?'

'Thank you, Zoe.' Ed smiled at her as she turned away to give them a little privacy. Lottie was not sure why; Zoe had seen them so often in this position at work Lottie was long over being embarrassed at her age.

'After you.' He held his hand out in front of Lottie and she started to walk off. He gently slapped her arse as she turned her back to him. She jumped back and shrieked out in shock. 'Laters, Mrs Dean!' he said and speeded up to catch her.

They found the party of people in question as they were putting on their coats. Lord Bennington had brought his son, daughter-in-law and his young grandson with him. His wife, Lady Bennington had passed away a few years before and he had been a very generous benefactor to Ed's charity ever since.

'Fantastic event, Dean. Real treat. Well done old boy. Here's a little something from Father Christmas.' He had a very well-spoken voice; deep and powerful. He put his hand in his pocket and handed an envelope to Ed.

'Maybe next year we will see you with an addition to your family?' He patted the small blond-haired boy lying in his father's arms, who was totally exhausted from running around all afternoon.

'Oh Pops!' the attractive young woman said, linking into his arm with hers once her coat was on. 'Give them a chance, they've only just got married.' She smiled at Lottie warmly.

'Man's got to protect his line of inheritance, hey, son?' He looked at his eldest, who seemed as embarrassed as his wife had. He just nodded as if not wanting to wake his own son in his arms.

'Lord Bennington, you are too kind.' Ed never opened the envelope, so was not aware of the amount that had just been pledged – he did not have to. It was never anything short of £50,000. He shook the older man's hand.

'Mrs Dean, it was an ultimate pleasure to meet you; this man is blessed by you, I hope you know that, Dean?' He looked at Lottie as he took her hand and kissed it gently. She smiled at him, his words still ringing in her ears.

Ed walked him to the door and Lottie watched as they went.

It was the first time in a while that she had thought about the miscarriage, and Bennington would have been right. Ed could have been organising this next year for his new family. Then she thought, is that why he has done this event in such a family way?

He walked back to her, asking if she was OK. She nodded and tried to skim over the conversation by saying she wanted to get a drink.

He never raised anything about the comments that had been made, but he could not help but think of them.

All the way home in the car, and as she lay awake that night after they had made love, she went over the tense conversation in her head. Was he trying to show what she could have, how her life could continue if she agreed to try for a baby again?

It had been three weeks after her miscarriage when they had both relaxed, sharing a bath back in Kent over a bottle of wine. Ed had finally opened up about his feelings and that he had not really thought about children before, but after what had happened he had taken to the idea more and more as time went on.

The conversation had revealed quite a change of heart for him, as the more he thought about it the more he wanted it. The more he knew he would be able to share some of Lottie. However, Lottie had seemed to become more relieved that she was no longer pregnant. She tried not to show it, but the conversation and maybe the wine had brought it out.

'I know, Ed,' she had said as she listened to him admitting that he had never wanted to share her, but a baby – it was different. She'd said, 'But it gives me some time and year or two to get working again and put into action some of the things I want to do before I become burdened.'

It had been that word 'burdened' that had silenced him. The conversation that night had stopped, and it was never reopened by either of them. Was he trying to change her mind in other ways; the family parties, his change around children, trying to fit in, show how good he could be as a father?

It was this and all the events of the festive season that she had played over in her mind as she made her wish on New Year's Eve. They watched the clock of Big Ben strike midnight from the penthouse roof where they were stood. They had been out at a party, but Ed had asked to be back at home for the witching hour; he had never done it before.

'I wanted to do this, our first New Year to be just us. We never know where we will be, or what we'll be doing together after that,' he said before they went out.

With her coat and her husband's arms wrapped around her, champagne in hand, they stood there listening to the distant chimes of the old master bringing in a new year.

Lottie made her wish, just before the arms around her moved, and that all-familiar smell and taste of him descended down onto her wine-tasting rich lips.

Chapter 2

Lottie put down the phone and looked through the glass partition into the office next to her. Ed sat in his chair, deep in conversation with the man who had arrived about an hour ago. She had not seen him before, but she had been told that he was one of the partners in the company lawyers; if she needed to know what was going on, she knew Ed would tell her. It was something he was getting good at now. At the start of each week, they spent a short time going through their diaries, setting things out that they both needed to do, but more importantly setting aside time for them to spend together, not talking about work.

As with all meetings the glass wall was brought back across to allow privacy, sometimes a godsend (she hoped on both sides) so that they could get on with things. It seemed that whenever they were in the office together and the doors were opened to make one big space, they ended up distracting each other in one way or another. The other, usually being taken into the bedroom on Ed's side of the room for an hour – or three.

She smiled at this thought as she looked at the door leading to the room that housed a large bed, with black silk sheets and a mirrored ceiling. Although she had never been very adventurous in the bedroom, of late little games had been introduced and she was beginning to become more at ease with some of the less-vanilla sides of sex that she had been used to in the past. His preferences of the past had never been discussed, but she was now aware that he had been very dominating, and it seemed that this side, on occasion, was starting to come back out. They had even joked about safe words, a memory that haunted Lottie from one of their first meetings when she had blurted it out about riding on the back of his motorbike. But their discussions were becoming open and honest, and her modesty, even her prudish side, was beginning to ease. Not that she was going to take part in anything 'dodgy' as she had put it, but she was coming into her thirtieth year, with the man she loved and trusted so why not relax and enjoy him?

The light on her phone went again and she picked it up.

'Mrs Dean, Mr Carter on the line for you,' Zoe said. Lottie smiled; she had not heard from Todd for a few days, so it was a welcome surprise to hear his voice when she asked for him to be put through.

'Well, Mr Dean, I will come back with all the papers drawn up next week, can we say the same sort of time?' the man in his late forties said, standing up to shake Ed's hand.

'That'll be great,' he said, taking the gesture.

'And you are sure that you want me to start this off? It is a vast amount, and a great commitment on your side.' He gathered a few papers into his briefcase while asking the question.

'I am sure of it,' Ed replied, eyeing up his wife and noticing that she was laughing to whoever she was on the phone to. 'I will see you out and we can check appointments with my PA.' He could also ask her who was making Lottie laugh so much; that little green-eyed monster had not totally gone away yet.

Once the meeting was set, Ed asked, 'Who is Mrs Dean on the phone to?'

Zoe looked up at him. She was aware of his little failings; always checking, asking. 'Mr Todd Carter,' she said back without showing any type of expression. 'Do you want me to interrupt?'

'No, I'll be back in a moment. Could I have some coffee?' He paused

'Maybe you could interrupt to ask Mrs Dean as well if you wanted?' She knew that this was code for, 'I hope that she is still not on the phone when I get back from the little boy's room, I want her to myself!'

When he had gone, Zoe stood up and through the glass mimed a cup to Lottie who put up her thumbs. The women had really hit it off, and they had established some secret codes and understanding of each other in the past few months.

Ed had said it was not really the 'done thing' but Lottie and Zoe had often gone for a coffee to get out of the office. In a way he did not mind so much if Pete or Phil went with them, and he knew she was safe, or at least was with people he trusted.

Zoe put her coffee on her desk and Lottie mouthed 'thank you'. She was still on the phone.

Ed looked across, almost disappointed to see this as he came out of the bedroom after using the bathroom. Within a second of deciding he would go into her, his own phone rang and he took the call.

Lottie sipped her coffee; she had made some notes in her diary, and sat back in her chair feeling quite pleased with herself. She started to doodle on the pad on her desk. It had been good to speak to Todd; his news was great, and she now had to think of her own next move to make his request a reality.

She saw Ed was on the phone, so she stood up with her drink and walked to the window. The day outside was dark, wet and cold. It was trying to snow, but it was more of a wet mush that fell from the grey sky. Only to be expected for mid-January, she thought.

The glass door slid open and she turned around. Ed was walking towards her, his own mug in hand.

'How is your day?' He wanted to ask how Todd was and what he wanted, but that would show that he had asked who she was talking to – a bit blatant.

'Good, better than the weather out there.' She tried to keep her answer light. He put his mug on the table and hugged her from behind.

'I can keep you warm.' He kissed her neck also looking out towards the murky weather.

'I am sure you can, Mr Dean, but your 11:30 appointment is due in any moment, so no ideas of that, just yet!' She smiled, leaning her head back to take the warm feeling of him on her, and he kissed her forehead.

'Um, I like that answer – it has promise of negotiation for later.' He smiled at her and she turned to kiss him on the cheek.

'Do you get something in your coffee that I don't, to make you have a one-track mind, Mr Dean?' she asked with a straight face.

'No, it's just what you do to me in those short skirts and see-through blouses. I really have to object to them for work, very distracting I have to say.' He ran his finger down the front of her blouse. It was slightly see-through, but not too much and the skirt was normal-length.

'It's not short!' Lottie protested.

He whipped his hand down to her skirt and pulled it up by a good three inches. 'It is now!'

She quickly pulled it down. 'Edward!' she exclaimed, 'Behave, sit down and control yourself!' She smiled, taking her seat behind the desk.

'Yes, Miss!' he retorted as if he had been scalded by his schoolteacher. He shifted in his trousers as he adjusted to make the allowance for the growth that had developed in his cock from touching her, and still talking to her, he sat down.

'I've just been speaking to Todd.' She opened the conversation freely with the information and took another sip of her coffee. He did the same and replied. 'Oh right,' trying to sound surprised., 'How is he?'

'I guess you knew he was on his way back to the UK again?' she asked, as she was sure Dorothy or Cory would have called to tell him.

'I had a text to say he was leaving in the next few days, but I never replied. I thought he would contact you himself, so I never said anything.'

It was almost as if he was justifying himself but he had genuinely forgotten.

'Anyway, he has asked me to meet him tomorrow for lunch, do you fancy it?' She asked him to go although hoping he would say no – but the offer was there.

'I'm sure you two want to catch up.' He wanted to say yes, but he had to try to keep up his promise to himself to let her do her own thing. 'You can catch me up with the gossip when you get back.' He impressed himself by how casual he sounded about it. Six months ago, he would be a raging mess agreeing to have let her go, but his New Year's resolution was so far looking good.

'Would Phil mind driving me?' Lottie asked as a peace offering, knowing that it was not an option anyway, but an understanding that Ed really would only let her go with a member of staff anywhere, at any time made her feel better for asking that he did not force her to do it.

'Need you ask?' he said, getting up from the chair opposite her, knowing she had only said it to make him feel better, which he did appreciate. 'If you let me know when you are on your way home, I will make sure Mrs B has supper waiting.' He kissed her head, as he saw Zoe showing his next meeting into his office.

'We won't be that late,' she replied. 'Maybe you could join us for a drink after you have finished, and we can go home together? I'll ask Zoe to book us a table somewhere.' She held his leg lightly as he stood by her side momentarily.

'Really, Lottie, have an afternoon to catch up with him on your own. I want to hit the gym and that will make me feel less guilty for not being with you.' He smiled to himself. Well done Dean, make her feel special, show her you are not possessive and that you still can exist without her for more than an hour. As he shut the door his inner self soon kicked in and he replied in his head, *Who are you kidding, Sunshine, you will worry every second she is not within eyeshot! You are getting better at this, but not that good so let's not get too carried away now!*

Lottie asked Zoe for a table to be booked, and Phil did take her the next day. As soon as the car had pulled up, Ed knew where she was and that Todd was waiting for her as she arrived.

They hugged and kissed before they were shown to their table. They chatted about various things, and the afternoon passed quickly. They sat at the bar and finished the wine they'd had with their meal. It was not late as Lottie had promised when she arrived back at the apartment.

Mrs B was in the kitchen and Ed had showered and was in his study making a call. She put her head in the door and waved at him; he blew her a kiss and put his hand over the phone.

'Hi babe,' he said, 'two minutes then I'm all yours.' She nodded and made her way to the bedroom to change into more comfy clothes.

Supper was served on the breakfast bar and, as they ate, she felt it was the right time to bring up the subject that she and Todd had discussed at lunch.

'Todd asked me to thank you for letting him stay in New York,' was the opener for the conversation. Ed nodded as he continued to eat.

'They have offered him a permanent contract. He wanted time to think about it, so he may only be back for six months. The professor requested him back to the UK for now as they have a couple cases that he wanted to try the new equipment on.' She paused to eat. 'I agreed to go back to work on Monday for two days a week. I need to keep my hand in, and it has been so long.'

Ed stopped eating and looked up at her. He thought that with all the work she was doing she had lost the need to also fill her time with the forensic stuff. He had hoped that that chapter of her life had closed. He tried to hide his disappointment in his reply. 'You said yes without asking?' He knew that had come out wrong as soon as it left his lips, so he tried to correct himself. 'I mean, you don't need my permission, just, well, did you not want to discuss it first?'

Something in her clicked and she put her fork down. 'You're right. I don't need your permission, and we are discussing it now.' Her tone did not change, but she was very aware that he was not happy.

'You said yes, so it is a pretty final decision not to be negotiated.' He took another mouthful of food to try to defuse a situation he could see arising. It had been a similar conversation a few months back that had made her bolt out on him for a few days, and it was an all-too-stark reminder of how that ended up.

'Sorry, yes. You know that I wanted to go back at some point after...' She stopped herself. 'Well, you know. If I get used to it again then I can take over from him when he goes back to America for a year or so.'

Ed looked up at the last bit of information. 'A year or so. Are you signing a contract or something?'

'I would want to make it more of a permanent arrangement; it was only a verbal understanding last time.' She could see that he was not happy at all. 'I will still be able to do everything at the office – the projects and the charity work,' she added as a sweetener.

'I have no doubt you will be able to cope with the workload, but I am not sure that it is...' he stopped himself. He was being almost word-perfect from the last discussion this subject had raised. He did not want her to be exposed to the risk of something going wrong. 'Cards on the table, Lottie; take the information and do with it what you will, I am not here to argue. I don't want you to do it, I don't like the idea of it, what it could expose you to, but,' this bit pained him to say and he bit his tongue as he did, 'if you must, then all I ask is that you are still able to do what we want, take time out for us, and that what we have planned will not have to be put on hold because of that type of work.'

She digested the comments. Did she want him to clarify what he meant by 'what we have planned'? Did he mean days out, holidays, weekends in Kent, or having children, starting a family and becoming trapped?

'It'll be as we do now. I will make sure that you know everything, where I will be, what I am doing day-to-day, and as I said it is only two days a week for now.' She realised what she'd said as his expression changed again.

'Two days for now. Are the goal posts moving already, without negotiation?' His irritation was clear as he stood up and left his plate by the dishwasher and poured more wine in his glass from the bottle on the countertop.

She followed him, emptied the leftover food into the bin and opened the dishwasher and put the plates in. 'If we get involved in something, sometimes, I may need to give a case more time, and I need to firm up a contract for pay and set hours anyway.' She wiped down the top and set the dishwasher going.

'Are you doing it for the money?' he asked. 'Don't you have enough with all this?' He waved his hand around as if to show off the empire they lived in.

'No, it's not the money and it never has been since I left Uni– it's the love of the job and my independence.' She grabbed a bottle of water from the fridge.

'I can get the independence bit, but you are my wife and I provide for you. Having a real job makes it look to others that I don't,' he added.

'And is this where the conversation really lies? You don't like me working as it does your male ego no good?' she snapped back now. 'Can't a high-flying billionaire also have a brainy professional wife to be proud of? Maybe you should have chosen a thick blond, who was out for your money to play the little woman.'

The conversation was now manifesting onto a heated debate, a row almost. If he had put his glass down on the countertop any harder, the stem of the crystal would have smashed.

'Damn it, Lottie. I am not arguing with you.' It was a contradiction, because he raised his voice sounding like he was in an argument. 'You know I respect and adore you for your intellect. Nothing makes me prouder than to stand by your side. I just know that I can't keep you safe when you are not with me.'

She needed to defuse the situation, so she walked up to him and put her arms around his waist. 'I'm sorry.' Why she apologised she was not sure, but it was a good place to start. 'I want to do this, Ed. You know I do,' was all she said.

'I know you do, but it doesn't mean I have to be happy with it.' He ran his hand through his hair. 'I want to make that clear.' She nodded. 'And another thing.'

'Yes?'

'If I had wanted a gold-digging little woman, as you put it, I would have found one years ago!'

'I'm sure you would have had a queue to have chosen from,' she said with a hint of sarcasm in her voice, knowing it was the truth. 'But I'm glad that you didn't,' she added in as a saving comment. There was a pause, almost as if the air might have been clearing, but he came back with his retort.

'Really?' he said. 'Sometimes I wonder?' He said it in jest, but it provoked her reaction.

'Edward, don't ever question how much I love you.' She stood up straight, letting him go from her grip.

'I was just joking, Lottie. Christ, if you think that I question your love I would never have just signed everything I own over to you!' He realised that he had not told her this yet, so should not be shocked by her reply.

'You what?' she asked. 'You've done what?' She was amazed.

'My meeting yesterday was to draw up contracts to give you everything if...' he paused, wanting to finish off by saying 'if anything happens to me' but he continued, 'you have half-control of everything now, and anyone will need your casting vote to change any one of the companies I have and you can make decisions in my absence if need be. You will be a complete partner while I am alive.'

'Well, you kept that gem quiet! It is a bit hypocritical considering our conversation about making decisions without any discussion first!' She referred to the opening line of the night's first topic that had got them talking. She was not mad, just slightly confused how they had come onto this conversation.

'I know, I had made an appointment to discuss it with you next week when Harris comes back with the papers, and technically as my next of kin you have everything anyway. It's just without this, some corporate lawyer could rule against you, and I do not want that.' He realised this was a big thing that would need spelling out to her step-by-step to allow her to understand. God alone knows it had taken him weeks to get it all straight with Harris and the solicitors before he could even agree to the terms. He had businesses that he did not know even existed.

'You're not ill, are you?' she asked with a sudden fear. 'You're not thinking of dropping down dead on me?' She almost laughed but knew it was not funny.

'No,' he replied smiling at her, 'just protecting my future, although there have been times...' He put his arms around her and kissed her neck as if in total submission that any argument, for whatever reason, was not on the cards anymore. 'There have been times when my heart has been near to bursting.'

'Smooth reply, Mr Dean,' she said, closing her eyes and accepting she needed things to slow down in her head. 'Seriously have you thought about this?'

'Oh, I have thought about this all day!' He continued to kiss her.

'No Edward, not that. I really don't want everything you have worked for handed to me on a plate.' She tried to get him to be serious, but the only thing he was doing was turning her on.

'It's not handed to you on a plate; it's part of being my wife, part of me, and if you stop protesting, I'm about to give you the rest of me for free too!' He continued to kiss her neck, running his hands along her side, and cupping her breast in one hand.

'Please don't think that the distraction is the end of the conversation,' she whispered as her breath started to increase. The words were muted by his mouth covering hers and kissing her hard. She responded and brushed her tongue along his teeth. He pulled her closer to him and she could feel the increased arousal in his groin, straining against the fabric of his trousers.

She ran her hands along his shoulder-line, and up through his hair as their kiss became urgent and more intense. He unbuttoned the front of her blouse and she allowed it to fall to the floor, after it was released from her skirt. Her full breasts were encased in a pure white lace bra. Ed bent his head down and kissed the line from her neck to her cleavage, pushing her ripe mounds together, gently rubbing her nipples through the soft material. They responded and became erect.

'Um, I still like the virginal white.' He slid one of the straps down her arm and pushed her flesh out of the supporting cup. He sucked hard on her nipple and she gasped as the tingle sent a wave of pleasure to her inner sex. She had negotiated his shirt undone and was rubbing his firm chest with her hands, slipping her hand down to brush over his fly to arouse the swelling flesh of his dick beneath. With the bra removed and discarded on the floor, he changed his attention to the other nipple, which equally enjoyed the attention of his hot mouth and sharp teeth as he grazed and nibbled at it.

The closing of the staff room door was a reminder that Pete was still in the apartment and could come into the kitchen at any time. Ed grabbed Lottie round the waist, lifting her and carrying her to the bedroom. She wrapped her arms around him and allowed her naked chest to rub against his as he walked. She kissed his ear and neck while he negotiated the pathway to their room, and he increased his urgency to reach the private location.

With the door closed, he set her feet down on the floor and removed her skirt. While on his knees, he kissed the line of her white pants across the top from hip to hip, holding her with his strong hands on her arse to steady her. The pleasure made her close her eyes and she parted her legs slightly as she could feel the blood rushing to her inner lips, making them swell. He continued up her stomach and she tensed the muscles, pulling them in to show a slight definition, a testament to working out. Licking and kissing his way up he found her right nipple and sucked it harder than before; he handled the other and squeezed hard with his thumb and finger. Lottie caught her breath, totally engrossed in the pleasure he was giving her.

She had not struggled with his gold and leather belt that was holding his suit trousers up, getting it undone with ease due to practice, and she unbuttoned the fly and slid down the zip. Although he had been to the gym, he had put formal clothes back on instead of the usual joggers, so he had tight boxer shorts on as well. She rubbed her hand over his large erection, allowing the cotton of the Calvin Kline's to create some friction, and the muscle in his engorged dick twitched as a response. She used her fingers to push them down, allowing her nails to just graze his skin, increasing the pain threshold a little from her touch. She bent down in front of him until she was facing his member, pointing up so strong it was almost touching his stomach. She smiled at him as she looked up and took the tip in her mouth, lightly rubbing her tongue along his very end. He grabbed a handful of her hair and pushed his head back with his eyes closed. She licked the pre-cum off him and tasted the salty liquid and sweet shower gel that still lingered on his skin. Easing her mouth further over him she took him deeper into her mouth as she started to suck. He drew breath through his teeth again and picked up the rhythm with his hands, helping her head move backwards and forwards onto him.

She used one nail to trace the line of the skin from the base of his throbbing mass over his ball-sack to the edge of his arsehole, and back. She felt his knees shake on the third stroke and he pushed himself in her mouth, making her gag. She withdrew to catch her breath and stood up. Kissing him, she pushed him to the edge of the bed and he lay down, with her by his side, their mouths not resting, their hands making contact all the time. She straddled him.

'So, Mrs Dean, you want to be in charge, do you?' he asked, looking up at her as her hair covered her face, the lace of her pants being the only barrier between their lower bodies. He pushed his hand between them and eased the material back to one side, allowing just a brush of his finger into her sex lips. She was wet and sticky, and he couldn't resist the urge to rub her opening while his hand was in that location. She dropped down onto all fours and kissed his neck.

'Not in charge, Mr Dean, just have some control,' she whispered in answer to his question. He guided himself into her and used her hips to sit her slowly down onto him. She was always tight, due his size, but it only took a few gentle movements for her to accommodate him. She was wet with her own pleasure, which acted as the natural lubricant they required. She bit her lip, pushing back up on her hands, resting on his chest so that his full length filled her. She let out a sigh as he pushed up hard, observing her face which was awash with pleasure, slightly pink on the cheeks and with the gratifying smile he had grown so much to love.

'Stop the lip thing, Mrs Dean, I need to concentrate.' No matter how much he controlled himself, one way to get him to shoot his load was when she bit down on her lip. She did it again in provocation, giving him a smile as she licked her lips, raising her hands and rubbing them through her hair. Her breasts pulled up tight and she wriggled her hips in a circular motion. This increased the pressure on her sweet spot, but also slowed him down. Using his abdominal muscles, he pulled himself upright to meet her face to face. The change of position deepened him in her and she jumped at the pain as he hit the back of her cervix with his large swollen head.

'I can't give you too much control, Mrs Dean.' He pulled her up and in one movement had her on her back, with him on top. They remained linked at all times, and just to ensure he was still in place he pushed down, and she arched her back to allow her hips to tilt to take him. He pushed her leg up, holding her under her arse and she crossed one leg over his back, pulling him down onto her.

Running her hands down his back she could feel the gentle beads of sweat as he increased his pace. She linked her other leg around him, making the rubbing of her clit more intense, and she rocked her hips up and down against his rhythm to build her own pleasure.

'I'm guessing you're doing your own thing.' He picked up on her greedy actions to ensure that she took her pleasure, so he grabbed one of her arms and put it above her head. It had been a breakthrough some weeks ago when Lottie allowed him to hold her wrists down when they made love.

'Maybe I should find something to keep these held tight permanently?' He lifted her other wrist above her head so she was secure under him, now not able to demand her own rhythm. 'Would you like that?' he whispered in her ear, nibbling her neck. She groaned in acceptance. 'I don't mind you having some independence, but you need to be reminded who really is in control.' He thrust hard with the last word and she opened her eyes sharply.

She was driven by her desire; the mounting climax was starting to pulse in her inner muscles and his words held no true meaning for her at this time. Her brain was fixated on her orgasm.

'Oh Ed, please,' she begged, trying to move only half an inch as his rubbing on her outer sex flesh was not quite enough to make it happen. He knew he was holding her back – he was in control of her. He smiled at her desperate request.

'Is it just here?' He moved one hand between them and rubbed her sensitive spot with his thumb, as it so desperately needed more attention.

'Yes!' she pleaded as he pulled away his hand. 'Oh, Ed, please!'

The gesture had taken her one more step closer but not quite, and she bit down hard on her lip. He released her other wrist and instantly she gripped his backside to get closer to him. He had to kiss her, taste that bottom lip, so he sucked at it and grazed it in his teeth. He knew she was there as she bucked and raised her hips, riding the tide of the orgasm, and he slowed his pace to allow it to be a longer pleasure. She gasped to catch her own breath, and he felt her go weak underneath him. Her internal pulsing had almost set him off, but he resisted as much as he could, not wanting to take the moment away from her. She opened her eyes, looking into his. They were like blue oceans, his hair a rugged mess, sticking around his sweaty brow. He was looking back at her, still gently rocking his hardness in and out.

'Relaxed, Mrs Dean?' he asked.

'Yes, thank you.' She ran a hand though his hair to give a clear view of his face, and strong jaw line. He pushed back on her hand and kissed it as it passed his face. 'I love you,' she said. Her words made him twitch inside her and she felt him on the tender, still blood-swollen area of her sex.

He lent down on her and softly whispered in her ear his reply, 'I love you too, Mrs Dean, with everything I am, and everything I own.' He started to speed back up, pushing deep inside her, he sucked on her nipples and pulled back as the first thrust of his release left him. He dipped his head next to her face and continued to empty his life into her. 'Now, now you have all of me.' He slowly pumped until he was spent. She kissed his face, and once his breathing returned their mouths met with a tender kiss that closed the carnal proceedings.

Taking time to get their breath back, Lottie laid in his arms, facing away from him, but cocooned in his powerful frame. He had started the conversation back up again about her working. They stayed in this attitude as they negotiated when and how it could all work. He was not entirely happy, but he was content that she would do as he had asked and follow the restrictions he had set if she was sure she wanted to go back there.

She closed her eyes allowing sleep to take over her; no one had won, and they had reached a compromise. For now!

'So, he was OK with it?' Todd asked as she walked through the doors to their old office in the DuPont Centre on Monday morning. Phil had dropped her off, not much of a compromise stipulated by Ed as she had now got used to having him around all the time. Though time would tell how weird it would be that a forensic examiner turned up in a chauffeur-driven Audi A9 to a crime scene, which would happen sooner rather than later.

'We talked,' she replied with a grin on her face remembering the sex it had led to.

'I'm sure you did.' Todd may have read her mind and she blushed slightly at his reply. Settling in as if she had not left, she turned on the computer.

'Prof wants to see us, I'll get some coffee and we can go in,' Todd said. She nodded in reply as she looked at her new name badge waiting for her. Dr Leticia Dean. Security needed the old one back, so she put it in her draw to give to them later.

Firing up the computer, she logged on to her emails. There were hundreds in the inbox due to the time she had been away, and it would take hours to go through them. The last one was only five minutes ago so she opened it up.

Enjoy your first day back, Mrs Dean.

E Dean CEO Dean Incorporated and missing you sitting next door.

She quickly typed back as Todd put her coffee on the desk.

I will try, just to note that until I get security clearance my new mobile does not work in the lab, should be OK after today though.

Lx

Her prefixed external signature was still set up and so sent out her old name: Dr L Jenkins

Within a second her inbox binged again.

Not changing your name, Doctor?

E Dean CEO Dean Incorporated hoping your IT sorts that out soon or I will be pissed off!

She quickly typed back.

Give me a chance I have only just sat down with a coffee!

Dr L Dean, very much wife and lover of Mr E Dean ESQ (better!)

It came back with the *bing* that made Todd tut as he knew who she must have been emailing.

Much better

E Dean – husband to Dr L Dean (AKA Mrs Dean)

She jumped up before it had time to distract her again. 'Come on then, let's get going,' she said to Todd, heading out the door.

She had agreed to do two days a week, although these would not be fixed. She'd negotiated some pay but was not pushy over this aspect of the job. She had been quite insistent that she had to limit the amount of work she would do in other police forces, if it meant leaving site and staying out, but she said it could always be negotiated. Both the professor and Todd had raised an eyebrow at the fact Phil would need to be security cleared as he would be driving her anywhere in the working day and be positioned outside until he was needed, but this was non-negotiable.

She signed the terms and contract after lunch. She scanned it in and sent it to Ed, not looking for his agreement, but wanted to show him she had kept her word about how much time she would be putting into it. She and Todd set about the first case that had been handed them by the police and they were soon back to old ways of working together as if no time had passed at all.

Her email back from Ed took longer than she had thought it would.

Our lawyers are happy with this, you are underselling yourself for the pay, but I guess you know that.

Mr E Dean CEO Dean Incorporated and lonely in his office. Husband of Dr L Dean.

She smiled at his reply but was pleased he had not made any comment that he was not happy with the documents. By 5:30pm Lottie was glad to be heading back home, and without fail her phone rang to say Phil was waiting for her without a second to spare.

Over dinner she resisted talking too much about work, but it was Ed who started her off and then could not shut her up about her day. She slept with a smile on her face and a warm strong arm around her waist; she was content.

Through into February it seemed to continue to work, planning days in the centre, time with Ed, charity work etc., and a bit of shopping where required. She was happy.

She sat at her desk in Dean, Incorporated, watching her husband on a sunny but cold morning mid-February. It was interesting to watch his body language when his client was another female, and this one had caught Lottie's eye as she went in. She was stunningly attractive, a little younger than she was, perhaps. Long red hair, cascading on her shoulders with pale freckled skin. A figure to die for (which Lottie thought never took hours in the gym to archive like she had to) well-dressed and presented in an attractive, but professional way. From his diary she knew she was a representative from an American company US Dean International had just bought out, other than that she was not sure why she was visiting.

Ed sat pushed back in his chair, one leg crossed at the ankle, occasionally putting his hand through his hair. His killer smile was on display and a gentle laugh at given times. She could not make out what they were saying of course with the screen up, but she could tell by the way the young girl looked at Ed, and played with her hair that she was attracted to him. She lent forwards to give Ed some papers. He must have got an eyeful of cleavage then, Lottie thought, as she had noticed the young woman's top was quite low. Ed flicked his eyes up, and then away again. Yep, he did, she thought as he looked away, then glanced in Lottie's direction. She looked away fast as if not paying any attention.

He browsed the paperwork, and the young woman got up and walked round the desk, leaning over his shoulder and pointing to something. Lottie was not a jealous type, or so she had thought, but she felt slightly put out by the closeness of the woman, and the way that she interacted with Ed. He said something to her, and she laughed, putting her hand on his shoulder.

Lottie tried to look away, but it was bothering her. 'Get a grip,' she said aloud to herself. 'He's the jealous one, not you.' She picked up her phone to make a call back to the architect to take her mind off what was going on next door. During the conversation, Ed stood up and turned the privacy blinds in the glass, but he did not sit back at his desk. Lottie could usually see the outline of him even with the glass frosted out. She forgot all manner of the conversation that she was having and was glad to end the call. She got up and walked to the window trying to see if she could see them in the room, but she could not.

Her palms itched. She was winding herself up now, and the more she thought about it the more she hated herself for even thinking it. 'What's got into you?' she said as she walked out of her own office to Zoe.

'Oh, Mrs Dean.' The surprise in her voice took her instincts to suspicion straight away. I need to turn my detective investigation head off, Lottie thought, but sometimes you just know when something is not right.

'Mr Dean done?' she said, going towards his door.

'Oh no, Mrs Dean, it's still locked,' Zoe replied quite nervously.

'Locked? Really?' Lottie was surprised too; he did lock it when she was in there with him, and they were not talking business! However, he did not it when he had a client, more for his own security so Pete could get in if needed.

'I'll buzz him if you want?' Zoe said as if that was what had been asked of her.

'No, I'll wait,' she said going to the coffee pot and getting a cup, trying to act calm.

She went back to her room and noticed the bedroom door had been opened, she went to put her hand on the adjoining door and then thought better of it. *Fool, don't read into this.* She cursed herself as she sat back down and sipped her coffee and tried to read the document on her desk.

It was about ten minutes later when the screen was unfrosted and Ed was shaking the young woman's hand. Just before she was leaving, he stopped her and handed her jacket to her that had been cast aside on the sofa. Lottie wondered when and why she had taken that off. She played around with the stress ball on her desk, but he did not come in. He just picked up the phone, loosening his tie as if he were hot, while he chatted to whoever was on the line.

This was a feeling Lottie did not like. Jealousy had never been a problem for her. The tables had turned, and she cast her mind back to several occasions when she had seen Ed act this way around her. Maybe it was the Dean name that had changed her?

She stood up and looked out of her window; the sun had gone in and the wind had picked up. She heard the adjoining door unlock, and she turned around. She had never noticed the inner door being locked before and her gut wrenched again with that unfamiliar feeling of green mist.

'Ready for home, Mrs Dean, I want to call it a day. Maybe we could go for supper out?' He did his usual walk up behind her and planted a kiss on her neck.

'If you want to,' Lottie said back.

'You ok?' He turned her quickly to look at her face. 'What's wrong?' he asked.

'Nothing,' she lied.

'There is, tell me.' He seemed to be wracking his brains why she was as off as this but could not get it. 'Lottie, something has made you quiet?'

'Did you have a good meeting?' she asked. It was not a change of subject, and there was a hint of sarcasm in her voice. 'Must have been a private thing for the door to be locked and the screen up?'

He took a moment to think about it and then a large grin came over his face. 'By god, Mrs Dean, is that a green mist I see in your eyes?' He was almost laughing at her.

'No!' Lottie snapped back.

'I think it is, or you wouldn't have mentioned it,' he smiled again, rubbing his chin.

'No, I just wondered, that was all. She was an attractive young woman.' She tried to shrug him off, but he caught her hand and turned her round.

'I do not share!' He took a breath, referring to a conversation they had had months ago about being faithful and how it was something he took very seriously. He continued, 'And I would never expect you to. I'm not sure if I am happy, you are jealous or a bit pissed that you think so little of me, and please, really, in the room next to my beautiful wife? I am not such a bastard, am I?'

'Sorry. My mind just got carried away and, suddenly, I couldn't see reason,' she said. 'I'm so angry with myself for even contemplating the feeling of jealousy, let alone that you would. It was a weird feeling that just sort of took me over.' She was finding it hard to justify herself. She had listened to him so many times trying to defend himself after acts of jealousy, and that in itself made her feel worse.

'My beautiful girl, how could I ever be tempted by anything other than the perfection I have right here?'

'Flattery will get you everywhere, Mr Dean, and that is what worries me.' She was talking about his silver tongue and how he could win a heart round even when it was as mad as hell.

'I am made of flesh and blood, I can't walk around with my eyes closed. First I would fall over, and second I would fail as a man. But there I can assure you, I would never want another woman, while you live and breathe, never, and then...' He had to stop as the thought of what he would do without her was just unthinkable. 'Then I would never want another if you were not,' he finished.

'Can we chalk this up to me being stupid?' Lottie asked, trying to find a way to change what now was a subject both of them did not want to think about.

'We can. But I'm sure there will be an occasion where I see the green monster. I have in the past to my cost, so can I put this one in a bag as a keep-sake, a get-me-out-of-jail-free card if you like. A negotiating pointer?' He smiled at her and pulled her face up to look at him.

'Yes, if you must!' She smiled back at him, still mad at herself more than anything.

'Right then, back to my original question. Supper out Mrs Dean?'

'Yes please Mr Dean, that would be nice.' He planted a kiss on the lips and pulled her close to him as conformation of the end of the conversation. Lottie promised herself that she would not do that again.

A few days later she got out of the car and made her way to the front door of the residential building. 'Thanks Phil,' she said as she left him to park the car. Smiling at the night watchman sitting at the security desk she made her way to the lift. She scanned her security card to allow her access to the apartment on the very top floor. As the elevator doors opened at the penthouse, the large wooden front door opened. She was thrown by the sight of the person leaving; she expected it to be a member of staff, not the red-head she had seen in Ed's office three days before. The young woman smiled and quietly greeted her – 'Mrs Dean' – not stopping to make conversation. Lottie nodded back, ready to speak but she was too late: the woman had caught the lift back down.

Lottie pushed the door handle down and walked in, leaving her bag on the side as usual. No one else seemed to be about, not even Mrs B. She walked past Ed's office, pushing the door open slightly, but he was not in there. She pulled the door to again and then made her way past their bedroom. She looked in and Ed was pulling a top back on over his head. He was home earlier than she expected, she was about to make her way to the sitting room, the door to which was closed, when Ed noticed her.

'Hey, you.' He walked to the door, straightening the loose-fitting top he had put on. His hair was still wet from a shower. 'Don't go in there just yet,' he asked her.

'Why, got someone else in there you don't want me to find?' The words came out without hesitation as she was confused; they never had people back to the apartment, clients, and was it a coincidence it was the same beautiful woman that had taken her attention a few days before.

'You saw Charlotte then?' Ed asked, knowing that the timing was not quite right, and she had not been able to get away before Lottie arrived.

'First name terms I see,' Lottie said, resisting the prying question of what she had been doing there.

'She had been most helpful,' he said with a smile. He walked to her and kissed her head. He held her hand and took her to the kitchen door, instead of going in through the large open-plan sitting room. The way that the apartment was laid out also meant that you could close off the sitting room from the kitchen. Lottie had only seen the accommodation like it once before as Ed preferred the large open space.

'Drink?' Ed asked, opening the fridge for a bottle of wine.

'What's going on?' Lottie asked as he took two glasses and poured without her giving him a reply.

'Nothing, why?' he asked, passing her the glass. There was a thud from the sitting room and Lottie looked up.

'Who's in there?' She walked to the door and Ed caught her hand as she aimed it towards the door handle.

'No one,' he lied, as there obviously was. 'Trust me,' he said, but he could see that she was fighting with herself. 'It's nothing sinister, Lottie, in fact I hope that you will like it.' He smiled at her.

Pete walked in through the other door. 'All done,' he said, then, noticing

Lottie, 'Evening, Mrs Dean.' Lottie smiled at him, now wanting to know desperately what was going on.

'Thanks, Pete. I had better show Mrs Dean in or I can see she will burst with worry that I have had some form of assignation with our young American visitor! A little green mist is starting to show again, I guess?'

'No, I just wanted to know what was going on with everyone looking guilty,' she added. Both men were smiling so it could not be all that bad.

Ed put his hand on the door handle and took both glasses of wine as he pushed the door with his hip.

'You came home just that bit too soon, I wanted to get everything ready before you walked in and suspected that I was up to no good again with the young red-head,' he smiled. 'You really must put that out of your head. Charlotte is part of a shipping company. One of the things they dealt with was antiques so I asked if she could get you something.' He pointed his hand over to the far corner of the room, where a large grand piano had been placed. The furniture had been moved slightly, but there was more than enough room in the apartment to accommodate it. A red velvet stool had a large bouquet of flowers on it; Lottie was almost rooted to the spot by the sight of the instrument.

'An 1870 concert grand, with hand-crafted turned lion legs in a pure rosewood frame. The pedals are 18-carat gold-plated, I had them re-gilded to make sure they were strong enough to be played. All restored and rebuilt and tuned, ready to use. It was made for and originally owned by a Russian Princess. In the 1900s it was lost for several years. Then, during the First World War, it turned up in a grand house in Germany. The scores written out by Princess Rosa are still in the seat, you can see where she made notes on the pages.'

He put the drinks down on the coffee table and walked over to the imposing instrument. Lottie followed him.

She ran her finger gently over the smooth wood. She could feel how warm it was to touch, as if it were alive. Several pieces of music had been arranged on the impressively carved stand, and the one on top was the music to the film *Pride and Prejudice*, the music she had played at the Tap and Tune the last time she was there. She smiled as she remembered the night. He had thought of everything! She felt guilty that she had contemplated he was being secretive, or even unfaithful. All to give her a gift that was so well thought-out; every detail had been paid attention to.

'Ed, she's beautiful.' She lifted the lid to reveal the gleaming white ivory and the ebony keys. He opened the lid to the body revealing the immaculate inner workings of the instrument, clipping it into the holder to secure it in the open position.

Lottie pushed her slender finger down onto one of the keys and the crisp note reverberated around the room in perfect tune. She smiled as the sound filled her, still leaving her finger in place as if she could feel it through the whole of her body.

'She took some finding. The right one I mean,' he said, looking at her reaction. 'I wanted to get something sooner, but when I knew this one was for sale, I had to wait. I knew it was the right one.' He moved the flowers from the seat and instantly Lottie sat down. 'She was originally made as a wedding gift; that was my intention too, but the restoration team had to wait for the right wood, and, well, I'm sorry it took a few more months to get here than I would have liked.'

'Ed, she's stunning.' She pressed another note, and the sound filled the room once more. 'I don't know what to say – thank you seem such small words for such a stunning gift.' She smiled up at him and he kissed her forehead.

'You can say thank you by promising me that you will play her often,' he replied as she continued to stare in awe at the gleaming, shiny wood. 'And to trust me sometimes with a secret, else I will never be able to surprise you with gifts.'

She stood up. 'You don't need to shower me with gifts,' she said. 'Not that I'm ungrateful, she is truly beautiful, and I will play her.' She looked back around almost as if to check it was real.

'Then I have two beauties in my home, what more could a man ask for?' He bent and kissed her lips, holding her in his arms. 'It is a gift for me too, to see you so happy, and I also get the bonus of listening to her being played. I was worried that it wouldn't fit in as the room is a bit too modern, but I guess something like this is a timeless piece. I looked at new ones, but they just didn't have the same appeal, or the same story. It's an investment, I guess.'

'She has a wonderful story and I want to find out more about her – something to tell the grandchildren,' Lottie said without a thought to her words.

'Grandchildren?' Ed asked, surprised that Lottie had made the comment.

'It's a figure of speech,' Lottie added, noting what she had said.

'Maybe we should practice getting their parents here, then?' Ed smiled at her, kissing her neck. There was a slight knock on the door and Mrs B cleared her throat.

'Supper's ready, Mr Dean,' she shouted out, 'don't let it go cold!'

'It will warm in the oven,' he said, continuing to kiss Lottie's neck.

'And I will still be here after supper. I'm starving.' Lottie kissed his cheek and pushed away from him.

'Are you turning me down, Mrs Dean, in favour of supper?' he asked, looking dejected.

'It sounds like I'm going to need to keep my strength up, so I had best eat.' She giggled at him as he chased her from the room.

'Too right you will!' He grabbed her and carried her to the kitchen table over his shoulder, gently smacking her backside as he put her down. They ate the food that had been prepared for them and finished the wine. Ed looked at her while she ate, and Lottie asked what he was looking at several times. He had replied, 'nothing,' and smiled. It had been the first time that they had even remotely mentioned the word 'children' since before Christmas.

After their meal Lottie put away the dishes and went into the bathroom to get ready for bed. Before she brushed her teeth, she took her pill, she shook her head as again she had forgotten it yesterday, and by the look of the packet the day before as well and she had missed a few at the start of the month too. She had to try harder to make it her regular routine. She was worried that she seemed to forget it no matter how hard she tried, so to make sure that there were no mistakes again she had booked an appointment to have an implant at the end of the month, so she would have up to six months with the peace of mind that a mistake would be as remote as possible.

Chapter 3

Lottie sat at her desk making the final arrangements for the charity event this coming Saturday. A small event by normal means, but important to her as she was hosting it for the Music Scholars.

'Mrs Hargreaves on the phone,' Zoe informed her on the intercom. 'Can I put her through?'

Lottie accepted the call and wondered why she had rung.

'Sarah, good to hear from you.' They had not spoken since Christmas, so it had been some time.

'Hi Lottie, thanks for taking my call.'

'Is everything OK?' Lottie asked. Their only connection really was Lottie's Pride, the horse who was still stabled and trained out of Sarah's yard she owned with her husband Joe.

'Good, thanks. Joe and I just wondered, we have a skiing holiday booked for the start of March. Joe's friend has pulled out with an injury and I just wondered if you and Ed would like to come for a few days, to make the numbers up. Joe's brother and his girlfriend are going and Johnny Skelton and his wife. I'm not sure if you ski; Ed and Joe did quite a bit in their younger years and it would give me someone to be able to hang around with as I am not so good. I tend to just shop or take in the sights more than get wet and cold,' she replied.

'Oh, um, not sure.' Lottie had been put on the spot.

'Sure, you need to ask Ed.' Sarah told her the dates.

'I would need to run it past him as I am not sure of his diary without asking. I wouldn't be able to do until the Wednesday, then it looks like we would have to be back for the Saturday anyway.' She wanted to sound as if it was not permission she was asking for but that diary space was the only thing that stopped her saying yes there and then. Although she had not skied since she was at school and it had not been the most exciting of holidays.

'No worries, if I email the chalet details. The weather has been great over there so far, and I would like to go through Lottie's Pride's running dates too, and catch up with you two of course.'

Lottie closed the conversation and put down the phone. She looked across at Ed who was deep in conversation in his meeting that seemed to be dragging on for ages.

Using the internet, she looked at the location Sarah had just given her. A private chalet in the French Alps, it had an indoor pool, hot tub, staff, personal bar, ski in and out to resort. It looked really nice. Maybe a quick break could be arranged. She would need to change some appointments and get some clothes, but that would be easy as it was still two weeks away. As soon as Ed had finished, she jumped up from her chair, got two coffees and went in to see him.

'Heavy meeting?' she asked.

'Yes, but successful, I think.' He rubbed the back of his neck and took the drink, and she sat next to him, leaning on his desk. Her usual position when she went in for a quick chat.

She outlined the phone call from Sarah as she sipped her beverage.

'I can change a few things, but if you want to, we could,' Ed said. 'Never thought about a winter break,' he looked up at her, 'or sharing a place with others while we are away,' he added. He liked the freedom to walk around in his own surroundings. More like he wanted to know he could have his wife anywhere without others to interrupt or listen in!

'I could have a look to see if there are any more apartments or places in the same resort?' Lottie offered.

'I doubt that there would be this time of year. Sounds like you would like to go?' He looked at his desk phone that was lit up with another call.

'I have to say I would need some lessons, else breaking my neck could be on the cards, although I like the shopping option Sarah mentioned,' she smiled. 'I will leave you to it and do a bit more digging.' She hopped off his desk and he hit the phone to answer. She blew him a kiss and he smiled.

He was right of course; no other places for miles around for the first few days in March. If they were going, they would have to stay in the chalet. Sarah did mention another couple who Lottie had not been acquainted with, but she was sure that Ed would know them. They carried on the conversation over supper, and it was agreed that they could go for a couple of days, although she was sure it was not worth lessons just for such a short time.

'We could run up to the dry slope on Sunday. I can't say it is like riding a bike, but you will soon pick it back up again. I'll be rusty. It's been a couple of years since I last skied,' Ed said.

'I bet you're saying that to make me feel better, get those skis on and you no doubt will be a downhill ski champion!' She laughed, as everything they did he had already done, and knew how to do well. Anything physical and he was in his element. 'Or are you admitting to getting older now you are almost thirty and not so fit?' she grinned, knowing this would provoke a reply.

'I can keep up with you any day, Mrs Dean.' He took a sip of his water and moved his plate out of the way.

'Really?' she asked, grinning. 'Remind me how.'

She knew that they had the apartment to themselves. Mrs B had gone, Pete and Phil had both taken some time out as her and Ed were home for the night and did not need the security detail. She jumped up and threw the tea towel at him. He followed her around the kitchen as she ran into the longue and around one of the large sofas. He followed, just missing her by a hair as he reached out to grab her. She squealed and jumped over the mat, picking up a sofa pillow from the couch and throwing it behind her to try to put an obstacle in the way. He batted it out of his way without any effort and reached for her again. She jumped over the other sofa to put the cream leather in between the two of them.

'Don't look so smug, you've only stopped to catch your breath,' he said to her, noticing her pink cheeks.

'I thought I had best let you rest!' she laughed back, starting to go back to the kitchen again, her socks and lack of shoes making the kitchen tiles slippery. She struggled to keep upright as she made her way round the breakfast bar. It was a bad move as it was a dead end. He lunged for her and she ducked; she had almost avoided capture, but he was too quick and grabbed her by the waist. She squealed again and as he picked her up she was wriggling and protesting to be put down. He threw her on the large sofa and she bounced as he let her go.

'So, who is the fit one?' he asked, pinning her to the sofa with just his legs astride her. He lifted his top over his head and pulled at the buttons on hers, not caring that they all ripped off as he was discarding the garment. She tried to tickle him, but she knew it was worthless. He was not ticklish, unlike she was, as she squirmed from side to side when he did the same. 'Stop it, Ed,' she said in broken protests between fits of laughter.

'Wish you had never started it now?' he laughed at her as she was getting out of breath. 'Want me to stop do you? I have not even started, Mrs Dean.' He pulled at her bra and released her breasts that were bouncing around.

Getting her trousers off was going to prove more of a challenge because if he let her go, he was sure she was going to make a run for it. He undid them and tried to push them down with one hand, but he could not. She wriggled and they went to her knees. A disadvantage for her as this stopped her going anywhere momentarily. She soon got free.

'I can see I'm going to have to tie you down!' he panted as she squealed. She made it to the other sofa, knocking the table out of the way as she went before he got on top of her again. This time she was face down on all fours. He grabbed her around the hips and pulled her closer, slapping her backside as hard as he could.

'Stay still!' He was amazed at his own power and was now sorry he had hit her as he left a red mark immediately on her bare flesh. He held his breath to gauge her reaction, but she continued to laugh and pretend to struggle.

He was so turned on by their game that he had to release himself from his trousers. He was fully erect and able to fill her from the position they were in, and he entered her without a second thought. He pulled her back onto him and she gasped in another tone as he penetrated the soft flesh around her sex. He knew he was being rough, but he was pushing her boundaries. She had become more experimental over the months they had been married. He took this as trust. She trusted him and knew he would never hurt her. All too aware of the occasion she had explained on her birthday, he never wanted to appear to be overpowering, but this was how he had had all sex until he had met her, and he had never lost the taste of hard play. He thrust into her again, pulling back on her shoulders. His legs were fixed by his trousers, and he masterfully was able to get them released and cast aside. She was just at the right height for him while she stayed on her knees, so when he felt her relax down, he slapped her backside again. 'Stay up!' he commanded, and she straighten her spine in reply and held on to the top of the sofa.

The adrenalin of the play was doing something to Lottie that she had not felt before. He had slapped her gently during sex before, but the urgency this time seemed deeper, more intense. She somehow liked the way it felt, the way that it had a direct blow to her clit that made her respond. She knew she was safe; it was rough but not unwanted. There was a difference. She was sure that if she said no, he would stop, but she did not want him to. She pushed back onto him, almost to reassure him she was ok, and she flicked her hair so it covered her back.

He took a handful of her hair and gently lifted it, and she pulled her head back and was close to his face. 'So tell me, Mrs Dean, do you want to play rough?' His voice was not the usual sensual Ed, it was the hard-ass Edward Dean. It was not a question at all, but a warning of how it was going to be. 'You have to tell me.' He did need to know because he needed to know she was OK, and that he was not hurting her.

'Yes,' she said, 'Yes please!' She was not sure why she said 'please' but it had just come out.

He was taken back with her request. Was that just a slip of the tongue, or did she know what he wanted to hear? He said in her ear, 'I'm going to take you, Lottie, you must tell me to stop if I hurt you.' This was a gentle request. 'Do you understand?' His blood was on fire, his heart racing. The thought of getting this far with her only added to the urgency of how much he wanted her. In the past five months he had done safe, loving-husband sex, but this took him back to wilder days, and had an added twist. The woman beneath him was the one he loved.

He reached his hand down under her and rubbed the inside of her leg, brushing her clit as he went past it. She bucked under him as the stimulation would have sent a pulse along the nerve endings. He had not forgotten how this played out, or what she would be feeling. Still trying to hold herself in place Lottie kept both hands on the top of the sofa.

As he thrust into her he rubbed harder, using one hand to take his weight and one to massage the swelling outer entrance to her sex. She was becoming overtaken by the feeling of pleasure. She was almost feeling ashamed that he was being so rough, and she liked it. Why had it taken all this time for her to respond this way to him? She knew deep down this was the sort of thing he knew as sex before they had met, but somehow it seemed OK to explore now. Safe. She dug her fingers into the soft leather as his thrusts were hard. He slapped her again as a stark reminder of what they must have looked like. Two rabid animals engrossed in carnal lust. Was it possible to behave like this as a married couple? She put the thought out of her mind as he put his hand up to her neck and added some pressure around her necklace. She gasped and he soon moved it.

'Sorry,' he whispered, knowing she was not ready for that.

He increased his strokes on her backside, watching as the pink flesh turned redder. His balls drew up and he could not stop his release. He had been overcome by her willingness to explore that he had forgotten his self-control. As he ejaculated into her, he reached up and pinched one of her nipples as hard as he could. Her inner sex muscles clenched so tight he felt them as the pain and pleasure pulsed through her and he thought he heard her swear as she orgasmed with him. Exhausted and out of breath, he withdrew and kissed her shoulders. She was breathing heavily too. She slumped to her side on the sofa, her eyes closed.

'You OK?' he asked in a soft voice.

She nodded and smiled. 'I'm not sure where that came from,' she said, 'but I take it you enjoyed yourself?'

'Sorry if I got carried away.' He gently rubbed her backside. He had left a mark, which was not his intention.

'You were not the only one.' There was a small rip in the leather sofa where she had been pulling and digging in her nails. 'You should be glad that was not you!' She smiled, knowing if she had been able to grip onto him it probably would have been.

He kissed her on the mouth, and he could see she was starting to feel the cold although the heating was on. He grabbed his top from the floor and pulled it over her head. Leaving the rest of their clothes there, he lifted her up and walked her through to the bathroom. Pulling up her hair into a bun to stop it getting wet he put on the shower and led her in.

'You need to warm up,' he instructed, stepping in when the water was hot and taking her with him.

As the water ran over her backside, she was aware that he had left his mark. But the pain was unusual; it made her smile, remaindered her of what they had just done. It seemed to turn her on again. He soaped her body and washed her down, gently with care and attention.

'Maybe you should teach me some more,' she said, breaking the silence.

'Teach you?' he questioned.

'To be more adventurous,' she added, not really knowing what to call it. 'I know we have, you know, done stuff, but,' she was red now, not from the heat of the water but the embarrassment of the subject, 'you know, I have always thought that you must miss...' She wanted to get out of the hole she felt she had dug for herself.

'I'm guessing I know,' he laughed. 'You're different Lottie, always have been. I guess you know me by now, and maybe my reputation in the past. I am more than happy in this department; making love to you is just that, the most intimate part of me and you. I have no objection if you want to play games, spice it up, but don't feel I am pushing you to something you don't enjoy.' He allowed the water to wash the soap off where he had applied it to her skin.

'I did enjoy it, should I be ashamed to say that?' she asked quite shyly.

'Not at all, we're consenting adults with respect for each other and, after all, this body is very perfect.' He kissed her nipples, getting his head wet in the flow of water. He worked his way back up to her neck and whispered in her ear, 'Why should you not enjoy the pleasure that it can give you, with a little help from me of course.'

She looked down at his growing arousal, amazed that he could perform again so soon, and without much provocation.

He turned off the water and wrapped a towel around himself. He took another of the warm fluffy towels and dried her down. Then he took her back to the bed wrapping her in the sheets to make sure she kept warm. He quickly went back into the sitting room and gathered up the clothes. As he came back to the room, he could see that she had settled and was starting to sleep. He gently climbed in behind her and wrapped his arms around her; she only momentarily stirred, and he lay and watched as she found her sleep.

He had been very tame with her, and in the past few months all thoughts of any other kind of sex had gone from his mind. He was sure that if in the first few months she had shown signs of wanting it rough or had been more adventurous he would have exploited it. But from the very beginning he knew she was not experienced, and that was almost one of the big 'turn on' points for him when falling in love with her. He had been more than satisfied and he thought he had moved on. It would worry him just how far they could go, if it sparked off his own tendency, and brought back the dominating person he thought he was leaving behind. He needed to speak to Dr Morgan about it, to see what he thought. They had worked hard on him putting this type of behaviour behind him. Could he emotionally afford to go back there?

As she had thought, Ed was a natural. Lottie stood at the top of the slope, looking down. She had hired skis and boots, but the reliable Bella had kitted her out in leggings and a bright pink and black jacket, hat and gloves to match for her first session on the Sunday afternoon.

The indoor ski centre was busy, but Ed had paid for a private session on the nursery slope, so she had it to herself. He was on the higher slopes and had left her with the young instructor, Shaun. He was patient and attentive, but she could not muster the courage to progress from the snowplough for fear of falling over. He suggested that she put her skis inside his and he pulled up close behind her, and holding her round the waist they went down the snow together to try to give her confidence. Once she knew she could make it the second time down he did not hold her so tight. It was unnerving to have another man so close; she smelt the unfamiliar scent of his aftershave, and the mild smell of perspiration from the exertion of his day's work.

He was younger, but only by about five years. Lottie looked around to see if Ed was in eyeshot; maybe a good thing that he was not. The third time down felt good, she really got the hang of it, but getting overconfident on the fourth run was her downfall. Tangling her skis with Shaun's she had them both over halfway down the slope. He landed on her with a thud, her face buried in his chest, their arms and legs tangled in a mess. She started to laugh, which he took as a good sign she was not hurt, but it did not help to get them up as he started to laugh as well. His face was a fraction away from hers, she felt his breath on her cheek.

'Mrs Dean, are you sure you are OK?' he asked, trying to get himself off her.

'Yes,' she looked into his dark hazel eyes, 'I just can't move.' She laughed, trying to untangle her skis. He got to his feet, unclipped her skis to help her and then offered out his hand to pull her up. He used his powerful arms and she shot up off the floor into them. He pulled the hair out of her face as she struggled to do it with her thick gloves on. 'Go again?' he asked. She nodded and brushed down her trousers.

By the end of the first hour her legs were burning, her thighs ached, she was using muscles she forgot she had. Standing at the top of the run she pulled off her gloves and rubbed the back of her legs.

'Sore?' Shaun said, pulling his gloves off and rubbing the back of her legs higher than she could reach herself in the restrictive clothing 'You will need to have a hot bath to relax you when you get home, or you'll not walk for a week!' She leant on her skis to stretch out the back of her legs while he rubbed them. She closed her eyes; the warming sensation was nice.

Ed looked over to the short slope again. He could see them at the top. His stomach turned as he saw the young man rubbing Lottie's legs.

He battled with himself to stay put. He knew that he should have been showing her, but it would not have been the best way for her to learn. But the closeness of another man to her made him grind his teeth. He spent another tormented five minutes watching as Shaun put his arms around her, placed his hands on her inner thighs, positioning her legs how he needed them, touching her upper body, her arms, her stomach. He was just too far away to see her face, but he could hear the laughter and tell by their body position that they were enjoying their time. He dug his skis into the floor and pushed back off. He would sooner she gets cosy with him than some French slime ball at ski school, he thought to himself as he went back up the slope for one final decent.

With the session over Lottie headed back to the car. After taking off her boots her legs felt like jelly, and the advice of a bath was going to be a welcome one when they got home. Ed was standing by the car; he had driven them to the centre, which was a few miles out of the city.

'I can see you enjoyed yourself,' he said, putting the vision of her in the arms of another man to the back of his mind for now. 'I booked another for Wednesday afternoon, if that is OK?' He popped the boot open and she put her coat and bag in the back.

'My legs need some soothing before then.' She rubbed her thighs through the jeans she had changed into as a small protest. 'Shaun said I should get another lesson, are you coming too?'

'He will have you all to himself, which I am sure will please him. Phil will come along to drive you, and he will ski. He's coming with us so needs to practice. He was an instructor in the SAS so if you need any more pointers that Shaun misses out, I am sure he will oblige.' Ed tried to make nothing of it, but the very comment was enough for her to know that he had seen her and Shaun.

'Do you want to use the get-out-of-jail card?' she asked, referring to the last conversation they had about who was jealous or not.

'Should I?' he asked.

'Not at all.' She leant across to the driver's seat and kissed him. 'You booked the next session after all, not me.'

'Point taken!' He smiled at her. She pulled out her phone and looked at her diary. She had the doctor's booked for the Wednesday also, and she saw that Ed had been in and booked the ski session in her calendar for after. She had told him it was just a check-up and no need for him to go, but she had spoken to them and booked the implant. He seemed happy not to ask any more, knowing that after all that had happened, she had been asked to go back for a few months just to make sure she was OK.

'You will have time to be in town, Phil's with you all day so if you want to shop or anything before just let him know.' It was if he knew that she was looking at the timings of her appointments.

'I'm good, Bella has a new on-line account for me so I can order and she will get it all sent over, but it's only a few days. I wasn't planning a new wardrobe.' The normal conversation continued as they made their way home.

The rest of the afternoon was relaxing, the bath had been a shared one, and the wine had gone down well. Lottie asked more about the other people who were going to be with them on the trip, and what to expect. Ed shared some of the stories of his previous winter holidays with her, and she had to admit she was looking forward to it more than she had been at the start of the day.

The week went by quickly. Lottie finished at the centre at 5pm, Ed was in the car waiting for her, the bags were packed, and the plane waited for them to arrive on the tarmac.

'Have fun,' Todd said as they left the building together. 'And come back in one piece,' he added, putting his hand up in the direction of the car as a greeting to Ed.

'I will, and if you get any more on the case just let me know. I have a feeling this one will have more than we first thought.' She stopped to add,

'It's going to take a bit more time to get to the bottom of.'

'Just have a good time and forget about this place for a few days,' Todd replied, waving her off towards the direction of the car.

It would be a long night of travel, so as soon as they got on the plane Lottie settled down to try to sleep. The private charter flight was like all the rest to Ed, but Lottie still marvelled at the luxury of the journey. The private bedroom was nothing like economy class. Being able to shower and relax made the whole jet set appealing to her, and it was a good place to start the break.

They arrived at the chalet late in the early hours, and they quickly settled into their room. Joe had waited up for them. The warm, soft bed was a welcome sight as they snuggled up for a few more hours sleep.

She woke up and Ed had gone, but not far; he was standing on the balcony looking out at the early morning sunrise. He was tapping away on his phone when she smooched up behind him in pyjama shorts and the ski jacket, and his shoes that she found by the door.

'Morning you,' she said, and he put his phone down and she slipped into his arms. He kissed her forehead.

'You'll freeze,' he said, noting her lack of attire. He pulled her closer to him and he looked back at his phone which pinged as another mail came in.

'Still working?' she said, hugging into him, noting that he was right; her legs were really feeling the chill although the sun was warming her face.

'Last one, I tried to get it done before you woke up.' He reached round her to send the reply and quickly tapped the keypad screen.

He looked back at her. 'Done.' He put it back in his pocket.

'I thought about buying a place out here, something about the clear air and fantastic view.' He brushed her hair that was still showing signs of her restless sleep away from her face. 'If you enjoy it maybe we should, the place is great in the summer too.'

'It is beautiful. I still need to get used to just popping over to places, as you put it, the travel does not seem to faze you.' She noticed how awake he looked. Full of life and energy considering they had been travelling for eight hours before.

'Practice from necessity, but I would sooner do it out of pleasure.' He hugged her again 'Hungry?' he added.

She nodded at him. 'Let's see what is on the menu.'

She spun round, unzipped her jacket and flashed her chest at him. 'This can be?!' Instantly, due to the cold, her nipples hardened. 'Still hungry?' she giggled.

'Oh yes!' He grabbed her and closed her coat quickly. 'I can see you need your first après ski lesson, Mrs Dean. The art of keeping supple before a good day's skiing is, well, where shall we start?' He bundled her into the bedroom and shut the balcony door with a crash. She bounced off the bed as he threw her back, starting his assault on her with the usual kisses.

As they walked down the stairs, they could hear the voices of the others. Lottie followed Ed, holding his hand as they walked into the large open-plan living space. The fire crackled and the other guests who were seated at the table were all eating breakfast.

'Morning you two, I hear you settled in ok, then?' Joe stood up with a grin on his face. Lottie felt her cheeks glow like a schoolchild who had been caught out.

'Ed, you know my brother Marcus.' Ed nodded at him and Lottie smiled. 'Johnny and Liz, this is Edward and Lottie.' Ed held out his hand to shake the young man's hand as it was offered over the dinner table, the ladies smiled and nodded. 'Julie, Marcus' girlfriend is about somewhere, and of course, the beautiful Sarah we all know.' He walked to his wife, who was facing the stove and putting syrup onto her pancakes. 'Eating her second breakfast, taking the 'eating for two' literally'.

As Sarah turned around it was clear what Joe had just implied. A neat, rounded stomach showed beneath her light jumper, which took Lottie slightly by surprise. She had not mentioned it on the phone at all. She glanced at Ed who seemed unfazed by the sight.

'You look well, Sarah,' he said as he lightly kissed her cheek then headed for the coffee pot. Lottie followed up with an empty cup, still quite surprised that when Sarah had asked them to come along, she had not mentioned to her that she was expecting, and that the fact she would only be watching and shopping had not had any meaning other than she did not like to ski.

'Good journey over?' Sarah asked Lottie.

'Yes, great thanks.' She sipped her coffee as a tall, blond, attractive young man walked into the kitchen from the room at the back.

'Lottie, Ed, this is Luca,' Sarah explained. 'He makes the most fantastic pancakes.' The young man smiled and showed his perfect teeth off.

'Good morning,' he said in perfect English, with a slight Austrian accent. 'Any meal requests just let me know, any washing, drying just leave it in the back.' He pointed to the washroom. 'I will be in every day to do the beds etc, so just let me know when you are about so I don't disturb.'

'He's amazing!' Sarah whispered to Lottie. 'Best chalet valet we have ever had, and quite an eyeful I am sure you agree?' She nudged Lottie's arm and winked. 'About time the boys got a taste of their own medicine – we usually get some busty blond that Joe ogles for a fortnight.' She took a mouthful of her pancake and Lottie just had to ask.

'Feeling OK then, how far gone are you?' Lottie looked at her bump, not realising that she did.

'Oh yes, 17 weeks, still OK to fly thank god. Sorry, I thought if I mentioned this you may be put off, although Ed was sure that you would be OK,' Sarah added.

It silenced Lottie. Ed knew and hadn't said anything. Why did she say he thought she would be OK, had he told her about the miscarriage?

'He never said anything,' Lottie said back to her, trying to hide her irritation. 'Why would I be put off?'

'I'm not skiing, so I didn't want to leave you in the lurch. I will still come up to the café and watch, but I tried it on day one and had a bit of a fall, so Joe banned me. Luca is good company though!' She smiled up at him and he gave her a grin back.

'Oh, we can still shop?' Lottie asked, relived that it was not the fact she knew about her miscarriage, or the fact that she too would have been around twenty weeks by now.

'Hell, yes we can,' Sarah replied.

Lottie took the pancakes Luca offered and smiled back at him with a polite 'Thanks'. She sat at the table next to Marcus and introduced herself to him. Ed looked up and gave a little confused look at her, to why she had chosen not to sit next to him. The seat was soon taken by Sarah, who sat next to her husband. They chatted about where they were planning to go that day and what they wanted for the evening meal. Joe attended Sarah, making sure she was OK with staying in the chalet for the morning. Lottie had been invited to ski, but took the schooling option for the morning, which meant the girls were going one way and the boys off on the other.

'You're annoyed with me, aren't you?' Ed asked as they got back to the room, sensing his wife's silence.

'Not really, just thought we had no secrets.' She carried on changing into her ski clothes.

'I was worried.' He walked over to her. 'Worried that you would get upset if you knew.' He stopped her hands from fastening her jacket and held them.

'Not as upset as not knowing, or you not telling me.' She carried on doing up her jacket, moving his hands out of the way. 'I'm happy for them, if it is what they wanted.'

'You say that as if it was not what you wanted.' He tried again to stop her hands to give him her attention.

'We've been over this. It was not planned, and what happened did for a reason.' She looked at him as to silence the conversation.

'But you are pleased now?' He pushed the question.

'Not pleased, I never said that. But it gives us a few years to have fun like we should be having now.' She moved to get her gloves and hat.

'It's not stopped Sarah. She still came on holiday and rides out most days,' he added.

'So, you brought me to see her to reassure me that in a few years, or if we ever have children, my life doesn't have to stop?' She was starting to get angry now.

'If we ever have them? What a statement. That sounds worse than in a few years.' He realised she was avoiding his eye contact. 'A few days ago, you were talking about grandchildren, you have sure changed your tune.'

'It was a figure of speech, I said that at the time. Ed, is this really the right time to be having this conversation?' she asked.

'It seems not,' Ed replied as a knock on the door came and Lottie answered it as a welcome distraction.

'Mrs Dean, the men are about to go. I will come with you to the lift.' Phil looked away as he got a stare from Ed. 'I'll be waiting outside then,' he quickly said, knowing he was an unwelcome guest at thc party.

Ed quickly gathered his things and walked back to her. He pulled her face up to him and kissed her lips. She responded by lifting her chin, but he could tell that there was no feeling in the gesture. 'I'm sure the conversation is far from over, but I need to go. Take care, stay with Phil, and we'll meet up in a few hours.' He kissed her again, but this time she gave into his touch and kisscd him back.

Lottie took the lift and there was silence in the cab, but the voices in her head continued the conversation. Had he been right that she was glad? She was getting her life back on track, enjoying everything she did, everything they did.

'Mrs Dean,' Phil held the door open for her, 'after you.'

The wind hit her face and it was sunny, clear and the air was clean because they were so high up. 'Beautiful, isn't it?' Phil observed as she stopped to look around. It was more the fact that she had stopped as her legs were shaking, and she was fixed to the spot. Looking down at how far she had to ski back made her panic. The small group including Julie and Liz had gathered a short way off, and the instructor beckoned them over to join them. Phil took her arm and steadied her while she pulled on her poles and took the first movement to join them. He smiled when she came to a halt on her own and then he stepped back.

'Glad you and your husband could join us,' the French instructor said. Lottie was about to correct him when he started talking to the group in French, then again in English. She noticed Phil check his phone, and then turn his back to the group. Lottie listened to instructions and then chatted to Julie, who also expressed she was nervous as this was her first time. That made Lottie feel better. 'At least the boys won't see me mess up,' Julie said, as if she was relieved it had turned out the girls were together.

After an hour, the weather had turned, clouds took the sun and at times it was cold. The runs they used were not steep, so they stopped often and worked down the mountain as a group. Phil kept to the back, and offered assistance to Lottie and Julie – much to the instructor's annoyance. They both took a few tumbles but nothing that was not laughed off. With a happy smile they arrived at the lunch destination, and it was not more than five minutes before the group of boys joined them.

A glass of wine with the meal relaxed everyone and conversation was flowing with the group until it was time to move on. They had planned to ski together, but the boys had found some fresh snow, and wanted the challenge. Ed said he was staying with Lottie but became the butt of the joke and gave in to the pleading to leave her with Phil, who seemed to be a better guide than the one they had had all morning.

'You've only got two days of snow, you need to make the most of it,' Joe had teased him. 'You have got all night to cosy up with her. Let the reigns go a bit, Ed.'

'Do you mind?' he asked Lottie.

'No, not if Phil doesn't, although it would be good for him to get a bit of enjoyment instead of hanging around with us females. Maybe he should go with you, show you how it's really done!' Lottie raised a mocking eyebrow and bit her lip. He kissed her, sucking on her lip.

'Steady, Mrs Dean, you could find yourself in trouble with such fighting talk.' He kissed her again and was the last in the group to leave them as he bid her goodbye.

The chalet was warm and welcoming when the girls returned. They were a good hour in front of the boys. Sarah had been shopping and helped make supper. Hot baths were taken and glasses of wine much savoured as they made conversation in the sitting room. Lottie noticed that a small patch on her arm was still hot and inflamed, although the bath water had cooled it down a little. The doctor had said that she may react to the implant, so for now she would just keep an eye on it. Most of the tee shirts and tops she had brought covered it over anyway.

The long day ended, and Lottie curled up in the bed first as Ed took another call. He was having trouble with his phone; he had even tried Phil's who was getting a poor reception too, due to the weather being bad and it had started to snow quite heavy after night fell. Lottie had offered her phone, but she had the same issues, and was asleep by the time Ed came back in the room.

Due to the increased snow, everyone had to stay lower down the slopes in the morning, so they all stayed together as a group. Ed was impressed by how much Lottie had come on. She showed confidence and better skills, but still had a stumble or two and he had picked her up, brushing her down each time. Sarah joined them for lunch, and as the weather in the afternoon seemed to get a little better the boys again decided to split away and try some more challenging routes. Julie stayed back at the chalet, so it was just Phil, Liz and Lottie who took the cable car back up to the far side of the mountain.

Phil checked his phone; he had no reception.

'We will only get one run in, Mrs Dean, this weather will not hold,' he warned, and she nodded. 'We may need to pick up the pace so that we don't get stuck, will that be OK?' Lottie felt that they could do it, and so took the hand-lift to the very top.

They hadn't done this part of the mountain yesterday, but the runs were just as gentle and quiet, and it was part of the resort that not many people used due to how easy it was. All things went well until Liz fell. Lottie was not sure how it happened as she was in front of them. Phil quickly went to assist her.

Frantically, he waved Lottie over. Looking back only 20 yards, Lottie could see that the cloud was covering the top of the slope and the weather was turning quite fast. She took off her skis and started to walk back up the hill to them. It was slow and hard-going on her legs. Phil was sitting on the ground by Liz, his face slightly panicked.

'She's been knocked out,' he said, not moving her. 'I'm worried that she's hurt her leg, and she seems really confused and dazed. I don't want to move her due to neck issues. I cannot get a signal on the phone – try yours.'

'I never brought it,' Lottie said. 'It was useless yesterday and I guessed you would have yours.'

'Shit,' he said, looking around to see if anyone else was on their side of the mountain. Not a soul for miles.

'We need to get some help, it's about an hour back to the chalet.'

'I'll stay, you will be faster,' Lottie said.

'I promised Mr Dean I would not leave you.'

'Then I'll go, and you will have to wait longer because I'm slower,' she said.

'But you will be on your own skiing, you could get lost or fall?' he commented; what a dilemma.

'We can't leave her,' Lottie said. 'We need to decide quickly.' She picked up the phone he had thrown on the floor and tried again – nothing. He pulled the rucksack off his back and took out the space blanket and a bottle of water.

'Put this around her so she's not cold.' He flicked the flare that he had put in his bag and ran to the far side of where they were and placed it on the ground.

'Maybe we should all just stay here, someone will see this,' he said, watching as the trail of smoke drifted off to the side the mountain. They waited, and they tried the phone again. Phil had dressed the cut above Liz's eyebrow, and she was talking to them now. The large swelling on her leg confirmed an injury, and she protested if it was moved at all due to the pain.

Phil had piled snow up behind them to give a little shelter from the wind, the snow was drifting and the visibility was low. He looked at his watch. The flare had gone out a while before. He had another but they only lasted 15 minutes and he wondered if he should waste the other just yet. Lottie shivered and huddled towards Liz to try to get warm.

'You need to move about, Mrs Dean, you're getting too cold.' He pulled another hot pack out of his bag and cracked it. The instant heat was welcome as Lottie put it down the front of her jacket. They had already used two for Liz to try to keep her warm. 'Here eat this too.' He passed her a chocolate energy bar. She did as she was told.

'We need to get her off this mountain,' Phil said, looking at Liz, who had drifted in and out of consciousness.

'Stay with her, I'll go. Once I am at the ridge there are bound to be more people about,' Lottie said, knowing someone had to do something. Phil tried his phone one more time.

'Are you sure?' he asked, knowing that this was the only option.

He needed to stay with Liz to give her support and if she did become unconscious again, he was sure that he would pick her up, overruling the leg injury to ensure that she did not get worse. He started to think about the way that Lottie should take to get her back. He then relayed this to her as she stood up and started to move to get the blood flowing around ready for her rescue mission.

'I keep the trees to my left, the edge to my right and at some point, I end up at the bottom,' she said, hoping that she was right from the talk they had had the day before; a bit of a survival course, Phil had called it. More like a precaution note from Edward to him before they set out.

'And the sunlight above that mountain, if you get to see it.' He passed her the water, his watch and another hot pack. 'Are you sure?' Lottie nodded. No, she was not sure, but it was the only thing that she could think to do. She set off, her heart racing and her hands shaking. Phil had pushed a map into her pocket of where he thought they were.

'The girls are not back yet, you're early,' Sarah said to Joe as he came through the door first.

'The weather is evil out there, so we came back.' He planted a kiss on her lips and smacked her backside as a loving gesture that he had missed her. 'We beat them back you lot,' he shouted through to the room where Marcus, Johnny and Ed were taking off their boots. Instantly, Ed picked his phone up and got a signal. He breathed a sigh of relief but on calling Phil the line went dead.

Ed looked up. 'Where did they head off to?' he asked Marcus.

'East side, top run I think.' He kicked off his boots and pulled his map out of his pocket to have a look – he had marked it that morning.

'No, they decided not to, as the other was longer but easier going. They took the lift and then would have buttoned it to the summit round here.' Johnny leaned over to point to the area where he saw them head off to the lift.

'I'm going out to have a look,' Ed said, putting his boots back on.

'Don't be a prat, man, the weather is unforgiving. Phil's with them, he will have sheltered them until it gives some, and slowed them down to get back safely.' Marcus looked at Johnny to try to reassure him. Joe had walked back in the room to see where everyone had got to.

Julie and Sarah sat by the fire. The boys were pacing the floor, looking out of the window from time to time.

'What is fucking taking them so long, how long does it take for them to get mobilised?' Ed said, referring to the call they had put in that they thought the group were lost, so mountain rescue had been called.

'You called them less than five minutes ago, Ed. Calm down.' Joe patted Sarah's leg.

As if he had willed them, a knock on the door revealed a three-man rescue team and search dogs. They were all dressed in the mountain rescue uniform, and the dogs had small survival packs strapped to their backs. They explained the route, and Ed said he was going with them.

'No sir, please stay here, the weather is easing, they will be easy to find.' The small team set off to join the full rescue team who had already set off up the mountain.

Lottie had done what she was told. She had set the watch Phil gave her to beep every three minutes. Phil said to get her bearings each time to make sure she was on track. Her legs were aching, and she was so cold she had lost the feeling in her fingers and several times she stumbled and fell. One fall had allowed her to face-plant the floor with a bang, and she felt the instant pain in her cheek bone. She winced and took some deep breaths, the thought of Liz just keeping her going. She had to get back as quickly as she could. She could see the cloud breaking the closer she got to the bottom. The cable cars overhead had stopped, so she was not able to alert anyone that way; she would have to make it further to the village.

She had been skiing for well over 40 minutes when a small figure appeared on the horizon. She waved and shouted and then she saw another person. She was so relieved when she saw that they had seen her. She made her way to them, and the rescue dogs dashed along and jumped up, almost knocking her off her feet. She was glad to see them, and they seemed to feel the same.

She quickly passed over the information about where she had left Phil and Liz and asked for them to go as fast as they could, explaining what she felt were Liz's injuries. They made a radio call now, knowing that there was an injured person, and one of the team asked for an ambulance for Lottie to go to hospital.

'I'm fine, I just want to get back.'

'We need to have you checked out, madam,' the young man said. 'I can see you have taken some falls on the way.' He indicated to her face.

'Please, just take me back to the chalet and bring back my friends, that is more important right now. We have no time to debate this,' Lottie insisted. She smiled at the young man, indicating this was not up for debate.

All the group in the chalet were looking out of the window and saw the helicopter buzz over.

'Why the hell have they not come back to tell us anything?' Ed was almost shaking with rage.

'They will when they know something, mate,' Joe tried to reassure him, as there was a knock at the chalet door.

Lottie sat on the top step taking off her boots; the rescue worker had taken her skis and planted them by the wall and the rescue dog continued to lick her and jump up her, and she managed a smile and to stroke him.

'Ed!' Joe shouted back as he opened the door and saw Lottie sitting taking off her skis.

'Oh, thank god, baby girl!' He ran out and sat next to her, hugging her. 'Are you OK?' He kissed her frozen nose and then tracked the coloured area on her face, that was starting to bruise. 'You are so cold; we need to get you warm and to the hospital and checked. What the hell happened?' He helped her to stand up and they made their way through the door.

'We need to check on Phil and Liz.' The rest of the group joined them, and Ed pushed past them to get her into the warm.

'We have located them, they are both being taken to the hospital. Are you sure that you will not go, madam?' the rescue member asked her again as he followed them in.

'I'm OK.' Lottie shivered, as she was starting to thaw out. Ed repeated the request and once more Lottie insisted she was fine.

'You need to get warm before we do anything,' Ed said. 'Marcus, if you find out where they have taken them, we can follow on.' Marcus nodded.

'She fell, Marcus. I never saw it. Phil was great and looked after her – she hurt her leg, and had a bump on her head, and we were worried to move her. I stayed as long as I could, but we had to make the decision to get help as no one seemed to come,' Lottie twittered on.

'I knew I should have stayed with you,' Ed said, passing her a cup of hot chocolate.

'The weather just turned so fast; the phones didn't work. It was no one's fault.' She sipped her drink and it felt good as it warmed her from inside.

'You did well, madam, to make it back down. The helicopter was able to see the flare, and the directions you gave us were spot on, saving us a lot of time.' He smiled at them. 'I will leave you now if there is nothing else I can do?'

'Thank you,' Lottie said, and the young man smiled and left with additional thanks from others in the room. 'Phil did the best he could, I insisted he stopped with Liz. He was giving her first aid and was more help to her than I would have been. We just had to make a call on it, and I said I would come back.'

Ed rubbed her shoulders and upper arms from behind and she winced slightly on the tender patch where the implant was. He noticed.

'Are you sure you're ok? Let me look at that.' He went to lift her top and she put her hand over it.

'I just ache, all that exercise. We should go to the hospital to see what's going on.' She smiled at him.

'I would sooner we stay here. Joe will report back,' Ed said, wanting to keep her in the warm.

'Please!' Lottie looked at him, her eyes desperate for him to give way.

She got her way. Ed took the car and they managed to make it to the next town where the hospital was, just as it started to get dark.

They were soon able to find Liz, and Phil had also been admitted against his will. He had hypothermia, mainly because he had taken off his layers to give to Liz, not thinking of himself. Liz had a mild concussion, the onset of hypothermia and a confirmed fractured lower leg. Marcus was with her, so Lottie went in to see Phil.

'You did well, Mrs Dean,' Phil said, wrapped in layers of sheets. 'Is he mad at me?'

'Phil, why should he be mad with you, you didn't do anything wrong. I wanted to go higher, I wanted to leave and get help.' She sat at his side. 'If he says anything, remember you are my friend, too.'

'I guess I'm losing my touch, all those years in the army, and I get stuck doing a small ski trip.' He coughed, and she handed him some water.

'You did great – judging by the other people who have been admitted tonight, it caught several people out, and in fact they are still looking for one couple. Your survival tips and the pack of goodies you carried saved us all. Not everyone would have been that prepared,' she said, trying to lighten his mood.

'Mr Dean.' Phil interrupted her as Ed walked in behind her chair.

'How are you?' he asked, a genuine spark of concern in his voice. 'They said that you did a great job looking after Liz – it could have been a whole lot worse if you had not been there.'

'I'm sorry, Mr Dean, that I put the girls in that situation,' Phil remarked.

'I have already said that this is not your fault, Phil,' Lottie interjected before anything else could be said. 'Ed, can we get Phil home early tomorrow, bring the flights forwards maybe?'

'I don't want to cut short your break, Mrs Dean. I will be fine once they let me out,' he protested again.

'With the weather being bad we would not have gone out in the morning anyway. I'll see what I can do.' Ed kissed her on the forehead. She looked up at him and smiled as he left the room, and he rubbed her shoulder, still grateful that she was OK.

'He's pissed,' Phil said.

'He won't be,' Lottie replied.

Back in her own bed, there was nothing like it Lottie thought as she pulled the sheets up around her. They had made it back a few hours early, but due to the weather most flights had been grounded anyway. Phil had been given some time off; he had been discharged later that night. Sadly for Liz she was still in France. They would not let her fly back any sooner than they had planned.

The shower stopped and Ed appeared in the doorway, rubbing his hair with the towel. She smiled at him. His face had caught the sun in the short time they'd been away. He had marks where his sunglasses had been, which made her smile more.

'What?' he asked, walking to the bed.

'Nothing, just admiring the view,' she replied, watching his powerful body flex and contort as the muscles worked as he dried himself off.

'You stay there. I will ask Mrs B to bring you some breakfast,' he said, sitting on the side of the bed.

'Are you going out?' she asked. He would usually bring her something if she was staying in bed.

'We said that we would go over to see Mum. You don't need to come, you should rest.' Lottie had forgotten about the visit. She pulled her arms out of the sheets.

'I'll come, if you give me a few minutes. Sorry, I had forgotten.' She sat up, pushing her bed hair out of her face.

'You don't have to, I would sooner you rest. It has been a stressful few days.' He leaned in to kiss her, putting his hand on her upper arm.

'Lottie what is that?' He looked at the large red mark on her arm, which had been growing in the past 24 hours, turning yellow around the edges.

'Just a reaction, made worse by a few knocks in the last few days. It'll go soon when my body gets used to it,' she said dismissively.

'Reaction to what?' He took a closer look, noticing the red circle around a white, yellowish dot.

'The contraceptive. I went for the implant, not the pills. It seemed a better option, with my forgetful head.' She tried to make light of it.

'Oh, I thought...' He sat back, pausing in his reply. 'How long does that have to be in for? I mean, surely if you are reacting that's not a good thing.'

'It has a life of about six months. They said it takes about a month to get used to it.' She answered his question, but she could see it was not a reply he liked.

'But you can take it out sooner, if you don't settle?' he asked, realising that six months was a long time, but not wanting to make a deal out of the timeline. Well, he did want to. He was disappointed she wanted to go back for more pills to be totally honest. He really wanted to see what happened, what was meant to be.

'I could, if needed, but the reaction is really not that bad.' She looked at her arm. She was lying. It itched and ached like hell. The whole top of her arm was hot to touch and she had thought about getting it out herself at one point it hurt that much, but she took some painkillers and decided she was sticking with it.

'Oh,' was all he said in reply. He needed to look this up on the internet. He was not happy she had not mentioned it before. He got up and went to the wardrobe.

'Stay here, I won't be long, no need for you to come.' He slipped his jeans on, grabbed some shoes and took out a top, pulling it over his head he brushed his hand through his hair. He kissed her on the cheek and left the room.

'Now he's pissed,' she said to herself, lying back down on the bed with a thump. She leant over and grabbed her iPod and put the earphones in. She closed her eyes and listened to music, relaxing. Her body needed to sleep and although she tried to fight it, she dozed off, then finally fell back to a full sleep with the music playing in her ears.

Two days later at work, Todd shouted at Lottie when she showed him her arm.

'For god's sake, Lottie, no wonder you look like...' He paused. She was pale and had a temperature. 'Get that out now, here give me a scalpel'

He was right it had to come out. The septic area on her arm was now something she had to address. Going to the doctor was something she never had time for, but this was not working; her body was rejecting it for some reason. 'You're going to need some antibiotics as well. Lottie, you of all people know that sepsis is a killer!' She felt the sweat on her upper lip: maybe he was right.

Chapter 4

March arrived and the social calendar was full; every weekend had something for them to do. They had a weekend in Liverpool during the Grand National. Sarah and Joe had a private box, with a couple of horses running on the Friday so they arranged to join them. Lottie found herself admiring her husband more than once; he was dressed in the finest black tails, with straight pencil grey trousers, hugging and tight around his thighs. He had rubbed the soft Indian silk of her matching grey dress, fringed with fake fur and a stole to keep her shoulders warm, commenting on how stunning she looked. Lottie had backed some winners, and some losers, but was up on the weekend. Never with big stakes, but she was able to add a few hundred pounds to her scholarship which was better than nothing.

Ed never said how much he lost, or won, but he seemed to be himself again. Attentive and loving, protective, and as passionate towards Lottie as ever.

They watched the boat race the next weekend, spending the day with some of his old friends from university; it was nice to get a glance of him with people from his past. He never really spoke about his school, or early years, but with his 30th birthday looming Lottie was trying to think what she could arrange for him.

She had called his mother, who said that she could not offer any thoughts.

'What do I get the boy who has it all?' she asked. 'Let alone give you any tips on what he wants,' she had said.

Ed's mum never had the heart to say to her what she was really thinking, and as she put down the phone Alice Dean recalled the conversation she had with her only son a few weeks before.

'It will happen when the time is ready, Edward. Don't rush her.' They had been sitting in the kitchen drinking coffee after they'd come back from skiing.

'I was so against it at – first sharing her, having to think of more than us. When the reality of it set in, after we, you know, lost the…' He did not say the word, he could not bring himself to. 'Well now I can't think of anything else. What could have been, how it would be, having to wait for so long with this implant thing.'

'And you have talked about this with Lottie?' his mother asked.

'Argued,' he explained. 'Not discussed. Dropped hints, not talked,' he paused, 'she just seems so against it, almost relieved that…' He stopped himself again.

'You are both young, you need to live,' his mother tried to reason.

'Nothing would have to stop. We could still live,' he argued.

'Oh, you think so. A child is a big responsibility for the rest of your life.' She took a sip of her coffee and Ed did likewise. 'You can still live, but do you really want to have a child and then just hand it over for someone else to look after, while you carry on?' She looked at him. 'I hated every second that you boys were away from me. Your father continued to live, too well as I remember. I, on the other hand, existed in the background.'

She walked back into the living room after she had finished her call with her daughter-in-law. Knowing that the one thing Lottie could give her son was something Alice could not tell her he wanted. They had to work it out for themselves and she was sure that they would.

The second to last day in March, Ed opened his eyes and felt the cold spot where he had left his wife when he closed his eyes the night before. He had to say they had drunk too much. They had been for an enjoyable meal with his mother and when they got back to the apartment Lottie had played for him. She had mesmerised him with her skill on the piano. She had explained over dinner more of the history of the gift he had bestowed on her, and he was touched that she loved it so much.

As he sat and drank whiskey he had become consumed in her playing. It had turned him on so much that, even with an excess of alcohol, they had made love until the early hours, which was why he had slept later than intended.

'Morning birthday boy!' she said, walking back into the room butt-naked. There was no one else in the apartment, so he was not worried that anyone else would see the beauty that stood before him. She had a red ribbon wrapped round her waist, with a neat bow on one hip.

'I didn't have a clue what to get you so I thought I would gift-wrap myself, then I thought well you can have me any time of the year, not just for your birthday, so I didn't bother to fully wrap!' She bit her lip and crawled onto the bed. 'I got you this, too.' She handed him a small gift.

'Um, I would sooner unwrap that in a moment.' He put the box down on the covers. 'First I want to unwrap this one.' He pulled at the bow on her waist and it came undone in his hand. She giggled as he pulled her to him, and she picked the ribbon back up. 'Well, Mr Dean, I thought that you could wear this,' she wrapped the ribbon round his head as a blindfold, 'and you can guess what I am doing...'

Ed grinned and allowed her to put the red silk around his head, she pulled it tight and pushed him down. He should have been the one doing this to her; the tables had turned, and he seemed to be at her mercy. She sat astride him and slowly started to rub herself on his chest with her chest. She kissed and whispered in his ear, 'What do you think this is?' She leaned over and he suddenly felt a soft touch, something running down his chest to the line of his pubic bone. He was not ticklish, but her touch, with whatever it was, made the hairs on his body stand on end. She blew on him as the hairs reacted to the feather that she was rubbing on him. He found it hard not to move his hands so he put them under the pillow, behind his head.

She swapped the feather for her fingernail. She ran it down his triceps which were bulging out in the position he was in and he tensed his stomach muscles as she continued down to the same spot she had stopped at before. Then she moved over to do the same on the other side, the feather first and then followed by her sharp nail.

She had no doubt that he liked whatever it was doing to him. His erection was full, touching the top of his stomach, just at the point that she kept stopping.

'Do you like it?' she asked breathing close to his ear. As he nodded, she licked around the curve of his ear lobe; he loved that. She bit gently on his ear and he almost moved his hands to grab her, but he restrained himself, allowing her to play her game. She leant over and grabbed a small pot of oil; she had put all the things under the bed the night before, in preparation for her treat to him. She rubbed her hands together and spread the oil over his chest. Under the ribbon he had his eyes closed. She rubbed down his thighs, just skimming past his prick each time making it twitch in response, wanting to be touched. As she rubbed down his legs she licked around his balls.

Now that was a surprise; she had done it before but the anticipation of not being able to see her was something he had not felt before. He groaned. *God, woman, I am going to get you back for this*, he mentally told her as he felt her gentle kisses working slowly round to his pulsing knob. He was almost willing her to go to it, *touch it for fuck's sake*! he wanted to scream. She moved away again. Working back up his body she bit down on one of his nipples, not hard, but enough to make it react and send the shockwave through him. He moved his hand to touch her.

'No, you don't,' she said, swinging herself around to straddle his upper body pushing her legs down on his arms, fixing them in place.

Her sex was just above his face, he could smell her sweet smell and he breathed her in. She kissed his lower hips, from side to side. He lifted his nose to touch her light hairs that covered her sex, he tried to lick her, but she sensed what he was doing and just lifted enough so that he could not reach his goal.

She kissed towards the end of him, and gently licked the small droplet of pre-cum. She opened her mouth and took him in. He tasted of last night's sex, and his salty mix of male scent hit her taste buds as she closed her mouth around him and sucked. He thrust up in her face, *at last* he thought, as she worked herself deeper with each mouthful. She used one hand to gently rub the lower part of him that was not in her mouth, working in time with each suck, covering her teeth she hollowed her cheeks to suck him harder.

He found it hard to restrain himself, and she lowered herself enough just so that he could rub her outer lips with his mouth, and he obliged, tasting her. She was wet, his pleasure was turning her on too. She rubbed her nipples on him, increasing her arousal.

She tasted more ejaculate from him, and she knew he was close. She stopped and turned herself around, straddling him once more, this time so that their sex areas touched. His hands reached out for her and she allowed him to rub her chest. He pulled on a nipple and she sucked in air as he tweaked it. She reached between them and guided him into her. She sat back as far as she could to take him all in, and started to wriggle around, up, down. She found it hard on her thighs, she needed some support, so she used his chest to push up. He held her hips and pulled her to a rhythm that had them both in time. He was taking over the assault as she became overcome with her own pleasure as well as giving it to him.

'I want to see you,' he said, 'I want to see your pleasure, Lottie'. She leaned forwards and pulled free the blindfold. She kissed him hard full on the mouth and sucked at his lower lip. She pulled back and smiled at him, the dimples in her cheeks showing as she flared her nostrils with increased breathing. She bit down on her lower lip as she pushed back her head and closed her eyes, feeling him so deep inside her.

He lost it, thrusting up, spilling into her without warning. 'Oh god, sorry Lottie.' He gritted his teeth as the orgasm pulsed deeper into her than he ever felt before. She squeezed her inner muscles to tighten around him, knowing that he would feel her. He closed his eyes and dug his hands into her hips as he shot up into her, thrust by thrust, leaving himself in her. As she felt him slow down, she gently rubbed herself over his dick, still hard. The increased pressure was a release for her, and she felt the slow, hot sensation of her own orgasm build deep within her. It crept up from the pit of her stomach and she let out a slow breath, as she pulsed. Her inner G-spot took the full pressure of his semi-hard cock, and it was enough to take her to the finish. She inhaled in short sharp breaths, and then let out one long breath as her body realised the full release. She smiled and opened her eyes. He was looking up at her.

'Happy birthday, Mr Dean,' she said, with the wicked smile he had seen in his head all the time she had blindfolded him.

'Thank you, Mrs Dean, I believe it is and will be.' He rolled her onto her side facing him and he kissed her.

She leant over and reached for the small present that had almost made its way off the bed. She giggled as she passed it to him. 'I hope that you like it. It's not much, but I really struggled to know what to get you.'

He took the gift and sat up, using both hands to open the box. As he lifted the lid, a solid gold pen was revealed. Inscribed around the lower part Lottie had had the words engraved:

My husband, whom I adore, your wife forever more. L xx

'I love it,' he said reading the words again.

'And we are still OK for a few drinks later?' she asked, hoping that the answer was still yes.

He felt the effects of last night's few drinks, but he was looking forward to a quiet night with Lottie. It must be his age, he thought to himself. *I can live with that though.*

They showered and made breakfast. Mrs B came in after 11 and wished him a happy birthday. They never did cards, but she allowed him a peck on the cheek as acknowledgment of the special day.

Lottie had arranged a shopping trip, and as the weather was nice, cool but dry, she quickly chatted to Pete about travel details.

After checking what to wear, they got in the car and made their way to Harrods. Bella was primed and ready to meet them as Pete opened the door.

'Achilles?' he said, and Lottie nodded. 'I'll call you,' she replied.

'Happy Birthday, Mr Dean,' Bella said, and he thanked her. She showed them through the Food Hall to the Oyster Bar. Other customers were seated around the bar, but six chairs were reserved. They sat at the end of the six, leaving the other four free, to give them some privacy.

'I tried to pay for all the seats so that it was just you and me, but it seems I don't have that sort of persuasion!' she said, leaning over to whisper. She was referring to the night that Ed had booked the whole of The Kensington just for them, to have a meal.

'I will have to show you that little trick,' he smiled at her, planting a kiss on her lips. A couple walking past looked at them, admiring the attention he was showing Lottie.

'Mr Dean, many happy returns,' the young waiter said, showing Lottie the bottle of champagne he'd fetched from the fridge below the counter. 'May I?'

She smiled, and he popped the bottle, pouring two glasses. She lifted hers to Ed and they touched. 'Cheers,' they said together.

Moments later a large tray of oysters was placed in front of them. A tub of the finest caviar and several small paninis, an array of salmon, all on wooden platters. Two ice cold vodkas arrived with another tin of caviar in the centre.

'Mrs Dean, do you want me drunk?' he said, looking at the fine food in front of him.

She leaned into him again. 'Not drunk, but I want you!' She lifted her eyebrows, and he used his hand to rub her thigh. He could feel the silk-stocking tops and the small button of the suspender belt beneath her tight skirt of the soft cotton dress she was wearing. 'Not that you ever need the help of oysters, but I am wearing the rest of your present!'

He took a deep breath in and shifted in his seat, knowing that he was aroused so easily by her promise.

They started to eat, and other diners occasionally looked over. One couple looked back at the menu, then they commented on the price of the food in front of them. Lottie smiled; she had not got used to money, but could see how it had its good points.

Bella walked over to them. 'How is it going?' she asked.

'Will you have a glass?' Ed asked looking at Lottie to see if that was OK. Lottie took a clean glass from the top of the bar as if to say 'of course it is'.

'Just a little, I'm on duty.'

Lottie poured her some and filled their own glasses again. They chatted for a while, and then Bella took a note from a young boy. 'Thank you,' she said passing it to Lottie. Lottie looked around after she had opened the folded note.

'Mrs Dean?' The attendant offered her a pen knowing from the headed paper it was a bill. She was just about to take it and Ed put his hand in his pocket.

'Here, baby girl, I have one.' He handed her the gold pen and took off the top. Lottie signed her name and passed the paper back to Bella.

'Beautiful pen, Mr Dean, a gift?' she said smiling. Of course it was a gift; she had helped Lottie pick it and been responsible for having the wording she had chosen inscribed on it.

Before Bella left, a hamper had been placed behind the counter, and Bella smiled at Lottie. Lottie smiled back and mouthed 'later'. She nodded back, without Ed noticing.

Conversation was light, people came and went at the bar next to them and others passed by. Lottie and Ed laughed, holding hands, him touching her leg, or rubbing her thigh and showing affection. They finished the fine food that was placed in front of them, and sat having a final coffee before Lottie said 'Ready?'

He had no idea what was on the cards for the rest of the day, but he did hope that no more alcohol was involved. Well, not just yet anyway or he would never last the night or make a good job of the second half of his promised present.

Lottie carried the basket, although Ed had offered. They walked out of the store and along the street towards Hyde Park. It was busy, with people bustling about everywhere. Cutting through the side road they soon reached the grass. Avoiding the people, joggers, bikers, and walkers all using the outside space on a sunny spring day, they walked to a flowerbed that had a small patch of grass in the middle and Lottie stopped.

She took the basket and opened it, taking out a warm blanket. She put it on the ground, sat down and patted the ground by her side. Ed lay on his back with his head in her lap.

'Now I know it is not a workday, but I wanted to run some things past you, is that OK?' she asked.

He turned his head to look at her. 'I suppose so.'

Lottie chatted about the hospital, how it was finished and they needed to go up to open it, what sort of event it should be, how to arrange it etc. She opened a bottle of spring water. Ed sat up to drink it, then settled back to the comfy position. She occasionally brushed her hand through his hair, and he took her hand and kissed it. They continued to talk, and the hours seemed to vanish. Although so many people passed them by, they could have been sitting alone in the world for all they noticed.

A chill had arrived in the air, and Lottie looked at her watch. She had a jacket on, but she could feel that it was cooler now the sun had dropped. She reached in her bag for her phone and texted Pete. Packing up, they walked to the corner of the road where he was waiting, holding up most of the traffic. The Bentley drove off but not in the direction of the apartment. Sure that the privacy screen was up, Lottie undid her seat belt. She had taken off her jacket getting into the car, meaning she had just the dress on. She straddled Ed.

'Mr Dean, the rest of your present...' She pulled her dress over her head to reveal a black lace bra and the smallest G-string Ed had ever seen. 'Would you like it now or later?'

He was amazed, almost to the point of being speechless. She had become so adventurous in the past few days. He took his gift; of course there was no point waiting!

After they had been back to the apartment to change and shower, Phil drove them back into town. He pulled up outside the Tap and Tune. The shutters were closed, but looking through the door it was easy to see that the venue was packed. Ed got out of the car and helped Lottie. As he opened the door, he realised that the place was full of faces he knew.

'Happy birthday, son!' his mother said as she kissed him when he entered. He looked round at Lottie.

'A quiet drink you said?' He was now on the same page – a surprise party, more like. Lottie smiled and bit her lower lip.

'Good or bad thing?' she asked.

'Ok thing so far.' He smiled and kissed her. Scotty rushed to him with two glasses of champagne and the guests started to greet him and pass on their birthday wishes.

Feeling at ease with close friends and family, he allowed Lottie to have conversations away from him, although he looked around the room checking her location often. Todd was there with his sister and Bob. Joe and an ever-blooming Sarah stood talking to Johnny, who had sent apologies about Julie, as she had to work late. Marcus and Liz were part of the group, although Liz sat on her own with her leg in plaster, not moving far and Marcus was taking full advantage of the free bar. Bella and her husband gave a wave and Lottie joined them, chatting for a long time about the day. Bella's husband was really interested in the story of her piano; he had worked with wood and appreciated such restoration work.

Several gifts and unopened cards had been left for Ed and Lottie took them out to the car. Phil came back in to help and when he noticed Liz sitting in the corner on her own, he asked if Lottie minded if he spoke to her.

'You don't need to ask me, Phil, please feel at home.' She pulled down the boot and locked the car. He had gone back in and she'd taken the keys off him. It was parked at the back of the bar in a quiet street. She thought that she noticed someone hovering; it had become dark and she was not sure if it was her imagination or if someone was really watching her. She flicked the key again to ensure the car was locked. The glow of the amber lights showed a figure standing at the end of the alley and she suddenly felt a shiver.

She pulled open the back door, it was the quickest way back in and had thankfully been left ajar. She pulled the door to, making sure that the lock on the crash bar clicked in top and bottom. As she walked away, she heard the door rattle. There was no handle on the outside of the door anyway, so even if it was unsecured, it would be hard to get in.

She walked through the small kitchen and back into the room, still looking behind her, and she bumped Todd on the arm.

'Lottie, have you seen a ghost?' She must have looked shocked.

'No, I just thought that someone was outside the back,' she smiled. 'Kids or something,' she said, dismissing it.

She looked around the room and smiled to see Phil with a glass of orange juice, talking to Liz. She guessed that they had not seen each other since the incident in France and imagined that it was nice for them to catch up. She did not go and disturb them, but sought out Mr Harris, one of the company's solicitors. She had met him as arranged to go through Ed's will and the asset details some weeks before. He was standing next to a young girl, who he introduced as his wife. Lottie could not help but think that the girl had to be her own age, and he was almost twice as old. It takes all sorts, she mused to herself, looking round to locate her own husband.

Ed was talking to young Simon who had come along with his father. She could not see his 'gramps' who had also been invited but watched on as Ed knelt down to his level and was in conversation with him, almost as if he were flying with his arms out, Simon copying his actions.

'I think he has a fan,' Alice said. Lottie hadn't noticed her walk up to her.

'Yes, although I am not sure who is the bigger kid sometimes,' she smiled, and took a sip of her now-warming champagne.

'They never really grow up, men,' the older woman explained. 'It seems only yesterday that he was that young.' She stopped a waiter and grabbed two more glasses, handing one to Lottie. 'I guess time flies and you don't realise it. He makes me feel so old.'

Lottie looked at the attractive woman standing next to her. She'd had Ed so young, under-18, and given that, she was nowhere near an age where she should see herself as old.

'Alice, you are beautiful, and certainly not old,' Lottie added, and it was a compliment that was genuinely felt.

'That is kind of you to say so, I guess the advantage of having him so young, but still, to say he is 30 makes me wonder what I did with the time.'

The two women spoke a little more, and his mother tutted as the paper planes they were making from the napkins showered the other small group who stood next to them. 'See, they never grow up!'

Liz caught Lottie's eye and she beckoned her over. Phil was still sitting with her. Lottie made pleasantries and asked how she was.

'Thanks to this wonderful man, doing OK,' Liz said with a smile that showed off her white teeth. 'I never got the chance to thank you either.'

'It was really all a blur; we just did what we thought was best at the time,' Lottie replied.

'Let me leave you, Mrs Dean,' Phil said, standing up.

'Oh, please stay,' Liz said. 'If that is OK?' She looked at Lottie, who smiled. 'I'll get us some more drinks,' Phil added and stood up, walking to the bar. Lottie noticed how Liz followed his every movement with her eyes, a look that had something, but she was not sure what.

'You and Marcus OK?' She was aware that they had only been on the break to try to patch things together, and he had showed her little if any attention during the course of the night.

'Not really, we came together tonight, shared a taxi really. I moved back home last week, we are taking it easy,' she explained. Lottie was not surprised.

'I found out he cheated on me, ages ago when we first got together. I tried to forgive him, but, well I know he looked like he cared when this happened,' she pointed to her leg, 'but at the first opportunity when we got back, he was seen out with her again. He denied it of course, but I really can't forgive him for that. He knows we are dead in the water, he just seems to want to hang on.'

Liz Morgan had her own small business at a fashion house and an unknown label called Miss M, designing clothes. Nothing large, or well-known but enough to keep her busy, and at her young age, if she had the right backing she could be successful. Lottie had commented on several outfits when they were away, all of which Liz had made and designed.

Marcus liked to play hard and lived off the handouts his parents gave him, or that he was able to get from Joe. He had worked for Joe but gave it up when he knew he could make more money on the betting side of the horses, rather than owning them.

'The drinking doesn't help, he gets a bit...' Liz stopped talking as soon as Phil came back into view. She would have finished the sentence by saying 'violent' but thought better of it. She smiled at Phil and thanked him as he handed her the fresh glass of orange juice. Lottie could not help but notice there was a connection between the two of them.

Oliver Matchin was a youngster that Lottie had started to sponsor before Christmas, with the hope that he would be able to go to the Royal Music School. He was only thirteen, and he was autistic, so he was labelled as having a learning difficulty, but, as compensation almost, he had a remarkable talent playing the piano. He was able to read and write music and, like Lottie, could hear a piece and then perform it on the piano from memory. He could also do the same on a guitar, violin and a clarinet, something that Lottie was amazed by. She had seen his application when she had visited the college. They had dismissed him due to his poor academic results. He was just the sort of boy who, given half a chance, would excel, even if he was never to be a brain surgeon. Lottie liked him and his mum from the first day they had met.

She had invited him and his mother along so that he could play as the final surprise. She had said hello earlier in the evening and as it grew close to 9 o'clock she noticed that they were talking to Ed. She went over to join them.

'Mrs Lottie.' He had taken to greeting her this way and she thought it was sweet. 'This is a great party.' He smiled a cheeky grin at her, something else she had found she warmed to after their first meeting.

'Thanks Oli,' Lottie replied to him. 'it's Mr Dean's night really though, his birthday treat.'

'I like treats,' Oliver replied, rocking on his heels. 'And birthdays, don't I, Mum?'

'Yes, sweetness, you do.' Mrs Matchin ruffled his hair and he smiled at her.

Lottie had learned that when Oliver had been born there were complications; he had been starved of oxygen for a time, and the learning difficulties had only shown as he started to talk, and when he went to school. The strain on her marriage had been too much and when Oliver was six, his father had left them. She had raised him herself, sacrificing everything, like a mother would and more. Lottie backing him had already helped her too. Unbeknown to Ed, Lottie had funded some weekend tutoring and for the first time in years, she had been able to take them both away thanks to the funds Lottie had put forwards. .

While Oliver had lessons, Lottie had been able to catch up with Sue, his mother, and they shared coffee and chats. She was seven years older than Lottie, and each year showed through her face. Lottie could not imagine how it must have been with such a demanding child, and on your own. She did not want to say that she felt sorry for her, but it made her think how hard her own mother had worked bringing her up alone, without any complications. It saddened her to think that society did not make it any easier, with little help from the state, and even less help from organisations who were not able to see past the fact that there was not natural perfection in every aspect of a child.

'Mrs Lottie can we…?' Oliver flexed his fingers.

'Oli!' his mother said.

'Oh sorry, it's a surprise, sorry, Mrs Lottie, Mr Lottie!' Oliver looked down at his feet and dropped his bottom lip as if to emphasise his sadness.

'It's Mr Dean, Oli,' his mum corrected him, rubbing his arm as if to console him.

'It's Edward, Oli, not Mr Lottie,' Lottie said, correcting them both with a smile in her voice. She held out her hand to Oliver and he looked up and smiled as if the last few seconds had not happened.

Ed looked a little confused but smiled at the greeting the boy had given him. Or was it the attention and obvious care that his wife was showing to the young man stood before them?

'Your last surprise is,' she paused. 'You tell him, Oli.' Lottie gently squeezed his hand.

'Mr Edward, we are going to play for you, the pieces of music Mrs Lottie got with her piano written by a princess,' he said in the best grown-up voice he could muster. His head was held high and his chest out proud.

Lottie had studied the scores she had found in the seat of the piano, and with a bit of digging, well, a lot of digging and as it turned out a bit of cash too, had been able to find more of her music. It was not considered that a woman should be talented enough to publish music back in the late 19th century and so she had written under another name. A man's name. The old, tattered sheet music Lottie had was only part of a romantic piece the princess had written for her husband. It seemed a perfect gift to give back to Ed, as he had said that he would enjoy her playing.

Oliver thrust some paper at Lottie, after he had reached under the table to get it and his violin.

'Ready?' she said, looking at him. His grin and hand pulling her to the direction of the piano was a very obvious yes – he was ready.

Only a few people saw them approach the piano. Scotty had arranged for it to be tuned and serviced in the last week, under the direction of Lottie. She sat at the stool and arranged the music. Oliver looked back at everyone and put his instrument to his neck. The first stroke of the strings was a signal he was going to start. The closing of his eyes was a transformation from a young boy to a talented young man.

Lottie followed his lead and started to bring the baby grand to life. She had to concentrate hard on the music as she had only played the piece a few times with Oliver; he had no music, but effortlessly created complementary rhythm to the slow lament that started the piece. His mother had followed them both as Lottie needed someone to turn the music and, as the first page turned, it was obvious that everyone in the room had stopped to hear them playing together.

Ed had to sit as his legs were in shock. His pulse raced and his nostrils flared with a passion he never had dreamt he could feel. He was not sure how to take his eyes away from her, but seeing the two of them, the young boy now standing directly at her side and Lottie in her familiar mesmerised state she adopted when playing, he thought that if he had not sat, he may have fallen. This proud, badass businessman had been reduced to possible tears. The lump in his throat confirmed that he was an emotional wreck. His mother sensed this and sat by his side. She smiled at him and he smiled back, not taking his eyes from the small, staged area where his wife was playing.

The back street was dark, and the assailant found that the toughened glass on the Bentley window was hard to smash. He tried the back window twice, only managing to crack it, not enough to be able to get his hand in. His intention was not to steal the car, but to try to get in to find and video the evidence that he sought.

Instantaneously the car alarm sounded, and he ran away from the area. Checking in his pocket that he still had the camera that he had taken photos with moments before, he headed away from the scene as fast as he could.

The sensor in Phil's pocket went off and he leapt from his seat, rushing as fast as he could from the bar to the location of the car without causing too much of a stir in the room that was still fixated on the music being played. Banging the fire door open he observed the car making a noise, looking around for anyone. He took his gun from his pocket and silenced the alarm with the key. With stealth he walked around the vehicle, but no one was around. He noticed the cracked glass and took out his phone to call Pete. Although he was on a night off, he knew he would want to be informed before the police.

'They are still inside, safe and unaware'? Pete asked down the phone once the information had been relayed to him.

'Yes. Whoever it was did not get in, but they must have cut themselves trying – there is a spot of blood on the window.' Phil noticed the small droplet with his flashlight.

'Keep them inside. I am on my way over. Is Mr Carter there?' Pete asked and Phil acknowledged he was. 'Get him out without making a fuss, then call me back and let me speak to him.'

Phil did as he was told. Todd was at first confused, but Phil fully explained before they had even reached the car, and Todd also spoke to Pete who was in his car on his way over.

Lottie and Oliver finished playing and the room burst into a round of applause. Oliver took a small bow, smiling from ear to ear. His mother was filled with pride and could not hold back her tears as the water trickled down her cheek.

Ed stood and walked over to his wife. He didn't speak, he just kissed her in full view of everyone in the room.

Oliver looked away, embarrassed, and giggled.

'Speech!' someone shouted, and Ed looked back at the crowd; he had temporality forgotten they were all there.

He held up his hand and shook his head. 'No speeches,' he said, holding Lottie by the waist.

'Oh, come on, man!' Joe shouted from not far away. The room fell silent in expectation.

'No speech, just a word of thanks to you all for tonight, it's been great.' He turned to Oliver and shook his hand. 'Thank you, Oliver, you played perfectly.' The little man grinned and took another bow, which made the room fill with laughter.

Ed turned to Lottie. 'Thank you.' He swallowed hard and looked deep into her eyes. She smiled at him, knowing that he would not say anymore in public, and he lifted her hand and kissed it. He whispered so that only she heard, 'My beautiful wife, I love you more than words, in fact I have none, but this has been one of the best days so far of my life. Without you, I don't breathe.' He kissed her hand again and she bit on her lip.

'I'm glad you enjoyed it,' she said. 'So catch your breath my love, I'm here.' She pulled him close to her and kissed his cheek, the small damp patch proof that he had wiped away a tear.

Outside, without any other guests being aware, Todd was looking at the car. He had rummaged around the kitchen to find some bits, and he was able to get a sample from the glass.

'Are you calling the police?' he asked.

'Mr Dean's call really,' Pete said back to Todd. Pete had turned up seconds before and caught the question. 'I'll give him a moment and then spoil the night. Can we get the story straight? Can you check this on the quiet and let me know, or do we involve the police?'

'Why so underhand?' Todd asked.

'Mr Dean has, how can I say this, upset people in his life. This could be kids chancing it. Or it could be something more – the car is very recognisable from the number plate. I have to say if it was a professional job, they should have known the car was bulletproof and would have used more than a stone to attempt to break in.' He pointed to the stone that Todd had picked up from the floor and wrapped in clingfilm. 'When the police become involved, it can add fuel to a fire and puts Mr Dean in the line of reporters and investigations, most of which he likes to keep quiet.'

'So, if I were not able to take this back to the lab what would you do?' Todd asked hypothetically.

'Pay someone else to find out and get any leads. Ask around to look at the CCTV. I have friends in the force, I call in favours. You are a trusted friend; this way I know you are on side, a favour for a friend, like staying in someone's apartment for months.' Pete added that bit as a sweetener, not as blackmail but as a reminder how things worked in this sort of world. 'Mr and Mrs Dean sleep safe in their beds without alarming them until there is any need, if indeed there is any need at all.' He played the Mrs Dean card as he knew how much Lottie meant to him.

'Fair comment. I can run these through on Monday and let you know.

I may need to prove why I want to see CCTV so I might have to ask you to deal with that side, although I will see who I can sweet-talk in IT. So, the story for now is…?' Todd asked.

'Kids trying their luck,' Pete instructed to both men, who nodded in acceptance.

'Phil?' He caught the man's arm as Todd and he were about to walk back inside. Phil turned around. 'And you were where while this happened?'

'Inside with Mrs Dean.' If he'd said 'and her friend', he knew he would be in trouble. 'At her request,' he added, as if it made it right. Pete just looked back at him. He would take the answer for now. He knew that Miss Elizabeth Morganas on the guest list and he knew that Phil had called her several times since she had returned from the skiing break. All Dean Incorporated employees' calls were tracked and traced if needs be. Pete had to be sure that Phil had not dropped his game.

Guests were leaving and the bar was closing. Pete stood quietly in the doorway. It was some time before he caught Ed's eye, but as soon as he did Edward beckoned him over.

For Pete to be there it was a given that something had gone wrong, and his first instinct was to look for Lottie and then his mother. Both women were present so what else could it be?

'Pete?' he said as a question.

'Mr Dean, sorry to bring you this, but it looks like the car has had an attempted break in.' He often found it best just to cut to the chase. 'Phil called me over to take a look.'

'Nothing taken?' Ed asked.

'No, it looks like kids, just damaged the glass,' Pete replied.

'Are you concerned it's anything more?' Ed looked at Lottie who was still chatting to his mother and Scotty.

'No, but of course I will look into it.'

'The police?' Ed asked.

'Your call, I would let me run with it first; the damage is limited, not even for insurance,' Pete added.

'OK good, thanks Pete, well handled. Where was Phil when it happened?' Ed asked.

'In here with Mrs Dean, at her request.'

'Oh yes, right, I did see him helping out Lottie. I'll see you tomorrow.'

'Yes, Phil's in the car now, waiting,' Pete replied and slipped out as quickly as he had come in.

Ed went over to the ladies and asked Scotty to help his mother with her jacket; they were giving her a lift back, so he just wanted to fill Lottie in before they reached the car. He had not seen the damage himself yet but could only say that it was not an issue for her to worry about. He also did not want to worry his mother.

As they walked back into the apartment, Lottie said, 'I saw someone you know, when I was putting the cards in the boot. It was just one figure, and it didn't look like kids.'

'You tell me now? Why did you not come back and say anything to Phil? Where was he anyway? Pete said he was helping put the things in the car.' Ed asked wanting to get the story straight.

'He did help but I took the last lot out.' She cut her reply short not wanting to say that he'd stayed with Liz. She was not sure if she should say that someone then tried the door when she had closed it. Her dilemma must have been noted by Ed.

'Anything else?' he said grabbing some water from the fridge.

'No, it just seems weird, maybe we should let the police look into it, get some forensic evidence.' She took the water he offered her and opened the bottle.

'Let's see how Pete gets on with it.' He came up to her and wrapped his arms around her waist. 'Anyway, Mrs Dean, thank you for today, I've had a great time.' He kissed her gently on the lips.

'Well, I wasn't sure there is anything in this world that I could give you as a gift, the man who has it all as your mother said, and she was right, so this seemed the only thing to do.' She hugged him back.

He looked her in the eye and smiled. There was one thing, he thought, as he put his hand over her shoulder, knowing now that the implications of the implant would prevent them for trying for a baby, sadly possibly for months. He wanted to say something, but it was late at night, after such a good day. It would undoubtedly start an argument, something he wanted to avoid; they were both tired and he knew it would get out of hand, so it would have to rest for now.

Ed put down the phone in the office and looked through the glass. It was Monday, Lottie was at the Centre but the news he had just received was good. He smiled to himself, picking up his mobile to call her.

'Hey, you,' she said as she took the call.

'Can we meet for lunch? I know I'm late in asking but I've got something to show you,' he asked, looking at the email he was about to print off on the screen.

'About 1:30 I suppose I can get away.' She looked up at Todd as if to ask if that time was all right and he nodded.

The date was set. Todd was grateful as he had tried all morning to get rid of her so he could run his tests. He knew that if he started on them, she would be asking questions as it was not related to what they were currently working on. He tapped the plastic and the hard stone in his pocket as a reminder it was still there.

Pete pulled up outside the Centre and went to the reception desk with Ed. Security phoned Lottie, who went down to meet them.

'It's just some salad Pete picked up, I'm afraid,' Ed said as he lifted the bag of food onto her office desk. 'I wanted to ask you about this.' He handed her a printed piece of paper and she read through as he got out the food and started to eat in the chair opposite her. She took her time to take in the information.

'This is really great, and you have spoken to him?' Lottie looked up.

'Yes, it has taken me a long time. I thought that I had friends in high places, but it seems not in the right departments for immigration. If you still want to go for the idea, I can get him over within a week.' Ed took another mouthful of leaves from the bowl and wiped his hands on the napkin, taking another piece of paper from the folder.

'We need, well you need to think about a contract, what you want to pay, terms and conditions etc. I didn't want to do it as it is not really my call, being your house, but if I put this down as a starter, the lawyers will draw you something up. But you need to be aware that it is only for a year; if it works out, we will need to see how we can keep him here longer.'

They were talking about Gerald, the housekeeper they'd had in the accommodation at their wedding resort. Lottie had mentioned that she wanted a housekeeper for the house in Kent, as they seemed to spend so little time there. She had befriended Gerald in the short time they were together and wanted to see if this could be the fresh start he needed. Ed had worked with Pete on background checks and what was involved in getting him over and it was something that he could arrange. He had spoken to him on the phone several times over the past month and, if they could get visas, Ed had booked a flight for the weekend for him to come over. They continued to talk about it over the rest of lunch.

Lottie added in, 'Thank you for thinking this is my decision, but Ed, as you often remind me, the house in Kent is yours too, we are in this together!'

Ed looked back at his wife. It was days like this that he knew in her face he could see his very future. He would stop at nothing to give her everything and he had to know that if he waited long enough, she would, without knowing, give him all he wanted too.

Out of sight of the dining couple a conversation was taking place.

'So, what have you found?' Pete asked Todd as they chatted in the corridor along from Lottie's office, knowing they were out of view.

'I've not been able to do it yet, she's been with me all morning. Let's go in the lab, keep an eye on them for me.' Todd scanned his card and Pete stood outside the door waiting. It was over 20 minutes later when Todd came back out.

'We have a sample, and I am running it now. I need to let the programme work though, it's being a bit slow.'

Both men looked up as the door opened.

'What are you two hatching?' Lottie came out of her office and saw the two of them together, and Ed followed her putting his jacket back on.

'Nothing we were just chatting.' Todd went red; he had always found it hard to lie to her. 'I'll show you out,' he said, walking down the corridor with Pete. When they were out of earshot he said, 'I'll call you as soon as I have anything.' Pete nodded.

Lottie and Ed said their goodbyes and she scanned herself back into the lab. She put her lab coat back on and poured two cups of coffee. She walked to Todd's desk and put his down. Out the corner of her eye she could see the lab DNA search computer flashing and wondered why as they had not been working on anything. She put in her password and looked at the results. She was still sitting in front of the desk when Todd walked back in.

'Anything you want to tell me?' she asked. 'I knew that you and Pete were up to something, why is this showing a match with my break-in at the flat and where did it come from?'

There was no need to lie – she would be able to search the file notes if she wanted, so Todd explained.

'I knew it wasn't kids,' she said, looking at the results again. 'It also mentions a cold case, closed but it will not grant me access. Should we be opening it up again?' she asked.

'We need the professor for that one,' Todd said. 'Maybe the two markers are enough to go on, after all it is a match with a case, but not a person or a name. We drew a blank with your break-in months ago, we will no doubt do the same here without any more leads.'

'But it does mean that someone may be targeting me. Is that not a lead?' She looked up at him. 'Someone did see me when I was out at the car, and they tried the door after I came back in.'

'Did you tell Pete this?' It was news to him, and he must have looked shocked.

'No,' she admitted. 'If we blow this up and tell Pete he will go to Ed. That will panic him, and I will be under house arrest if he thinks there is a problem. I really don't want that.'

'But say this is true and you are someone's target, should he not know? Pete and the team need to be made aware. God, Lottie, I don't want anything to happen to you, and this could be serious. There's a lot of time between the two events, but we can clearly see they are linked in some way.'

'So, we look into it more before we make any rash decisions,' she said.

'And I tell Pete what?' Todd asked, knowing that he had to report back to him.

'That there was no match,' Lottie said.

'I'm not going to lie about something that could lead to you getting hurt.' Todd stood up and came over to her.

'If whoever broke into my flat wanted me that bad, they would not have taken three months to have another go,' she explained.

'Unless they have been inside or something,' Todd added.

'And if they had been, we would have their DNA match from the police record data base,' Lottie quickly replied.

'Maybe they have been somewhere else or planning something in that time.' Todd scratched his head. 'I would hate for something to happen to you, Lottie, you know that, and if something did and I knew we could have stopped it I would never forgive myself. Plus, your husband would have my balls on a plate within hours!'

'Look, just tell Pete that nothing came up. Let's leave it as it is for now and I will ensure that I take extra care. If we find something else, well then, we can tell Ed. But I can just see that he will never let me do a thing if there is the smallest chance that someone is out for me, and that includes working here. I don't want that to happen.'

'Lottie, I hate the fact that we are lying,' Todd said.

'Not lying, just not telling them all the facts until we have some solid evidence.' She paused. 'Come on, you know that speculation can be just as damaging.' She tried to appease him. 'If we ask the prof for the other case notes, I can almost assure you that Ed will find out.' There was a moment when their eyes met, and she tried to appease him with a smile.

'How?' Todd asked.

'Long story short, Ed makes good payments to the Centre to ensure that the prof follows my work closely for this very reason. I'm living with that as a compromise, and I can assure you my husband knows I'm not happy about it, but we have had to give and take a little to allow me to keep working.'

'You mean you have had to give, and he takes, is more like it', Todd added still very aware of the controlling nature her husband had.

'No, there are things I know he would sooner I do, or not do.' She picked up the file and placed it on the bottom of the in tray. 'Make the call to Pete, let him know you found nothing to note, and that you will monitor it closely.'

Not wanting to and knowing deep down it was wrong, he did as she had asked. How could he not – he loved her. Always had, and always would.

Chapter 5

Lottie and Ed met an overwhelmed Gerald off the plane at Heathrow on the Saturday night. They drove over to the house in Kent and spent the rest of the weekend with him. The contracts were drawn up and they went through everything, making sure it was a good arrangement on both parts.

Agnes had been reserved in her judgement, saying that someone local would have been better, but Lottie really wanted to give him a chance. He had left everything back home to do this and promised her that he would take very good care of the house.

She settled him into the spare room, and on the Sunday, they arranged for her car to be brought back over for him to drive. He was nervous about this as he had not driven outside his own township, so Lottie said that he could have some lessons and they could apply for his UK licence when he felt happy.

He would need to be able to get about to shop and to have something to do other than spend days cleaning, gardening, and doing DIY jobs that had been put off for far too long. They went down to the pub for a late lunch on the Sunday and he met some of the locals. A mixed reception from some which annoyed Lottie and she made this known, but others welcomed him to the village.

Although Lottie wanted to get back to work on the Monday, she was still worried about him being on his own in a new place. Agnes said she would pop in, once Lottie had convinced her it was the right decision all round. And on the Wednesday, Lottie was going to go back over to see how he was settling in, as they headed back to the city as planned.

'I can't come with you, Lottie,' Ed said, 'I have to be in the office. Can't you wait until tomorrow?'

'I will only be gone one night, and Pete will be with me, seeing as Phil is on a few days off.' She pleaded with him as they stood in the kitchen after their supper.

'Can't you just–' he was stopped short by her kissing him.

'No, I can't. I'm a big girl, and it is only one night,' she said after backing away from his lips. 'You know where I am, who I am with – you may as well shackle me to this sink!'

'The thought has crossed my mind!' he said with a cheeky grin. 'Several times,' he murmured under his breath.

'I am sure it has, and not just to satisfy yourself that you know where I am!' She bit her lip, hoping that the subject was changing in her favour.

'Mrs Dean your mind is purely one track. I was not thinking of anything rude.' He paused. 'But now you talk about it...' He grabbed her around the waist. 'I can just see you in a short apron with not much underneath.' He slapped her backside in a playful way, and she giggled.

'Black stockings and a whisk?' She picked up the kitchen utensil and slapped it on her hand. 'I am armed and ready for you.' She smiled at him, wriggling out her of skirt and unbuttoning her shirt. She had a black set on underneath.

'If I had known you had that on under there, we would have missed dinner that's for sure!' Ed said, rubbing his hands along her thigh.

'Uh-uh, don't touch, you haven't been invited!' She slapped him with the whisk, and it made a noise on his arm. 'Sorry, that was a bit hard!' She looked at him apologetically and he laughed.

'Sorry, Mrs Beaten! I did not know I needed an invite to touch my wife.' He unbuttoned his shirt, revealing his well-developed chest, and then pinned her to the side of the worktop. 'You were saying about an invite?' He started to kiss her, along her neck and down the front of her chest, between her breasts. He mauled her left breast with his hand, while he kissed the other through the black lace, making the soft material grate against the end of it.

She held herself back on the worktop and dropped the whisk she had been holding in her hand. As he kissed her other breast, she rubbed one hand through his hair, allowing the pleasure to run from her nipple down to her inner thighs. She used a hand to pull off his shirt, assisting with the buttons on each wrist. She rubbed her hands along the tops of his shoulders, tracing the line of the muscles as they moved gently as he continued to kiss her neck and shoulders. He dropped the bra straps down one at a time kissing the line where they had been all day.

One simple move allowed the back hook to part and she was free. He stood back admiring her full form, kissing at each nipple in turn and watching them react to his touch. Lottie could feel his rise in pleasure and rubbed herself across his groin. He traced his way with a flutter of kisses down her stomach, which tensed at the sensation. She naturally parted her legs, and he hooked the simple black lace pants in each hand and lowered them to the floor.

She pushed her head back as he kissed the outer mound of her sex, lightly covered with dark hair. She had recently had a bikini wax, and the skin was still very tender.

Pushing his head harder to her he used her arse to get more pressure, and he allowed his tongue to slip into her warm sex lips. She smelt sweet, and he licked her and absorbed her moisture on his tongue. She was increasingly turned on as he reached for her inner area. Leaving her black stockings and suspender belt in place he rubbed up her legs, along and up her inner thigh until his thumb brushed her cleft. She opened her legs slightly more.

'Is that an invite, Mrs Dean?' he asked, sensing that she wanted his touch in this intimate place.

Lottie looked across to the large expanse of window, and she could see their reflection from the internal light and the dark sky outside. It was like looking in a mirror. She looked at the way he nestled into her groin, his back and shoulder muscles working as he moved and turned, translating the movements through his tongue to her. She caught her breath at the idea that someone outside may see them, a slim chance as they were so high up, but it was the thought of how it would feel for someone to be watching this act. She dug her fingers into his hair and pulled back his face, wanting the chance to kiss him. She also needed to slow down as she had felt the stir of her climax low in her stomach and knew that if he continued this pace, she would not last more than a minute.

As he stood and reached her face, she made eye contact with him and kissed his neck, reaching for him. She rubbed the material of his trousers, the large, pulsing member hidden behind the fabric. She fumbled with his zip as she carried on kissing him, tasting herself on his smooth lips. .

Releasing his trousers and boxers she massaged his prick, taking it in one hand and wrapping her fingers around him, pulsing up and down to a gentle rhythm. She shot her eyes back to the reflection and smiled at the image she saw.

Ed caught her looking at their refection in the window. He smiled to himself – was it the thought of someone watching, or the observation of them pleasuring each other? Whichever it was he liked the idea and had on occasion been to watch a live sex show, although it had not turned him on as much as watching her at this very moment. He pulled her chest up so that he could suck on her hard nipple, biting the end, licking it, and soothing away any pain it might have caused. He did it again, and each time she tightened her grip on him as the pulse ran through her body. He kissed her and she sucked his lip, almost biting it as he pulled back. He had lost all hope of restraining himself, knowing that his hard, purple shaft was letting his closeness to orgasm out, as she rubbed the specks of pre-cum off, using it to lubricate the constant wanking of his shaft that she was performing effortlessly. If he did not have her now, he would spill everywhere.

He knew that the worktop was too high for her to sit on it, so he pulled her back and turned her round, controlling her like a rag doll. Spreading her legs and pushing her forwards exposed her arse, framed with the black elastic of the suspender belt. She gasped as the cold marble top touched her naked upper body. She spread her arms out to try to hold herself off, but he was so close and with his weight on top of her she was not strong enough. Bending his knees slightly he placed himself at the entrance of her sex and thrust up, holding her waist to give him more leverage. She was tight, hot, wet and he pushed up harder again to force his way. The breath left her body as he pushed, and she gave a pleasurable scream as he stretched her to accommodate his size.

She gave a little turn of her head to get a look at them once more in the reflection.

'Do you like to watch?' he asked her. 'Do you like to see me mounting you, entering you and filling you to the core with my throbbing knob?' He spat out with each breath as he continued to pound into her.

'Yes,' she said, catching her own breath, aware that she had uncontrollable pulses in her inner muscles.

'Would you like to watch someone else like this, would it turn you on?' She was not sure how to answer, as she had never thought of it before. He slapped her backside hard. 'Answer me'.

She jumped, not expecting the slap but noting that it increased her aching between her legs. 'I, I don't know,' she gasped out in honesty.

'Maybe we should try it,' he said in her ear. He kissed down her neck and reached between her legs to rub the soft spot at the entrance where his shaft was rubbing in and out. She pushed her head back and he knew he had found the tender spot, where the nerve endings were. He felt her knees shake and he used his other arm to keep her upright. As her inner muscles clenched, she called out as the wave of her orgasm hit her. She gasped as each wave felt like it burnt her skin, her face red and her chest rising and falling quickly with the need to fill her lungs with oxygen. Her movements eased and he pushed her forwards, taking hold of her by both hips. He pushed her into the worktop watching as her flesh slapped against his upper legs. His balls tightened and he listened as she gasped with each application of force.

He was so deep inside her, and he looked at her slender legs covered with soft black material to try to prolong his moment, but it had the opposite effect. He squeezed his butt cheeks in his last effort to wait as he knew she was growing close to coming for the second time, but he was not able to.

With a grunt he shouted out, 'Lottie, oh fucking hell!' His heart rate rose fast and he sucked in air, as much as he could to keep his breathing going.

Each powerful thrust almost lifted her off her feet, until he was spent. He pulled her close and kissed her neck, and she put her arms around his hips, all she could reach from that position, as a gesture of closeness. As she straightened it was hard for him to remain internally attached and he withdrew, his dick still semi-hard. He turned her around, pulled her close and kissed her. He reached for some kitchen towel, and gently wiped her between the legs. He had filled her so much and as she remained standing, she was not able to keep his seed inside her. She took his hand and continued to wipe herself slightly embarrassed he was doing this intimate task from their carnal act. He sensed this and said, 'Let's have a shower.' He picked her up, leaving the aftermath of their passion on the kitchen floor.

He would clean it all up once they had got ready for bed. He knew that it was embarrassing for the staff to hear them, and he was careful that they did not see them. The thought that Lottie wanted to watch a sexual act was something he maybe wanted to explore. As long as it was to watch and not to be watched he could live with that. She was for his eyes only.

She went off to Kent as planned and safely returned for her meeting at the Music School on the Thursday. On Friday they went out for a meal, and as they sat drinking coffee she wanted to ask if Pete had found out anything else about the attempt to break into the car.

'No. He said that all his leads have drawn a blank so we will just put it down to kids, although I told him you saw someone.' Ed took another sip of his drink. 'He had a look at the CCTV. I'm not going to ask how he was able to get hold of police footage from the streets of London, but there are no cameras directed at that area anyway. There were lone people around at the time in other streets, but no one looking suspicious, so we just need to be careful.' It was the truth. Todd had told Pete what Lottie had asked and, of course, this had been passed back to Ed.

April was an uneventful month of work, dinners out, social functions and events and as the first weekend in May arrived, Lottie was ready for the opening of the hospital. She had taken Zoë's advice and they had used an event coordinator, a lot easier all round and to make sure that none of the funding came from the charity, Ed paid for their services himself.

They were booked into a local hotel for a few days, just to make it easier logistically, so on the Thursday Lottie spent the morning with Bella going through clothes and outfits. They were travelling up to Yorkshire on the Friday morning, so there was time to spare for a last-minute shop.

'Mrs Dean,' Bella said as Lottie put her handbag on her shoulder to leave. Lottie stopped and turned around with a smile. 'You know what we talked about a month or so ago? Well, our chief buyer is in the store today, and I was not sure if you would have the time to meet him. I haven't made any arrangements, but I can phone through – he will be free for you.'

Lottie quickly computed in her head what conversation Bella was referring to. She had been chatting to Liz about clothes, over the past few weeks they had had a few conversations by phone, even one chance meeting, although Lottie suspected it was no chance as Phil did not seem surprised that they were at the same venue. Lottie had commissioned a few bespoke outfits and was really pleased with them, saying that they were as good as anything she had purchased, and if only Liz could get in with an exclusive shop, she could do well. This conversation had been passed with Bella, who it seems had taken it further.

'Oh.' She looked at her watch; they had made good time choosing her outfit for the event. 'I can do another half hour, I'll just let Phil know.' She picked her phone up and spoke to him; he was, of course, happy to wait. In the meantime, Bella had called the store office and was asked to take Lottie to the Champagne bar where Mr Sovan Blink would come to meet her.

She instantly noticed the tall dark-haired man approaching her. He was dressed immaculately with a dark blue pinstriped suit, cut to perfection, with the most fabulous shoes and matching pink and blue tie. He held out his hand way before he got to her and introduced himself, in a French accent.

'Mrs Dean, I'm very pleased to meet you.' His smile seemed genuine. 'My Bella here has been explaining about the possibility of introducing a new fashion label in store, and I wanted to know more.'

'Well, I can't speak for Liz, I mean Elizabeth, but it would be fantastic to maybe meet up and go through some of her designs. I find them awesome – well, of course your range here is wonderful, too,' she added quickly. 'But I am all for trying to help a friend.'

'As a very valued customer,' he was thinking that maybe he should have said 'with a stinking rich husband', but he had to reappraise his first impressions of her, now that they had met in the flash and he could see that she was an independent person, 'I value your opinion.'

Lottie carried on talking, and he listened with genuine interest. The more she spoke, the more captivated he became with her. She was not just a trophy wife, he thought, after listening to her reasons and the business proposal that Liz and she had talked about.

'It's a bit cheeky of me, I know, but I am sure that Liz would love to meet up, maybe we could even do a fashion show or something – for charity, of course – and invite a few people to see if there is a real interest. What do you think?' She bit down on her lip out of habit, as her brain was in overdrive about the possibilities this could open for her friend.

Wow, he thought to himself, the papers did her no credit; what little you saw of her in them. There was much talk of Mr Dean, the bad-ass businessman, but this beautiful, clever independent woman was fascinating, and the lip-biting thing… well, it would drive any breathing male insane. Dean, you lucky bastard! the Frenchman thought, ensuring his lewd thoughts were his alone. He composed himself to speak.

'I realise that you are pushed for time now, but I would very much like to meet for lunch, dinner maybe, with your friend of course to discuss your ideas.' He paused; his dark brown eyes seemed to burn into her flesh, and she felt a sort of magnetism in his soothing voice that she knew was wrong of her to think. She fumbled with her wedding ring, maybe as an unconscious reminder.

'Can I offer you another glass?' He pointed to the champagne bottle.

'Thank you but no. I will ask Liz to send you over some of her portfolio. Can I pass on your details?' she asked.

'Of course, please take my card, Mrs Dean. I am happy for you to contact me and arrange something, for next week maybe. I am back in Paris for the week after that, although I could easily arrange for you to come out to my home if it pleases you better?' He took a pen and put a number on the back of the card. 'My private number, and home phone just in case.' He smiled at her and she felt her cheeks warm. Is he flirting with me? she thought.

'I am sure we can find something for next week,' she replied. Even if she wanted to, she really could not see herself trying to persuade Ed; it had been hard enough for him to let her go to Kent on her own for one night. Paris, with a French man, for a meeting – *yeah, right*! She would have to dream on for that one.

'*Enchanté*,' he said, kissing her hand. 'I look forward to your call.'

Lottie stood up and made her way to the front of the store, and after a call to Phil he picked her up. She quickly text Liz, who confirmed she was at work. They started to make their way back to the apartment when Lottie called to the front of the car.

'Phil, can we quickly call round to the fashion house? I know I am cutting it fine, but we should be able to spare half an hour?'

He looked in his mirror. He hated going off plan, but she was right; they were doing well for time. 'No problem. Is Liz, I mean, does Miss Duke expect you?' It was a silly question; of course she did not but he was thrown by the fact that he would see her again.

'I just texted her,' Lottie said with a smile. There was more to his tone of questioning than he was letting on, and she was now intrigued by it. He focused on the road ahead and made a call to inform Pete there was a change of plan for Ms Dean. He smiled as they headed towards the intended destination.

The warehouse was small, down one of the back streets in the city. Phil opened the car door and said he would wait in the car for her.

'Come in, I'm sure Liz would love to see you,' Lottie exclaimed, and he did not need telling twice, locking the car he followed her up the stairs to the small office.

Amongst mannequins and rolls of fabric, sketches and designs, sat Liz at a desk alone.

'Hi Lottie, this is a real nice surprise,' she said, then she looked at the male companion. 'Hi Phil,' she said in a higher-pitched voice. He smiled at her and Lottie could see there was something there that lighted his day. Phil did not really smile, well, not at work anyway.

Lottie started to explain about her meeting with the smooth Mr Blink and Liz showed excitement about a possible meeting.

'Really, Lottie, you could arrange this for me?' she asked.

'I will set things going, but you will need to do all the talking. I said to you if I can help in any way then I would. I've found the Dean name in this town can get you noticed in higher places, so it is not really me, but the name tag.' She smiled. 'But for you my friend,' as that was what she had become over the past months, 'I will do all I can. It's a shame that I'm not around for the weekend, we could have got together and chatted a bit more about this.' Then she had a thought and came out with the question. 'Are you busy Saturday night?'

'Nop, nothing but a TV dinner for one, why?' Liz replied.

'Well, why don't we see if you can come to Yorkshire, have a night of glitz. I could do with a friendly face there. Why did I not think of this before?' She paused, thinking about how she would get up there if they were leaving in a few hours. 'Give me a moment.' She picked up her phone and started chatting to Zoe. Instantly as her attention was turned, Liz started to talk to Phil. Lottie was listening to Zoe, but looking at their body language. Yep, something there, she thought to herself.

'Right, I have a room for you on Saturday night, I just need to get you some transport. Phil?' She looked at him. 'Bit of a trek. We can get you to York train station for just after 3pm, but then you will need a lift. Can you do it?'

He pulled out his phone where the planner for his life was stored. 'Should be able to, Pete and I are on shift all weekend, but by then Mr Dean and you will not need both drivers, and for CP you two will be together.' He almost smiled again. Lottie looked at Liz.

'What do you think? Can you wow us with one of your designs and that stunning figure of yours? Get a few pictures in the magazines that will be there, that would impress our Mr Blink.' Lottie was now thinking what Ed would say to her plan.

'Lottie, you think of everything, how do you do it? Make the world stop and turn the way you want it to?' She hugged her friend.

'I have a good tutor, believe me! It must be rubbing off!' She laughed. but it seemed to be true; money could get you everything you wanted. 'I am sure that you and Phil can finalise details.' Lottie grinned. 'Do you have each other's numbers?'

One said yes, the other no. She laughed and raised her eyebrows.

The spare room had been laid out with clothes and bags half-packed. Mrs B had arranged everything that had been asked for and Lottie's bags from today's shopping trip had been placed in the room, and the dresses had been hung up.

'Hey, you,' she said, kissing her half-naked husband as he walked out of the shower into the room, his hair still wet, body glistening with droplets of water. 'Good workout?' she asked. She had arrived home before him and he had jumped into the shower after a quick hello as soon as he got back.

'Punishing.' He said his trainer had worked him hard as he had missed two sessions already this week. 'But I feel good now.' He looked at the amount of clothes she had in front of her. 'We are only going for two days!' he said, drying his hair.

'I know but I am not sure which to wear, what looks good on me?' she asked holding one dress up to the mirror. 'This?' He shook his head. 'This?' She held another, and again he shook his head. 'This one?' The new one from today.

'Ummm...' he mused. She grabbed the last one and held it up pinning her hair up. 'This one?' He shook his head again.

'None of them. Really? I have to wear something.' She looked confused; they were all beautiful and more than expensive.

'Now, I have a vision – you not wearing anything. That would get the charity bash off to a great start. In fact,' he stood up and started to unbutton her top, 'let me see how that looks!' He pulled at the thin top she had on and she grabbed his hand.

'No, Ed, please.' She looked at him under her eyes. 'I'm on,' she almost whispered. Although they were married, she still felt it was not right, almost embarrassed to have sex during her time of the month. They had done it once before. It had been a mess and she hated herself for a while after, then they had talked about it and she thought he had understood. This month she was not heavy at all, hardly anything really, in fact just a tiny bit of blood first thing this morning, but there was a punishing pain in her stomach. Maybe it was another side effect of the implant, or the fact that it had been taken out, thanks to Todd, and her body was confused. She needed the period before she could start taking the pill again.

'Shower is still warm,' he offered, kissing her neck, knowing it was the mess she disliked, not his touching her or the offer he had made.

'Sorry.' She hated turning him down, more for the fact that she would miss out on the pleasure of getting to feel him inside her. 'A couple of days,' she said.

'What about this?' he asked, and they looked down to the growing mound under his towel and he smiled.

'Can I put him on hold?' she asked not daring to touch him.

'I will see if that can be arranged, Mrs Dean, for you.' He kissed her nose and sat back down, understanding her, but frustrated nevertheless. She smiled at him and held up the first dress she showed him again. 'Not going to be able to put him on hold very long if you wear that!' he stated as the dress was low cut at the back, and would show off her full chest and her silky shoulders. 'In fact, I'll have Pete bring up a boiler suit for you, that may have the desired effect!'

She picked up the empty toiletry bag and threw it at him, but he ducked, and she missed. 'Edward, be serious, I need to pack!'

She slept some of the way. Ed had made some calls, emails and read some paperwork. She had raging stomach-ache although she was now not bleeding at all and he had asked Pete to stop at a service station to get some painkillers. It was the only break in the journey, and she took the opportunity to get out and go to the toilet and stretch her legs. She walked back to the car, still not getting used to the fact that people sometimes stopped and stared at the Bentley, or the fact that Pete opened the door for her, like royalty. Ed jumped in by her side and passed over a bottle of water, a pack of ibuprofen and a large chocolate bar. He knew her well when she felt like this; it was all a girl needed! She took the tablets and settled back into his side, offering him the chocolate as she snapped off another piece and let it melt in her mouth. He put on the iPod and selected a classical piece; she smiled at his change in taste of music. Was that her influence, or did he really enjoy it? She was relaxed; this was a good start to the weekend. She knew it would get hectic from then on so took the time to close her eyes.

There was a crash on the motorway and it held them up, crawling along in the traffic. Although the air con was on, Lottie opened the window to get a fresh view of their location. As the smoked glass rolled down without effort, she looked across at the car next to them. A young boy in the back of the car waved at her and she smiled back.

'Poor soul looks bored,' she said to Ed. He leant forwards slightly to see who she was talking about, and smiled as a little hand waved at him. He waved back and the boy grinned. The boy turned his face back around in a flash to the front where a woman and man were sitting, as if one of them had said something to him.

Edwards's heart sank; he knew that face, one of fright, not boredom. The Bentley moved forwards slightly and Edward got a look at the male driver. His cheeks were red, his scowl dominating his face and his mouth moving fast but without sound, his hands banging on the steering wheel and then gesticulating to the traffic in front. Ed had a sudden flash back to when he was young, being driven back to school.

His mother would be crying, his father shouting at her, making the crying worse, and at him for no reason. He held out for Lottie's hand and gave it a squeeze. He had no idea who the people in the car were, where they were going, or what their lives entailed, but he knew he would never allow a child to suffer. He hoped one day their child or children at that age would not know that the world could be so cruel. The boy wiped a tear from his little face, still looking forwards. Ed used his button to pull the window shut; he could not look any more. His stomach knotted with rage, for the boy, or for himself he was not sure.

Once they had left the motorway the traffic eased, and they were at the hospital sooner than expected. Lottie had been right to think that it was going to be a rush from then on. The charity event was in a posh country club/spa hotel a few miles away, and they would be coming back on the Sunday to officially open the hospital. The royal visitor was due for 11:30, to unveil the plaque and then have lunch with them and a few other VVIPs after a quick tour of the place. Lottie didn't recognise it anymore as the old farm, it had changed so much. It had almost been a year since they had met, and how everything had changed in that time. She smiled, wondering what her grandparents would think now. She held back a tear when she thought what her mother and father would think of her now, too.

She sat on the step in the sun outside waiting for Ed to come back to the car. Maybe she was dreaming; could one man really make this much of a difference to her? Maybe she was over-emotional due to her time of the month, but as Ed joined her she quickly looked away, not wanting him to see her face, as she was sure that he would notice she was having a surge of emotions, all be it good ones though.

The long, dark slate grey dress covered her shoulders with a fine veil of see-through silk, which flowed down her back. Her arms were covered to the mid-elbow, and her hips defined by its flattering cut. The diamonds she wore around her neck and wrist were the birthday gift she had received. Ed had kissed her and complimented her more than once before they left the room, and so the party began.

There were smiles for the camera, handshakes for the paying guests, polite cheek-kissing for the wealthy funding benefactors, and hugs for the few friends that had been invited.

Sarah and Joe had come up, and of course Liz, but those were really the only friendly faces she recognised. Walking around with just orange juice she felt comforted that Edward never left her side. He did this sort of event with effortless ease. Ed made polite conversation with everyone, even politer chatter to those pledging larger sums of money. Smiles and a show of teeth that would win them over, she thought to herself, and most of the women, regardless of age, fell instantly under his charm.

They all said, 'Mrs Dean, we are pleased to meet you', but she was sure that some of them were not, and would surgically remove Ed from her hand or waist given half the chance. Wealthy widows, married women and kept women alike, she was sure that she never knew why he had chosen her. She had not felt this uneasy for a long time, maybe it was because she had arranged it all and wanted it to go well, and she felt that she was being judged in more ways than one.

'Relax, you,' Ed whispered, noting that her hand was getting tighter around his. She smiled unconvincingly at him. 'Baby girl, it is going perfectly, you should be proud of yourself.' Even though he had smiled at everyone else, the one he gave her made her take a breath. It was the deep look into her eyes that came with the smile he had reserved for only her that had a calming effect, and it was only then she took his advice and swapped her orange for a glass of golden bubbles of the Champagne offered to her by a young waiter.

'You look amazing.' Liz walked up behind her and they hugged. Lottie let Edward's hand go to move to the side of the group he was talking to. He looked over as if to approve of who she had found to talk to and continued to talk business once he was happy she was still not far from his side.

'And this, will blow Mr Blink out of the water,' she said, referring to Liz's dress. A pale blue over-lace number, short on one side, showing a good deal of leg, and touching the floor on the other. The contrasting sleeve length was one long on the opposite side to the leg length and short the other, adding dimension to the design.

They chatted about a date for next week, and when they were joined by Sarah and Joe, the same polite welcome was given.

Sarah was in full bloom; the dress complimented her growing figure. 'This is one of Miss M's,' Sarah said. 'She mentioned to me about your little venture. I have to say I'm very excited for you both. I had to join in; not that I want to monopolise your ambition, but there does need to be a good range of 'plus size 'clothes for this type of event. I had such a job shopping around, maybe they think all pregnant ladies wither up and die the second they get the tiniest bit fat, and the social and fashion life stops too!'

Lottie thought about it. Not that she had ever looked out for maternity clothes, but now she gave it some thought she had never seen anything like that on the rails of designer wear that Bella and she had spent hours looking through. In fact, she had at times not been able to fit in some of the items as she was too big! Size 6 and below only. No wonder some young girls had eating issues and food phobias.

'Maybe you are on to something there,' she said out loud, transmitting her thoughts to the rest of the group.

'Really, Lottie, you think?' Liz said.

'Hey, I want a share in this million-pound company, my idea!' They all laughed, but the grey matter was going around in Lottie's head and it took up the conversation until they were joined by Ed.

'Watch out, Ed, I can see Mrs Dean taking over you as the richest ball-breaking business bad ass guru in London,' Joe said, shaking Ed's hand as he joined them. 'There will be no family time for you when she is flying high, bet you would not like being a 'kept' man eh?'

'Joe, stop teasing Edward, you wish that you could be a 'kept man', that's all,' Sarah said, leaning in to give him a kiss on the cheek.

'I'm going to be a modern man, making bottles, cooking, night feeding, nappy changing – maybe occasionally,' he said, 'so you can happily go back to work,' he added. 'We can watch TV, shop, do the gym and get our hair done just the same as you women fill your days!'

'Male chauvinist pig.' Sarah slapped his arm playfully.

'Be careful, tiger, that's how you got like that in the first place!' He gave her a cheeky grin, pointing to her stomach, and she looked away from him.

Lottie felt embarrassed for the two of them. They were a great couple now she knew them better, although she was not sure what type of life they did lead, and with the insinuations to their sex life, they seemed very open about it. She found her mind wandering slightly back to Ed's conversation about watching someone and she could not help but think, was this how he knew them in the first place?

'Do you think, Lottie?' Liz asked, and she broke her train of thought.

'Sorry,' Lottie said, 'miles away.' Liz repeated her question, and this time she paid attention and replied. They continued to talk until it was time for them to eat. As they walked to their table Ed asked, 'You ok? You were miles away back there for a moment.'

'Yes,' she said, smiling back at him and not daring to say where and what had been on her mind at the time.

Dinner consisted of fine food, fine wine, and good varied conversation from all at the table. Ed pulled out his small piece of paper and looked over the few words written down. The event organiser had said that they were ready for the speeches and he took one last gulp of his wine. The toastmaster introduced him, and the seated guests applauded as he took to the stage. Once the clapping had quietened down, he began to speak. Thanking people for attending, he outlined the work and the future plans for the hospital. Then finally he said,

'And of course, my final and most heartfelt thanks must go to the one remarkable person who has made not only tonight possible, but the whole project. My beautiful wife and business partner, Mrs Leticia Dean.' He pointed over to where she sat, and the room followed on with applause and Lottie felt her cheeks go red as people looked over and nodded to her.

'Go up and say something,' Liz whispered.

'Not a chance,' Lottie replied. 'It's bad enough he had to mention me. I wouldn't know what to say, even if I made it there alive in these heels to the stage. I would fall or do something embarrassing.' She smiled as the room still had vibe as Ed closed his speech with a simple, 'Thank you.' He came back down and joined them.

He stood behind her chair and kissed the top of her head and she looked up at him and smiled, not needing to say a word.

The next day was also a success and Lottie was taken aback by the royal visitor; he was so down to earth and easy to get on with. He made conversation with both Ed and Lottie as if they had known each other for some time. She had worked with Clarence House on the timings of the event, itself a military operation to the last minute and smallest detail.

It was late in the afternoon when they checked out of the hotel to head back home.

'Phil took Liz back an hour or so ago,' Lottie said to Ed as she got in the car.

'Right.' He carried on looking at his phone.

'Are you not interested?' she asked.

'About them?' he asked, putting his phone down. 'What about them?'

'You know,' Lottie said.

'I don't know, or I would have said so. What about them?'

'They've been seeing each other,' she said. The following day had confirmed this. They did not see her as she came out of the gym early in the morning. As she went back to her room she had to go past the corridor where she was staying, and she'd seen Phil leaving Liz's room.

'He's allowed a life as long as he does not drop his game during work time,' Ed said, looking back at his phone as the car set off.

'It's sweet don't you think?' Lottie said, noting his lack of enthusiasm. 'The way they met,' she added.

'I wish them all the best, and I suppose if you are going to be working with her more then he will get the opportunity to see her more.' He put his phone down again. 'I'll make it clear to him, though, that he had best not drop his game because he is otherwise occupied.'

'Did you drop your game when we first got together; were you preoccupied?' She linked her arm to his and snuggled into him on the back seat.

'Slightly, I guess,' he said, looking away from his phone and trying to play it down. Slightly was a huge understatement. There were days when he'd had nothing else on his mind but meeting her again, or getting to see her, wanting to know where she was, what she was doing; it became an obsession, and still was.

'Only slightly?' She looked at him and rolled her bottom lip in a childish way to display disappointment. He leant over and kissed her.

'What do you want to do next weekend?' he asked, changing the subject completely.

'Have a rest, it's been so hectic. I wondered if we could go back to Kent,' she replied.

'But can we stay around town the weekend after?' he asked, referring to London.

'Yes, why?'

'I have a surprise. It's almost a year since our first meeting, unofficially.' It was the meeting in the bar that he referred to. 'I just need you not to book anything, and I hope that you enjoy it.'

'I need more information than that, what to wear, shoes etc,' she said.

'I will sort it all,' he said with a smile. 'And no matter what you do that's as much detail you are getting.'

'Are you sure? I can't get an insight' She took her hand and rubbed it down his chest towards his groin.

'Low blow, Mrs Dean,' he said, not stopping her. 'But I will not give in, even if you...' his words stopped as she stroked him. 'Don't start something that you can't finish,' he said, referring to the fact that the weekend had been a dry one for sex, as Lottie was not only exhausted but waiting to come on.

She pushed the button so that the privacy screen was secure. 'Who said I couldn't finish it?' she asked, unzipping him and positioning herself so that her head was in his lap. With ease she found her target, swollen and pulsing with anticipation and excitement, and she gave the head a sudden lick.

'Mrs Dean, try as you may,' he held his words and she took him in her mouth and sensually sucked him, using one hand to tuck her hair behind her ear, giving him a better view of what she was doing, 'try as you may I am not going to, sssss...' He made a sucking noise as the air passed through his teeth and he closed his eyes as she made her way up his chest with one hand and with precision found his nipple and gave it a hard squeeze.

'Fuck me!' he said as the pleasure spread like a wildfire through him.

'I would love to, Mr Dean, but for now, I offer you this.' She took him whole again and rounded his now fully-erect cock with her mouth, and using her fingers she massaged his balls; he had moved and spread his legs to allow her better access. She used her tongue to stroke his tip while her mouth fucked him in a rhythm that was increasing.

'Mrs Dean, you are bad, bad.' He shook his head, knowing that he was only going to be able to wait a few more moments before she got a mouthful, if not two, of his wet salty seed.

The frustration of the weekend, the constant wanting her, seeing her naked in the shower, lying next to him, sleeping softly in bed draped over him, dressed and being adored by far too many other men, all pent up in him over the last few days meant he was struggling to hold his own composure.

He tried to slow his breathing, but as he looked over her body, her position had made her skirt pull up around her thighs showing her long legs and he could see the black lace at the top of her thin, barley black stockings. Her chest pressing against his own thigh gave away the hard firmness of her nipples and he resisted the urge to replicate her actions in finding one to tease or pluck at. The very thought of the hard, dark brown flesh made the hairs on his arms stand up, and he throbbed in her mouth as the assault on his shaft never wavered or stopped the whole time.

He was so deep in her throat that she gagged slightly as he pushed up into her face. Controlling her breathing she never faltered until she knew he could take no more.

His urgency for release was noted by her as he held her head, assisting with the constant rhythm of her full lips, which were now burning from the constant friction.

'Lottie!' He pulled at her hair as if to signal that he was about to explode. She took a breath, and he filled her mouth, swallowing him down to allow his full need to be expressed. 'Oh, baby girl.' He put his head back on the seat and the realisation that he was sitting in the back of his car, with his wife buried deep in his groin slowly flooded back to him.

Lottie lifted from him and smiled. Ed pulled her face to his and he kissed her, tasting all that he had given her on her lips and in her mouth as he thrust his tongue into her. He reached over and pulled one of the tissues out of the side console, and she wiped her mouth.

'You may be finished, but it's not over,' he said. 'I will remember this, Mrs Dean.'

'I hope you will, Mr Dean.' She gave him a smile as she sat back up and he adjusted his trousers to allow his still semi-hard cock to be caged once more. 'And the very thought that you may have caved in and told me more about next weekend was never my plan!'

'Good, because it will take a lot more for me to spoil the surprise.'

'Well, now I know that you have upped the game, you may have to leave it with me!' She bit down on her lip and raised her eyebrows, picking up the magazine that had been left on the consol.

'I love you,' Ed said, reaching back across for her hand and placing a kiss on it. 'It's been an amazing weekend.'

'I love you too,' she replied, settling into the long journey home.

Chapter 6

Lottie sat watching and listening to Liz who was going through detailed designs and a business plan with Mr Blink. The meeting had been set for Thursday, and after meeting up with Liz the day before to go through some ideas, Lottie noticed how confident Liz was with him although she had expressed that she was nervous ten minutes before he arrived.

Lottie observed a man in the corner of the hotel restaurant, who seemed to be looking over at them a lot. She had not recognised him although she thought she knew him. Every time she tried to look and take a better glance he turned away.

The meal had been good, it always was at the Grosvenor, but she was still struggling with stomach cramps. Not that she was worried that her period really had come to nothing. The wound on her arm where the implant had been had become sore, possibly to the point of still infected. She tried to bathe it, and kept it hidden from Ed, but she had made up her mind that she was going to have to go back to the doctor.

She took another glance across to where the guy had been sitting, but he had gone. She put the thought out of her mind and tried to focus again on the conversation over the table. She quickly realised that Mr Blink had a knack for flirting and Liz seemed to be under his spell. How would Phil feel about that, she thought to herself.

She was not sure why she could not keep her mind on the task in hand, but from getting up this morning she had not felt 100%. When Ed asked, she said that she was just so very tired. Although he had said to call off her lunch appointment and stay at home, she'd really wanted to make the meeting for Liz, who was very excited and also seemed to have some really good business ideas.

'So, Mrs Dean, you are able to put some backing into the label?' He was referring to the finance arrangements.

'Yes, Miss Duke – Liz – and I have discussed how much would be needed to get the ideas off the ground,' she replied, snapping back into the here and now.

'And even if we do not go for the range, you are still sure that this will work?' he asked.

'I have every faith that it will work, so yes, if Liz wants to branch out, I will back her,' Lottie added, taking a final sip of the coffee she had ordered, now quite cold. 'Although Liz will still have full control in everything,' she said and smiled at her friend.

'And your husband, he is ok with this?' Mr Blink looked up from the papers he had in front of him.

'Why would he not be, this venture is in my name.' Lottie held his gaze and he seemed to look away.

'I am sure that any branch of the Dean name can be a great guarantee that the venture will work.' He took in a breath. 'So, Miss Duke, do you think that you can supply our demand?'

'Yes, as it says in our business plan, we can supply a range of maternity wear, possibly even new-born and an infant's range, as well as classical designs for evening gowns, many of which would be bespoke.' She had her fingers crossed under the table and looked at Lottie for support.

'Look at a possible winter collection. We aim to purchase these around August to go into the shop for late September. The idea of a fashion show to launch your brand is an excellent one. I have contacts that I am sure will be able to come and support.' He put all the papers into a pile and knocked them together on the table. 'I am interested, Miss Duke, and I look forward to seeing you again, and working with you in the future.' He stood up and shook her hand. He took Lottie's hand and kissed the back of it. 'Mrs Dean, I hope to see you soon also.'

As they sat and watched him walk out of the room, Liz smiled. 'Did that go well?' she asked Lottie.

'It seemed to, though I have to say I am no great business leader. There is lots to think about and organise. I wanted to do a fashion show for the Dean trust, so it seems a good place to start.' They continued to talk about the logistics of this, timings and all the elements required to put something on. Lottie had not noticed the time until Phil walked over to the table. She noticed the way in which he greeted Liz, and she smiled to herself; it was nice that they had struck up more than a bond.

On the drive home her email alerted her, and she looked at her phone. It was the doctor's reception letting her know that she could go in a few days for an appointment. There was also a missed call from Gerald, so she called him, and they chatted for the rest of the journey. It had been nothing important; he was just checking in with her really, and reporting back on some of the jobs she had requested on the house.

The night passed without anything of note. Lottie filled Ed in on all her events of the day, although she omitted the details of her appointment booking in two days' time. They chatted about his day and agreed on plans for the rest of the week. Still working on the fact that they would go to Kent on Saturday morning, Lottie phoned Agnes and caught up with her. They then went to bed as every other working couple, falling to sleep quickly, Lottie resting in Ed's arms.

'Mrs Dean, sorry to say we have to take a re-think on the type of contraceptive. The implant was not working for you. We knew that this was a possibility, but the implant clearly has caused an infection. It was a good job it came out before it caused blood poisoning,' the doctor explained as Lottie pulled her top back on. 'I need to give it a clean out and ensure that the device is fully clear.' Lottie had already been scolded for allowing Todd to remove it.

'Today, though?' Lottie asked, thinking how she was going to get Phil to wait any longer without having to report back with his location.

'Yes, I have asked the team next door to clear the area so I can use the operating room. It will only be ten minutes maximum,' he said, washing his hands at the sink in the corner of the room.

'And a coil can't be fitted until I have had another period?' she asked, using all the information he had given her during her examination earlier to try to come to a solution.

'I would say another two months to ensure that you have a normal period lasting longer than this one. Do remember though, you are not covered and must take other precautions. Does this pose a problem?'

Not that he was a guidance counsellor, but she knew regardless that she had confidentiality with him. Lottie explained her concern about getting pregnant again, and the fact that she felt Ed had different plans. The suggestion of using condoms would, she was sure, lead to heated discussions about having children and starting a family. She even explained that was why she had not told him where she was now.

Although he could not offer her any advice, he was keen to move her to the sterile room to check out where the implant had been, and she had no option but to ask Phil to wait.

'Pete?' Ed asked enquiringly as his right-hand man walked into the office. Pete explained as tactfully as he could that Phil was sitting outside a doctor's surgery in Harley Street waiting for Mrs Dean and then braced himself for the fall out. As expected, Ed jumped up asking all manner of questions that he did not have any answers for. He just opened the door and followed his boss as Ed made his way down to the car, knowing he wanted to be taken there to find out what was going on himself.

'I thought she looked ill,' Ede expressed as the door shut. 'Fuck it I should have known, who is this doctor?'

Pete relayed the name and Ed punched at his phone to look at the web site. 'Gynaecologist!' he said as he read through the text. 'And she is not answering the phone?' Ed looked towards his driver who was making as much progress in the traffic as he could. 'Any idea why Phil evaded letting you know they had this appointment?' Ed asked, his anger now clear.

'No, Mr Dean,' Pete replied. 'Maybe a check-up so he did not see the relevance?' He tried to smooth the way for his colleague, knowing that he would need to mediate when the two men came face to face. 'You do know that any appointment will be private and that you will not be able to go charging in,' he finished to try and explain that he was aware that Ed would do just that.

'Her location is relevant at all times. He needs to remember that. You should have a check on him all the time.' He changed the subject to the fact that he may not be able to get into the surgery. 'I am her husband. They will let me see her,' he spat out, still trying her number on his phone with no reply. 'Can't you get there any faster?' he shouted out. Pete just let him get it out of his system, thinking that this would be better all round.

'Mrs Dean, I am sorry, I had to let them know. You know that the car is tracked and all I said was that we had been held up at the appointment. I guess Pete tracked the car and saw the address.' Phil had come into the entrance to meet Lottie as soon as she said she was on her way out. The doctor had been right; it had only taken a few minutes to dress her arm. It had been her following conversation with him that had held them up.

'You know they are on their way here now?' He looked so apologetic that Lottie smiled back at him. 'I have been asked to stay put till they arrive.'

He opened the car door for her, and she got in the back. 'He will be mighty pissed off with me, again.' The man mountain that he was, now looked like a sorry schoolchild. His job really was his life, and he knew just how verbally volatile Ed could be if he was not in control.

'It's ok, I've got this,' she said to Phil. 'It's my own fault for not coming clean last night with Edward when we chatted through our plans for the day. When he kicks off just leave him to me, please don't listen to any abuse or threats he makes to you. You have only done as I asked.' He closed the door behind her and waited on the side of the road, not getting in and ignoring the fact that they were parked on a red route and should have moved off straight away.

The black Bentley had hardly stopped before Edward Dean jumped out the back and rushed over to the car. Phil hesitated in opening the door. The look he got shot him to ice and Ed beat him to the door handle.

'You wait there!' Ed jumped in beside Lottie who had been looking out the back window, slowing her breathing down ready for the argument that never came.

'Lottie, are you OK? What are you doing here?' Ed asked in a remarkably calm voice, grabbing out to hold her hand.

'It was just an appointment that took a bit longer than expected. There was no need to rush halfway cross town!' She laughed out of nerves more than anything.

'Are you sure? Why didn't you say you had an appointment? What was it for? You're not...?' he stopped. Since seeing the name of the doctor, noting he was well known for the care of expectant mothers and new-born babies, Ed had only been fixed on this page of the website, not looking into birth control, or any other gynaecological service that was on offer.

'I had to go in to see about the implant, you know in my arm. I was reacting to it.' She took a breath. 'That's all.' She watched his face for any indication of his mood, though she did not say it had been out for some time thanks to Todd's handiwork. 'I would have relayed any information tonight if you'd needed to know it. Did you think I was...?' She took a breath as she saw the page open on his phone he had in his other hand showing the services of the surgery she had just been in. 'You never thought I was pregnant surely? You know I've been on, well sort of.'

'I wasn't sure what to think, to be honest.' He stopped himself again. 'Well, you know, you said you felt ill this morning and I just needed to know you were OK.'

'So, you jumped to a conclusion?' she asked, 'and rushed over here in a state, and didn't think that I would say something to you if I thought it was important?'

'Well, you have been so secretive about the implant I wanted to find out for myself,' he retorted.

'I have not been secretive. I just knew you would not like the alternatives, and given how hell bent you have become on having a child I didn't want to bring it up again.' She shot the words out without a thought to how he would react.

'Hell bent on having a child. Christ, Lottie that is a statement. One that almost hurts. You say it as if it is a crime for me to want such a thing.' He was taken aback by her coldness to the subject. It stunned him to silence and she knew that the wrong thing had been said.

'We have broached the subject, almost skirted around it on more than one occasion. You showed and voiced your opinion when you noticed the implant. I didn't want to bring it up again as I know that you are not happy with the fact that I am starting to find my way again. I am happy with the way we are.' She looked away.

'So, you finally admit that you are happy that you lost our child?' he asked straight out.

'I never said that,' she replied, looking back at him. 'Don't twist my words!'

'But you don't deny it,' he said back.

'We've been over this.' She felt her voice break.

'But you can't bring yourself to admit you are relieved?' he asked again, almost forcing the question.

'What do you want me to say? Yes, I am glad that things turned out the way they did?' She pulled her coat around her trying to distract from the conversation.

'I want you to be honest with me,' Ed said, 'I have admitted to you that I was shocked at first, then deeply saddened when I realised how much I wanted it.'

'And now you are annoyed that I don't want to even risk it for a few more years because I want a life of my own.' She paused. 'I am only asking for us to wait, but you can't do that, can you?' She felt a hot stain on her cheek. 'Is it the fact that you are not controlling me, or the fact that you can't get what you want?'

'Neither. It is the fact that we have had to have this conversation in the back of a bloody car, outside a doctor's surgery that I knew nothing about.' He sat back in the chair, his back stiffening.

'So, it is the control thing. The thought that I make my own decisions to control my own life, my own body really?' she asked.

'We are going round to a dead end with this conversation. Can we just go home?' he asked, his stomach seething with a rage that he was not sure how to control.

'And finish a conversation that will only end in the same reply?' Lottie asked, now clearly distressed.

'No, Lottie, talk about it like adults who love and care about each other.' Ed tried to hold her hand, but she pulled away.

'Bottom line, Ed, regardless of where we talk about it. I don't want to plan to have a child yet. I need to work, find my way, do some of my own things, enjoy our lives. For one moment do not question my love for you but I need you to stop having me followed and watched every minute of every day. I feel smothered, even if it is because you don't want anything to happen to me. It would not surprise me if the guy the other day at the restaurant was not someone new working for Pete making sure I was exactly where I said I would be.' She saw the expression on his face and stopped talking.

'What guy the other day?' he asked, looking concerned. 'Something else you omitted to tell me?' He picked up his phone and started a short text.

'Yes because I seem to have lost my sense of knowing what I should or should not be doing for myself,' she answered him.

'But what guy?' he asked again as the front driver's door opened and Pete jumped in.

'Some guy stood at the bar in the restaurant for about half an hour and just watched us. Well, me, just watching me.' She said the last two words quieter as the car started and they moved away from the curb.

'And you wonder why I am concerned. Some random guy has tabs on you, and you fail to mention it.' He pulled down the screen so that Pete was able to listen to the conversation. 'Lottie, what did he look like?'

'What does he matter? You have again skipped from the real reason you stormed over here.' Lottie looked out of the window at the passing buildings.

'Lottie, please, what did he look like?' He tried to be as calm as possible. 'It's important.'

'And changing the subject from the original one is not?' she asked, looking back at him. 'He was about your height, blonde, rough shaven but well dressed. He never smiled and I was not close enough to see any more. If I had to say if I had seen him before... I think I have somewhere.'

'Anything else, Mrs Dean?' Pete asked from the front in a stern voice.

'No, why?' Lottie asked the new person in the conversation. Neither Ed nor Pete replied. 'So now you have your secrets,' she added frustrated towards the direction of Ed. 'Hypocrite!' She forced out the words and looked away. 'You know maybe if I give in, be tied at home and become a nobody, baby-making wife, you will share more with me!' She was angry as the words came out.

'That's not the reason I want you to have my children and you know it. This conversation has become out of hand for both of us.' He moved towards her again to take her hand.

'So, don't treat me like the brain-dead fool that you obviously do. Have some respect for me. Something is going on here.' She again refused his hand, or any affection he wanted to show her.

'Better you be a brain-dead fool instead of just dead!' Ed knew that he released the words in anger and shot Pete a look as if he knew he needed to say more now.

'Mr Dean, it is clear that Mrs Dean needs to know more, for her own safety, if not her sanity. There are a lot of words being exchanged in anger and I think it is clear that we need to discuss this more, when everyone's temper has calmed down.' Pete never moved his eyes from the road.

'At last, a sensible person has a reply!' Lottie exclaimed.

'OK,' Ed replied, 'But please, Lottie, I love you so very much, you must always know and remember that, whatever happens, or is said, however you feel I need to know you are with me. If we wait for children, then I have to get over that fact. You have your reasons, maybe I have mine.' She allowed him to hold her hand. 'I never thought it possible to love someone this much, and you are right, I want it all. I want to give you it all and I have a habit of not wanting to wait, for anything.'

'A sensible reply, at last!' She kissed his hand, trying to show him that she understood, even if she didn't really.

They had parked the car at the apartment and made their way to the penthouse. Phil had driven behind them all the way, and then quickly chatted to Pete as they got out.

Lottie smiled at him as he walked over to his own car; apparently his services for today were no longer needed.

'Pete, you are not angry with Phil are you? It was me who asked him to keep my location today quiet, even though he objected. I may have bullied him into it.'

'Mrs Dean, he has always kept me in the loop in some way. He is one of the best. I have no doubts that he's off home to get some sleep. You'll see him tomorrow.' He said it as if he knew what Lottie was thinking, worried that Phil may be reprimanded in some way for the instructions she had given him.

All three of them returned to the apartment in silence. Mrs B had been in and gone, so they made their way to Ed's study. Ed took off his jacket and pulled off his tie, unbuttoning the top of his shirt. He sat in the large leather chair at the back of the desk and turned on the computer. Pete pulled up a seat around the side of the desk and offered it to Lottie. He left the room and went to the kitchen, preparing coffee to bring back through.

Ed looked up at Lottie; they still had not said a word after getting out of the car downstairs.

'I am sorry about today,' he said, tapping his password into the computer. 'I guess I overreacted.'

'Maybe a little,' she replied. 'But I should have been more honest with you.' She smiled at him. She was slightly nervous about what she would hear in the next few minutes.

Pete put the coffee and mugs down on the table and started to pour. Lottie went over and helped, taking Ed a coffee back to his desk for him. As she placed it down, he put his hand on hers and looked up at her. She smiled at him and bent down and kissed his head, smelling the sweet, clean smell of his shampoo and the all-too-familiar aftershave.

'I'm not sure where to start with this. Pete, shall I start off and you fill in any bits I have missed?' Ed asked, as Pete took a chair and pulled it up closer to the desk.

Ed took a breath. 'Some of this you know, so please excuse me if it is old ground, but I want to paint the picture from the off.' He took a sip of the coffee. 'You know my father had some business acquaintances that, some may say, were not so straight? Well, his death was in question for some years. Something at the time I was not really bothered about. Over the years my family have had various death threats, old employees, pissed-off businessmen who felt they had been hard done by, all of which had been dealt with or went away. In the latter years, with the help of Pete, I have been able to deal with these, and more I'm sure that I don't even know about.' He shot Pete a look, but he remained expressionless.

'Just before my brother,' he faltered, 'Mitch, had the accident, my mother received a threat that something would happen to him. He would not accept any help from me. I was out of the country and had been for some time. I never took it seriously, but maybe should have in light of what happened.'

'You said that it was an accident; the court had ruled accidental death?' Lottie interjected, giving Ed time to take a breath.

'I never really believed them, and spent months trying to get more information but nothing seemed to come of it. Pete followed up on any leads, but they all seemed to be as dead as my brother was. A few months after you and I met, I had another letter.' He turned the laptop round to show Lottie the document that had been scanned in.

Do not get too close or you may lose her too!

She looked back at Ed and turned the computer round, removing the words from her view.

'I had no option but to pull you closer and, in your words, smother you from the word go. I knew I wanted you from our very first meeting. Then I got these.' Ed pulled out an envelope and scattered pictures around on the desk. They were all of Lottie, mostly going to or from work. Some of her flat in London that she had rented for a few months before moving in with Ed. Again, the computer showed the document that had come with them.

If she gets too close, she dies.

'This is the reason I did not want you to look into any old cases that may relate to my family. The reason that the professor has been paid to monitor your work, and maybe the reason I wanted you to stop working if I tell the honest truth.'

Lottie looked up at him, her stomach tightened and her heart was racing as she looked at the photos again, remembering the places she had been, the times and dates that these must have been taken. A cold shiver went down her spine. She thought she had always been so careful. It had been known in her line of work that people got upset with convictions that her investigations and police work had caused, but nothing on this scale.

'Too close to what?' Lottie asked both men in the room.

'We have no idea who it is, Mrs Dean; the threat can be from anywhere, anyone,' Pete said, seeing that the photos were now starting to distress her. He pulled them together in a pile and put them back in the envelope.

'Was my flat break-in related?' Lottie asked.

'We're not sure,' Pete replied. 'Same with the car a few weeks ago, although we have had photos taken of you playing on that night, so I am guessing that someone was around,' he finished, not showing her the photos he referred to but pointing to the next brown receptacle on the desk.

Lottie felt the colour drain from her cheeks. 'They are related,' she said in a slow, low voice almost as if she did not want the men to hear her say it.

'Say that again, Mrs Dean,' Pete asked.

'It is related, I mean, they are,' Lottie corrected herself.

'How can you be so sure?' Ed asked, looking at her. She took a breath. Now she was the hypocrite as she had asked Todd not to mention this to anyone because she knew that the overprotective husband would kick in – but it seemed now he had a real reason.

'How do you know, Lottie?' he asked again, moving round to the desk and sitting in front of her.

Lottie wiped her mouth with her hand and looked under her eyes at him like a scared child about to admit to stealing sweets. 'Because the DNA is the same.'

'Mrs Dean, there was no match. Mr Carter confirmed it,' Pete interjected.

'But you asked him not to say anything, I presume, because you knew we, I, would pull the reigns tighter around you?' Ed said in a caring and apologetic voice.

'I'm sorry to have kept it from you, but yes.' Lottie knew this was not the time for holding back information; she had to be honest no matter how painful it felt. 'Please don't blame Todd; it was me who asked him not to mention it.'

'I blame myself,' Ed said, getting up from his perch on the desk and taking in a heavy breath. 'If I had been honest with you, then you would not have felt the need to withhold this from me.' He slumped back into his chair.

Pete pushed one last pile of papers towards Lottie and she looked at the message on the top.

Another family member to take care of?

The letter was attached to a magazine article that had been taken just after they married speculating that the new Mrs Dean may be expecting due to the speed of their wedding. It was the article that Mrs B had tried not to show Lottie one morning at breakfast. Lottie glanced at the documents and pushed them back over the desk. A heavy lump in her throat prevented her from speaking.

'You know it all now,' Ed said, looking at Pete who nodded and left the room without a word. 'It does not excuse the fact that I, how did you say it, smother you, but may explains a little towards why I do?'

Lottie remained silent, putting all the pieces together in her head. Ed looked at her. 'Say something, Lottie,' he almost pleaded with her.

'The incident with the police, from Monaco, is that also related?' she asked.

'I have no idea, why do you say that?' He pulled down the screen of his laptop, not wanting to look at it anymore.

'Just a thought,' she replied.

'Lottie?' he asked, to warn her not to hold anything back.

'No really, it was just a thought. We found DNA there too but struggled to find a match, it was–' she suddenly stopped but then carried on, 'It was none of the ones we checked.'

'And who did you check out of interest?' He leant forwards on the desk and placed his head in his hands, looking at her.

'The teams, Stephen, Pete, yours,' she said openly.

'Mine? Why the hell would you check mine?' He raised his voice slightly but was not irritated.

'To be sure. You have to admit, there was an altercation in which we were involved, then the guy ends up dead! It had to be looked at. The French police thought that it was of interest and that's why they visited you. I needed to be clear and have the facts.' She looked at him directly. 'It's what I do, it's my job. Maybe I need to check again,' she finished.

'Well, thanks for the trust.' He pushed his chair round so he was only half-facing her now.

'I think we both need to take some time to digest this, but I have to ask, where do we go with this from now?'

'Business as usual,' Ed said. 'But maybe now you will totally understand why I need you so close.'

'How can it be business as usual? Don't you need to get to the bottom of this?' Lottie was amazed that he would let it lie.

'Pete has it in hand; if he thought it was a real threat then he would say something. He is one of the best in his field.' Ed rubbed his face again.

'Rubbish. It needs to be dealt with. I am not saying Pete is not a good close protection officer, but I refuse to be the target of some crazed idiot. Especially if that is the real reason why I feel so constrained in everything I do. I'm not walking around looking over my shoulder every day or being cooped up in a building and ushered from one place to the other with some sort of threat hanging over my head. I do not want to fear for your, mine or anyone's life. This bully needs to be stopped.'

'No, Lottie, you are not getting involved.' He stood up and walked to the window.

'Because it is too dangerous, or because you don't want to know the truth? If there is no threat, then you will have to let me have my life,' she paused and then said, 'back.'

'We are back to this again, aren't we?' He didn't look back. 'I want you close, not for any other reason than I love you and never want to see you harmed.' He walked over to her and she stood up to face him.

'I know, but how much better would it be, knowing the answers to so many questions, putting it to bed once and for all?' she questioned, trying to find his better nature. 'Then we can get on with whatever our lives have in store for us.'

'Trust me if it is not this nutter, then there will be another. You will find out that there is no love lost in business, if you piss people off.' He lifted her face and looked into her eyes.

'Then we face it together,' she said, smiling at his deep eyes, lifting a small lock of hair away from his face. He bent slightly and kissed her. 'And we must try not to piss people off in the first place!'

He laughed. 'Are we OK?' he asked with a smile, and she nodded.

'If you had woken me this morning and said that today would have panned out like this, I would never had believed you. It makes me not telling you about the doctor seem so inconsequential now,' she added, trying to give it some perspective.

'But does it not all boil down to both of us needing to be honest with each other?' He took her hand and held it to his face. 'Me about this, and how I feel about starting a family, and you, feeling suffocated and needing your own space?'

'I have said it often, Ed, my independence and space is no surprise to you. I have tried to compromise.' She pushed back slightly from his embrace.

'OK, so I take the blame. I can't get over being dominating, getting what I want, being obsessive, all of which you have accused me of in the past. I accept it all, but please, Lottie, I need you most of all, and I will not do anything to jeopardise that. I accept we do need to get through this, but I don't want you to be involved.'

'I am already involved, just by being in the photos, Ed, just by this being aimed at you via me. You need to understand that I had a life before we met, and this sort of thing is not new to me. I may not have been a badass business billionaire to piss people off, but I have had my share of threats and nutters after that little bit of revenge. You need to know that the only way it stops is to bring it to the surface and remove it.' She was the one to move away now and look out of the window.

'I can't take that risk,' he said, following her.

'But you risk millions every day?'

'This risk is far bigger than that, Lottie, be real. Money can be replaced, but not people, not you, my family.' Ed held her from behind, wanting her to know that he was there for her more than anything.

'I know but it is just like a business deal. Whoever this is they want something, they have an agenda. We need to find it, research into it, get the facts, plan how to face it and how to take it out.' She stayed facing away from him but lent back into his arms so that he knew she wanted him close. He paused in thought.

'I don't like it *at all*,' he said, emphasising the last two words, 'but with everything, I can see you have already made up your mind that you are going to do it.' He sighed. 'And so I guess I have to go along with it, although you need to know I am not happy about agreeing to this. At least I know what you are doing, and that you won't keep anything from me?' The last bit was a question more than the statement it was intended to be.

She turned around to him.

'I'm not pressuring you, but it seems that there are questions that need to be answered. I will ensure that nothing else we have planned stops. It is important that we carry on as normal so that no one suspects any change that could lead them to think we are investigating. I will be careful. I need you to agree that Todd can be on board and brought up to speed, but that is all. It could be someone close to us so the fewer people that know the better. The professor needs to know that you are happy for me to carry out my full workloads, maybe even investigate old files.' She kissed his lips gently, letting him know that they really were OK, and that the request for old case notes could mean looking into his brother's death again. 'And whatever comes up, we hit it face on, truthful and with no shadows regardless of what skeletons fall out of the cupboards. Is it a deal, Mr Dean?' she asked.

'I suppose it is non-negotiable?' he replied.

'There could be room to compromise. It is dependent on the findings, or who is doing the negotiation and what their tactics are!' Her reply was based on the fact that she felt him slowly start to kiss her neck.

'Would this work?' he asked, moving his soft breath and silky lips round to the hollow of her neck.

'Possibly, it is totally dependent on your next move,' she said, closing her eyes to his touch and the hot feeling he left on her skin. He moved his hands along the line of her stomach, round to her firm ass and held it tight. He used his mouth around her ear and then kissed her hard and full on the lips. He opened her mouth with his tongue as his kiss gained urgency. She replied and allowed him to thrust into her mouth. She moved herself into his space and rubbed herself onto him. His body responded instantly, and she felt his groin swell.

'Is this a good first move?' he asked, rubbing his hand over her top, seeking out the hard mound that was her nipple.

'Certainly is a good opener, you have my attention. Now you need to show me your bottom line, and the assets I stand to gain.' She ran her hands up his back and through his hair.

'That can be arranged, Mrs Dean.' He lent her back against the window, crushing her as he kissed her again, continuing the urgency from his lips as before.

A door in the apartment closed, a reminder that they were not alone. Ed picked her up and she felt the strength of his chest holding her as he carried her to the bedroom, closing the door behind him.

It had been almost two weeks since she had felt his touch on her intimate places, and as he slipped a finger between her sex lips, her body quivered. Ed had her pinned down on the bed with his legs over hers as they both lay naked, kissing, caressing, touching each other. His full erection strained against her leg and hip as he rubbed himself on her. He was soft and caring, paying attention to her every need. He left kisses over her chest, and gently sucked each nipple until they were firm and throbbing with desire.

He kissed her stomach, tracking the line of her muscles and she arched her back as his hot breath reached her panty line. Releasing one leg he pulled it up and parted her, kissing the soft flourish of dark hair that covered the secret area his tongue was aiming for. As he brushed across her, he felt the wet, sweet moistness of her arousal and he licked her, just pushing into her enough for her to tighten her inner muscles in response with a soft moan.

He needed to be inside her. Otherwise he would burst, it had been so long. His thick member throbbed at the thought of her being filled by him. He needed to restrain, as he wanted the moment to be hers and last longer than he knew it would if he took her now. He pushed his face into her to allow his tongue to penetrate as far as he could. She bucked and pushed at his head to create the rhythm and friction she needed to reach her own climax.

The heat growing in Lottie's stomach sent waves of elation down to the area where her husband was licking, sucking, and nipping. He was focusing on the most sensitive area of her body, creating a new height of pleasure. She rubbed her hands up her own chest, finding that her nipples were still hard as rocks and sensitive to her touch. She squeezed one, allowing the sensation to spread through her. Ed noticed and lifted his head.

'Mr Dean, don't pull out mid-pitch. I still need to see all the business plan.' She had her eyes closed but could feel him move up her body. His head hovering above her hands as he watched her fingers dance around the dark hard buds.

'I don't want this to be a full takeover plan though, Mrs Dean, I want to remain the lead share holder.' He replaced her hands with his mouth and sucked as hard as he could and swapped his mouth with two fingers that thrust into her with ease. Lottie shot her eyes open, at both sensations given to her at once. He looked up at her face; her cheeks were pink with a growing pleasure. She bit down on her lower lip and let out a slow breath as he used his third finger to rub the nub of flesh at the opening of her sex, his fingers still searching out her G-spot.

Oh God, he could not hold it. He licked his lips as he watched her bite down on her own, crazed by the pleasure he was giving her. He felt the end of his dick moisten and he knew that once her soft pulsing cunt swallowed him, he would spill. She needed to be closer to her own climax if he was not going to overtake her on the ultimate release. He carried on increasing the stimulation on her highly charged and sensitive nub, she squirmed and dug her hands into the bedclothes.

'Please Ed, oh please,' she groaned out.

'Tell me what you need to close the deal, Mrs Dean.' He breathed the words into her ear, and she pulled his head down to face hers.

'I need to you to take me, please I am begging you, Ed.' She licked at his ear and kissed his neck. He pulled her towards him, navigating his own body over hers as he kissed her with such force that he felt her teeth cut into his lower lip. In a seamless union he pushed as she raised her hips and their bodies joined. He thrust into the moist, wet area feeling her pulsing sex engulf him. He pushed down on the bed with his hands to look at her, and she pulled at his lower back to ensure that all his full throbbing length was inside her, tilting her hips so that he reached the deepest part of her, sending hot pain each time his whole body-weight drove into her.

Sweat ran down Ed's back. He was trying as hard as he could to hold off, but the rush of blood to the area encased by her body confirmed that he was spent as he exploded and ejaculated deep inside her.

'Oh shit, Lottie, I can't hold for you.' He ducked his head down as he felt his life pump into her, each thrust digging deeper.

'Oh, baby, don't worry, I'm there!' she panted out, digging her nails into his back as the first shock wave of pulsing confirmed that her climax was about to explode as his groin rubbed on the very nerve endings of her over-engorged sex nub. It was as if her world blacked out for a split second, and she screamed out the gasp of pleasure that rocked through her body. Ed was spent, his seed and her come making her so very wet and slippery. He carried on rubbing his cock as hard as he could into her so that every second of her pleasure was felt. He kissed her nipples, and they were so sensitive that she almost recoiled at his touch, as if it were too much to cope with.

Her breathing slowed and he slowed his rhythm, also catching his breath, his semi-flaccid cock gently rubbing in and around the entrance to her. Small shock waves still pulsed through her as she kissed him tenderly on the mouth, and his dick made gentle contact with her nerve endings that felt like they were on top of her skin, not under it.

'I love you,' Ed said, rubbing small strands of damp hair away from her face. 'Please always remember that. You are my everything. I am nothing without you.'

'I love you too, Edward Dean.' She reached up to kiss him, soft, tender, and peaceful in his touch. He rolled to her side and pulled the sheets up over them both. Lottie lay on his chest, wrapping her legs around him and he pulled her closer with one arm, rubbing the soft skin of the arm that lay across his chest with his other.

'Together we face this, please let me do this one last job, however long it takes. Cards on the table every time and then we take whatever life throws our way, agreed?' Lottie said, muffled by his chest.

'Agreed, Mrs Dean.' He planted a kiss on her head and put his head back on the pillow musing at her words 'one last job'.

'Then it is a done deal, Mr Dean! And as always, a pleasure doing business with you!' She smiled as she jumped up so that she was over the top of him and their faces met for a final kiss to seal the deal for sure. They enjoyed a shower before finally going to bed. Lottie soon found sleep. Ed lay awake listening to her words in his head: 'One last job'. He hoped this was not going to be the worse decision of his life.

Chapter 7

Life would go on, but not quite the same, as there seemed to be an air about everything that Lottie did for the next few days.

They had talked more with Pete about the way to move this forward and agreed that they would go to Kent as planned for the weekend and then when Lottie went back to the DuPont Centre on Monday, she would ask Todd to meet up with them all to discuss a plan to follow up all the current leads to give them a starting point.

Ed drove them down to the house; Pete was on call, but it was right that his team had some time off. After all, no photos or reference had ever been made to the house so it seemed to be a haven, although Pete had said that they must never drop their guard while they were there.

Gerald was pleased to see them and was excited to show them the handy work in the house and garden that he had done since their last visit. With a little negotiation, Ed was happy for Lottie to spend an afternoon with Agnes; it was only tea in her house, after all, as she had explained. He took her and then filled his afternoon working. When he collected her, they had planned a visit to the pub for dinner, and so Agnes's family joined them. It was the first time in a few days that things had felt as normal as they were going to get.

As with all their free time the weekend passed quickly, and Monday soon came around again. The routine of going to work started for them both, and as soon as Lottie got to work, she took Todd to one side.

'Todd, Edward and I wanted to ask if you could join us for dinner tonight or tomorrow?' she asked as they sat drinking a coffee.

'Oh, yes, nothing planned for me,' he said. 'Not bad news I hope?'

'Well, I'm not sure, something we need your help with really. I don't want to go through it here, only so that Ed can have his say, but it is sort of to do with work,' she continued.

'You have me intrigued now,' he said back at her. 'Tonight I can come over after work, or I can get changed and pop over for about 8pm?'

'I don't mind, you could come back with me. Pete can drop you home later. If you need to shower and stuff Mrs B will have one of the spare rooms ready.' Todd and Lottie always kept spare clothes at work as after post-mortems often they would shower and change.

'It's not anything dodgy?' he asked.

'No, but I need you to help me.' She did not want to raise any alarm bells with him, it was bad enough having a protective husband, and an overprotective work colleague and friend was not one to add to her list.

'Are you in trouble?' he asked, 'are you in any danger?'

'I don't want to go into it too much here, it will become clear once we have explained.'

'Well, yes, of course I can come back with you if it is easier,' he replied, waving to his assistant who signalled he had some post to collect.

'Can you get us external access to the files and computer systems?' Lottie asked.

'This sounds serious. I can but I will need to sign out a laptop and a pass card; what should I say it is for?' he asked.

'The current case? Can we say we are working at home?' She did not want Ed to speak to the professor yet because she wanted to draw all the information they already had, so she was not sure of an excuse.

'Don't worry I will get us in, leave it with me.' Todd smiled at Lottie. He was getting used to the underhand tactics employed by Dean Enterprises following the car incident, and he was guessing this had something to do with it.

He knew that anything Lottie asked for he would go out of his way to get or do. He would always be there for her no matter what. Now she did not need him for anything else, this was the way he could show her just how much she meant to him.

Ed had phoned to say that he would be back within the hour, as Lottie and Todd arrived at the apartment. Mrs B had made up a spare room and put out towels.

'Help yourself and make yourself at home,' Lottie shouted as she went through to the kitchen to get some coffee.

Todd walked around the large expanse, amazed at the apartment that was nothing like the one he had stayed in in New York. He marvelled at the piano in the living room, guessing that no expense had been spared for Lottie, as he could not see that it had been bought for any other reason.

As he walked through the rooms, he could only guess how much the place had cost or was worth.

'You're in this one.' Lottie caught up with him in the second sitting room and walked him out to the corridor, pushing open the door and a large bedroom opened up in their view.

'I'm just going to change. Coffee is on in the kitchen if you want some and Mrs B has left out some cake.' She smiled and vanished off along the corridor to her room and closed the door.

Todd dropped his bag on the bed and made his way to the bathroom. This alone was the size of his flat, and as he turned on the shower and undressed, he could hear Lottie singing to herself as she was doing the same, not too far away on the other side of the wall. He closed his eyes and thought of her, his mind wandering to the days when he had shared a shower with her. The heat rose in his gut and the blood stirred in his groin. He wanted to bang his head on the wall to get the thoughts out of his head. She was so physically close to him but so very far away. He knew this, and had to live with the fact. He tried to let the water wash his mind clear.

He pulled the towel around his waist; it was short and only just did up, revelling the top of his leg as he walked back through to the bedroom. He could smell the coffee and he made his way back out, without thinking where he was.

Standing with his back to the door he stood at the worktop and looked out of the window at the high roofline across the town.

'Oh, sorry!' Lottie said as she entered the room and saw him in his towel. She averted her eyes, but not before she noted his powerful figure. Strong arms, tight abs and defined legs, a hint of a tan and a tattoo she had not noticed before. Todd pulled his hands close around the towel as if he could hide his modesty with the napkin he had been given.

'You've seen it all before as I recall,' he said, referring to their intimate times, with a smile to his face.

'Yes, but not for a while,' Lottie replied, keeping her eyes firmly up. 'And not this.' She pointed to the tattoo on his arm, then moved in closer for a better look. He pulled his arm round so that she could see, and she moved closer still. She smelt the shower gel, one that Ed used occasionally.

Todd flexed his muscle and the outline of the fair maiden on his arm seemed to come to life. She was dressed in a flowing red dress; on closer inspection she could see that around the back of his arm was an outline of a man holding out his arms.

'That's beautiful, what does it mean?' She never gave him a chance to answer when she followed the red skirt around to the hands of the man – he looked like he was letting go. 'That must have hurt; the skin is thin around there.' She moved her fingers over his warm skin until she could also feel his breath. Todd tried to look away, but she was so close to him.

His heart raced; he felt the heat in her touch, not just on the skin under his tender, sensitive arm, but in his groin once more.

'Does it have a meaning?' Lottie asked again, looking at the words. 'My Latin is not as good as it should be.' She was looking at the short verse that had been scribed under the feet of the man.

'Yes,' he said, trying to put some distance between them now, hoping that he would be able to get dressed and hide the fact that her very touch to him was electric; after all these years, wanting her had become worse.

'I get the word 'love', I can't quite see the rest, is it...?' She was just about to manhandle him round the back so that she could read it all when Ed walked into the doorway. He stopped and they both shot their heads up.

'Hey babe.' She looked at him with a genuine innocent face. 'I was just admiring Todd's tattoo.'

'Excuse me,' Todd mumbled. One look at Ed's face was all he needed to remove himself from the room, embarrassed. Ed noted the words on his arm as he walked past. Translated, they read, 'My heart, my lost and forever love.'

'I am sure every husband wants to come home to see his wife admiring a naked man in their kitchen.' He walked over to her and pecked her cheek.

'It's only Todd, Ed, let's not do the green monster at that!' She laughed and kissed him as a proper greeting. 'Want coffee?' she asked, grabbing a mug. 'How's your day been?' She chattered on as if there really was nothing wrong with what he had seen.

Not just his wife touching a man who was clearly aroused and semi-naked, but someone who shared her intimate secrets, someone who knew her only how he wanted to know her. He could not, as hard as he tried, push the image out of his head. He thought, how are they at work? Do they share this intimacy there? His stomach turned and he could almost follow Todd into the room and beat him to a pulp for getting so close to her, throw him out of the apartment and tell him never to get within a mile of his wife ever again, but he could not. He knew how much Todd meant to Lottie and he could never upset her that way, though he knew he would never totally accept Todd still being in her life. Her words broke into his thoughts.

'Ed. Hello? Back to earth, Ed.' Lottie held out his coffee.

'Sorry, just lost in thought.' He tried to keep as calm as possible as she genuinely did not seem to be phased by what had happened; he on the other hand, was boiling inside.

'What thoughts are they?' she asked, sitting on a stool.

'Nothing,' he replied, moving away from the counter.

'Ed, share secrets, remember!' She referred to the pact they had made to say everything to each other regardless. He took some time to think about his answer; he would have to carefully reply. He took a breath.

'How would you feel if that were a woman – my ex for example?' He kept his voice calm and matter of fact.

'Point!' Lottie said. 'Sorry, I didn't think. Todd is such a dear friend, but I never look at him that way. I'm sorry, it was insensitive of me.' She walked over to him and gave him a reassuring hug, and he kissed her head.

'You may want to know that he stills looks at you that way,' Ed said, not holding back now, although he did not say that he thought the tattoo looked very much like her and the words could clearly refer to her too.

'Sorry?'

'You can clearly see when a man is turned on, you know.' He looked down at his fly and wiggled his eyebrows. Lottie got on the same page and blushed. 'And you, young lady, had that effect just then!'

'Sorry, I never...' She stopped as Ed put his hand on her shoulder to indicate that Todd was making his way back to the room. He bent and kissed her cheek.

'Just remember I'm the lucky one you do it too all of the time, Mrs Dean!' He slapped her backside as she turned around and put some distance between them.

'Noted, Mr Dean,' she said back as if in code. She wandered off to get the laptop and papers they needed to work through to bring Todd up to speed.

They were going to work in the small sitting room; it felt less formal than the study. She made a note to ensure that she watched how she was around Todd. She did love him, but not in that way and she did not want to do anything to hurt him.

Todd did not look Ed in the eye as he picked up the coffee that he had poured out earlier. Ed felt the thing to do was to start the conversation and let it pass.

'Thanks for coming over Todd, I hope we have not put you out.' Ed felt proud that he had dealt with the situation as well as he had, the importance of this was much greater than the huge green-eyed monster the scene had arisen in him moments earlier, he thought to himself as the voice of reason.

'No it's fine, really.' He sipped his drink and managed a smile.

'Shall we go through? Pete has arrived, and I am sure you are wondering what this is all about.' He nodded in the direction of the sitting room. As they walked in Ed smiled at Mrs B who had returned to cook dinner.

'Give us about an hour, Mrs B,' he said.

'Shall I bring in fresh coffee at any point, Edward?' The friendly housekeeper smiled at him, knowing that he'd told her a time and that meant not to disturb unless required urgently.

'No, but the bottle of '68 red and three glasses and some water for Pete would be nice to start with,' he smiled back at her.

'I will follow you in.' She rushed in the direction of the kitchen to pick up the items requested to make sure that she did not disturb the start of whatever it was they were meeting about.

They all took a seat and once the drinks had been served Mrs B closed the heavy doors behind her.

'Well, Todd, you must be wondering what this is all about,' Edward started. Lottie had sat next to him, allowing Todd to sit on the other side of the small table with Pete. She thought it was better that way after the recent events.

Edward took his time to explain the past, relaying the story again, much the same as he had done to Lottie some days before. Todd showed signs of concern and panic at some of the photos, knowing he had been there and not noticed anyone, or anything.

Todd relayed findings of the DNA reports and fired up the computer to confirm things they had found in print.

Lottie felt it hard to talk and Ed put his hand on her knee several times to reassure her. Handing over the pregnancy article seemed to affect her the most and at this point she said, 'Another drink anyone?' her hand on the second wine bottle using the corkscrew to open it. Pete took his water; he never touched anything on duty. Lottie refilled the three glasses but was the only one to take a drink as soon as the glass was full.

She finished the glass of deep red wine in a few mouthfuls and then asked, 'Todd, can you open case 039/234 14,' she filled her glass again, 'and look at the results of the DNA. If memory serves me right 004/5 came back as no known match but run them with case 067/224 14.' She seemed to take on a new dominance now with another glass of wine inside her and a full working head mode on. The numbers were nothing to Edward and Pete but represented case numbers and codes.

'Your flat break-in,' he typed the numbers, 'and the stolen notes on the dead French man,' Todd said out loud as if to let the others know what he was looking for. 'Let me just hit search.' He tapped in a few more letters on the keyboard and then 'Enter' as he sat back a little and picked up his drink. Lottie poured another, as if she knew already that she would need a drink to face the results. Ed noted how much she was drinking and that it was not normal; he felt the tension that his wife was feeling.

'Stolen French notes?' Ed asked as he picked up what Todd had just said.

'Well, not technically stolen, just borrowed, copied to our files and then used.' Todd smiled, remembering how they had been able to get the information from Interpol without going through the usual channels.

Another day he had loved working with Lottie.

'Needs must sometimes!' Lottie said, looking at Pete who had a dry smile on his face as if approving of her methods.

'Just like borrowing our DNA to compare them with?' Ed asked, and this time Pete frowned, 'Yes, yours too.' Ed looked at Pete when he said it.

'Bingo!' Todd said, jumping back in his seat. 'Well done, Lottie it's here, how did you remember that?' He typed a few more things into the computer and more results came up.

'How can the dead man be the one who broke into your flat, Lottie?' Edward asked, jumping in without getting all the facts.

'It's not the dead man, Ed, it's the person who we think, well we are almost sure was the killer,' Todd replied.

The room went silent. Lottie took another gulp of wine and looked at the computer screen that Todd had turned around. She picked up the laptop and put in on her knee. Edward looked over her shoulder, although the data seemed to be a blur to him. He too found the need to take his wine and contemplate the facts that had been found.

Lottie scrolled through the post-mortem pictures. Edward was not ready to see the shots of the dead man and was fixated on Lottie zooming in and pressing the keys to the computer as easily as she played her priceless piano. He had never seen this side of her at work before, and now, he almost felt why she needed to keep doing it. She was good, as impressive as ever.

'See, look Todd!' She jumped up and moved in close to him, pushing him along on the couch so he could see the screen. All concerns from earlier gone with regards to his contact.

'Lotts, it's no match.' Todd lent over to her, pointing to the screen and tapping a few more keys while she held the computer on her knee. 'Nothing on the NDB UK,' he said. She entered in another few words. 'No, nothing there either.' He continued to talk to her as if no one else was in the room and they were back in the centre.

'The guy has no criminal records?' Pete interjected, wanting part of the action too.

'No, Pete, we tried that, it would be easy if he had; auto-DNA helps.' Todd carried on looking at the screen; his leg was touching Lottie's and neither seemed to notice or make any effort to move.

Again, Edward felt a twinge of their closeness. He hated it when Todd called her 'Lotts'; it was an old form of endearment, and it just did not feel right. He pulled his shoulders back and said to himself, get a grip, Dean, they are working, nothing more, and be pleased he thinks so much of her – at least he is one person we can take off the suspect list. He filled his glass again and took another large gulp.

'We need the older notes, archive, past stuff to push the search out wider,' Lottie said, pumping the keypad once more. 'Grrr, I can't access, my code needs the professor to authorise.' She shot Edward a look.

'I'll ring him,' he said, grabbing his phone from his pocket.

'Got him on speed dial?' Todd asked, and Ed quickly replied, 'Yes', not noting the mocking sarcasm Todd had had in his voice when he'd made the statement. Todd raised his eyebrows at the reply.

'Damn, no answer. Could he still be in the office?' He was dialling the number even before Todd answered.

'Some dinner tonight, I guess he will be offline for an hour or so, but...' Todd pulled a dongle from his pocket and attached it to Edward's laptop. 'Can I?' Todd asked before taking the equipment on to his own knee. Edward nodded and pushed the equipment over to him.

'No!' Lottie exclaimed. 'Todd Carter, tell me you haven't!' Lottie looked at him and he smiled.

'Well, in for a penny in for a pound. I'm sure that stealing the passwords of all the top bods is illegal, but I won't tell if you don't. This way we cannot be traced either, or so Sasha in IT said. She was more than willing to pass them over!' Todd was too deep in tech land, pushing keys and opening documents to notice the following comment.

'Best not ask what methods of persuasion you used!' Edward said under his breath. Lottie caught the comment and followed on with, 'Whatever methods he used, we are in.' She jumped over to the other computer again and tapped the code that Todd relayed to her. The process was repeated several times as page after page of documentation started to appear on the screen.

'How far back should I go?' she asked.

'As far as you can,' Pete replied.

'You are going to have to go year by year with that refined search, it might take a few hours otherwise.' Todd sat back with her again. 'I should have brought the cables to dual process, it would have been quicker,' he added.

'What do you need?' Ed asked and Todd explained the wires required to link the two computers. He got up and went to the office. This was something he did from the desktop to the laptop sometimes so it was not long before he came back.

Quickly they started to work through it when there was a knock on the door. Pete opened it up and Mrs B informed him that dinner was ready.

'Let's eat and leave them running, just on the DNA driver to start with,' Lottie said looking at Ed. 'No point sitting looking at the screens and letting the food go cold.' They moved to the kitchen where the food had been laid out, and made polite chatter and filled up drinks while they ate.

'Impressive, although I never doubted it,' Ed said, leaning into Lottie while Pete and Todd were in conversation about some CCTV links or stuff that did not interest Ed. 'You make a good team,' he said looking over to Todd, 'I can see why you are so passionate about it all; the life of crime solving would suffer a great loss if you followed my request to stop doing it!'

'Is that the wine, or an understanding husband talking?' she asked, biting her lip and raising her eyebrows.

'Maybe both, but the husband is asking you not to bite that thing.' He put his finger on her lip, and she sucked it.

'And for god's sake don't do that or those two will have to do the rest of the night's work without us!' Ed flared his nostrils as a warning that he was not joking.

Todd glanced across to see the pair of them chatting like love-struck teenagers. Pete also looked up to see what had taken Todd's attention. It was not the first time he had seen the way that Todd looked at Lottie. Some months ago, the thought crossed his mind that Todd might be somehow involved, but then had to rule him out as the threats had come way before Miss Jenkins had come into Ed's life. And after their last few meetings when Lottie had been in a room with Todd, he was sure that everyone had one goal; keeping the person they loved safe. He was not a physical threat to his employers, but Pete was sure he was a mental one to his boss. He could see Edward's face when Todd was in the room, even more so today when they had been brought together in his own home.

Clearing the pots away to the dishwasher, Ed's phone rang, and he looked at the caller ID. He took the call and started to walk into the other room.

'Professor, thank you for returning my call so late,' the conversation started, but Lottie never heard any more. She moved back to the computer and found that there was some sort of match. An archived file, but only within the last few years. She entered the password and looked at the screen.

'Oh God,' she said out loud, and Todd walked over to her, closely followed by Pete.

'What you got, Lotts?' he asked, sitting by her side. He looked at the opening lines to the first document, and Lottie quickly scrolled through to others including pictures and photos of an accident scene.

'I had a feeling that this was something months ago,' Todd said, 'but I got denied access even with the home office passcode, so I never pushed on with it. It seems that only the prof's code would open it fully.' He looked up at Pete.

'We can't fully investigate or reopen without the family's consent.' Todd looked at Lottie.

'Well, I had better ask then,' she replied, standing up and looking to Pete for some reassurance. He nodded as she started to walk into the room where Ed had taken the call, but he walked back in before she had made it two steps past the sofa.

All eyes fell on him and he looked blankly back at them all.

'What, what have you found?' he asked, knowing from not only Lottie's expression that something had come up, but Pete always had a look of concern that just clicked with Ed the second he saw him. 'Anyone?'

Todd quickly tried to close the photos, just leaving the opening coroner's report page on show. He stood up and along with Pete they went back to the kitchen and closed the door. Lottie walked to Ed and held out her hand.

'No easy way to say this, but...' She sat him down and pulled the screen in his direction. He read the page. 'We should not open it without your written consent,' she said, not saying that she had already skimmed through the photos and seen some pictures of his brother, both at the accident scene and the post-mortem stage. 'And your mother's,' she added quickly.

He took in a deep breath and rubbed his head. She put her hands on his knee and smiled at him.

'Edward?' she asked, to see if he was ok; not to ask for the consent there and then.

'Open it,' he said, looking at the screen.

'We need it in writing from your solicitors ideally, Edward, and your mother needs to know,' she replied.

'Open it,' he said, and in a flash he leant forwards and pressed the enter button. Todd had tried to close the photos but failed. Within a second Ed was looking at a photo of his brother. Taken at the scene by the pathologist, his damaged body fully exposed as he lay dead in his car.

'Edward, no, close it please.' Lottie pulled the laptop screen down to remove the image from view. Ed just stared at the space the machine had taken up on the table, his eyes reddening and his hands shaking in rage. He had never seen the evidence files, and even with all the investigating he had paid for after the verdict of accidental death, he had never seen any photos. The last time he saw his brother alive had been several weeks before the crash had happened. Now he had the image of the mangled mess of a body that had been left on the side of the road to die. He finally closed his eyes, almost shaking his head to remove the image.

Lottie held him in her arms, his head buried deep in her chest. She rubbed his hair to try to soothe and calm him. She was not sure what to say, or how to react to this sensitive issue. It was Ed who uttered the first words.

'How is it linked, Lottie?' he said.

'I am not sure without going into it, but my first thoughts have to be with DNA found at the scene.' She looked at him, her heart heavy with the pain that she knew he was feeling. 'Reopening this case will be hard for you, for us all, but it is the only way I can be sure or have any more clues.'

He nodded to her. 'I'll get Mum to sign whatever you need. I will contact the solicitors first thing. Just promise me one thing.' He looked at her and she nodded. 'Don't think bad of Mitch, whatever you find, and don't be afraid to share anything with me even if you think it is going to hurt to know the truth. I want to know and after all this time, I can't think of anyone better to get the answers than you.'

'I know it is going to be hard, and of course you will get to know as much as we do, but for now, let's just leave it. Let me get to work tomorrow and follow the normal course of investigating this. You said we must act normal, hard as it is going to be, but we need to. It may take weeks, months to conclude everything. I must ask you to be patient and not to expect answers straight away. I will email your solicitors the request form and once we have it back, I will carry on. Agreed?' she said, looking for some sort of pain relief for him.

'OK,' he simply replied, standing up and walking to the drinks cabinet, pouring a large whisky. He stood and took the liquid down in one swallow, then poured another. He looked out over the town, shrouded in lights illuminating the streets below.

Lottie looked at him as she hit the send button to their solicitors; he poured his third drink and took it down as swiftly as the first. In their time together, she had not seen him drink so much so quickly, but she was aware that in his time of need he found that alcohol was his mistress. She would not stop him but did want to make sure that he was OK. This could be a long night.

It was around 3 am that Lottie woke. Edward was not in bed; he had to still be in the sitting room where she'd left him when she said she was retiring hours before. He had remained there with the half-demolished decanter of amber liquid next to him.

She pulled on her light dressing gown and padded her way into the sitting room. A single light was on, and she looked at the large sofa where Ed was laid out, an empty glass on the floor by the side of him. He was asleep. She went to the spare room and took a blanket from the closet. As she walked back, she noticed the other figure sitting in the chair in the corner, and she jumped slightly, not wanting to wake Ed, although she was sure that the amount of whiskey he had consumed would not allow him to rouse for a few more hours yet.

'Pete, you made me jump!' she said, looking over to his direction.

'Sorry!' he whispered back, looking over to her. She pulled the blanket over her husband and gently kissed his forehead.

'Was he OK?' she asked, referring to the few hours after she had left him.

'He lost it about an hour ago, and you're going to need more whisky I am afraid,' he said, referring to the decanter that was now empty on the side. 'This could be a hard time for him again, but I am sure he will be fine. I'll stay here until he wakes, you get some more sleep.' Pete smiled at her and she pulled the gown around herself, noticing that she had very little on underneath. 'I will make sure Mrs B has some strong coffee and painkillers ready for when he wakes up.'

Lottie mouthed 'thank you' to him and walked back to her bed. The rest of the night's sleep was hard to find, she did doze but could not rest completely.

The noise of the shower woke her; she must have found some sleep, although she did not feel like she had. The tall figure standing in the shower had their head fixed against the wall and was just letting the hot liquid spill over their body. Lottie almost wanted to smile, knowing that if his headache was as half as bad as that which she could imagine, he was going to be feeling rough.

'Hey, you!' A muffled voice came out over the waterfall and he pushed his head around the shower screen. He looked drained, eyes red, skin glowing from the heat of the water.

'Morning,' she replied, as she slipped off her nightgown and stepped in beside him. The large shower was big enough for both of them and she held him in her arms, the hot water soon engulfing her too. Silently she started to wash him as he stood with his eyes closed allowing the fragrant bubbles to wash over his skin.

'Guess I had too much!' He finally broke the silence.

'Guess you needed it?' she replied.

'Not as much as this.' He kissed her hard on the mouth and she could still taste the harsh liquor he had consumed on his breath. Once he let her go, he looked down at her. 'We will be able to find a way through this, won't we?'

'Yes. We carry on doing what we do every day; this case will be just like any other for Todd and I, and we will work on it together.' She carried on kissing his shoulders, getting wetter with each mouthful of water.

'But it's not like any other case; it's very personal and I'm not sure I want you to be exposed to that, or any risk that may come with it.' He just stood with his eyes closed.

'I know you don't, but I promise it will be OK,' she said, not really sure how it would be if she had to make some decisions and follow the path of a normal cold case. It could mean that they exhume the body and carry out further tests. How could she share that with Ed? It was if he could read her mind as he replied.

'I don't want...' he stopped. 'I don't want him dug up,' he said thinking about his brother's grave and what would be left of him. 'Not unless you have to,' he added.

'Let's see how we go. We have a lot of questions to ask, papers to go through first; it will take a few weeks. I said I would not work more than three days a week, regardless of the case. A change in my workload could trigger off someone. I know that you don't want to hear this, but I do think it is someone close, someone that knows us.'

He looked at her, stopping her kisses. 'What makes you think that?' he asked.

'I just have a gut feeling. They know where we are, what we do,' she replied.

'Then we have to change what we do,' Ed added in quickly.

'No, we don't – we have to become clever and expose them. First thought is that this is DNA-related, but without them being on any police database a lone profile is not enough; we need a name.'

She turned off the water and stepped out of the shower, putting a towel around her. Ed followed, grabbing a towel for his hair, rubbing it quickly and then wrapping it around his lower body. Lottie admired his form as he stood looking for his clothes, and by the fact that he was not at his wardrobe she knew he was not going into the office. He pulled out a tee shirt and pulled it over his shoulders, making his muscles define in the action.

'So, exposing them, bringing them out into the open, puts you in danger?' He walked over and sat on the bed as if the act of half-dressing was already too much for his hungover body.

'It could take months, but they have to slip up at some point.' She helped herself to her underwear and put the little white lace items over her body. Ed held out his hand and she walked over to him. He traced his finger over the line of her panties along her pubic bone and she felt her stomach muscles react with his touch.

'If I didn't have a marching band in my head, these would not be here right now,' he said, smiling, although it looked like a forced smile.

'And if I didn't know that the band was in residence you would not have made it out of the shower!' She ran her fingers up his thigh towards the parting of the towel that was exposing the hint of his dark pubic hair.

'Well, you could stay and have a duvet day with me. I'm hoping it'll finish playing once Mrs B rustles me up some breakfast and coffee!' he smiled, running his hand up to her left breast and cupping it softly.

'I want to go to work and catch up with Todd.' She ran her fingers through his wet hair. 'I want to ensure that we do this properly, set a game plan.'

'It's not a game, Lottie,' he said back to her. He knew the stakes were high, not only for what may happen, but for the emotions it was bound to bring out about his brother.

'I know that, and I cannot really imagine how you or your mum are going to feel about it at times. I'm not sure how I would feel if it brought up things about my mum, or dad for that matter; the past is buried for my folks, sadly. I have no questions on why they passed, well maybe one. Why they were taken from me so soon. But I will stop this for you, for us.' She bent and kissed him.

He pulled her close and kissed her stomach, feeling the soft downy hairs that covered her skin. He breathed her in; he knew she would do this for him. That gave him a feeling of guilt, because if the truth be known, it had been what she did for a living that had added to his list of interests before he had met up with her. But from the very first time they spoke he knew that he was not going to use her in this way, to get to know her just because she could find the answers to his brother's death. It was the fact that she was so very different that instantly aroused him. He had mused at her innocence, been physical destroyed by her sexuality, and as he was reminded every second of every day, she'd soon become the very air that he breathed. She dominated his life. If this shit had not come along, he would never have asked her to investigate his brother's death.

He pulled her closer, almost crushing her. 'Steady, Hercules, still need to breath here!' she smiled, trying to lighten the mood.

'Sorry!' he said, letting go. 'No, really, I am sorry, for putting you through all this.' She moved and sat by his side. 'Don't you ever wish we could just be a normal couple?' he finished.

'What, with 2.4 kids, a semi-detached house in Watford and a Flymo!' She quoted the national average Joe Blogs according to the government with a smile on her face.

'Maybe. I never thought I would want to be, but if it means we don't get this type of hassle... then I would give all my money away and keep just you, 2.4 kids, a semi-detached and a Flymo!' he added quickly. 'Well, the kids bit when you are ready of course, that was not meant as an added pressure. And I like living in the city close to work and having the option to spend time in the country at weekends. And I love my job. It has taken me years to grow what we have.'

'And so, with success comes the added stress, but between us we are strong enough to overcome and cope with anything. How boring would it be to just eat, sleep, work, repeat every day, of course unless you don't sleep! I suppose that is how the 2.4 kids come along!' She turned his face to her and kissed him. He pulled her to his arms, and she fell back on the bed and giggled.

'Point taken.' He kissed her again and then rubbed his head as a reminder that the increased blood flow to the area now he was laid down increased the intense throbbing he felt. Lottie sat back up.

'I need to get moving. Phil will be here waiting for me soon.' She walked back to the wardrobe and grabbed the clothes for the day. 'Changing the subject, are we still on for your surprise at the weekend?' She was aware that last night had changed his mood, and he was feeling down, not just hung over. Before they met, he would have been the first to admit that he lived, thrived on the thrill his business gave him, the power he had over people. The sexual drive he had, and how he needed to have full control of everything.

'I suppose you are going to say to keep normality going,' he smiled. 'Although there is nothing normal, in some people's eyes, in where I intend to take you,' he said, remembering his promise from a few weeks before.

'So, let's not just eat, sleep, work, repeat, let's live!' She turned around for him to zip her skirt and he stood up, obliging. He planted a kiss on her neck.

'I love you, Mrs Dean.' He folded his arms around her, aware not to pull too tight. She had given him the reality check he needed. 'You see the good and positive in everything. I'm sorry for my pessimistic mood.' He stopped as she put her finger over his lips, turning to him.

'I love you, Mr Dean,' she smiled, and reached on her toes and kissed his nose. 'Do we have a date on Saturday then?'

'We sure do,' he replied.

Lottie and Todd found an area to chat privately about what they would do next. There was nothing really until the formality of paperwork was over, although illegally they had already gained access and it had to be done correctly as to not to arouse any suspicions. They already had some cases that needed to be worked on, so it became business as usual for the next few days. All this was explained to Ed and Pete, and everyone seemed happy to let this run along.

Lottie's conversation with Agnes had not given anything away, although she knew her best friend would never be a suspect; in fact, no one on her side would even focus on the questioning but keeping it to a limited need-to-know number was the first part of the plan.

Saturday evening came and Lottie was out of the shower, finishing her hair.

'I'll let you get dressed,' Ed said to her. 'The car will pick us up at 9pm so if you need any help give me a shout.' He pulled a box out from the bottom of his wardrobe, leaving Lottie sitting at the dressing table looking over at him as he retrieved the item. They had started to shower, but it had soon turned into the most fantastic sex session, and she now questioned if she really wanted to go out, she was so relaxed.

'Your outfit,' he said, opening the box and kneeling close to her. Lottie pulled out a pair of lace hold ups, a black leather basque, and a tight skirt to match that also laced up with no zip. The shoes at the bottom were ridiculously high and she looked around in the box for anything else.

'You need this, too.' Lottie looked up at the black mask with diamante and feathers, and something else. Ed reached over and put her diamond choker around her neck and did up the clasp. Lottie pulled the top up; it was not going to hide much. 'No bra then?'

'And no undies either,' Ed added, pulling a black suit from his wardrobe and choosing a plain black tie and white shirt.

'Really?' Lottie said she held up the skirt, wondering how she was going to cover herself with the small item.

'Really,' Ed said back with a smile. 'You said you were up for this, Mrs Dean, so no questions. Do you need me to stay to help you get into it? He asked almost fully dressed himself.

'I am guessing Mrs B or Phil would not want to lend a hand!' She stood up and looked at herself in the mirror.

'No makeup,' although she wore very little anyway, often none at all, 'and hair must be up,' Ed added.

'Anything else?' Lottie asked sarcastically.

'No other jewellery,' he said, adding gold cufflinks to his shirt.

'I'm not taking my rings off,' she said, pointing to her large glistening engagement ring and the gold and diamond band which sat proudly next to it.

'And I would hope not,' he said, walking over to her. 'These stay very firmly on at all times, and not just tonight.' He lifted his own wedding ring hand up and took hers and kissed it. 'I meant bracelets, earrings,' he added as he took the stockings from their box and pointed for her to sit down.

He dressed her like a child. Pulling at the laces ensuring that they were tight, but not uncomfortable. When he had finished, she tottered over to the mirror to look.

'Tell me that this is a fancy-dress party!' she exclaimed. 'One where I hope we sit down because too much walking and I will break my neck!'

'It's not a party, nor is this fancy dress.' He passed her mask and pulled another out of his coat for himself. 'It is an exclusive club, and everyone will be dressed the same. There is a strict dress code, and when you are inside the mask stays on, at all times.'

'Even if the rest of the attire comes off?' Lottie said, biting down on her lip giving him a seductive smile.

'Yours, Mrs Dean, will not be coming off while we are out, but yes, if applicable others in the room may only be wearing this.' He flared his nostrils at her biting down on the lip he had sucked and licked only minutes before and put the mask around her head. 'Although, keep it on when we get home, bite that lip again and I guarantee it will not be long before it's on the floor,' he said, feeling the arousal at the glorious sight in front of him.

She turned around and wiggled her arse at him, and he slapped her butt and due to the fact that, as she had put it, 'there was little more than half a meter of material to the whole outfit', his hand left a mark on her skin.

'Don't make us late, Mrs Dean, we have a table booked!'

'Maybe later then, Mr Dean?' She rubbed up next to him, totally aware of the rising temperature in the room that seemed to come from them both now they were dressed. She made sure that her thigh rubbed just in the very spot where his trousers were starting to strain at the groin.

'No maybe about it!' He grabbed her by the chin, holding her to the spot as if touching any other part of her body would have been his downfall. 'You're so fucking hot I can't believe I'm letting you out like that.' He took away his hand and pulled her long winter coat from the closet. 'Put this on,' he said, almost as a demand.

'Regretting starting this already,' she said, doing as she was told. 'I won't see the green-eyed monster tonight will I, even a blind man would be forgiven for not noticing there is not much about this?' She pointed to the outfit before she did up the coat.

'I am sure a blind man would shoot his load at the very thought of seeing it! I will try not to get pissed off with others ogling you, just promise me if you don't like it, you will say and we will come home. Likewise I will try to contain myself, but I have to say, the thought of men seeing you like...' he stopped. 'Looking like that has made me change my fantasy completely. I never want to see you with any other man, dressed or otherwise.'

'Looking is all they can do. You, Mr Dean, get the pure pleasure of unwrapping and touching.' She bit her lip again and flashed at him, opening the coat to show him her long slender legs, encased in raw black silk. Her tiny waist was pulled in, and the basque was pushing her full plump breasts up, almost showing the tops of her nipples.

He could not believe that she seemed to have changed personality once the clothes had gone on. He never thought she would enjoy the way she looked, or want to be looked at like a slut.

He could not contain the fact that he needed to fuck her here and now, again, until she begged. If he did not do it in the room, the car ride would be hell, and not long enough to do what he wanted. Then he would have to sit there, for what he knew would be several hours, eating with the hardest knob he had ever felt in his trousers. He had hoped that the hour of love-making before they went out would dampen his amour, but there was no chance of that with her in that outfit – if anything, it had made him worse.

'That's it we're not going!' he said. 'I'm not going to be able to control myself, not to strip you and take you on the spot, or to lay out the first guy that even blinks towards you.'

'You must have thought you could when you arranged all this, you must have taken...' she paused. 'Other women there. What makes me different?' She was slightly disappointed at the thought now of not going but had to agree she did not want a pissed-off husband. Although they were risky sometimes at their choice of sexual locations, it had never been in full public view, always safe places, private places. But that was the thrill, the whole point, to see if it was like she thought.

'Women who I never cared for, maybe.' He was brave but followed the agreement not to lie, even if the other person did not want to hear it.

'Fine, Ed we won't go. I'm not pushing, I just thought it would be fun, different, and as you said we can come home whenever we need to. Pete will be outside I have no doubt and I promise to behave, and only do as you tell me.' She batted her eyelashes at him, and he pulled her a face.

'OK, you win. I will test my control to the limits, but you asked for whatever comes from this.' He buttoned the last black catch on her coat and kissed her face. 'Ready?' he asked, and she nodded.

The car pulled up in central Soho and a door guarded by a man mountain was the only indication of any activity in the area. For the last twenty minutes Ed had sat holding Lottie's hand, but keeping as far away as he could. He still knew that this was a bad idea. He had informed her of a few of the club rules while they had been en route just so she knew the etiquette that was required. Mask at all times, no one uses anyone's name even if you know them. While there is any show on in the main area everyone must remain seated and as quiet as possible. No fornication in open areas unless indicated by signage (that one interested her). No drugs both prescription or recreational/illegal will be tolerated by any person including staff. The staff are randomly drug tested and at the request of the management guests will be tested on site. Any advances or unwanted attention must be reported to a member of staff, although he had said 'sod that' where Lottie was concerned. She was almost commanded that she told him first, although he did not intend for her to be off the end of his hand all night. As they got out of the car Ed flashed a gold card at the man on the door, which he looked at, smiled, and welcomed them in. He pulled Lottie's mask over her face and put his own on. She smiled at him, although it covered most of his face. She could still see his ruffled hair and dimple in his chin, although as the room got darker, she soon found it harder to make out clear shapes and faces. As they ascended the steps the lights dimmed more, and Lottie concentrated on the steps down in the silly shoes she had to wear. Another man dressed the same as the first doorman appeared and visually checked them both, and without a word he nodded and opened the large red doors.

Music started to drift towards them, and a figure appeared.

'Good evening Sir, Madam, may I have your coats?' He held out his hand as Ed passed his first and then helped Lottie take hers off. She felt like she wanted to cover herself back up but soon pulled her shoulders back and took a deep breath as the attendant didn't seem to bat an eyelid at her apparel.

Another well-dressed man approached them as they walked down a dark corridor to another door, and he opened it and showed them in. The music was louder now, and Lottie tried to adjust her eyes as quickly as possible as the room opened up in front of her. It was dark, with a red glow to the lighting.

'Evening Sir, Madam. Welcome to the Coven Club. I will be waiting on your table tonight, please may I show you the way.' The young girl was clad from head to toe in latex, her mask totally covering her face. As other guests now came into view, it was quickly apparent to Lottie that everyone was dressed totally the same as they were. Not just the masks, but the suits and shirts for the men and the outfits for the ladies. Interesting, she thought as Ed held her hand, leading her through the little groups, or couples that were already placed at their tables or private booths.

'Who should I address tonight?' the girl asked. Ed quickly answered, 'Me, at all times.' She smiled although it was hard to see. She simply said, 'Sir' and lowered her head. He placed a drinks order, and she went off without a word.

'OK?' He looked at Lottie as they sat in one of the booths in front of a large stage that was currently blacked out. The only item on it was a large leather sofa.

'It's very dark,' she said back as she slipped in behind the table and fixed seat. She was glad in a way that as she sat the skirt did not cover her nakedness. She noticed that Ed never made the effort to look down at her legs and partly uncovered pussy.

She was also glad it was warm in the room. She looked at the list of house rules on the table, all of which Ed had explained before. She smiled to herself and wondered how many times he had been there before to have remembered them all.

The girl appeared with a bottle of Champagne and two glasses. 'May I serve you now, sir?' she asked.

'You may, the lady first,' he said, still holding Lottie's hand. 'And we are ready to eat,' he said, no please or thank you. It was not his style, as he always had manners Lottie thought to herself; one thing she loved about him.

'If it pleases you, sir,' the voice said as she left the bottle in the ice bucket placed on his side of the table. Lottie caught a quick look at the girl; behind her mask she had strong features and the small cut out areas showed her soft eyes. Lottie guessed she was young, not just from her figure, but her voice and what little she could see of her skin. A small freckle by the side of her mouth was the only real feature visible and quite distinctive.

Lottie looked back to Ed and took her glass to drink. As she did, he squeezed her hand hard, and she shot him a look.

'I never said you could have a drink.' His voice was stern and scolding.

'Ed, really, I never saw that in the rules,' Lottie almost laughed.

'And you took no notice of the "not calling anyone by their name" rule seriously too, I see!' A hint of sarcasm in his voice as he turned over the rule sheet on the table and thrust them in front of her. Through the dim light she carried on reading.

If your master gives an order then you must obey, if you fail at any time your master can choose to punish you, either at the table, or in private. No punishment must disturb the other guests.

She carried on reading the list of punishments.

Spanking, sitting at your master's feet for a designated time, being muzzled, requesting a leash to be fixed to your master's hand or the seat for a period of time.

As she kept reading her eyes got wider and the punishments became more risqué. The realisation of what type of club this was seemed to really kick in. She was sure under the mask she had gone white, wondering if this really was a good idea, and if she should have taken Ed at his suggestion not to come. She was starting to be out of her comfort zone.

'As it is your first time, I will let you off, baby girl,' he said with a smile. 'Relax, I have already said I would not want anyone looking at you, let alone bent over the table showing the world that beautiful white ass being slapped until it went red!' He smiled and took his drink, taking his mind off the very thought as his dick stirred in his trousers once more.

'Sorry,' she whispered, biting her lip which he could see under her mask.

'I will let you off on one condition,' he said, leaning back to her so she could hear. She nodded. 'You don't bite that again all night,' he put his finger on her lip and she moved her teeth, 'you know I am trying to control myself and that,' he tapped it, 'does it every time so you're not helping.'

'Sorry!' she said again, this time not doing it, although it was a force of habit for her. 'I'm not very good at this am I? I shall be shackled to the seat and flogged before the starter arrives if I'm not careful.'

'I never said that you would not get punished, I just said not here!' He took another drink and looked ahead of him. Lottie felt her stomach churn, and somewhere deep inside her she quite liked the thought.

As they ate the delicious food that was brought to them, Lottie noticed at various points both men and women seemed to be carrying out some of the punishments she had read through. A man sat and ate his food from his plate on the floor, while the woman rested her foot on his shoulder. She mused at how uncomfortable it must be for him. Ed noticed her looking over in their direction.

'He could be a high court judge for all you know,' he whispered in her ear, 'or a famous rock star!' He took a mouthful of food. 'Or one of our solicitors, or my bank manager.'

'You don't know that they come here!' she said in a low voice.

'Don't I?' he mused, finishing off his steak.

'If you do know them, they know that you come here too,' she said back.

'Before I met you, you know they must have,' he simply said, 'but it is the unwritten rule that you never tell, and if you do then you don't get back in. Some people, well everyone here actually, likes that anonymity, don't you?' He asked, 'Would you like to go to your next fashion show, or shopping and get stopped in the street and asked how you liked your night out at a BDSM club? Not everyone in the world thinks this is right, or just a bit of fun. Not everyone here is with their wives or people who may understand.'

'I have to say it is rather a shock, but we are adults, and we make our choices,' she said.

'Not everyone is as accepting of this kind of behaviour, some people think that dominating people are mentally disturbed, outcasts to society, sick or evil in some way,' he said. He pushed his plate away as an indication to the waitress to take it. Without fail she appeared. 'If it pleases you, may I take them, sir?' she asked. 'Yes,' was the reply.

Lottie looked at him and listened to his words as her plate was taken too. Is that really what other people thought of him or how he saw himself, remembering all the conversations they had had in the past. She felt saddened for him and squeezed his hand as if to reassure him in some small way that was not how she felt at all. He looked at his phone and as if to change the subject he said, 'Bloody thing I can't get a signal down here.'

'Do you need to make a call?' she asked.

'No, just need to know that Pete is still outside. The show is about to start, so remember if you don't want to stop and watch just let me know, and we will go.' She nodded her head, 'I'm good,' she replied, and he smiled.

Ed looked around him; he was not looking for anyone in particular, although it was hard to make out faces even if he was; that was the point. Luckily, the fact that he was on edge had taken any sexual thoughts from his mind, in fact he was now convinced that this side of his life was well and truly over. He would do anything for Lottie, indulge her in anything, but this, this was now truly not who he wanted to be. But he had promised to share everything with her, let her know everything about him, so he had to go through with it.

Before the lights totally dimmed Lottie looked over to a man sitting alone to their left. He had looked over several times before when they had been in conversation, and she wondered if he was annoyed at the fact they were talking. Although she was sure they were not loud, in fact she could hardly hear anyone else's conversations, those that were having one anyway. As the light faded the stage was in darkness. When the single white light returned a young couple had arrived on the stage. They were dressed as every other man and woman in the room. Nervous, excited, embarrassed, Lottie was not sure how she felt, or what she expected was about to happen, so she moved closer to Ed, who still had her hand in his. He put their hands up on the table to give her more room but not letting her hand go.

The light must have blinded the couple, probably stops them from seeing the audience, she thought to herself. Soft music played in the background but apart from that you could have heard a pin drop. The couple did not talk. The man started to caress the woman, but their lips never kissed. Slowly, the sexual act started to play out, soft at first, but then as the dominating man took over, he chained the girl to the sofa. Lottie instantly thought how awful it must be to be bound, not being able to get out, and she tried not to have a flash back of the time she had felt so scared. Her breathing increased and Ed looked at her. She tried to smile back, knowing that this was nothing like the situation that had happened to her all those years ago. This girl showed no resistance – she was not being forced. She tried to calm herself and watch on; she turned her head, and again noticed that the man was watching her more than the stage.

Focusing now on the sudden smack of flesh she jumped as the girl received a slap from the leather instrument in his hand. Ed put his hand on her arm, and she looked at him briefly. Soft whimpering noises were all she could hear now from the girl, not pain, but something more. Lottie could almost feel each blow, and the muscles in her lower stomach twinged; she clenched them, knowing that in some way this was turning her on. The more she watched the more she recognised some of their own sex play that had slowly and willingly spilled into their lives. It is normal, she said to herself as if anything they had done had not felt normal anyway.

She released the grip on Ed's hand, and he must have felt her relax as he did the same too. She had noticed him look at his phone one more time but was now quite transfixed by the display in front of them. Oral sex performed by them both, various positions that increased the stimulation of them both. She could not help but feel her own nipples straining against the leather corset, or how her upper legs were damp from her own arousal. How she felt when Ed did this to her. As the man kissed the girl's exposed nipples, Lottie found herself take a sharp breath, as if it were her on the stage feeling the electricity shoot through her body.

Ed looked out the corner of his eye, not wanting to draw attention to the fact that he was watching her. He had tried to think of other things but had given in several minutes earlier when he knew Lottie was relaxing. His dick felt so hard under the table that he could have sworn he was jammed behind there by it. His trousers needed to be undone or he would scream with the pressure soon. It was not watching the stage, but watching her that was doing it for him. Her sudden intake of breath had confirmed that he was leaking out pre-cum. It was like a wet dream, ones he'd had when he was at school, but he was well and truly awake.

Lottie unconsciously had moved her free hand from the top of the table to her knee; she felt her hot bare skin and started to rub. She had watched porn before; Todd loved it. She had not seen the attraction herself, but here, live, only feet away from them it was different. She rubbed up her leg, skimming her sex with her hand. Out of the corner of his eye Ed noticed this and almost shot from his seat. He contained himself and took her hand from her leg and put it back on the table.

'Keep it here, babe,' he said, not that he ever wanted to deny her pleasure, but if she did touch herself, he knew that she would regret it tomorrow, feel embarrassed. No, fuck it, he thought, it's not what she does to herself that will make her feel embarrassed, it is what I will do to her myself at this fucking table if she carries on! He tussled with his thoughts.

At some point that he missed that the couple on stage had joined. She was bent over the sofa, and he was entering her forcefully from behind. Every breath, every plead for more or agreement of pleasure could be heard now. The slapping of skin on skin, the continued slapping of leather on skin brought the whole show to a climax, as both of them screamed and grunted out. Pulling out of her he freely ejaculated, covering her from behind, spreading his seed all along her naked back. He carried on using his fingers in her to ensure that the same completed pleasure was achieved.

Lottie held her breath; the lights went out and as quickly as they had appeared on stage, they had gone. The main room lights turned up slowly allowing Lottie to come back to reality. She slowed her breathing and looked at Ed.

'Can we go?' he asked.

'Yes,' she said, 'Oh god yes.' She moved out of the booth one way and Ed went the other. He was gone from sight, but she did not see him shoot off to fix the bill. It was the only moment they had been physically parted all night. She smoothed her skirt, well the small amount of fabric that you could call a skirt. She moved to the side of the booth where she thought Ed had stood up from, but he had gone. She walked to what she remembered was the door and suddenly two arms came around her waist. The black jacket sleeves and the white shirt looked the same, but the cuff links did not match; they were nothing like what Ed would wear and there was a strong smell of cigars. She turned around to see a man, same build and size as her husband, same mask covered his face, but his hair was different, and his eyes were distinctive.

'Mrs Dean, we meet at long last, in the last place I would have ever expected to,' his low voice said, as if he did not want to raise suspicion.

Lottie's legs moved as fast as she could, but he held her arm momentarily before allowing her to get away. She had only taken two paces and she looked back. He was gone. Whoever it had been had gone and all she could see were others in the room, and they all looked the same.

She shook her head; had she still been in some transfixed state? No, she thought, who the hell was that?

'Lottie?' The voice this time she knew and the arms that held out for her she wanted. 'Lottie, baby, what is it?' he asked, taking off his mask.

'Sir, Mr Dean, your mask,' one of the doormen said as they made their way towards the exit.

'Fuck the mask, man. Lottie, slow down, are you OK?' The two doors opened, and she stopped and turned to him as soon as she was through.

'Sorry, I couldn't catch my breath. I'm not sure if I panicked as you had gone or was so overcome by the whole thing!' He took off her mask and the attendant said, 'Sorry, sir I had no idea it was you, but advise you to put on your masks on in the club.'

'I advise you to shut the fuck up and get our coats,' Ed spat out totally focused on his wife not any etiquette or rules to stop him.

'I looked round and you had gone,' Lottie continued, almost physically shaking.

'Sorry, I said I would catch the bill.' He pulled the coat offered on an outstretched arm around Lottie's shoulders and put his own over his arm. 'Are you sure that is all?' He punched some keys on his phone, still noticing there was no signal.

'Sorry I never heard you, like I said I was lost in the moment or something. I feel such a fool for making a fuss,' she said, walking up the stairs and using Ed to rest on as her shoes were as bad going up as they had been a few hours before going down. As the top door opened the sudden rush of air was a welcome relief to her; she had not felt stuffy but suddenly craved the fresh air. 'You are sure that is all it was?' he asked again, putting her coat on fully for her now. His phone beeped to acknowledge that a signal had finally sent his message, and within a second their car pulled slowly around the corner of the street.

'I'm good.' She reached up to kiss him to confirm her statement, although she guessed inside, she would kick herself for not mentioning the guy, whoever he was back there.

'Fancy a drink somewhere?' he asked.

'You are joking me right, dressed like this?' She managed a smile at his suggestion. 'Although I'm sure you know a few bars in this area where this is not considered risqué?'

'Positively tame compared to some!' he joked back, feeling happy that she was OK.

'Home is fine for me, not sure how much excitement I can take!' She moved to the car as Edward leant over her to open the door.

'If it is straight home, a lot more excitement I hope after that little warm-up display, and your current get up!' She got in and he pushed in after her.

'Warm-up display?' she asked.

'Oh yes, that was just the start, three more acts and then it really does get jaw dropping, even I could cringe at some of the things you would have seen.' He paused and looked through to the front of the car. 'Hi, Pete, home please,' he said, putting his arm around Lottie. She smiled as her Edward was back, manners and all. She put her head on his shoulder. As she closed her eyes, she thought that the guy in the room must have seen them before they went in or something. She never gave him another thought, or a mention as they arrived home.

As the hot feeling of her climax reached through her body, Lottie opened her eyes to see her husband above her naked body, thrusting himself into her. Sweat had gathered on his forehead. It had not taken them long on arriving in the apartment to make their way to the privacy of their bedroom and become entwined with each other. The urgency of their need had been clearly brought on through the events of the night. Unstrapping her outfit had become so slow that Ed used small nail scissors from the bathroom to just cut it off. Both consumed by their passion they used and enjoyed each other with an urgency that increased the intensity but did not remove the intimacy. Wanting to be so close, closer than it was physically possible to get.

As her inner muscles spasmed Ed gritted his teeth knowing that his own release was not far but wanting her to take what she needed from him before he could be spent. Digging in her nails Lottie grasped him and lifted her upper body up in a reaction to her lust to get closer to him.

'Lottie!' he called out as the pain from her nails and the rush of blood drained him, and it felt as if the only body part he could feel was his shaft exploding into her. He let out grunting noises as he pumped away. She felt a second surge of electricity hit between her legs and she braced him around the waist, pushing the direction of his thrusts inwards more, rubbing her G-spot that quivered, sending the spasm to her legs. It was the most frenzied and noisy love-making session they had ever had, not allowing their bodies to stop violently shaking or moving for what seemed minutes. That was the sheer moment that they became as one, as if no one else on the planet existed, and they needed no one else in their lives.

Moments of silence passed in total contrast to the last half hour. They just held each other as if psychically communicating. Neither had any comprehension of the time; it had been dark when they fell onto the bed, curtains still open but as usual as no one could look in. The darkness of the room was only broken by stolen light from the city below; like them, the city was still awake. Ed broke off the embrace, asking if she needed a drink.

He returned moments later, naked and carrying two bottles and a glass of milk, as per the request from his former question. Embracing the refreshing liquid, they took a moment of calm before it started again, a soft touch, a kiss, an intimate touch and before they knew it, they reached the height of complete togetherness, entwined and entangled in lust, passion and love-making again.

Chatting until the streetlights faded, if either one had dozed, the other had watched over them. Ed looked over at the time when he heard the door to the apartment close. Sunday quietly drifted over them, and as if a jailer had a key to their room, they never left until the fragrant smell of a late lunch reached their sanctuary.

'We should get up and eat,' Ed said, 'come for a shower.'

'If you want to get up and eat, you had best shower alone, I will have a quick bath,' she grinned. Moments later as she entered the bathroom the water was already filling the tub for her. 'Who needs food, then?' Ed said with a smile, already sitting in the steaming hot tub filling with fragrant bubbles.

Mrs B placed the food in the warmer; it was clear that they were not making it for dinner, so she left, humming to herself as she could hear the laughter and jovial voices of her employers taking a bath. Chatting as if they had never had a conversation in ages, catching up like old friends with so much to discuss, so many things to talk about. She closed the door with a smile of contentment on her face for them.

Chapter 8

Two whole weeks had passed, and Ed and Lottie were getting ready to go around to see his mother for Sunday lunch.

'What are you smiling at?' Lottie asked as she caught her husband watching her as she put up her hair, making the final adjustments to her dress.

'You,' he said simply.

'Why?' she asked smiling. She knew why.

'This time last year, you would not believe how nervous I was at meeting you,' he said, ruffling his still-wet hair from his shower.

'You came in all guns blazing, Mr Dean, you knew what you wanted and took advantage of me.' She bit down on her lip. 'And you have had your way with me ever since.'

He swooped down on her like a predator picking up his prey.

'A whole year of my life consumed by you, and it feels like a lifetime.' He kissed her neck; she still wore the necklace he had given her, and he looked at it as nothing else now other than a gift, for the woman he knew he would love for the rest of his life.

'Is that a good lifetime, or a sentence?' she asked, joking with him.

'For all my lifetime,' he said looking back at her in the mirror. Despite all the revelations that had come out over the past few weeks and the work on the case, the increased tensions that had built up since they first agreed to see this thing out, they had never felt so relaxed with each other as they had of late.

'It could not go by without giving you something today.' He passed her a box from his side of the bed. She opened it. It was a small, paper dove.

'Paper for our first anniversary,' he said. She looked almost puzzled. 'Paper is one of the old traditional gifts.'

'What is written on it?' she asked, making out that some of the writing looked like hers.

'It's the bit you dropped out of your bag and I picked it up. It was the clue that you were going to the Tap and Tune,' he finished.

'Where you were stalking me!' she said.

'The very same.' He jumped off the chair. 'It took me hours on the internet to find out how to do that. I have wasted a whole tree trying to get it right!'

She placed it on the dresser in front of her. 'I haven't got you anything.' She was almost disappointed with herself. With all the work she had not forgotten, just had not found the time.

'Don't want anything really,' he said. 'It's not your proper gift,' he said, reaching in his pocket for something else. She turned around on her chair.

'Really Ed, you give me too much all the time,' she said, standing up to take out of his hand what he was offering. She opened the envelope. 'More paper?' she asked, looking inside. 'Tickets to the opera.' She looked again. 'In Italy?!'

'Yep, next weekend. I thought we could get back into normal life properly, we both need a break from it all. Don't tell me that you have to work, we both know the score. I want you to find out who this idiot is, but we have had nothing to go on, nothing has come back from all your hard work, so a quick break will refresh us for what is to come.'

He went over the details of when they flew and what was in store for the rest of the two days away as they made the short drive to his mother's.

It sounded less like a break the more he explained what he had planned. While they were there, his mother seemed happier with the idea of the investigation. She had signed the paperwork, but was upset that it had to go this far. They had agreed not to talk about it as they had driven over but she had brought the subject up. Lottie made an excuse to wash the pots, although the dishwasher really did the work, but she wanted Ed to have some time alone with Alice as she could see that she was clearly upset by all the events.

It was only on the drive home that Ed explained what they had chatted about, and Lottie felt guilty in more ways than one. It would be her finding things out, things she knew one day they may not want to hear. She had to stay detached, leave the personal side out of work, and leave work out of any personal time they had together. It had been something they had chatted about long and hard.

The program of events for their weekend away was as punishing as she knew it would be. Sitting at her desk on the Monday morning, she felt drained and totally exhausted.

'Well, if that is what a weekend away does, I would sooner stay at home,' Todd remarked, walking into her office and passing over his shop-bought coffee for her. 'Here you go.' She took a mouthful, but it tasted funny, so she made a face.

'Too smooth after that Italian soup they serve up out there I guess.' Todd noted her face.

'Yes, after a day I sort of lost the taste for it, but it does keep you awake.' She smiled and took another sip, but it really turned her stomach.

Uh, I guess with your husband in tow, you don't get much sleep anyway! he thought to himself and a twinge of envy kicked into the thoughts of their love-making sessions he knew without doubt would have taken place. He smiled at her. 'Want something else?' he asked, 'Water?' He pulled a bottle out of his bag and she took it from him. They caught up with the work he had done on the days she had not been there, but there was nothing new to report.

Sometime later in the day after lunch Todd spent time in her office on his laptop.

'Do you think there is any mileage in getting him out of the ground?' Todd asked straight out, pushing himself from his chair. Lottie looked up at him. He had Mitch's case file open.

'I really don't want to until we have a solid case of why we are going to do it.' She sighed. 'I can't see what more evidence or information at this point I can gain from it, and the impact on Ed, well you know what it does to families. If I can, I want to avoid it.' She smiled at the young lab boy, Eric who walked in while they were talking and she turned back to her desk. Todd pulled his screen down.

'What are we working on. Anything of interest?' he chirped up. Fresh from university last month he was keen to work with them both. He was over-enthusiastic sometimes and Lottie had noticed how he seemed to linger around them. Keen, she just thought. They both replied, 'No' together.

'Mrs Dean speaking.' Her mobile had rung, and she scrabbled to pick it up. Not recognising the number, she took the call. 'Oh yes, I have forgotten. That will be fine,' she said and put the phone down. Quickly scrolling through her phone calendar, she realised that she had not made a follow-up at the doctors; it was a good job they called to remind her that the seven-week appointment was due. She made it for the following Thursday. She would have time between her meeting with Liz and a quick catch up with the music college. She made a note to ensure that she reminded Ed, too.

Over breakfast on Thursday, they swapped appointment details. She had already told Ed about the doctors and met with a frosty reply at first. He asked the same questions again.

'Do you want me to come with you today?' He took another mouthful of his granola, keeping it as casual as possible.

'No, we'll head over straight to the fashion house, and then I am having afternoon tea at the college. I'm good to meet you here later as we planned.' She took another sip of her juice. She left her toast, not feeling hungry.

'More coffee?' Mrs B held up the jug and Ed passed his mug over. 'Mrs Dean?' Lottie smiled and declined.

Liz had been pleased to see Lottie, although Lottie smiled when Phil asked if he could come in with her.

'I know about you two,' Lottie said as she took the stairs when they first arrived. 'You don't have to make any excuses up, Phil, I think it's great.'

'I guess Mr Dean will not be so understanding,' he replied.

'I guess Mr Dean will have to live with it; work and social lives should be separate. Liz is perfect for you, and you are a great catch for anyone, so don't tell Mr Dean I said that, and your secret is safe with me.' She smiled at him as he opened the door to the office for her where Liz sat, studying her computer.

Lottie had taken some time out to look at the completed dresses already, waiting for the up-and-coming fashion show, when her phone rang. Todd's face and number popped up and she took the call.

'Lottie, you need to see this,' he said, almost whispering.

'What have you found?' she asked.

'Can you come over?' he enquired. 'I know it's your time off, but you do need to see this.'

'You're not alone, are you?' she asked.

'No,' was his simple answer.

'When?' she enquired, gauging the urgency.

'Now. The body is in, not sure how long it will be until they move her!'

Lottie replied that she would come in, and cursed under her breath. She would need to cancel her other appointment on route back to the centre and make it for another day. Doing this, she was disappointed that she could not get in until the following week. She agreed to the date and they continued. She asked Phil to let Ed know of her change of plans, just saying that she had been called back to the centre.

Ed was in a meeting and took the call. He knew that Lottie could fill him in if he needed to know, but the rest of the meeting was quite a blur in the anticipation of what had been so urgent that she cancelled her appointment.

Todd took her to the quiet room as soon as she arrived and put a case note file in front of her. Lottie took time to read through it and looked at the photos.

A young woman, early twenties, had been found of a drug overdose – nothing new there. Police were not suspecting any foul play. They said she was a prostitute and she had recently had sex with several people it turned out. As Lottie read on, a picture in her mind was developing of the girl and then she saw the words 'Coven Club' worker. She looked at the girl again. She was not sure why, but she thought she recognised her eyes.

'Can I see her?' she asked Todd.

'I have not been asked to look at anything. Dom from the Met has, but they are full and asked if we could chill her here until they contact relatives. So I quickly pulled up the files. It would arouse suspicion if we had to go over there to look at her, but as she is here you can go down and have a look.' He urged her to keep reading. 'Have you found the match yet?' he asked, almost in triumph that he had, and she was taking some time to get there. Admittedly it had been the search on the computer that had found it for him, not having to read hard copies. He could not wait any longer; he sat by her side and took the file and flicked the page in question. 'DNA,' he said, pointing to the area on the page. 'Small trace of semen DNA.'

Lottie looked at him and a sudden surge of nausea came over her. Whoever had been with her, slept with her, maybe even killed her, had been in her flat, damaged the car, and potentially been the one sending the threats.

'When was the body found?' Lottie asked.

'Date of death was last Saturday, well, the early hours of the Sunday morning. She was not found until the evening when her friend called round to go to work.' Todd looked at the computer to get more information.

'Can I get that lot printed off?' Lottie said, 'So I can take it home and keep working? Are there pictures of the scene? What was the original report detail base? Was she a known drug user?'

'Wow, slow down Lottie, I have only one pair of hands.' Todd looked up at her. 'She will be here for a few days yet; her folks are in America and they can't get over here, and even when they do, she will stay here until they can arrange to take her away.' He went to the printer to get the photos he had just downloaded. 'I will take what I can get in the next half hour. You can have a good look through it over the weekend and then on Monday, if you have to, we can take a look in more detail.'

Lottie looked at her watch. The afternoon had flown by and she knew that she would have a waiting car at 5pm.

'Have you got photos of the scene too?' she asked, looking quickly through the papers he handed her. 'Just coming through now,' Todd replied, repeating his trip to the printer.

'Hey, you guys are busy again, we don't often see you, Mrs Dean, on a Thursday,' Eric said as he came into the room. Todd looked at Lottie and she smiled replying, 'I forgot some things that Todd asked me to look at. Nothing from work, it was for his brother. Some printing I said I would do for his bar, don't tell the prof, not really appropriate use of staff time or centre resources!' Lottie tried to lie as fast as she could and hoped that he believed her.

'Oh, ok,' Eric said, walking off. 'Call me if you need a hand with anything though,' he said, leaving the room.

'Well, that was easy!' Todd said, still tapping away on the computer.

'What was?' Lottie asked.

'Lying!' he simply replied and looked at her under his eyebrows.

Lottie tutted. 'Can we call your friend Max and see if we can have a chat?'

'Will he not want to know why we are interested?' Todd replied. 'It seems an open and shut case to them.'

'Um, maybe too early for that, but it may come to it, and how can they have closed the case? Surely the DNA would show up to them and it would cause alarm bells?' Lottie stood waiting for the last lot of printing.

'The police are going with junkie pro, who shagged about, I guess.' Todd did not mix his words. 'The sort of place she worked does evoke a certain type of person.' Lottie shot him a look. 'What do you mean by that?' she asked.

'Oh, Lottie come on, the Coven Club, full of sex pests and sickos who like to play a bit rough. Don't claim to be so innocent that you have not heard of it,' he retorted and then said to himself, ask your husband. I am sure he will enlighten you! Todd smiled at his first reply.

'The girl could have been working hard to move on, better herself. And maybe she did not do drugs or take every guest of the club home?' she said, knowing the rules, but she was not going to let on.

'So why did she OD on hard class As, and a lot looking at that blood count. I guess the rough sex thing, you would put down to her being raped, forced against her will, not taking a rich psycho home for a bit of extra BDMS that his wife does not know about to earn a few quid for her next fix.' Todd passed her the last of the printing.

'Maybe yes, I do think that,' she said with honesty in her voice.

'Live in the real-world, Lottie, it is not all roses and enough money to get you anything you want.' She let that comment go. 'It's also not always as simple as people think, not as black and white as it seems!' she said, grabbing her bag, ready to leave. 'See you Monday, and thanks for this,' she said, 'enjoy your weekend.'

'You too.' He watched her leave.

God, he loved her. He knew she was so innocent, her outlook on life so simple, and that made him love her more. The job offer he had been given in America needed to be replied to by the end of next week. How could he let her go again and now when she needed him the most? For once in his life, he could help her, be close to her, give her something that she needed. Even if she did not need him in other ways, how could he leave her at all?

He had cried when she got married, knowing that she was now beyond his reach. Knowing that any hope of them being together was so very far away. Maybe the best place for him was miles over the sea so he could start again, find his own happy ever after. His sister had been right; working with her and being so close would only make his fascination worse, and it had. He lay awake at night, knowing she was in Ed's arms and it pained him so much. Not just that she was not with him, but knowing she was with a better man. Not just because Edward Dean had everything to give her, but he told her and physically showed her he loved her. Dean had grabbed her while he'd had the chance, claiming her, not foolishly letting her go as he had years before.

This case could take months to see out; she needed his help but, what was in it for him? Miss the job opening of a lifetime and regret that as well? No woman that he loved and no top of the notch job either. He took a deep breath and pondered over her words about not always black and white and wondered how much more he could do tonight to help her get through this. That was another thing about her; once she had her teeth into a case, she never let it rest until it was concluded, that is why she was so good. That's why he loved her. She never let go.

'Hey,' Ed almost greeted her at the door as if he had been waiting. He had of course, all afternoon to ask her what was going on.

'Oh, I'm beat!' she said, kissing him and taking off her shoes.

'Want a coffee?' he asked, letting her get settled before he bombarded her with questions.

'No, is there any of that Jasmine tea?' She walked to the bedroom and changed into jogging bottoms and a loose top. The weather was nice, and the sun shone through the kitchen windows out onto the balcony as she walked back in. Ed was just putting the tea bag in the bin. 'Thanks,' she said as she sat down, dropping the large folder on the table.

'Is that why you had a change of plan?' He had chosen his words carefully, not saying she had cancelled the doctors for something more important.

'Yep, and it could be the opening that we needed.' She pulled the folder towards her.

She sipped the hot liquid. He had put some cold water in it, and she smiled that he knew how she liked her drinks. It was sometimes the fine details that made her love him, not the thousands he spent on gifts and weekends away.

'Do you want to grab dinner before we have a look though? I have not been through it all yet. Todd gathered as much as we had so I could bring it home.' She could smell something nice. No doubt Mrs B had made it for their tea, but to be honest she was not hungry. She had a sick feeling in her stomach, tied up with the questions and anticipation of what she was going to find. She knew Ed would not have eaten so maybe they needed to first. 'You are starving I presume,' she said as she opened the oven door. Behind her he was putting out two plates and she served up the pie. As they sat at the breakfast bar, Lottie pushed most of her food around the plate; as fantastic as it smelt, she just did not want it.

'Eat it, Lottie.' Ed had noticed. 'I know you want to crack on but passing out mid-way is no good for any of us!' He had finished his plate and was getting a glass of wine. 'Want one?' he asked. She shook her head, saying that she still had her tea, although now cold. It somehow tasted better like that.

'You know that by showing you these I am technically breaking the law, and my professional code of conduct?' she said, settling it all out over the floor in the living room. It was a method she liked to adopt to put a timeline to the information or create some form of group in her mind.

'I'm hardly going to say anything, am I?' Ed replied. 'To be honest it would help if I knew what I was looking for!' She smiled at him as he looked at the pages of words and reports.

'The pictures are more graphic, are you sure you want to see them?' She was worried it would evoke the memory of Mitch. He nodded and she followed her method of spreading them out.

'Do you recognise her?' Lottie asked. He shook his head. 'Look closer at the mouth.' She shuffled to him and lent over his shoulder and pointed out the contours of her delicate features. He still shook his head.

'If she said, "May I take your drinks order, Sir?", would that stir any memories?' Lottie lifted her eyebrows with the question.

'No!' Ed said, instantly realising she meant the waitress from the other night at the club. He looked again, trying to see through the paper as if he would get a closer look. 'No, is it really her?' he asked, almost in disbelief.

'I totally think so. It was the same night we were there; something about her smile, and her kind eyes made me recognise her, then Todd gave me this.' She passed him the profile of who she was, where she worked etc. Ed took the time to read through it.

'We're not jumping to conclusions, are we?' he asked.

'Coincidence is easy to discount, my old professor used to say that to me. If you have a hunch, check it out, you are 9 times out of 10 to be right.' She put her hands on his shoulder as her stomach rumbled. He looked back at her.

'You should have eaten more food!' he said.

'I will get something later before we go to bed,' she replied, already scrambling through some documents she also wanted to show him.

The night ran away with them. She had taken her time looking through everything, explaining as much as she could to Ed, trying to build up a picture. He had been to the kitchen several times to fill his wine glass, and took Lottie some water and toast, that again she hardly touched. Finally, way past 1am in the morning he got her to come to bed. He had early meetings, and she could pick it back up. She put the files in the wall safe. Ed had questioned it, but then could see after she explained why she thought it was the safest place for them. They snuggled up in bed and Ed lay behind her. He felt how hot her skin was; she was almost sweating.

'Are you coming down with something? You're on fire,' he said.

'I feel OK, just exhausted, and it is hot in here.' She kissed his hand and closed her eyes. Ed frowned as he did not feel overly hot – the room felt just fine.

He was up and showered before Lottie even opened her eyes. She seemed to ache all over and felt lifeless. Ed came back in the room and she was still tucked up in the sheets, dozing.

'Stay there sleepy head, and rest. I need to get off.' He kissed her head, moving a lock of tangled hair out of the way. She nodded to him and said there was no need for Phil to hang around as she was not planning to go out all day. Ed agreed and said that if she changed her mind to call and Pete could come over.

She slept until after 11am, when she woke to hear Mrs. B pottering around, clearing up.

'Sorry, Mrs Dean, I never meant to wake you,' she said, giving her a smile.

'Oh, that's OK, I really should get up.' Lottie looked out over the sheets and slowly came to life, finding that the shower helped once she had made it into the bathroom.

It was the start of another busy weekend. They had two charity dinners and Ed had arranged to meet Simon and his father for a boy's toys day on

Sunday. Some time ago Ed had bought him a remote-control helicopter, and since then he had changed his fascination from cars to anything that flew. In Edward Dean style he had gone one better and promised them a flight in the company helicopter. Lottie had filled her days with shopping and meetings since they had last sat down together, and hardly looked at the files, knowing that the information was not going anywhere.

'I'm not sure I feel up to a joy ride,' Lottie said to Ed as they pulled into City airport.

'I can't let them down now,' Ed replied, looking concerned. He had noted that she left most of her breakfast. Although she did not mind flying, the helicopter rides were always more of a challenge for her.

'If you go, they will not be let down, I can ask Pete to drop me back home once I have said hello.' She smiled at him and he frowned.

'That means we don't get to spend the day together.'

'You have had me all weekend so far, and more than once in the literal sense!' she grinned back to him.

'What a joy that has been.' He hugged her and kissed her hard on the mouth, reminding him of their passionate night. 'Thing is, I think on Tuesday I've got to go over to Japan,' he sighed, as his comment came out of the blue. 'And I just wanted to go and get back as quick as possible. With your workload, against my better judgment, I was not going to ask you to come as it will be hours in the air. You are already exhausted, and I don't want to make that any worse.'

'Well, Mr Dean, I am impressed you are willing to give me up.' She smiled. A few months ago this would have been a heated discussion and he would have insisted she be with him.

'Don't be fooled. I am not doing it willingly; every bone in my body wants you there, safe, not out of my sight, but I have taken a reality check and know what will be, will be. Our fate is in our own hands no one else's. I respect and admire your work and the decisions for you to carry on. How important your independence is to you. So, therefore I will bloody worry and constantly fret for every second I am away, and Phil will not be out of your sight for the whole time. But I will man up and live with it!' He kissed her again. 'That's why when we do get time together, it is so very special.'

She almost had a tear in her eye for some reason that had made her feel emotional.

'You said last week that I give you too much, but what I really don't give you is what you really want – trust, space, independence. The things that do not financially cost, but have no doubt, they are costing me very dear in my head.' He tapped his forehead as if to reassure her of his words.

'I understand that, and,' she took a breath to stop her crying, 'I appreciate it totally.' The car stopped, and she looked up to see Simon and his father already standing on the tarmac. Ed squeezed her hand. It was clear to see the excitement in the young boy's face, he was hopping up and down and clapping his hands. The smile on his face was enough to outshine the sun and bring it crashing from the sky. He hugged his dad's legs and his dad hugged him back, ruffling his hair and waving over to the direction of the car.

Lottie thought to herself, it is so special to see such joy, to be able to give a child that much love and happiness. She swallowed hard. 'I'll come with you. How can I let the little man down? I have to warn you though I feel as sick as a dog, so the pilot had best make it a smooth ride.'

He kissed her forehead. 'I will make it as smooth as I can.' Part of the fun was he was going to fly them. It had been a while since he stretched his well-earned pilot's wings. Lottie had thought to herself when it was first suggested that the whole day was going to be more fun for Ed than for the guests really, and she was right.

He did have to go on business, early on Wednesday morning, but the timings were tight ensuring he was back in the UK for the dinner hosted by Lord Bennington. An invite that could not be missed by the CEO as

Edward's was the only charity Lord Bennington supported and supported very well.

With military procession Ed and Lottie had swapped diaries. Ed was taking no chances that he would not be able to contact her, and both Phil and Mrs B at home and the office staff at work well prepped about what was to happen while he was away. He had even called Todd and asked to ensure that he looked after Lottie, inviting him to stay if required so they could carry on work in the safety of their home. He hoped that would not be needed, but it was impressing Lottie with his whole new attitude, as hard as it was for him deep down.

Uneventful was an understatement, but Thursday afternoon came around and Lottie had got no further with her investigation and was realising how much she was missing her husband during his time away. Talking on the phone and the Skype link, just was not cutting it.

She was even chatting to him on her way to the doctors before he got another internal flight. The reception in the car was not very good, but they were able to catch up from their conversation only a few hours earlier. She smiled at Phil as he dropped her off.

'Go and get a coffee. I can call when I'm done. I'm not sure how long I will be,' she said, closing the door.

'Next appointment is at 3:45pm, Mrs Dean.' It gave her well over an hour.

'Yes, and I know that you are really keen to see Liz, I have not forgotten.' She smiled at him. 'In fact, why don't you go over there now? I can catch a taxi over.'

'No can do Mrs Dean, but I really appreciate your thoughts,' he answered without falter, knowing that his balls were far too attached and very precious for him to have said yes and something happen to her. Not again, not on his shift.

'Just a thought!' Lottie said, smiling back at him.

Within the hour she walked out of the large external wooden door back in the London street. Cars came past her, buses and people all going about their normal lives. Each person having their own agenda, taking no notice of each other. She looked down the road for the car; nothing either way. She started to walk in the main direction of traffic and found herself crossing the road. How she was not hit by anything was a miracle; two cars sounded their horns, one cyclist shouted abuse to her and she had no recollection of how she got to the other side.

She sat on the stone steps of an office or apartment and stared at the cars.

The Bentley pulled up alongside her and Phil opened the door.

'Mrs Dean?' he said, encouraging her to get in, and she just seemed to levitate from the step to the car. She never spoke. It could have taken an hour for Lottie to arrive at the warehouse. She could not tell. Her body was going through the motions of being there, but her brain was totally disengaged. Greeting Liz, she sat, hearing what she was saying but as if it was through a distorted old gramophone.

'Lottie, where are you today?' Liz finally asked, sensing something was wrong. 'I know you miss Edward, but he will be back soon.' The mention of his name suddenly made Lottie snap back and she had a rising urge in her stomach to be sick. She ran to the direction of the bathroom and vomited.

'You OK?' Liz asked when she finally returned.

'Yes, I've just been to sort out my pill and...' Lottie started.

'I was sick after I had my first one, it's strong if you have not had it before.' Liz carried on looking through the dresses on the rail. It was her intention for Lottie to wear one for the dinner. Lord Bennington's daughter-in-law had also shown an interest in the range and Liz wanted Lottie to be her mascot as such. 'How about this one?'

'Umm,' Lottie answered her, not really knowing if the dress was black, blue, or bright orange.

As she tried on the dress, her phone rang. Liz shouted through for Phil to answer it, and he informed his boss that he was outside the fitting room and could she call him back later? Ed was happy with the reply, however he worried it would be a few hours until they could talk, and it was.

Lottie had gone to bed soon after 8pm. She ached all over; she was just drained. Mrs B was still in the apartment, clearing away the food. None of which Lottie had eaten, although she managed the cup of tea. The more she looked at the photos and at the scene, the more she could not see anything. She was looking for that little something, something to give her a lead. Mrs B knocked on the door and arrived with some toast and peanut butter. She smiled.

'Try this. I notice you left your dinner, although Phil seemed to have a good appetite, even if you have lost yours.'

Lottie smiled as she put it down on her bedside table and the smell of the toast hit her nose, instantly making her feel hungry.

'Thanks Mrs B.'

'Mrs Dean, your phone is still in the hall on charge. Phil will keep his ear out for it.' Then she turned around and said, 'And if you need to talk to me while Edward is away, please do think of me as a friend and share any troubles or concerns that you have.'

Lottie looked at her not knowing what she could be referring to. How could she help with what was going through her mind?

'Thank you, I'm fine. I will get my phone before I go to sleep,' Lottie replied.

'Yes, I am sure you are, but I have heard that before from you. Well, my dear, you know where I am. If that is all?' Mrs B walked over to the door.

'Thank you.' Lottie smiled, still looking at the door long after it had closed. She drifted off to sleep and when Phil took the call from Edward, he told him that Mrs Dean was asleep. Ed was content to talk to her in the morning if possible, although he left a text for her to receive, endorsing that he missed and loved her.

Chapter 9

Lottie smoothed the fabric over her hips and followed the careful stitching over her waist. The raw silk was a dream to wear, feeling warm, but cooling to touch. The dark blue full-length dress was a perfect example of the skill Liz had for design and finish. She smiled to herself, knowing it would be a success for her. She looked at the message on her phone again. Ed had sent it while she slept last night. As soon as she had woken, she sent him another, but guessing the time difference would put a delay to any further communications for now.

During the car journey he called quickly to say he would be with her in less than an hour. Her stomach still turned with anticipation, knowing when she would get to see him again. Pete drove and Phil was her escort until Ed arrived.

'You scrub up very well!' Lottie said, making small talk in the car as she looked over to the CPO. Although he always had a suit and tie on for work, there was something about a man in a black DJ and bow tie, more James Bond Agnes had always said. It suited both Phil and Pete down to the ground as they were in effect their own MI5.

She was not late to the party, but the room was already full of faces. Some she knew, some she had no idea who they were, but they knew her. She chatted and moved around the room with ease. Far more confident than the last time Ed had been away, and she had had to go to a function on her own where he was joining her later. Although that ended badly, she hoped that this one would not, but she could not help but have a feeling of deja-vu.

Sitting eating her meal, Phil stood as the dessert was cleared away. She had tried to eat, but found it hard to stomach; the dress was tight and the food rich and too sweet. She glanced as he moved, thinking he was going to the toilet, but as the person sat back next to her, the sudden smell that preceded him made her smile and she instantly knew her husband was back and in the room. Despite everyone verbally greeting him, he took no time in taking her hand and planting a firm kiss on her lips, whispering in her ear, 'You look stunning. I have missed you, Mrs Dean.'

'You too.' She smiled and for the first time in two days she was clear in her mind.

He was desperate to talk to her, hold her, touch her, have her, but the conversation and present surroundings did not allow him. Soft music started to play, and a young boy sat at a piano playing after dinner music.

'Do you dance, Mrs Dean?' a voice said behind her and both Ed and Lottie turned to see Lord Bennington.

'I do, my lord,' she said smiling, offering him her hand.

'Dean, do you mind if I steal your wife?' Bennington asked, although it was not really a request.

'Not at all, Sir,' Ed replied, standing as a gesture of respect for the older man. Inside he shouted as loud as he could, No! I have not seen her for days! He helped Lottie stand, holding on to her hand and squeezing, reluctant to let go and watched her walk to the small area of the dance floor.

Although the other guests kept him talking, he faced the area they had walked to and watched them dance as a couple. Bennington was a fine, middle-aged older gentleman, no threat on the 'running off with your wife front' not from age, or wealth for that fact. Ed could outstrip him in both departments. The envy was that he was not holding her, he was not the one they were all looking at holding and dancing with the most stunning creature in the room.

Lottie chatted with ease. He was such a gentle man in every sense. They swayed more than danced, and she giggled at his jokes. Ed rubbed his hands as Lottie's dance partner's son walked over to him.

'I am sure the old man will not mind, you know.' He paused and nudged Ed's arm.

'Sorry?' Ed said. 'Evening, Bennington.' Holding out his hand in greeting to his old acquaintance.

'If you butt in, I can truly understand why you would want to.' The remark was not meant in any other way but that he could tell Ed wanted to be with her. 'I can only go a few moments without Em.' He smiled in the direction of his wife who was busy chatting to a group of ladies. 'And Father is not as young as he once was, it's not so good for him to be on his feet too long, especially as he still thinks he's twenty!' The remark was aimed at the fact that Lord Bennington was swirling Lottie around like a teddy boy in a dance hall.

They came closer to the edge of the dance floor and Ed saw his chance to take over. With a polite bow he took Lottie from the older man, who patted him on the back and wished him luck. 'Worn me out, boy, hope you have better luck and more stamina than I have!' Then with grace the older man withdrew and allowed Ed to hold the most precious object in the room.

Every other woman was draped in gold, diamonds, or the like. His Lottie, so simple in her dress, positively plain in comparison some may say, but she still shone above them all to him. He had enough stamina to take her right there, several times he was sure.

'At last, Mrs Dean.' He rubbed the soft fabric at her lower back, and pulled her hand into his chest, resting her head on his shoulder. Her mind finally at peace with some of the decisions she needed to make as she listened to the beat of his heart.

'You look so glowing, somehow different,' he said, running his hand along her collarbone and down her arm. 'I hope that you have not been working too hard, but I don't want to know about that tonight.' He added that final remark as he did not want to spoil the moment. He knew if she had something to say that was important, she would.

She turned her head back around and softly kissed his chin. 'Ed,' she said in a soft low voice. 'Ed, I'm...' He ran his hand down the side of her face and she kissed his hand turning her face to it, making her stop speaking. Suddenly without warning or indication, she jumped back and exclaimed, 'Cuff links!'

Several people close to them looked around and Ed looked as confused as if she had grown two heads, and he held her at arm's length. Before he could even question her, she held his wrist and said again, this time in a lower voice, 'The cuff links, that's it!' The information that was going on in her head, seemed to compute and be seen through her eyes, oblivious to where she was – this was her Eureka moment. When she sobered from the thought, she looked round her and went really red, knowing that she had exclaimed this out loud, and it was not her intended conversation when she had said his name, far from it.

'Sorry.' She smiled, embarrassed or pleased with herself. Nothing else was in her mind now she knew she had found the connection.

'What about cuff links, what were you going to say?' Ed enquired, aware they were on a crowded dance floor and he looked like he was holding on to a crazed woman, not his calm, serene siren he had seen earlier.

'Sorry,' she started again; it had taken this time to get it clear enough to put into words. She gestured for them to walk to the corner of the room, find a quiet spot. When this was achieved, she needed to get this out before it went again from her mind.

'I was looking too deep, and the clue was there all the time. I saw the same cuff links, that night, on someone in the club.' This would have been the time to say 'the guy who knew me', but she diverted from the truth a little.

'What, the same as mine?' Ed had a flash of panic, but he was not sure why. These were the ones he always wore, the crest of his brother's army regiment; they had been Mitch's.

'No, not yours, silly!' She smiled and snorted slightly at the thought. 'On the side of the girl's dresser,' she carried on, 'there was a pair of male cuff links, some form of crest, different, like a family crest. Well, I say a pair,' she never took a breath, she just carried on explaining. 'That's the thing, they were not matching.'

'Not all cuff links match, some cheap novelty ones are designed different, to be odd,' Ed explained, but made the comment as he was interested in her discovery.

'I know, I know, but when I say different, I mean not totally in design. As if they were a pair once, years ago and for some reason one got lost or maybe damaged and the owner had another made to match, but it did not truly match.'

'Can you see the detail in a photo or something?' Ed asked, wondering if he could look, or they could find a goldsmith or something that could give a clue to who it was. He had not wanted to talk about her work tonight, or the case, but he found himself needing to.

Lottie recalled the photo. It was more the full view that she got of them personally from which she remembered the detail, and she could only slightly tell from the photo that they were not the same.

'Maybe a digital camera will enhance them,' she said, still with the excitement of her breakthrough evident in her voice. She had mentally left the dinner and had her head fixed on work.

'If you are so sure, you can look on Monday. Lottie, you can't do anything sooner.' Ed smiled at her, so amazed at her, so in awe of her mind for detail. 'Was there something else you were going to say,' he paused, 'before this outburst of utter revelation?'

She looked back up at him. 'Oh, oh no!' she stuttered. She had not forgotten, just got lost back in the moment. Pulling her close they returned to the event, although it was clear they both really wanted to get home. Lottie to show Ed the photo, and Ed, well it had been five days without her, so there was only one thing Ed wanted to do with Lottie.

Once in the privacy of their own four walls it did not take much to guess who got their wish first. It was late, and Lottie was easily persuaded to look at the photos after breakfast. He needed to send a few emails just to tie everything up from the last two days, so he said she would have an hour or so then.

'So, for now, Mrs Dean, come here.' He pulled her to him in the hallway and before she knew it, he had picked her up in his arms and taken her through to their bedroom.

'Smuuuuer.' He breathed her in as he unzipped the back of the dress, kissing her neck. She instantly closed her eyes and laid her head to the side of his shoulder, like his action was hypnotic, and his touch electric. 'My perfect wife!' he said, cupping her breast, feeling it respond directly to his touch.

He rubbed himself into her backside, not just to stimulate his rising erection, but to give her a reminder of what she had missed, and what she very soon would be getting. Slipping her arms from her bra, he then moved down to lift her free from the fine delicate lace that covered her intimate areas. As her panties fell to the floor, he rubbed his hand along her stomach. It felt tight, swollen but she never moved from his touch so it could not have been painful, nor did she object in any way to him carrying on. Just the opposite in fact.

Spinning round on her bare feet she tugged at his shirt, and made easy work of his trousers. Leading him to the bed, he sat down first as she straddled him. Kissing his head, she made sure that his face was pressed close into her chest. The open invite could not be missed to lift one of the plump mounds to his mouth and suck. She slightly recoiled; they felt tender, but not too much that she needed him to stop.

She slipped further down his body, taking care to kiss each area where his muscle flexed and relaxed. Using one hand she pushed him back so that he was resting on the bed. She placed her hands either side of him and kissed his stomach; his defined abdominals contracted and formed a perfect arrow to where she headed next. She always called them the 'lickie bits, which lead to heaven!'

As she took his pulsing head into her mouth, he pulled at her hair. 'Lottie.' He sucked the word through his teeth as she encased his fully erect dick in her mouth. The first stroke of her moist lips took her part way down and then the next she felt him hit the back of her throat.

She gagged slightly but prepared for the next suck, hollowing her cheeks as she totally took his length. As she moved her head up and down, she occasionally flicked her tongue, which aroused the end of him, tasting the salt he was releasing already.

Dropping his head back on the bed he could see her in his mind's eye. Her hair draped over him, her hands massaging his ass and his balls. He could feel her rubbing herself up and down on his leg, her breasts gently hovering over his thighs, occasionally brushing hard to ensure her nipples still felt the pleasure.

'Turn around, let me taste you?' he asked and with the precision of a praying mantis, she moved around his body without losing focus on him, still sucking, licking.

He pulled her up to his face and instantly thrust his tongue into her. She was wet and smelt musty, sweet. He put pressure on the entrance of her sex, and used his nose to rub her sensitive nub, while his tongue was as deep as he could get it. Noises like a hungry animal came from him and she was finding it hard to fully concentrate on her task in hand, as the muscles of her sex contracted and went into spasm due to his hard, furious assault.

She let out a little whimper, smothered by the engorged dick she had in her mouth. She was breathing hard and now finding it hard to keep up her rhythm at all. She replaced her mouth with her hand, cupped round him, rubbing him up and down. She was able to catch her breath, only to gasp again with the pleasure he was bringing her.

I can't keep this up, he said to himself, I have to feel her. He lifted her off him as if she were a rag doll and flung her on her back. Driving in between her thighs, his legs pushed hers to spread her out under him and he kissed her face. Their flavours mixed, each other tasting themselves in the kiss. Lifting her arms above her head, he held her down easily with one hand, and the other he used to guide himself into her pulsating pussy. He was large and she arched her back as he used his weight to force himself into her. Although he a light hold of her hands, she was able to move one down and put it on his hips, to slow his thrust down, to ease him more gently into her.

'Please be gentle,' she whispered.

'Sorry,' he softly said, guessing her action was to slow him, so that he did not hurt her.

They writhed in each other's pleasure, kissing, stroking, pulling, holding each other through the bonding and binding of their bodies. Lottie climaxed with soft, slow moves of her hips. It went on and deep, deeper than she had felt before. He pulled her so close to him and lifted her off the bed, he was holding her with one arm, and she ran her hands through his hair, still feeling her inner muscles contracting.

'I love you, baby girl,' he said, 'this does not get better. My life could not get better. There is nothing I need, nor want more than this,' and with the statement he came. His thrusting was still slow and deep as he ejaculated inside her, and he felt the hairs on his arms stand up. He flared his nostrils as he released her and himself back to the bed, being sure not to crush her; he had used his strength to fill her with his salty seed and was truly spent.

Rolling over, holding her in his arms, they lay silent until they both found sleep that was needed to seal their true bond.

Light poured into the penthouse the next morning. Edward had been up for over an hour when she padded into the kitchen, in the same shirt he wore last night.

'You look... how can I say this without getting punched? Awful!' He winced at his own words, knowing that they were said with love, but truth.

He was right, she would punch him, and she did playfully on the arm. 'Thanks!' She stuck out her tongue. 'I love you too!'

'I should damn sure hope you do, Mrs Dean.' He pulled some pancakes out of the oven and put them under her nose. Lottie felt repulsed by the smell and had to swallow hard to keep from retching.

'You hardly touched a drop last night, in fact I never saw you with a drink. Do you feel OK?' he asked. She could see he was pouring her a coffee.

'Not for me, water is fine.' She stood up and grabbed some from the fridge. 'I'll have a shower and make another entrance. See if I can look better next time round!' She moved quickly as she needed to reach the toilet. Now she knew that she was going to be sick.

After half an hour she emerged, refreshed. She made the same entrance and Ed still had his head in his laptop.

'Ta da!' She smiled. 'Better?'

'Babe, you looked awesome the first time, now I have perfection once more.' She had not noticed Mrs B in the kitchen.

'Your pancakes were cold, so I did you this, Mrs Dean.' She handed Lottie some toast and jam and a cup of tea. 'I'm guessing they will go down better?'

'Thank you.' She sat at the stool and watched Ed work for a moment. The morning was warm, so she went to the large doors and opened them, taking her toast with her. Even though the sun was out, a cool breeze swirled her still-damp hair and she mused out at the city. Wondering how many people were just waking up or going to bed. What their lives held for them, or what they wanted out of life.

Resting her tea on the balcony she took in a deep breath. The food did make her feel better. Closing her eyes, she listened to the bird song, the filtered sun's rays hitting her face. Ed had been right; life could not get any better, what more could she need or want. What more than she had already. She turned her back on the world and lent against the balcony and watched as Ed put down his laptop screen and jumped from the stool. He walked out to her.

She observed that he looked good in everything; particularly nothing. But there was something about the relaxed Sunday Edward Dean that really did it for her. Maybe it was the fact that she knew very few people ever saw this side to him. His baggy tracksuit bottoms and white tee shirt, bare feet, usual hair all ruffled and hand-swept. Her Mr Dean. She smiled as he took her in his arms, and she put her empty cup down on the table next to her.

'Happy?' she asked.

'I meant what I said last night.' He kissed her nose. 'I could not be happier.' He pulled her close and she resisted him, wanting to look at his face. There was a pause as he looked at her. 'What, are you not happy?' He looked puzzled.

'I am happy, very.' She bit down on her lip, smiling.

'What, Lottie, tell me!' He looked her in the eye, but her smile was now making him nervous.

'I bet you a pound you could be happier,' she said, still smiling at him,

'I bet you the entire sum of Dean Incorporated's bank balance and your pound that I could not!' He grinned. 'After all it's all yours, so I have nothing to lose!'

'So, there is nothing in the bet for me?' she asked.

'That's because I could not want anything else in the world.' He pulled her to him again, and this time she hugged him back. The same blackbird Lottie listened to before was back, sitting and watching them, singing to its heart's content. Ed kissed Lottie's head and smoothed away the hair that was blowing in the breeze. Lottie said something in a muffled voice, and he did not hear because her face was so tight against his chest.

'Sorry?' he said, letting her go a little so he could hear her, 'I didn't hear that.' He looked at her face and he could see the tears rolling down her cheeks. She was not sure that she wanted to say it again. She could have said something else, but she found the words coming out again.

'I'm pregnant. I'm going to have our baby.'

He looked at her and words didn't come from his mouth. The moment was silent, for what seemed an age and then he spoke.

'Lottie, I don't understand, I mean... Oh my God, really? You're joking with me, right? That's fucking brill!' He paused mid-word, looking at her. 'This is good, right?' He was physically shaking because tears were still streaming down her face, and the sudden thump of his heart stopped as the contemplation of her not wanting it hit him like a train. 'Oh, baby girl, please tell me these are tears of joy.' He wiped one away from her cheek. 'Oh please!' He was desperate for her to reply. He was crazed by the thought of what she had just said but hanging on a line, awaiting her reply.

She slowly smiled at him. 'I had no idea. You know how I felt about this.' It was still not the reply he was looking for. 'I was waiting to go to get my pill and I guess fate played her hand. Maybe I was being lazy, or maybe,' she paused, 'maybe it just feels right!' Her smiled extended.

'Oh God, really, it's what you want?' he asked again to make sure he was not dreaming.

'You said a few weeks back that whatever our lives gave us we would tackle together. Well, this just seems like the next thing.' She looked back out over the city. 'I guess if we had planned it, I would not ask for it just now, but I have to say, I hope that you are not disappointed in me.' She looked back at him. 'I tried to tell you yesterday. I never meant to keep it from you. I found out on Thursday but there was no way I was going to tell you on the phone or by text.' The words stopped as his mouth covered hers, kissing her full on.

'Oh God, Lottie.' He fell to his knees and hugged her around the waist. 'You have well and truly made me the happiest man on this earth, thank you.' He carried on kissing her stomach. 'I guess I owe you a pound!'

Mrs B looked on from the kitchen and smiled to herself. I was right then! she said to herself, looking at Ed hugging his wife around the waist, kissing her stomach and guessing at the conversation.

Ed picked her up and took them over to the outdoor sofa where he sat her on his knee. 'I can't believe it,' he said again, 'I guess I am broke now you won your bet!' Lottie laughed at his reply, and no more tears fell from her eyes. 'I need to tell Mum,' he said, still so excited.

'No, not yet please, let's just keep it to ourselves for a while.' She was so mindful of how so very delicate this could still be. 'Just for another month, until, well, you know.'

He did not know to start off with; if he had a megaphone, he would have stood on the balcony and shouted it out for the next 24 hours so that the entire world knew, but then he saw in her eyes why she wanted to be cautious. Of course, she was right.

'Are you OK, I mean you don't feel ill, do you?' he asked. 'Oh shit, last night, I'm sorry.' He referred to their love-making where she had slowed him down, the recollection that he was sure it was the sort of thing that could have led to the miscarriage last time.

'I'm not going to break,' she said, noting his caution suddenly with his embrace being released.

'Oh, Lottie, I still can't...' He kissed her again wanting to say 'I can't believe it'. 'When, how?' he started to sober up slightly with the euphoria pacing through his head.

'They said just over seven weeks, hyper-fertile he said and well, Mr Dean, if you don't know how, then maybe I should show you!' She started to kiss his neck and run her hands along his thigh.

'Lottie, you know what I mean. I have complete clarity on how, every mind-blowing second.' He took her hand from his leg knowing that he would give away the arousal that she instantly gave him with every touch.

'I hope that you don't think that this changes anything, and you are going to deny me this tempting body for the next eight months?' She entwined her fingers with his and kissed the back of his hand.

'It does change everything though, Lottie, everything,' he replied looking seriously at her.

'Please.' She jumped up from him and walked back towards the balcony. This was exactly what she knew would happen. 'Don't you even think about mentioning what I know is now going through your mind. Do not come out with the bull about having to keep me safe, and the very mention of you saying that I am not going to keep working through this, I swear Ed, this is the very reason I was–' she stopped.

'The very reason what? You were not going to tell me again, or you were glad about last time?' Why the sentence came out of his mouth at such a fantastic moment he was not sure. He had been so elated 30 seconds ago. He could feel a new emotion inside him that he had only felt for a passing moment before, so why should he not want her to be safe and deliver the one thing he wanted as much as he wanted her in his life?

'I told you why I have held off saying anything, and that comment was a low blow. If it was something I did not want, I would say so, but, and it was you that said it, we could still live. My work is part of my life.' She shunned his advance to touch her.

'But your work, the shit we are having now, is personal. Not just the normal 9 to 5 office job; come on, Lottie, admit it. You will, I am sure, get close to something soon and whoever this fucking prick is, they will stop at nothing to hurt us, you, both of you.' He said it as kindly as he could not wanting to spark any further row.

'Please don't think so little of me that I would for one moment put our unborn child at risk knowingly. What sort of heartless person would that make me? Stop to think that if I had been so hell bent on not getting pregnant, I would have insisted they put another implant in or something, instead I wanted to wait, see what happened. On Thursday I still went in there thinking we should give it a try, and I was not going to do another course of pills, that's why the cancelled appointment was not really a big fuss for me the week before. I know how much this means to you, but that was when I thought you had finally got it. Knowing how much my independence means to me.' Lottie stood tall pushing her shoulders back, she had a sudden wave of nausea from her stomach to her mouth, she was sure it was just the high emotions. 'All those conversations, sharing, telling each other everything how we felt was a waste of time!'

'I had finally got it, as you put it. I just can't put us through the loss. You know that I hate even the remote chance you could be hurt, but I have let you carry on. Now the stakes have just increased by well over 100%, it's not happening!' She looked at him and pushed passed his powerful frame back into the apartment. She really was going to be sick now.

'You let me carry on? Like I needed your permission!' She was getting really angry now and feeling sick just made her speak without thinking. 'Same old, same old control freak,' she said walking towards the bedroom with a bit more speed than before.

'And do you know what?' he said calling out after her. 'Same old, same old Lottie thinking it is always right wanting to get your own way, it's not too dissimilar to you being a control freak you know!' The door slammed in his face and if he had not stepped back, it would have hit him. The lock clicked as he tried to open the wooden obstacle that had been slammed seconds before.

'Lottie!' He knocked on the bathroom door. 'Open this, please. I do not want to fight about this, but please see my point of view.' His inner body said, 'I give you five seconds and the fucking door is coming down, now open it!' 'Lottie,' he said, keeping his voice calm and trying not to alert everyone in the apartment. Pete had already put his head through the corridor to see what the commotion was and been warned off by the look Ed had given him. He could have the door down in a second, but he crushed his fist up and punched out at the wall. He heard her being ill and put his head against the door.

'Lottie, please, just let me in.' He wanted to sit with her, tell her he was sorry. The toilet flushed and the door lock clicked. He hesitated and slowly pushed it open to find her leaning over the toilet, kneeling again on the floor, once more retching.

'Sorry,' she said, wiping her mouth, 'Attractive I guess?' Ed held her hair back. 'I guess I'm taking 'in sickness and health' a bit too far?'

He could not help but laugh at her mention of their wedding vows.

'You are still ever beautiful in my eyes. I only wish I could do something to help.' He passed her a face cloth as the next wave of sickness came over her.

Standing up, she pulled down the seat and sat on it. 'Let's not argue about this; we will forever agree to disagree. I can pass some of it on to Todd, but there are things he cannot do. We are getting so close, I know it. Phil and Pete just need to be up to speed. If we put this on hold for the best part of a year, we will let it go cold, and then anyone will struggle at getting to the truth.' He was holding her hand. Every inch of his body wanted to say no, no fucking NO!

He knew how so many people he had dealt with in the past felt. When he wanted to get his own way there was never any talking him around. He had gone from being dominating, to totally submitting to her every whim; he could not say no out loud, as much as he tried.

'I give in.' He held up his hands. 'Again!' he paused. 'I can't see you this upset on top of feeling so ill. If you do anything that remotely puts you in danger, I will chain you to the apartment walls myself.' She smiled at him but refrained from kissing him until she had cleaned her teeth.

'Now can you please let me spoil you and take you out somewhere for lunch? Let me show off my pregnant wife?' He leant against the sink waiting for a reply. She rolled her eyes at him as he rubbed her stomach with one hand. The smile on his face was electric and she could not help but to put her hand on his. 'Not sure I could stomach lunch just yet, but a change of scene would be nice, and if you drive, then we can chat along the way.'

Chapter 11

'So, you think you have found the cuff links?' Lottie asked Todd walking back into her office, only taking seconds to put down her bag and pick up some papers and start scrolling through them on her desk. It was Tuesday morning and she had called to say she would be late, as Ed had totally insisted he take her to the doctors to see if they could ease the morning sickness.

'Late night was it?' he asked looking up. 'Some excuse that your billionaire husband had some papers for you to sign! You'll say the dog ate your homework soon, just say it, Lottie – you overslept!'

'Whatever,' Lottie replied, knowing that she wanted to tell him, but they had promised no one would find out. She had tried to prevent Ed saying something to Pete and Phil, but then knew why her husband had been so insistent. They could be trusted after all. And, well, Mrs B, it was clear from her response that she already knew before they'd uttered a word, but for now that was it, only the chosen few shared the happy news.

Todd spent some time getting her up to speed. They were going to look at the dead girl that afternoon, but he had worked on the cufflinks and could not find a match.

'The digital enhancement does show you are right, they are the same, but have different colours; well spotted! As for the design it is a coat of arms. I investigated it and there is nothing registered as official. I checked out a few websites to see if there is a national register, but nothing came up. I guess that if you know the design, you know the person. All I can say is he has bad taste. I would not be seen dead in them.'

Lottie looked at Todd dressed in jeans and a tee shirt that looked like it had last night's tea down the front.

'Oh, so he has also committed crimes against the fashion police? Take a look at yourself?' Lottie joked, lightening the mood in the lab. She soon changed the conversation back to the cuff links. 'I wonder if we could ask the people in the club if they recognise them?'

'Oh, and how do we find out a guest list? I looked into the club as well, and I have to say it was *very* interesting. Maybe we should go and see if we can find out for ourselves.' He raised his eyebrows.

'In the name of research, I guess. You were the one that said it was for pervs and sickos.' She piled papers up as she read through them.

'Interesting shows though, got to be worth a look. I wonder how you get a membership?' He tapped at the computer and found the title page for the club.

'You have to be invited,' Lottie said, without knowing her words came out. Todd almost had his jaw on the floor.

'Lottie Jenkins, you dog!' It clicked in his head as he said her maiden name. 'You know all this because you've been!' He knew his jaw had dropped, then came back to the reality of who she was married to. 'Oh My God! Lottie, you have, tell me you have been?'

'I have and the fact that I got married and changed my name means I went with my respectable husband.' She felt she was blushing. He ran around the table like a child. He could think of names he would call Edward Dean, and many of them were not respectable.

'I am not sure I need all the details, but go on, do tell. Oh, hang on,' he paused, 'That's how you recognised the...' He stopped mid-sentence. It was coming together for him. 'You saw the guy; the cuff links reminded you.

Shit, Lottie, you met him there?' He rubbed his face. 'We need a guest list for that night'.

'No shit Sherlock, but as you pointed out, it's not easy. Anyway, I may not recognise his face again, even if we got names; it could have been any of the men that night.'

'The police would get one. It narrows down the list of suspects though.' Todd started to dial the phone and Lottie pressed the receiver down.

'Don't get them involved yet, it's not enough.' She looked at him.

'I can't see any other way,' he replied as Lottie picked up her phone. 'What are you doing?' he asked.

'Well, my 'Sysco husband' became a member, maybe he knows a way.' She turned her back on Todd as the call was answered almost instantly, with a question about whether she was OK.

Averting Mr Edward Dean having a heart attack every time she called him was going to take some getting used to, but once she had confirmed she was OK and said there was no need to panic every time she called, she explained they had a few questions and could he join them for lunch. Although it was only an hour away, they agreed to meet up away from the centre, so Todd and Lottie locked away the files in their office and made their way to the car.

'Thanks for keeping me in the loop,' Ed said to Todd when Lottie had got up to go to the toilet.

Todd was desperate to ask about the club, but knew it was not a wise move. When Lottie had asked, Ed had simply replied 'I will have Pete look into it,' and nothing more. He was not sure if this was some form of code, that members were not supposed to talk about it or embarrassment that Todd was prying into their private life.

'Ok?' Ed said to Lottie, standing up and pulling out her chair as she came back to the table. She had managed to eat and was grateful that the tablets the doctor had given her seemed to take away the physical sickness for a while.

'Sure,' Lottie said, swilling down the rest of her ginger tea she had ordered instead of coffee.

Todd and Ed said goodbye and Lottie kissed Ed as they made their way to the car.

'Check your email, Mrs Dean,' he said. 'Call me when you get back if you can, or I will explain at home.' She looked confused but left their conversation at that.

Once they had settled, Lottie only had half an hour before they were due in the autopsy room. She entered her password and then opened Ed's email.

It was a list of everyone who was a member of the club. 'Pete works fast,' Lottie thought, pushing the keys to open her phone to call Ed.

'How did you get that then?' she asked, getting it in before he could ask her if she was Ok for the hundredth time today.

'I own it!' Ed came straight out with the reply.

'Edward Dean, really?' Lottie was not sure why she should sound so surprised.

'I won it in a bet, years ago, well, before I knew you, Lottie.' He felt he had to say that, but she really did not care. 'We played cards one night, someone owed me a lot of money and they could not pay up.' He paused only slightly. 'Money was money really, and the books looked good; it is a good business. That's why I kept it,' he said.

'Not for the lifelong membership then?' Lottie had a hint of sarcasm in her voice.

'Well that too!' he replied back, and Lottie tutted down the phone. 'Only joking, because it makes a fortune, Lottie. I wasn't joking when I said that some well-heeled people keep up the membership. I have spoken to Freddy the manager and he has agreed to meet me. I have not said anything, just said it was for a catch up really. I wondered if we could show him the cuff links. He does get to know regulars in his own way.'

'You don't think that would set alarm bells going?' She worried that she did not have enough information yet to blow open the chance for whoever it was to know they were getting somewhere.

'No, he knows what it is worth to him. He will not say a word,' Edward replied, and their conversation ended with a loving goodbye.

Lottie stood in the shower at work, washing the thoughts from her mind about what she had just seen. The poor young girl, the rest of her life to look forward to and someone had taken it away.

She had spent hours looking over the body, and something was bugging her. Blood results had come back but something did not make sense. Quickly going back to the lab, she pulled up some more results and milled them over in her mind.

'I wasn't aware that you had a cold on the slab,' Eric said to Lottie as he walked in. Lottie pushed down her laptop screen and turned to face him.

'The Met called, just asked me to look at something for them. The judge wants to make his call before the parents arrive to collect her.' She hoped this would satisfy him.

'Just a junkie OD'ing then?' he asked.

'Seems so,' Lottie replied. He seemed to hover around in the doorway. 'Anything else?' Lottie asked. He replied 'Nope' and reluctantly walked out.

She pulled out another file. She looked at his name: Michael Dean. She looked back over his pictures. She had a lump in her throat because the more she looked, the more she thought about Ed and the pain this had caused for his family. Mitch had many of Ed's facial features and her skin went cold knowing that she was looking at the uncle of her unborn baby. She closed the file quickly. She had seen enough for today.

Saturday morning came around and she woke to find she was alone in bed. Ed had mentioned that he wanted a gym session and she guessed she had slept through him leaving.

Showering and finding a loose-fitting day dress, she went through to the apartment kitchen, and all was quiet. She looked up as Phil popped his head round the kitchen door.

'Sorry, I heard someone; I didn't mean to disturb you,' he said, just about to walk off.

'No problems, do you want anything?' Lottie asked, pointing to the kettle she was boiling to make tea. She had a hunger and was pleased to see Mrs B had left the fridge well-stocked. The tablets seemed to be working and finally she'd found her appetite.

'I'm good thank you, Mrs Dean,' he replied about to walk back to the staff room.

'Don't run off, sit and chat to me,' she said and although he looked uncomfortable with the request he did.

Lottie chatted about Liz, and Phil seemed to open up after a few minutes. She talked about the fashion house and the show. She asked about his family and she learned more in the half an hour than she had known in all the time he'd worked for them.

There was a knock on the door, and Phil jumped up. No one was expected, but to get up to the apartment they needed to get past reception, and no one had called. He approached the door and looked through the spyglass; hand on his shoulder holster, he supported his firearm.

Opening the door Todd walked in expressing his greetings.

'What brings you here?' she asked, knowing that he usually called if he wanted her.

'Lottie, I need to tell you something, can we talk?' Her mind completely went to the case. 'Yes of course.' She took him through and they opened the kitchen door and went onto the balcony where she thought it would be quieter.

She was devastated. She had tried not to cry when he told her, but as soon as he closed the door to leave, she ran to her room and fell on the bed, crying. She exhausted herself through tears and must have dozed off because it was there Ed found her when he returned home. Mrs B had told him where Lottie was and at first he left her to rest, after he'd been informed of the visitor, the nature of their conversation and the reaction it had had on Lottie. He went back into the room and sat on the bed. The movement must have stirred her, and she started to cry once more.

Apologising for her emotions, which seemed to explode again, she explained what Todd had been round to talk about.

'He goes tomorrow.' She sat in the middle of the bed, wrapped in her husband's arms. 'He accepted the job last week but has left it until the day before he goes with his bags already packed to tell me. How could he do that, just drop me the bombshell?' Ed tried to console her, but had no words that seemed to comfort her. 'He had the cheek to ask if I would ask you if he could stay at the flat. You will have to ring and tell him if you want him to. I don't want to talk to him. How he can just walk out when he knows I need him so much? I really don't know him like I thought I did.' She took a breath. 'He knows that he is my best friend and he never even told me he was even looking for a job, let alone accepted one and bought plane tickets, ready to go.'

The words cut deep in Ed's heart, jealous of how much this friend, this old lover, meant to Lottie, but also that he had asked for him to look out for her, pick up on anything that may lead her into danger. Too damn right he would ring him, but not until he had calmed her down. Not until he knew what he was going to say to him with a clear mind. He was pissed off and for sure was not going to allow him to stay in the apartment, but then as he had listened through Lottie's sobs, she was right. They would know where he was if for any reason the case moved on and they needed to get hold of him again. He would do it for her, not him. He made the call later in the evening. It had not been an easy one.

Todd never said the real reason, that he loved her so much he had to go. He took the ear-beating that Ed thundered down the phone about how upset she was, but he explained that he had to take this and move on with his life. He knew that she would solve the case without him and at a moment's notice would help as much as he could thousands of miles away. But he had to do it for his own sanity. This of course was not explained to Ed; he reasoned with him that it was a professional move and surely Ed would understand about the world of work and business.

Ed finished the call and made a few others to clear his diary for the next day. He would take Lottie back to Kent, catch up on some of their time, cheer her up. It was when he put the phone down that he heard her playing the piano. The saddest tune he had ever heard; in fact, it made him shiver. He let her play on, not just so he could listen, but to give her time to get it out of her system. When it fell silent, he went back to the living room where she sat in the dark, with a glass of milk in her hand.

They sat together watching TV, and conversation was hard. Lottie was a mile away in her thoughts. When he went to bed, Ed looked over to the score on the top of the immaculate instrument. 'My Lover Lost' was written in old handwriting and was the piece she had been playing. He looked closer at the name who had written the tune; it was the princess who had originally owned the piano. He hoped that he was wrong to think that this was how Lottie felt about Todd leaving, but more importantly he hoped that she did not remain in her melancholy state for too long; she was more delicate now than ever before.

The suggestion of a trip to Kent went down well, and after the first day Ed embraced the fact that he could work remotely away from the office with the use of his tablet, phone and laptop, making the decision to stay another day an easy one. The prof was OK with Lottie missing work; well, he had no choice really when Edward phoned him. Agnes was thrilled to see them, although kept in the dark about the baby. Lottie found that so hard and understood how Ed must feel about telling his mother, but they had decided to wait to say anything and that was that.

Gerald had overhauled the whole house and the gardens looked a picture. She had really enjoyed him showing her all his handiwork and sitting down with him, catching up. She was pleased to know he had settled well and that he had made friends in the village. He often walked along the country lanes, and even asked if he could get a dog to keep him company, something Lottie thought was a really good idea. They shared a drink and Lottie stayed sitting in the suntrap, making notes and writing as Ed popped his head over the fence from a run. He loved the countryside, and admitted getting lost in the isolation, and the peace the country could bring.

'What you up to?' He grabbed some water and walked to her side, kissing her head and looking at the scribbled paper.

'Just making a mind map.' She never looked up at him.

'Working?' he asked.

'Yes, sort of, I never brought any notes home because I did not know we were coming, but I often find that by doing this I can piece things together.' She carried on writing.

'Has it worked?' he asked, not bothering to look at the scribbles as they would mean nothing to him.

'Not really sure but...' She stopped, watching as he gulped the water down and wiped the sweat from his brow on his tee shirt.

'What?' he gasped, after taking the rest of the water from the bottle.

'I am going to have to use your permission mandate.' She did not want to use the words 'exhuming authorisation document' – it sounded so insensitive, although there was no way to make it sound any better. She wanted to get a look at his brother's body to see if, although committed to ground several years before, it held any more clues. Edward closed his eyes and shook his head. He'd known this day would come.

Returning to the centre on the Wednesday, she spoke to the professor about what she had asked for. This was going to raise questions and Ed had agreed to pay for a private company to do what Lottie required. He was not going to be taken back to the centre; the professor had arranged for him to be taken to Oxford, where Lottie could work without questions raised.

'You have an idea what you are looking for, don't you?' the professor had asked her when she first spoke to him.

'Yes,' she replied, not going into any more details.

'And you say that this could raise the case again, as you suspect foul play?'

'As I explained, Mr Dean has had some threats and I think that this could be related. Opening it up could be a problem for us all, so your professional code of silence and help with this is welcome.' They had continued to chat in his office with the door closed.

'Mr Dean is a loyal donor. I admire him allowing you to work on this which is so personal, and I understand how sensitive cases can be, so Lottie you have my total support and anonymity.'

She totally believed she could trust the professor, as she had explained on the ride home the day before. Apart from this the subject had been quite muted since she had first mentioned it. Without Todd she needed some help, and she never mentioned she had a theory to Ed, because for now, it was just that.

She kept her promise that she would only work three days a week at the centre, which was a good thing as it would keep their lives normal. Lottie was still busy with her charity and the fashion house, which, since the fashion show, had taken off in a big way. Liz had emailed to say that several local boutiques were interested, and one had placed an order for some sample ranges.

The weeks rolled by and Lottie's birthday was celebrated with a weekend of luxury in the Lake District and more gifts than she knew what to do with. It was very different to the year before, with one exception; she was pregnant again. This time quite happily and she was now starting to show signs – her best jeans did not fit, and she had the start of a very small, rounded stomach. No one else knew yet, so when Ed handed her a small, neatly-wrapped parcel, he did so in the privacy of their bedroom.

He had been shopping for an eternity ring, and while walking back to the car had been side-tracked by a small boutique. The assistant was dressing the window with baby clothes and he was drawn to have a look. The young girl smiled at him as he looked in, turning red-faced as he seemed to stare at her, or so she thought.

He looked around him like a criminal about to pounce, looking more like he was going to do over a jeweller, not walk in off the street and buy a garment for an unborn child. His stomach churned; he was so tempted to get it. He wrestled with how Lottie would react to it, as they had said to hold off buying anything until they made it official, but the little romper suit was so sweet. It would soon be her 12-week scan, so he thought, why not?

He opened the door and went in. There was a sweet smell, of what, he was not sure, but it was clean and pure. Babies, he thought, do they have a smell? There was a young woman looking at maternity clothes, showing her full bloom to everyone, lovingly smoothing her hand over her stomach as the assistant helped her choose. His mind wandered quickly to Lottie's new business venture in fashion for maternity wear and wondered if she had been thinking about starting a family even then. His train of thought was interrupted by the same young girl who had been in the window.

'Hello, Sir,' she said. Immediately Ed felt out of his depth. 'Are you looking for something specific today?' she asked. As he looked at her, she blushed as his blue eyes seemed to set her alight inside and she tried not to make it obvious that she was looking at his strong body, dressed in his all-too-familiar white shirt, tie, dark pin-striped suit, that fitted every curve and dimension of his body. Normal rough loose hair, which he ran his hand through, pushing it back on his collar, more from nerves than to make him look presentable.

'Um, yes, sorry,' he stuttered. God, he did not even know what the little suit in the window was called. 'The baby...' Did he call it a thing, a dress? 'White one in the window, with the bear on the front?'

'The new-born romper,' the assistant helped him out, guessing he had no idea, but she did not mind. He was brightening her day up.

'Yes,' he said.

'Is it new-born, a larger size or small?' she asked.

'Not born yet,' he replied. 'No idea of size.' He was the one to go red now clearly showing he was out of his depth, as he moved to the side to let the other shopper out, opening the door for her as he was standing close to it, having not taken more than two steps into the shop yet.

'I see,' said the assistant, looking up the shop for her colleague who was now free, happily folding the items that her customer had not purchased. The young girl handed him an identical item from a wrapper she had on a shelf behind her.

'First one?' she asked, trying to stimulate a conversation, as she did with all customers.

'Um, yes.' Ed must have looked so strange as he stood feeling the tiny item that he held in his, what seemed like large, oversized hands. Could a baby really be that small? He almost said it, but was fearful of looking even more stupid than he felt. Of course, they are so small, Dean, you arse, or they would not make them this size! his inner self said back.

'Is it white that you are looking for, or blue, pink maybe?' the young girl asked.

'Not sure, it's... they...' He stumbled for words. 'We don't know yet.' His stomach turned over again.

They had not even had a conversation of what they hoped for. A boy. Oh god, yes, he thought again to himself, a boy. Then his heart pulled in his chest with another thought; a girl, the perfect image of Lottie, dressed in pink, spoilt to the point of obsession as she was. Oh yes, a girl.

'Well, white is always a good colour for any new-born.' The young girl tried to ease what now seemed a one-way conversation, and she almost smiled.

Healthy, yes, oh my god yes, I do not care as long as it, they, are both healthy. His mind raced, talking to itself. He could feel a bead of sweat running down his back. The very thought of something going wrong. He almost felt the colour drain from his skin. He had never felt so emotional, never felt this strange feeling inside him of overwhelming love for something he had not even got.

'I will take it please.' He handed it back to the young girl. She gave him a smile.

'I'll wrap it for you. Anything else today?' she asked whilst taking care to wrap the tiny bundle. He shook his head, but a small white rabbit seemed to smile at him. It had been strategically placed at the counter, just like sweets at a supermarket checkout, to make the wide-eyed children beg their parents to buy them some until they gave in to shut them up.

'This too,' he pointed, and she quickly put it in a bag with similar care. He took out his card and made the transaction. Ever attentive, the young girl spotted his name. Handing him over his purchase she smiled. 'Thank you, Mr Dean, and good luck!' The comment passed him by as he was now intent on getting out of the shop alive. Courtesy made him reply thank you, but he never turned around as he left.

Million-dollar deals had been easier, he thought as he swiftly walked back down the road to where he had asked Pete to wait.

'OMG, did you see him!' The assistant who had been folding clothes came closer to look out of the window as Ed walked off, more to get a view of his backside than anything else.

'Sure did. I thought I recognised the face, hard to forget being that drop-dead gorge!' the other girl said back, joining her ogling friend at the window. 'Mr Edward Dean. His wife is the one doing new maternity wear; remember that flyer that came around last week?'

'Well, lucky Mrs Dean is what I say, oh, can you imagine waking up next to that sex god?' she giggled, walking away now he had gone from view.

'Not sure I would want to sleep if you get my drift!' The girls giggled at the reply. 'But seeing as he was buying that, I guess the lucky cow does not get much – sleep that is!' She emphasised the last words and they both laughed again.

'Edward. We said we would wait,' had been her reply as she opened the package, cross-legged on the bed.

'I know, but look how sweet?' He picked the rabbit up and wiggled its head around. He said, in a childlike voice, imitating the soft cuddly toy as if it could speak, 'I'm so sweet, don't be mad with Edward!'

Lottie took the toy from him, laughing out loud and shaking her head.

'What have they done with my husband? Quick, call a doctor, he has been possessed by baby brain!' She pushed him backwards and he fell onto the bed. She straddled him and pressed the rabbit into his chest.

'If I got that on camera, I could blow every business deal you want to make in the future out of the water. No one would believe it was you under that soppy exterior!' She poked a finger at his hard chest muscles, then rubbed it smoothly. She instantly felt aroused by the way he felt.

He had got the notion into his head that she had suddenly become so delicate that he had protested every time she had made any sexual advances towards him. She craved his body, his touch. In her powers to persuade him he had remained constant, adamant that he would hurt her, or the baby. Her advances were caught again; he knew her too well. He did not push her away; he just held her hand, stopping her touch from affecting him.

'Oh god, roll on tomorrow,' she sighed and rolled off him, rabbit still in hand. 'I know, not until we have spoken to the doctor, I get it.' Her voice was disappointed and her nipples, skin, and sex was frustrated. 'Or not!' she said in a lower voice, but intending him to hear.

He raised his eyebrows.

'You get your way with everything, Mrs Dean, but not this. I am holding fast.' He kissed her nose and sat up, moving to the edge of the bed. Lottie draped her arms around his shoulders. 'I know,' she said, drawing out the words, licking around his ears, as to add to both of their frustrated misery. He had to move; he was good, well OK, at resisting her, but even the chastity he had brought on himself was wearing thin, and when she did that, he had no hope of keeping his own promise.

'Have you thought about it?' he asked, changing the subject.

'Every day!' Lottie knew he was not on the topic of their carnal relations, but could not help herself from teasing him.

'Lottie! I mean the sex of the baby, not the sex that you are thinking about!' He lent against the dresser, keeping his distance from her. She lay on her side, propping herself up. Her long hair covered her hand, brushing down against her shoulder; she looked so alive, so amazing. He had to breathe and concentrate to take his mind off the increasing size of his dick in his jogging pants. He was pleased he had some room to move around in them, or she would see it, he was sure.

'I guess,' she replied, knowing he wanted a sensible answer, and she rubbed the little suit with her hand; it felt so soft.

'Well?' he asked, 'Do you want to know?'

'I'm not sure. Some part of me does, but then it is all about the surprise.' She unknowingly rubbed her stomach and Ed smiled to himself. 'Do you?' she asked back. He moved from his place as she got up from the bed and walked towards him. He held out his arms and he pulled her to him, quickly turning her round so he was only lightly pressed against her back. He laced his arms through hers and they both rested their hands on her stomach. He resisted kissing her neck, but he breathed her scent in, closing his eyes.

'I don't know, maybe when we see...' He stopped. Do you call it 'it'? he thought to himself. 'Maybe when we see a picture on the scan, we will be able to decide?'

Ed held her hand for the entire journey, and as they pulled up at the Harley Street destination, he gave her hand a squeeze and they made their way out of the car for the appointment. He had to admit he was excited and nervous at the same time. Questions had gone through his head all night, preventing a peaceful sleep. He had written some of his questions out on his phone to make sure that he did not forget to ask.

Once inside he was able to ask the doctor all his questions, although he felt slightly embarrassed when Lottie had stepped out of the room to get ready for her scan. He loosened his tie and his top button as he felt he was starting to sweat, even though the room was temperature controlled.

They made general chat, and the middle-aged doctor expressed that Ed had no need to panic; Lottie was in good hands and all the first signs of the pregnancy had been good. Their chat meant that Lottie would already be getting ready for the scan and it was not something Ed would want to miss.

They walked into the examination room and Lottie was sitting with a younger girl beside her. She lay on the bed with her tummy exposed, glistening in gel to ease the scanner over. She was looking at the large TV screen, smiling, and the woman was pointing at various areas of the dark and light images that were constantly moving. As if his feet had rooted to the spot, the doctor gave him encouragement to go and join them. Once Lottie noticed he was by the door she lifted her hand to invite him over. There was a seat by the bed, but he chose to stand.

'Mr Dean, as I just explained to your wife, if you look you can see the arms starting to form fingers already. A strong heart and, oh, we are moving again, come on, don't hide and be shy for your daddy.' The girls laughed and Ed felt his knees give way under him. Thank god for the chair now, as he needed the support. He kissed the back of Lottie's hand; she had not taken her eyes from the screen. Lottie was using all sorts of medical names and terms, which the young nurse was commenting on. He was lost in this little image glowing and flickering in front of him.

'Do you want to know the sex?' they were asked as the young nurse moved the probe around, seeking a better angle for the image. 'This bump's a wriggler!' she said.

'Ed,' Lottie said, smiling at how lost he was in the image. He snapped out of it and shook his head slightly.

'Is that a no?' the nurse asked.

'No, I don't know. Lottie what do you think?'

'You don't have to make your mind up now. We can have a look later, when we may get some better images and a clearer idea,' the nurse added, to ease their decision.

'I like the surprise for now,' Lottie owned up. 'If Bump stays genderless, we can have more fun thinking of names,' she smiled at Ed. 'That OK?'

'Yes,' he smiled at her and kissed her cheek.

'Want the image downloaded?' the nurse asked, and Lottie nodded.

'Can you really do that?' Ed enquired. 'I thought it would be an old-fashioned picture.'

'Technology, Mr Dean, you can have Bump as a screen saver if you want.'

As Lottie put her clothes back on Ed went back through to the doctor. The image he had looked at earlier was playing again on the PC for the doctor to look at.

'Well,' he started as Lottie joined them. 'Everything is fine at this stage. We will programme in your next appointments, Mrs Dean. Pleased the medication worked for the morning sickness, are you still taking it?'

'Only if I need to, it's not so bad now. Found a ginger drink a friend recommended to me. It tastes nice and seemed to work as well.'

The entire appointment really seemed to go over Ed's head. The grin on his face seemed to have been fixed through the whole process. They walked out and the sun was shining. Pete had not been able to park close, and as Ed got out his phone he said, 'Do you want to walk a bit, or should I get the car. It will not tire you out?'

'Edward Dean, you heard what the doctor said. I am fine, the bump is fine, I will not break, and it is safe to have sex, so walking is OK, although I feel the urge to get the car and go straight home to follow through on the first bit, as that is more than OK and desperately missed!'

Ed laughed. 'Mrs Dean, what has come over you, you are insatiable.'

'I can't even blame the hormones, as I have always found you irresistible!' She started to loosen his collar as they stood there in the street, pressing into him close and kissing his neck at the same time. Ed sent the text asking for them to be collected. The moments they had to wait made several passers-by giggle, and one guy said jokingly, 'Get a room!'

'Pete, can we go to Mum's?' Ed asked as they got in the car. Lottie's face dropped as she'd been sure they were going straight home.

'No problem, Mr Dean.'

Ed looked at her. 'What?' he asked, smiling at the face she was pulling.

'You know what,' she replied.

'Oh, come on, you said as soon as today was over I could tell her.' He looked at his phone, noticing several messages had come through.

'Today is not over in my book!'

He moved her hand as she slid her nails up the inside of his thigh, the target his semi-hard dick. 'Half an hour that's all, promise.' He fluttered his eyebrows and Lottie slumped back in her seat.

They did spend half an hour with his mother, who was so overwhelmed she cracked a bottle of Champaign, disappointed that they had not told her before, but she totally understood why. Although the fact that they had asked that it was still not to go public was annoying as she could not wait to tell her friends at bridge and her afternoon club, and lunch club and every other meeting she went to, to fill her days.

As promised, they did go home after the bottle was emptied. Because of the tea drinking that Lottie had done she dashed to the loo as they walked in, and Ed vanished into his study, picking up and dialling his phone as soon as he got in the door. Lottie looked in at him and he held his conversation to tell her he would try not to be too long she went outside on the balcony and called Agnes. She had to hold the phone away from her ear for the best part of ten seconds as her friend was as excited as Ed's mother had been. She promised to keep a lid on it, but insisted that if they were not going home to Kent that weekend, she would come to London. Lottie loved the idea, with no choice but to stay with them, of course. Lottie also asked if Agnes would mind bringing Gerald; it would be great to go to Battersea to get him a dog, and it would save one of the guys making the trip both ways.

Although she had not spoken to him since he had left, Lottie left a message for Todd to call her back; looking at the time difference she presumed he would call once he got the message later in the day. So, the next few days were set out, and Lottie started to look back through the notes she had brought home until Ed finally emerged. She quickly put them away; he never asked her what they were, and he guessed it was something she did not want him to see willingly and knowing that they had repatriated his brother he could only assume by her sad smile that she was trying to protect him as best she could.

'No work now,' he said to her as he joined her outside on the seat.

'No just me and you alone at last.' The staff had gone or were in the staff rooms.

'And bump!' he said with a smile. 'Yes and bump,' she replied. Lottie explained about their weekends guests and although Ed had planned a meal out, it was nothing that the guests could not join in with.

'I wanted to give Gerald a tour of the city before we go to the dog's home,' she said.

'I am sure Phil can do that.' Ed seemed to think it was a good idea.

'If you don't want to tag along, I understand,' she said, noting that by the fact Phil was nominated to drive, Ed would not do it, which was her intention.

'I can go to the gym and have some boy time,' he said.

'Are you sure you trust me out of your sight?' She leant into him, rubbing his leg and he pulled her over until she was on his lap.

'I am sure as long as you don't come home with the cutest puppy in the world, and its six brothers and sisters!' He smiled, knowing if she did, he would not really have too much objection. Although they had talked about getting a dog, they had agreed that the penthouse apartment was not really the place for one. He lifted her shirt and rubbed her stomach. It was still sticky from the gel. 'Fancy a bath?' he said.

'I'll put the water on!' She jumped up leaving him to close the door.

He went to the bathroom, which already smelled sweet from bubble bath that had been added to the steaming water, with another glass of Champaign. He handed Lottie a glass of milk which she placed on the small glass and gold table that sat by the tub in the centre of the room.

'Not sure I will get used to the no alcohol thing.' She lifted her shirt and dropped it to the floor.

'I will pour this away if you want, so that I don't tempt you.' His offer was genuine, although he was still in the mood to celebrate, albeit alone. He put the glass down on the same receptacle and took off his top.

'Come over here and take my mind off it!'

He was not going to turn down the offer as she now stood in just her white lace panties, brushing her hair and putting it up to prevent it getting too wet. He stood and admired her body, which he was sure was changing. Her pert breasts had developed, if it were possible, into fuller round moulds, and her nipples had become darker. Her little bump showed from what was usually a flat stomach, and he smiled when he thought of the contents. Snuggling into her neck he started to kiss her, running his hand round her waist and along her stomach. The other hand ran up to encircle one of her breasts. She put her head back onto his shoulder and closed her eyes. She had craved for his touch, his skin against hers. He reached round and ran his hand under the silk to find her most private parts. She opened her legs slightly, inviting his touch without restraint.

Pushing her backside into him she could feel the growing tension in his trousers, her struggling to reach behind to tussle with his belt and zip. Doing this pushed her breasts out more and he squeezed them knowing now that they were fuller, heavier. He stepped out of his trousers and she quickly turned around seeing him standing in front of her with crisp white CK boxers on that clung to his very form. She ran her hand down his pecs and along the line to his stomach, towards his V-line which vanished under the cotton garment.

He pulled her face back to him and kissed her with urgency. She rubbed her hand over the material, making the friction on him increased with the pressure. Releasing his lips from hers she ran her hands down his sides, kissing the centre line she had felt earlier, and on reaching his V-line she pulled at the pants to reveal her long-awaited prize. His shaft had become fully erect, hard, and throbbing; it was just tempting her to lick it like an oversized lollipop, so she did. She opened her mouth and at first just took in the top of him, licking her spittle away as she withdrew, then she placed her mouth over him all and took as much as she could, slowly drawing back to his tip. He put his hands onto her head as if willing her to do it again and she did, licking at the top with her tongue but keeping him firmly in her mouth. She continued the process several times before she felt an increased salty taste, reassurance that he was becoming aroused beyond wanting to stop. With each suck her cheeks hollowed, and the sensation was not only stimulating for him, but she felt her inner muscles around her sex clench and tighten. She knew that as he had not been with her for a few weeks his large member would stretch her, and although the doctor could see no reasons why they should not have a normal sex life, she was aware that he would hurt her, so she needed to be ready.

He had to get her away from him or it would be game over. The sensation of her lips, her tongue on him was divine and any selfish man would have allowed her to stay on her knees while his dick fucked her face, but he knew it was not just about relief. His true climax, the deepest sensation of gratification, only ever came when he was encased in her sweet, hot, throbbing pussy. He still had doubts if he could do it without being rough; could he hold back to ensure he never reached that deep inside her to do any harm?

Lottie stopped and eased herself up from the floor, kissing her way back up to him. She walked over to the bath and slipped her pants down and got into the water, kneeling up so that Ed could sit down and put his legs out under her. She straddled him, and gently rubbed herself up and down his shaft, allowing him to open her outer lips and rub her highly-charged tender nerve endings. He took her lips and sucked, kissed, and licked them. Tasting himself on her plump, soft pink skin. He allowed her to work herself on him, knowing that the hot water would relax her, open her more. Using one hand he cupped her breast and slowly licked around her fully erect nipple. He gently sucked and got no resistance, so sucked again. She closed her eyes, the bolt of electric shot to her core and she pulled in her thighs, tightening the grip on his legs under the water.

With the other hand he found the area between her legs and he gently eased one finger into the entrance. She pulled away slightly to stop rubbing herself on him, to accept the intruding digit. She sat down on him, feeling the tender flesh around his hand expand with ease, and he rubbed, nudging another finger into her when he felt her relax. She started to writhe on his hand, forcing the water in the bath to move with more effort, small splashes going over the edge to the tile floor below. She sucked at his lip as he kissed her, and she gasped as he pinched her nipple a little harder that he had before. He moved his hand and directed his cock towards her opening. Like a hungry animal she accepted, and sat on the engorged head.

'Slowly, baby girl,' he reminded her, not wanting her to be slow at all really, but knowing that she was so needy, wanton that he had to show control for them both. She lowered herself, accepting his girth, as slow as her body could, but her mind was enraged by him, and the pressure building in her sex felt like she would explode if she did not have him now.

'Oh God, please Ed, please.' She threw her head back and pushed as much as she could to get him deep in her. He was crushed between the marble bath and her hot, expanding, welcoming sex and he could not help but thrust. He held her hips to ensure that he could control her and the depth that he reached. He slowed her, stopped her pumping up and down on him and controlled her. Her body reacted by prolonging the burning sensation she was having at the start of her climax, but it came back as he took her hard nipple in his mouth and sucked hard. 'AuGh' she cried out and the spinning sensation in her stomach moved to her sex and she came; without control it took her over.

He totally slowed her pace, allowing each agonising pulse to run through her, to satisfy her need, and the long wait of wanting him. The disadvantage to Ed giving her what she wanted was he could not control his own lust, and he found that the increased tightening of her inner muscles only led to his own release, as she slowly lent against his shoulder, with her head resting on the side of his face, her orgasm stringing her along. He pumped himself into her, teeth clenched, nostrils flaring, eyes closed as the energy left his body. His breathing coming in gasps, quiet and deep. Their movements eased, until they sat joined by their sex, entwined in each other's arms in the hot water. Their kisses deep and lingering. He softened inside her, but remained nestled in her, until she moved. She slipped around to lie on him and the water flooded her upper body as he moved them both further down in the bath.

'You OK?' he asked, running his hand across her stomach.

'Mmm.' She let out a long sigh. 'I have missed you, Mr Dean.' She was so relaxed, she could have dozed off.

'Was I gentle?' he asked, stroking damp hair away from her neck. 'It still worries me.'

'I am totally exhausted, relaxed and infatuated with my husband. Bump and mother are doing well, although mother may need an hour or two to recover for a replay!'

'Close your eyes then my love, I will wake you in an hour!'

She splashed water behind her and giggled. He held her with one arm, with the other he leaned to reach his drink and took a sip of the now-warm, expensive, semi-sparkling wine.

It was only about ten minutes after that Ed realised she had really gone to sleep, and although he did not want to disturb her, he had to, as the water was going cold, and their skin was beginning to wrinkle. Encouraging her to stand he helped her out of the water and wrapped her in a large white towel. Picking her up, he took her through to the bedroom and placed her on the bed, the sheet already turned down.

'You can't get in wet, Lottie. You need to dry.' He patted her skin, and she made the effort to do the same.

Her dry and tucked up under the sheets, he went back to the bathroom to tidy round. She was sound asleep when he returned, so he picked up his phone and sat naked on the bed next to her, looking at his emails, and watching her sleep. It was a few hours before he got into bed and he too drifted off.

Waking, he found she had gone from the bed. Pushing the sheets back he walked to the bathroom, her towel was still on the floor and he picked it up. Grabbing a tee shirt, he walked to the sitting room where Lottie was on the floor surrounded by photos. Looking closely, he saw a gruesome picture of his brother, and another. He was drawn to pick one up and look closer. It was a photo of a fully decomposed body taken during the second autopsy. He looked at it closer and the image of his unborn baby seemed to merge into what he could see.

Lottie took the photo from him and handed him another. It was of the girl in the club, lying dead on the mortuary slab, cut open. He felt his stomach turn. Lottie stood and smiled at him and without a word handed him a letter, with the words, 'They are all going to die, everyone you love Mr Dean, just like these two.'

He threw the letter to the floor and as the large window was open in the apartment the breeze pushed the papers around on the floor. He tried to close the door, but it was stuck, when he turned around Lottie had left the room, a pool of blood on the floor where she had been sitting. He called out her name, but she did not walk back in.

He quickly went to the door and followed the trail of blood to their room. As he opened the door, she was lying in bed holding a bundle in her arms. As he looked closer it was the smallest baby, almost deformed. Lottie smiled and handed it to him, but he could not put out his arms to take it.

'I died because of you.' A little hand passed him a note with these words on. Sitting next to Lottie was his brother, blood soaked on his face he handed Ed a note that said 'I died because of you.' He looked around the room and Pete was in the corner; he had blood running down his face, and he gave Ed a note saying 'I died because of you.' Ed put his hands to his face and screamed.

'Edward, what is it?' Lottie's soft voice said to him, and he slowly opened his eyes. He looked around him; the room was exactly the same as it had been in his night terror. She was dressed in the same nightshirt she had worn in the dream. He was sweating, confused, and disorientated.

'Edward, were you dreaming?' She held out her hand and he touched her. She smiled at him and pulled him close. 'Was it a bad dream?'

He had not had such vivid terrors since his father died. He had been teased at school about the circumstances that his father had died in, suspicious, some sort of gangland gunfight as the story went. He took a deep breath.

'It's OK,' Lottie said. 'We are here.' She kissed his head. 'Would it help to tell me about it?'

'No,' he said. 'It was just a bad dream, all the things we are dealing with coming back to me all in one go, it means nothing, nothing to tell.' He paused. Could he say he had seen his dead baby in her arms? No. Could he say that he had seen his brother, and his mind had somehow brought his death back to him? No.

The dream had clearly shaken him, and as they dressed for the day, Lottie tried to take his mind off everything. They were having a weekend with friends and as planned Agnes and Gerald had arrived and the fun and catching-up soon began.

Walking around the pound, looking at all the dogs, made Lottie sad to think that so many animals were unloved. She had to make the effort not to just sign the blank cheque Edward had given her and tell them to put whatever sum they wanted on it if it could help them all.

Edward had called them explaining that they wanted to take a dog home, but it seemed that even he was not able to persuade the powers that be to change the rules that the prospective new home had to be inspected and checked before they would let any animal go. Gerald fell in love with a large, longhaired German Shepherd, who was three years old and had been mistreated by its owners. He was very wary as they passed the cage, but as soon as Gerald spoke to him, it was almost as if the dog heard something in his voice that he knew was kind, and he came to the fence and licked his hand straight away.

That was it, decision made. He was content that the following Monday someone would come out and look around the house. He had asked Lottie if he could keep him in the house downstairs only, and then make an outhouse for him. She agreed, knowing he was really starting to feel at home in Kent, and not only was the house well looked after, but it seemed to be working for him too, getting to know people and having a great life, not seen as staff at all, just a live-in friend.

As they sat in Kensington eating lunch, Lottie looked at her phone and replied to a message from Ed. He had not planned to muscle in on their day but wondered if they would still be in the restaurant for the next hour, as he could join them after all. As they had only just ordered, they put the food on hold giving the waiter Ed's order too.

On one of her frequent trips to the ladies Lottie noticed a guy at the bar; she was sure she recognised him, but tried not to stare. He was with a group of quite loud men dressed in suits. She could hear the laughter but not the conversation as she walked past, some of them turning their heads to notice her.

She walked back past the group and headed straight to the table, thinking nothing else of it. Too much water and tea would soon have her travelling in that direction again, and she was sure she would be able to get another look at him. Something about his features she recognised.

Once Ed arrived they started to eat, and Lottie tried a few times to look over, but the guy had left the group which continued to get noisy, shouting and heckling the staff. Twice they were asked to be quiet by the manager.

'Do you know any of them?' Lottie asked out of the blue.

'A few faces I would say that I have been introduced to, but I really don't have any dealings with them, why?'

'I just wondered,' she replied.

She had walked over to them again for the fourth toilet stop since they had been there, but no one said anything directly to her.

'Why did you ask, have they said anything to you?' Ed asked as she returned. He had watched her go past them all, noting the way they looked at her.

'No, just thought 'boy's day out on a Saturday getting drunk,' would have been the sort of thing you got up to a few years ago?' she smiled at him.

'May have been, but not here,' he replied, taking a sip of his mineral water. Although Agnes was the best way down her bottle of wine, Ed had chosen to go for the water option with Lottie, a sympathy vote she had said when Agnes offer him a glass and he declined.

'Not posh enough for you?' she giggled.

'No, just the opposite, if you want to get thrown out of one of the places you own, it does not look so good for the staff, or other guests.' He leaned in close to her. 'Not that I ever have been thrown out of anywhere for being drunk and disorderly, you understand!'

'Yeah, right, Mr Dean, pull the other one, I know that's not true,' she smirked, shaking her head at the fact that he owned this place too. She really did not know the extent of his wealth.

'Well not for a long time. I am a reformed man!' Ed kissed Lottie's cheek and she blushed as Agnes made a comment about putting her down in public.

Ed looked over at the group. A few names came to mind, and one of the guys smiled at him and he acknowledged them with a nod. He was glad to see one face not there, who he knew was part of their crowd.

As soon as the meal was over, Ed left them to it. Phil had a list of places they wanted to go and see, and so they started a tour. Agnes had insisted on shopping, so the only place Lottie would go would be Harrods. Bella was pleased to see them all, although it was clear the opulence and extravagance was too much for Gerald. They took a quick walk around Covent Garden, and ended up in Carnaby Street. Phil had been trying to follow them and get the car in the right location, but it was just too busy.

They ended up in a cafe at the back of Liberties waiting for him, and Lottie saw a face out of the corner of her eye. The guy from the restaurant. Had he been following them? She was not sure whether to ask Agnes if she had noticed him, so thinking on her toes asked the two of them to get together for a photo, so that the guy was in the background. Hard to see, but she could work on that on the computer on Monday. Maybe he would show up on face recognition or something. It was too much of a coincidence that he was there, so he had to be following them – he had to have been.

Chapter 12

The guests had all gone and Monday morning brought a return to work for them both.

Lottie walked into her empty office and put down the tea she had made in the small kitchen. Some items of post sat on her desk from the few days she'd been off, and she set about looking through them. The one document which she had been waiting for all week, she opened last and it took some time to look through.

Making sure this was not on the top of her desk, she downloaded her pictures from the weekend. The one that she wanted the most was transferred to the computer and sent through a recognition programme. It was taking some time, so she left it, looking again over the notes she had unlocked from her office filing cabinet.

Her desk phone rang, and she looked to see that the professor was calling her. She picked up the phone and they chatted.

'Easier if I show you,' he said, 'Can you pop in?'

With that she closed the laptop and put the files in her drawer. She passed Eric in the corridor, who had a hand full of papers. 'I will leave your post on your desk, Mrs Dean, although I am not sure you have anything,' he said as he walked past. 'Is the door locked?' he asked. She said it was and he would need to wait until she got back if he needed a key.

Their business took only half an hour, and on the way back Lottie went to the ladies before going to her office. She returned to find the door unlocked and Eric sitting in Todd's old chair. She looked at him, amazed.

'How did you get in?' she asked.

'I've got Todd's old key code. Security said it would help me get around the place, so they swapped it over.'

'Oh.' She was a little surprised as the labs were strictly for the doctors and authorised staff. She looked over at her laptop that was still closed down, and the files were where she left them.

'You still keeping busy with stuff then, now he's gone?' Eric asked, standing up from the desk, referring to Todd.

'Yes, still got a few things to do.' She tried not to give too much away with what she was working on. He walked to the door.

'Let me know if I can help,' he said, smiling back. She thanked him and said that she would be OK for now. She unlocked her cabinet and walked over and closed the door. She called down to security and asked to see how long Eric had been in her room. The guard was able to see from the time codes he had been there for under half an hour, so just after she had left really. She asked him if it were possible to cancel his access to her office, and he said he would need this to go through the professor, so she sent him an email straight away.

She sat at the breakfast bar with the photo of the guy in her hand. She had shown Ed and he had asked Pete to come and take a look.

'No, Mrs Dean, I can't say that I have ever seen him around here or the office. You say that you have seen him more than once?' he asked. Ed was not impressed that she had not said she had seen him before at The Kensington, but even less so that Pete had not seen the guy at all.

'I cannot see how, in this huge world our paths would cross so many times, if it were not for any other reason than he was making them,' she said.

'I will have the whole team on this, so they know the face,' Pete said. 'Can I have the copy?' He held up the picture and Lottie nodded.

The club was dark, and the music was loud. Eric sat at the bar, waiting for his cousin. He hated the fact that he was being blackmailed by him, but if he did not want his parents to find out about his growing habit, then he had to do what his kinsman asked.

When he left Uni, he was surprised that his cousin, well his second cousin actually, had been in touch. Eric only used mild drugs at weekends, like most of his friends, but one day, out of the blue he was approached by a guy who said he was a friend of the family and one thing led to another and they had ended the night in a seedy bar, sharing a few lines of coke. The guy had photos from the night and sent them through to his relation. He had sent him a note saying that his secret was safe with him, as long as he kept his eyes open for anything at work involving the Deans. He was not sure that he should do it but guessed that as the favour came with a regular supply of coke, he was onto a winner.

The tall blond guy walked over and sat next to Eric, and he felt the hairs on his arms stand up.

'Well, cos, we meet again.' Eric held out his hand to shake the offered limb of the person he really did not recognise from years before. He guessed as kids they may have known each other but he could not remember. He was related somehow on his father's side, and since he had walked out on them years ago, his mother did not keep in touch with any of his family. His mother would kill him if she knew he was talking to him, but not quite as disappointed as she would be to know he had a habit, one that she was helping to fund with regular payments to his bank account that he knew she could not afford.

'What do you have then?' the guy asked, waving at the bartender to get whisky for them both.

Eric did not drink the stuff so cringed when the amber liquid hit his throat. 'I am not sure what Mrs Dean is working on, but I was able to get a glimpse at something and your name came up.'

'My name, why?' the man asked.

'I don't know, I had to put the files back. It was a newspaper report, I think.' Eric felt his hands shake.

'Well, find the files then, get me them. Remember your mother has a weak heart – this could finish her!' The glass was slammed back on the bar as the guy stood up. 'Or she may have a horrid accident while out shopping, or at her bridge club; she does like her Sunday strolls in the park, doesn't she? She should be very aware that people get mugged, or a lot worse in the early hours of the morning, you know!' He turned and Eric felt brave enough to grab the guy's arm.

'Don't you threaten my mother!' he said.

'Oh,' the guy laughed, 'You're either a brave little boy or stupid. Or what? You will hurt me?' In a swift movement the guy had Eric's arm around his back and was pushing him up against the bar. 'Threats like that can also get you very hurt, you need to make sure that you control that habit. Mummy would be devastated if her beloved boy was dead of an overdose now, wouldn't she?'

The bartender walked slightly closer and said, 'Take it outside gentlemen or I will call security.' The guy released Eric and he rearranged his jacket. 'Next week at the latest I want to know what is going on,' and with that the figure walked away. Eric took a deep breath. Oh shit, he thought to himself what am I going to do?

'Edward wants to go racing on Sunday, so we are dropping in on Saturday for the night, is that OK? I am sorry it only gives you a few days' notice,' she asked Gerald as she sat at her desk late on the Wednesday afternoon before she left work. 'We will be with Phil, and I am asking a friend along, so can you make up the staff and spare rooms?' Lottie asked, knowing that only one of the beds would be slept in really, as Liz was coming along for a fun weekend too.

'I'm pleased he is settling in,' she said, referring to his new companion. The new friend had arrived that morning from the kennels. She had been really surprised to hear that another call from Edward, along with another cheque, had speeded up the new arrival of Apollo, just the day after the home visit.

She put down the phone and picked up her bag, gathering the papers she wanted to take home. The rest she locked in her safe in the office.

'Have a good 'rest of the week off'!' Eric shouted through to her when he could see that she was heading out of the office. 'Will do!' Lottie shouted back. She knew he had been listening when she was on the phone. As she walked out of the door, the security guard stopped her. 'A courier just dropped this off for you.' Lottie thanked him and looked at the postmark. Manchester Police was the stamp. She didn't open it, simply pushed it into her laptop bag and walked to the predictably waiting car, with the door held open and Phil greeting her as usual.

Friday afternoon was warm and sunny. Lottie was rushing to get packed for the weekend but becoming more depressed the longer she stood in front of her wardrobe with nothing fitting her.

'Well, dear, you look wonderful. I never thought you had enough skin on your bones anyway. How can you say you are fat!' Mrs B was folding and hanging the clothes back up as quickly as Lottie was trying them on and discarding them.

'Oh, little bump, you are causing your mother some frustration,' Ed said. He had been listening and watching with a smile for a moment before he walked in on the conversation. His grin could have lit up the whole room. He put his hands around Lottie and rubbed her stomach. 'Baby girl, just go and get more clothes.' He kissed her. He had just arrived back from the office and after another kiss he made his way to the shower.

'Not going to have time before we go tomorrow though,' she shouted, as the water started to cover his body. With a watery reply, he shouted back at her, but she had gone out of earshot. She shook her head and quickly picked up an item that had been discarded on the floor, changed and then walked into the sitting room. She had picked up his shirt from the floor and put it on. Loose-fitting and smelling of Edward Dean, his aftershave, and his own smell from a day in the office, crisp and distinctive. Finally, she felt comfortable in something. He came back to the sitting room where she sat with a cup of tea. He was dressed in joggers with no tee shirt, hair still wet and tumbling towards his neckline, and with a smooth hand he pulled it back from his face.

'Put a belt on this and I could be comfy.' She stood up and went to the kitchen to get him a drink. He followed her through. Looking at her long legs, he followed the line up with his eyes. Even now her little bump showed in that, he thought to himself.

'Well, I have no objection, but you could have chosen a clean one,' he said, turning his nose up. She sniffed at the sleeve. 'Oh, it just smells of you,' she said back.

'That's why I had a shower! Has bump affected your sense of smell too?' He laughed, taking the hot coffee she passed over.

'It's nice,' she said, sniffing again. 'It makes me feel safe,' she said and when she looked at him his smile had gone.

'And when don't you feel safe, Lottie?' His question was suddenly quite stern.

'I don't mean safe, I mean, secure, happy, homely.' She really had chosen the wrong word to say.

'If you have any issues, you must let me know. Pete has been looking at new staff for the team, all I have to do is say the word and we can increase security, get more staff to watch if you have any concerns.'

'I don't, I never meant the word safe as you have taken it. Slow down, Mr Paranoid. I am fine.' She kissed him as a way to ease his mind. 'I am guessing by the fact your phone is going you have bit of work to finish?' She changed the subject, and Ed apologised and nodded. 'Go then. I wanted to make a call too, so I will get dinner ready for an hour's time but no later as I am starving!'

She picked up the phone and dialled the number for New York. She had put off contacting Todd and had sent him an email instead of calling him. From his tone in reply, he seemed fine, and was settling in. Although he had said the use of the apartment would only be for a few days, he was still there, and Lottie felt better knowing he was, at least it was one less thing for her to worry about.

She had explained all her findings so far and had asked him to mull them over. She wanted to hear his voice, as well as take his advice on how to move on with the case. What Lottie was proposing to do would, she had no doubt, bring things out, and if this person were exposed, there was no telling how it would go.

As he answered the phone, they made small talk exchanging pleasantries. She had not told him about the baby; she was not sure why, but she just had not. She was still on the phone when Ed came back into the room, and Todd could tell by the way Lottie had started to change her answers to his questions, that she did not want to talk about it with him around.

'I take it by the way your voice sounds, Edward is back in the room?' he asked.

'Yes,' she simply said.

'Well, Lottie, you need to tell him. The information from the police does seem to stack up that the drugs were the same. Something added to them that seems to be a trait or a trademark from one specific dealer. The guy, who you said you have seen following you, has links to a drug deal a year or so ago. Now you are asking me to investigate this shipment that went wrong last year, and this guy, Edwards's old friend. It does all seem to be more suspicious than coincidence.' He paused. 'You will take care. I really think if you are planning to go back to the club and see if you can recognise this person, you should go with Edward, and so he needs to know.'

'I know, I just need to get some more solid evidence before I go...' She stopped as Edward came back from the kitchen with a drink in his hand. 'Back there,' she finished.

Ed mouthed to her who was she talking to, and she put her hand over the phone, but so Todd could hear her, 'It's Todd, just seeing if he is OK,' she said. Lying, she said to Todd, 'Edward says hello, anyway I should let you get back to it.'

'Lottie, promise me you will tell him your plan.' Todd expressed his concern again.

'Ok. Will do,' she said in an upbeat voice.

'Don't say it just to make me feel better, please do it,' he pleaded.

'I hear you, speak soon,' she said. He said goodbye and Lottie hung up.

'I never knew you were calling him today,' Edward said.

'Yes, he sent me a mail, saying how great it was over there so I thought I would just catch up.' She snuggled down beside him, and he moved his arm so she could get closer.

They chatted for a while. Lottie tried to focus on their weekend, but she had made up her mind now how she could pull this off. Sadly, she reflected on how easy it was to start to lie to everyone again.

They arrived in Kent late on the Saturday afternoon. Liz had loved the house and the village and was excited about having a weekend away. Although Phil had driven them, Edward invited him to the pub for an evening meal, which pleased Liz, and with a bit of persuasion from Lottie to get over the fact that the two of them were an item. He had reinforced to her that work was work but to anyone looking in the room, that was packed with locals going about their business enjoying a Saturday night out, they looked like two young couples socialising.

Lottie loved Apollo. He had been timid at first but seemed to recognise her as soon as they had arrived. Gerald had not finished his outside pen, so the new canine friend was staying in the utility room, but as Lottie sat on the couch that was in the open plan dining area, he made his way onto her and put his head on her knee. She was drinking a glass of milk before she went to bed; this had become a habit lately. The dog seemed to edge his way further onto the couch, resting his head on Lottie's stomach, and he licked her hand that was laying over the bump and nuzzled at her.

'He can tell you know,' Gerald said, observing the behaviour of his new friend. He had been told about the baby and though he was to keep this to himself outside their family, he could talk about it now as they were alone. 'They can sense it. Back home they become very protective you know, of mother and baby.' Lottie smiled at him and stroked Apollo's long fluffy ears. The dog responded by putting his head to one side, as if he liked the attention. She gave his muzzle a kiss and pushed forwards to get up. 'Apollo,' Gerald said, clicking his fingers to get his attention. Amazingly, after only a few days, he responded to his new master and he moved off from his position and placed himself at his side, allowing Lottie to get up.

'He is good for you already,' she said, putting her glass down on the sideboard, referring to how responsive he had already become.

'He will love his new home, just as much as I do, Mrs Dean.' Gerald took the glass in a second and put it in the dishwasher. 'Thank you both, for what you have done for me.' She could see in his eyes he genuinely meant it.

'I'm just glad we have you looking out for us. You're all part of our family now.' She smiled at him again. 'Have a good night's sleep,' she called back, making her way to the stairs to join Edward, who had gone up to have a shower.

The sun shone and the crowds had come out for a day at the races. Luckily for Lottie, Liz had come armed with a selection of dresses, which hid the 'bump', and made her look fantastic, not pregnant. A floppy hat with feathers had been tried on in the house, but once they reached the course, the light wind had proved a test that she was not prepared for. It kept blowing in her face, so it came off and was left in the car. They had hired a full box in the executive enclosure, and Lottie was pleased to see Sarah and Joe had already arrived. Ed had obviously been in contact with them as they both congratulated her as she arrived. Their new arrival was at home with the nanny. This was the first official day out they had spent as a couple again since his birth. Joe was taking advantage of being away, as the drink was already flowing, but Sarah was less sure about leaving her newborn and had her eye on her phone for most of the time.

Lottie's horse was in the third race, so they had enough time to eat and mingle before they had to go down and meet the jockey. She hated the attention and although the race meet was not the most prestigious in the calendar, the course was busy and lots of eyes were on them as she walked into the ring.

'You've got a good chance here, Lottie,' Joe whispered to her, 'The favourite has pulled out, your odds will be falling soon, so go place your bet quickly.' He pointed to the row of bookmakers standing along the line of the fence.

'I'll come with you,' Ed said after she told him she was going to place her bet. 'I can manage!' she said as it was only a few yards away from where they were standing. What could possibly go wrong? she had exclaimed to him and rolled her eyes. So, armed with her own money, she walked to the row of stands, looking more at the friendly face than the odds, or the name of the bookmaker where she would deposit her cash. Really, she did not have a clue what she was doing as she approached the young man who had a round, red smiling face as he greeted her.

'£200 to win on number 4,' she said. The line had been rehearsed all the way to the stall in her head so she did not get it wrong.

'There you go, my lovely.' He passed her a small piece of paper. 'All the best, you have a good eye for the horse and a good chance, you could break my heart and the bank at those odds.' As he spoke the teller behind him lowered the odds and new figures flashed on the electronic board behind him. She smiled to herself as she walked away.

The crowd was large, people waiting to put their money on, and she jumped as another voice directed his question to her and said, 'Mrs Dean, backing your own horse, is that a clue for me to place my money in safe hands?' She looked up and observed the tall blond-haired man. She thought she knew him, but only his eyes seemed to stand out for her. They were cold, cruel but distinctive, un-reactive and pin-like, as if their owner had taken some form of drugs. What totally stood out for her was the smell of his aftershave. The unforgettable, strong smell of cigars, stronger as he had just stubbed one out on the floor. She noticed the dark-blue pin-striped suit and purple tie and lilac shirt as an afterthought.

Every hair on her body seemed to stand up, and her face drained as she realised this was the guy, the man in the club, the one who had known her before. He'd been dressed as the rest of the men in the club, but his eyes she would not forget. She seemed to be rooted to the spot and her mouth wanted to say some words but did not move to project them out.

A young man pushed past her and he knocked her betting slip out of her hand to the floor. She quickly looked down to where it had dropped as she was aware that the slight breeze could possibly blow it away. Her attention was taken by the butt of the cigar. As she bent down to pick up her ticket, slightly groping around people's feet, in a flash of inspiration she also took the stub. Securing the paper in her hand she used it to wrap the smelly deposit and stood back up, turning back round to where the person who had interrupted her had once stood, but he had gone.

She tried to look past everyone in the queue, she thought she saw him go back into the main stand and so she started to walk over towards the area. As it was a nice day, not many people were hanging around in the area, only those eager to get a drink from the bar. She quickly scanned the room but could not find him. Had he gone upstairs? Surely, he was not that fast. She followed one of the signs to take her to the stand outside. Even if she could not see him maybe she could look out over the crowd. She made her way up and blinked in the sunlight as she came out at the top. Allowing her eyes to adjust to the light she started to look around.

'Can you see where Lottie went to, which teller did she head for?' Ed said to Joe, noting that she had been gone longer than he expected.

'Just down in the ring I think. She had best hurry or she'll miss the race, they are making their way to the start line.' He pointed to the horses running past them up the course to the starting post.

'Phil,' Ed said, gesturing with his head for him to come over.

'Mr Dean?' he said, arriving at his side in a second. Edward asked the same question and Phil looked over to the teller where he seen Lottie hand over her money. He visually traced the suspected way she would have taken to get directly back to them, but he could not see her.

'I'll go and look,' Phil said, heading off as quickly as he had said it.

'Maybe she went to the toilet?' Liz said, knowing that Lottie had paid several visits already today. 'I'll go and have a look, she won't want to miss this.' The large screen was showing that most of the mounts had reached the start line and they would soon be loaded into the stalls. Liz had offered to look thinking that Ed was anxious that Lottie would miss the race, but he was as ever concerned that something had happened to her.

Phil made his way back and looked directly at Ed, shaking his head. Ed took out his phone and called her number.

The public stand was packed with people as the race was about to start. It had been like a sudden surge that seemed to come from nowhere in particular, but the crowd engulfed Lottie. She stepped down a few rows, where everyone was standing. She looked at the back of several men, wearing similar tops, but none the same. She was glad that they were in the owner's private area. It was so busy and she had become almost disorientated. It was loud too. People laughing and shouting in the excitement of the day. She looked up and noticed the big screen; the race was about to start, and she knew she had to get back to Ed. She battled with people who seemed not to see or hear her try to move past them. She said sorry to everyone she had to push past. At one point she had been totally turned around and headed back up two steps just to get past one large group.

'She's not in the toilet, Edward,' Liz said, getting back to see that the last horse was in the stall and the excitement of the commentator confirmed they were under starter's orders, and they were off.

'No answer!' Ed punched his phone once more to call for a third time.

Lottie felt as if someone was behind her, but she did not turn around. In front of her the crowd seemed to move aside, almost involuntary. A large bulk of a man physically moved another out of the way. He used some choice words, but he never flinched, his prey in sight. Lottie felt a hand on her arm, and she looked to see Phil parting the crowd, showing her the way down.

'Stay close behind me, Mrs Dean.' Lottie turned around and there he was, the man she had been looking for, several steps up behind to her left. He had been behind her all the time. She stumbled and put her hand on Phil's shoulder, still trying to look at the person she had set out to find, but just as before he had gone.

'I'm on my way back,' Phil said, and Lottie could see his phone to his ear. To her it felt as if she had been gone seconds, but as they walked back through the guarded gate, Edward pushed past his close protection officer to assault her with questions.

'Where the hell did you get to, Lottie?' He pulled her to him.

'Sorry I got lost.' She almost started the lie as she cast her eyes over the spot where she knew she had last seen him. 'I...' she faltered, trying to explain what she had been doing, 'I went to get the ticket and I needed to go...' She stopped.

'To the toilet again!' Liz tried to finish her sentence for her, thinking it would calm the situation down as Edward was clearly angry or concerned about the fact that she had just simply got lost.

'Yes,' Lottie retorted quickly, 'the toilet.' She squeezed Ed's arm. 'Sorry.'

'Well, Mrs Dean, you missed that then.' Joe walked to them all and pointed to the screen where it announced that 'Lottie's Pride' had won by a clear head. 'That will make you richer, Dean, for sure,' Joe mocked, knowing that Edward had put a lot of money on him, even before the start of the day when the odds were almost twice as high as the final figure. 'Nine grand plus at a guess.'

Edward had no concern with the race, or the money. He could tell by Lottie's face that something was not right. He put his hand around her hip. 'Lottie?'

'Not here,' she said, knowing that a lot of attention was about to fall their way. 'Honestly Ed, I will tell you but not here!' She smiled at him, 'I'm fine.' She was right; people were clapping as the horse came back towards the enclosure and Joe said that she would have to go and get the winner's cup.

'No please, Joe, please go for me, Sarah, please tell him to go for me,' she pleaded, not wanting the attention, knowing that somewhere out there in the thousands of other people that were standing around there was one person she did not want to see her. 'Please,' she said, as Edward looked at him, his eyes asking the same request but with more of a command.

'OK!' Joe put up his hands to give in. He enjoyed the whole event and atmosphere really. Sarah smiled and he pulled her towards the winner's stand and the horse who was still highly strung from the race, steaming from the water that had been splashed over him.

From his high vantage point, Lottie's mystery man looked over to the winner's crowd. He smirked, noticing that she had sent someone else in her place. He took a deep breath, drawing in the smoke from his cigar and smiled; he had seen her pick up the stub and was glad she had followed him. He was going to try to get it back from her, but the meathead had reached her sooner. Edward Dean had his arms wrapped firmly around his wife in the ever-protective role that he played, and their heads were close as if they were sharing secrets. Well, Dean, you have a definite weak spot, it is a shame she will get herself in trouble for being so nosy, not matter how you try to protect her. I have your weakness, old friend. His train of thought was interrupted by the group of men he was with. 'You jammy git, you had that one, didn't you?' one said to him and he laughed. 'I got to her yes!' A slight smile crept across his face.

Lottie pulled Ed to the side and he put his arms around her shoulder so that she could speak in a low voice.

'Ed, don't draw attention to us, but the guy,' she stopped and looked around trying to locate him. 'The guy from the club, that night, who spoke to me, he is here.' She immediately put her hand on his arm to control the explosion she expected. 'He spoke to me again. I tried to follow him, but I lost him,' she said, knowing he would blow not only at the first sentence but the second one too.

'Jesus, Lottie, you followed him?' He took a breath in trying to control himself, knowing that Phil was watching them closely. 'What the hell were you thinking?' he tried to keep his voice low, but failed as Liz looked over to them too, along with several other people. He smiled at them, trying to remain calm, but the fire in his stomach burned far too hot. 'Why did you not come straight back, or answer your phone?' he asked, 'What would have happened to you if he had...' He did not finish his sentence but continued the questions. 'What did he look like, can you still see him?' He had noticed that she seemed to be looking in the main public stand.

'I recognised his eyes, they were...' she paused, 'cruel, evil, totally drugged-up I expect.' She finished with the statement that really made Edward shake.

'Oh, and that makes me feel better, knowing that you felt he looked evil and drugged-up but you still bloody followed him!' Ed tried to look around but had no idea who he was looking for.

Behind them the celebration of the win was carrying on. It could have been a million miles away for Lottie. She had totally forgotten.

'I'm sorry. I guessed that maybe, well if I could try to get something else to work with then maybe it could all come together.' She looked at her phone, seeing the missed calls. 'Sorry I guess I could not hear it.'

'What would come together?' Ed asked. She had started the conversation now and she knew that by the end of the day she would have to bring him up to speed on everything she had worked on over the past few weeks. Maybe the plan to go back to the club on her own would be one small detail she would leave out after today's episode, but she knew that they would not see the rest of the racing and the day was over for them.

She fumbled in her bag for her ticket and slowly unwrapped it. The smell was sweet, and the ash had covered the numbers and print on the small betting document. She had not got it out ready to collect her winnings, but to ensure that she still had the evidence.

'What on earth?' Ed asked, looking at the discarded item. 'That's a cigar butt.' He had been known to have had a cigar in his time. He hated the taste and had not tried it again, but he could tell that the brand was not a cheap one.

'He put it out, just before he spoke. I can get some DNA hopefully,' she said, fumbling in her bag for a pack of tissues. She took them out and placed the butt into the little bag. 'I don't think it has got too damaged, I should be able to work with it.' She looked at the ticket. 'Not sure they will want this back though!'

Joe walked back over to them and they stopped talking. 'I don't know what is going on with you two, poor timing to have a domestic, old boy.' He lifted up a crystal goblet as a celebration to Edward. 'You did well though, Lottie, whatever has taken your attention had best be worth it because today you have just earned a fortune and could stand for a lot more. Lottie's Pride will sell well if you want to get rid of her.'

'Joe, don't put us out of business,' Sarah butted in, referring to the fact that they stabled a winner now, and it would make them a better option for other owners to place their rides.

'Some guy came down said his manager wants to buy her, offered a ridiculous price.'

'Where is he?' Lottie asked.

'What are you thinking?' Ed asked, straight away knowing that look on his wife's face was not on the same conversation as Joe.

'There!' He pointed him out and immediately Ed and Lottie turned around to see him. She almost looked disappointed that it was not him.

'No,' she said to Ed.

'Oh, it was a generous offer,' Joe replied, taking the no as her answer not to sell, not as it was aimed at Ed.

'Well, let me have that then, if you don't sell, you will still be better off cashing in the winner.' Joe took the paper from her hand, he could see it had ash on it. 'Did we lose you for a crafty fag, Lottie?' he joked, but soon stopped smiling looking at Ed's face. 'Ok I get it, sense of humour failure all round, am I the only one happy about this win?' He wandered off to the stalls to cash in her winnings.

'We are going,' Ed said loudly so that Phil got back with them. He had kept close by with Liz, but knew they needed space.

'Mr Dean,' he said in reply.

'Sorry to spoil your fun, maybe you could stay with Liz, and Edward and I can get a taxi back?' She was thinking then they could talk.

'Mr Dean?' he said the same words but now as a question. He knew his work came first but it would have been nice to spend more time with Liz. Edward brushed his hand through his hair, gathering his thoughts. He nodded in agreement and took Phil to one side for a chat.

'Sorry for spoiling your day,' Lottie said to Liz.

'Are you and Edward OK?' her friend asked.

'Yes, we just have some issues, not serious, but work stuff,' Lottie said back.

'Sounds serious for you to miss out on all this; your horse won, and you don't look bothered. Gosh Lottie, you must have got a fortune on your bet too.'

'I am happy, just sometimes work comes first.' Lottie tried to convince her friend everything was OK. She knew that Phil would not utter a word about this to Liz or anyone, so she tried to convince her friend with more conversation that things were OK until the boys came back to talk to them.

Joe gave her a large envelope before they said their goodbyes. He had been right that Lottie's Pride was a good bet. One positive thing from today was that Lottie had over five grand to put in her trust fund, but it was sadly overlooked by the other event of the day that remained the topic of conversation for them both on the journey back to the house.

If she had her way, they would go straight back to London so she could look at the stub, work on it to see if what she truly believed would turn out to be right. But she would have to wait; it was not practical to go back today, it would be too late at night, and for now they could just take in the events and work through her plan if she turned out to be right. She left the evidence in her bag, sitting on the kitchen table.

They sat in the bath, enjoying the closeness of each other's touch. The water was warm and smelt sweet. The bubbles covered them and as Ed sat behind Lottie, her cocooned in his arms, he flushed the water over her with the bath sponge. Everyone else was out, not yet returned from the races, and

Gerald was walking Apollo, so they relished the time to be alone.

'I could get used to this,' Ed said, brushing her hair away from her face and kissing her head. 'I was thinking, maybe after Bump is here, we could think about making this the more permanent place, a family home, and keep a smaller place in London, sell the apartment. It is not very family-friendly, more of a bachelor pad.'

'What about work? You need to be in the city, and I don't want to commute to the centre.' She sensed he had given it more than just a thought with his confident tone.

'We will do two or three days there, then the rest of the week here. I wondered if we could extend the house, maybe add a bigger pool, some outhouses for the staff,' he carried on, moving the water around in the bath.

'So, you have done more than randomly thought about it then?' She said what she was thinking a few moments before.

'I have been trying to get work to a stage that I can do most of it remotely, yes.' He lent back in the bath.

'So, you can be a stay-at-home father then?' She laughed, envisaging him with nappies and washing in hand. Then finished her comment with Not!

'Don't laugh, but sort of yes. I know you want to carry on working but I don't want to just share you both, I want to be part of it. This place is so peaceful, a great family home.'

She rubbed his leg that was tucked over hers. She could not disagree with him on that score. She had so many happy memories of her own childhood here.

'We could sell it and start again, find something as nice but closer?' She hoped that he would not say yes. She could not really think about selling her home, it was too precious, but she had to put it out there as he was willing to sell the apartment. His reply was really pleasing to hear.

'Lottie, no, it's a wonderful home, your home, our home, it holds such memories for you, and me now. We could make it fit all of us.'

'How big does it have to be when you say all of us?' she asked.

'Well, Bump will need a sibling!' he said, rubbing his hand over her stomach. She smiled but did not want to rush plans; it was OK thinking of the future but there were some big issues for the here and now to deal with.

'I'm not dismissing anything, Ed, but it's a long way off.' She rolled herself over in the bath so that they were face to face. 'It's good to know what you are thinking, but can we hold the thoughts of increasing the family just yet, well unless you are talking about practicing!' She smiled as she ran her hand up his leg and rubbed the top of his thigh, gently placing a kiss on his neck, licking around the lobe of his ear. She moved her legs to straddle him; it was tight in the bath but achievable. She sat upright and rubbed Bump. 'After all it seems practice does make perfect!' She smiled and lowered down onto him, kissing his chest, seeking out his left nipple and rolling her tongue around the now pert end of skin.

'Mrs Dean, I am not sure I can improve on perfection, although I have to admit your tactics for persuasion are somewhat hard to resist.' He drew her head back up towards his and kissed her.

'That is not all that appears to be hard,' she said, using her body to rub against his dick, which was on its way to being fully erect. She placed herself so that her sex took him by his engorged head, lowering herself slowly down to take his length. His size made her gasp, and he used his hands to take her weight.

He lent back as much as the bath would allow to admire this vixen riding him. Her full breasts started to bounce as she closed her eyes, absorbing the pleasure into her mind. The pure lust for him aroused him more and with each solid stroke he knew she would ruin him before she reached her own goal. She held onto the sides of the bath as her movements became more urgent, and as she took her weight, he released one hand to reach for her breast. He was fixed on the mound wanting to suck and lick this tempting object, so he satisfied himself by rolling it between his finger and thumb, a sensation that was plain to see sent excitement through his hungry sex-driven wife.

Lottie changed her movements between up and down, to a circular rub when she was totally full of him. His pubic bone met hers and allowed her very sensitive nub to be massaged, causing a spasm in her sex muscles. She took another gasp as she felt the heat rise in her thighs, her stomach tightened, and she pushed her head back in total acceptance that he had her on the edge of a climax.

Sensing she was close he took her weight again, and stopped her rubbing the spot that would trigger her.

'Oh, please?' she begged, opening her eyes to see this tanned, dark-haired Adonis, his arm muscles flexed, his abdominals taut, controlling her moves, and she just had to kiss him. She dipped her head down to meet his lips, and she whimpered as he kissed her, finishing off with a small bite of her lower lip. She made a sound as she sucked in the air past her teeth and pulled herself close to him to kiss his neck, feeling his wet hair on her face. He whispered in her ear, 'Baby girl, go slowly, don't be so greedy.' She bit his ear and he sensed slow was not her game. Her playful bite had would have him eating his words as such stimulation rocketed to his dick and it throbbed, indicating the very start of his climax into her. She moved to the other side of him, and the gentle release of her weight allowed her to sit deeper onto him, twisting her hips again to get the position of him in her she wanted; she circled her hips and he felt himself give another thrust. 'Please baby girl, I can't hold on for you.'

'Then don't,' she whispered in a deep sexy voice, inviting him to fill her with his seed. 'Don't hold back.' He knew he had to. If he thrust and forced her as much as he wanted to, he knew he would hurt her, and remove every drop of water that was already leaving the bath and soaking the floor of the room. He squeezed his eyes closed in the vain attempt to hold himself back. His mind's eye was his very enemy as he could still see her image before him, twisting and swaying on top of him. The soft round tits made more delicious by her current state, the fact that she carried his child itself took him to euphoria and he grabbed her backside in an attempt to control some of what was about to happen.

The control of his legs and the power he had to contort her in the position showed his physical fitness. Lottie clenched her inner muscles, knowing he would feel the increased tightness around his cock. She smiled with pleasure as it responded with a thrust and a pulse as if it acknowledged her need. She felt his hot mouth take one of her nipples and she opened her eyes to see his face latched on to her. The roughness of his tongue, lapping round the sensitive bud sent a message to her sex, she contracted her muscles again, but this time involuntary. As she gasped in pleasure, she felt the heat rise to her neck and cheeks; he held the nipple firmly in his teeth, and flicked his tongue violently over and over the end. He had total control of this now, the rhythm, the speed. She dug her nails into his back, making him jolt back to reality. The pain was not unwelcome, but it proved to be the start of fitting the final piece into the carnal act.

He clenched her in his legs and in one movement, with the little water for buoyancy that was left in the bath, he rolled her and put her under him. She scratched her back on the tap, which was in the middle of the bath as she rolled over. She felt the pain, but her mind was too enthralled with the sexual passion she was fixed on, ensuring they did not lose the body friction that was stimulating her to the climax she craved.

With better control of her he pushed himself down, careful as ever in his mind that he did not crush her. He smiled to himself amid the mind-blowing sensations she was giving him, that he could feel her increasing swelling belly on his stomach, confirmation that he could not be any more content, happy in his life. She wrapped her legs around him, positioning her hips slightly better, and again she started to moan as her release clearly was about to show. He had been able to hold off. Minutes ago he thought he would not be able to, but the warm throbbing he could feel around his dick, the picture of pure lust and passion on her face, and her gentle moans confirmed she was there. She held the bath, and he instinctively speeded up, thrusting into her. She screamed out, 'Aah, Edward!' In fear he had hurt her, he stopped and apologised, and she clutched at him desperately. 'God don't stop, not now!'

No more encouragement needed, he was content it was not real pain, but passion that had made her call out. He relaxed his hips and drilled down into her. The spasm and throbbing that her climax released was strong, stronger than he was sure he had felt before. Her grip on him internally rippled through to his inner stomach.

'Lottie,' he said as almost a warning that he was not holding back. The bath almost seemed to pound with his thrusts, coming loose from the floor mountings and it took all his strength not to drop on her and pump as hard as he could.

His nostrils flared and he grunted out her name again as he flushed his come into her, and with every thrust she held on. He was deep inside her and she could feel it more now her own pleasure had stemmed; she tried to put some space between them by pushing back on his hips. At one point she winced he pushed her so deep and it was the first time she ever thought that they needed to slow down.

'Edward,' she said, pushing back again on his hips, knowing he was overcome by pleasure.

'Sorry.' He took the hint of her pushing back on him and he slowed his depth and pace, which only prolonged his release. Sounding more like a child than a sex-crazed adult he whimpered as his final life seed passed to her. He was barely inside her, but the stimulation of his engorged head made his arms quiver, and he shook as if someone walked over his grave. She pulled him close and he gently pulled out of her.

They were naked and wet, no water in the bath except for about an inch.

Breathless and panting for oxygen, he placed his head on her forehead.

'Oh, baby you are...' he paused to get more air and lifted from her. He pushed back onto his knees and helped her up in the bath. His face dropped and he had a look of horror as a droplet of water-diluted blood trickled down her leg. She smiled at him and froze as she looked at his face. 'Edward?' she asked in an enquiring voice, 'What?' She looked down to where his eyes were looking, and she noticed the slight trail of blood.

'Oh my god, Lottie, you are bleeding!' He looked in the bath to notice the slight pink tinge the water had taken on. He had to steady her as she froze to the spot. 'Oh God I knew this would happen, that fucking doctor was wrong!' He stood up with her and pulled her to him. 'I knew this would happen,' he repeated, 'I am such an idiot, a selfish fucking idiot. I was too rough and oh God look what I've done, I've...' he stopped again, 'Are you in pain, is Bump OK? Oh God, shit!' He grabbed her a towel, leaning over and then helping her out of the bath.

Lottie felt fine physically, no pain, and she could not work out where the blood was coming from.

'Sit down. I'll call an ambulance. Oh, fucking shit,' he said, rushing into the bedroom to get his phone after she sat on the bath edge.

Lottie looked at the blood and wiped herself between her legs; there did not seem to be any more. Unwrapping herself from the towel, she noticed a small speck of blood on the back of it. She stood up, her legs shaking, she was not sure from the shock or from the experience she had just shared with her husband. She looked again at the towel, then turned in the full-length mirror and looked at her back. She could see the mark where she had felt the pain; the tap had caught her and taken off the layers of flesh, releasing a line of blood. The water had just made the amount look worse than it really was.

'Edward!' she shouted, trying not to sound alarmed, 'It's OK.' She started to walk to the bedroom to intercept a panicked emergency call but was too late.

'Lottie?' he called back, quickly moving his feet whilst hitting the 9 button repeatedly.

'Don't call, it's not what you think.' She turned around to show him her back. A low voice on the other end of the phone could be heard. 'Hello caller, what service do you require? Hello!'

He rushed to her to take a better look at her back, the relief that washed over him making him forget he had the call open and he put a finger to the tender spot. 'Are you sure this is where the blood is from?' Lottie almost laughed with the reply.

'Yes,' she said, pointing to the phone in his hand. 'The call.'

'Sorry?' he asked, not realising what she was saying to him.

'The emergency call!' She pulled up his hand and took the phone. 'I'm sorry, there is no emergency I am OK, I'm so sorry my husband reacted too quickly, we are both fine.' The operator asked if she was really OK again. Lottie presumed that some people really were prevented from calling the emergency services for whatever reason when they needed them, and she had thoughts of domestic violence go through her head. 'I am fine, honestly, it is an overreaction from my protective husband.' That may have not sounded so convincing, so she added, 'I am expecting but he got the wrong end of the stick with the situation, nerves I presume!' The operator was happy for Lottie to hang up, but not before saying she must call back if required and that they had the phone number recorded. Putting the phone down on the bedside table, Edward asked to see it again and asked her for a third time if she was sure.

'Yes, I'm fine babe. I felt it catch my back, but, well I was a little carried away at the time to notice fully!' She rubbed his arm to try to appease him.

'We must be more careful. I can't think about what I would do if...' She stopped his words with a finger on his mouth.

'I know,' she said, softly placing a kiss on his lips, his face still quite white from the panic. 'Neither can I.'

Chapter 13

Placing the cigar butt under the microscope she tried to remove the outer layer. This would be the bit that if she could, would get the DNA. Annoyingly they had arrived home after lunch on the Monday, and when she phoned the centre, the professor said not to come in until the next day, as they were not over-run with work.

So, she had set off early and been at her desk since 8am working on the item she hoped held the key to who the person was. This was one step closer than she had been weeks ago at least.

By late afternoon, the results had been emailed to her, and yes, she was right. The same person who broke into her flat, the car, been with the poor dead girl and for some reason been at the scene of Mitch's death was the same as the guy who had spoken to her twice now. She had a thought over dinner, she had wondered if from the item they could get any other results and so had sent off some other checks. The toxicology would not be in until tomorrow, no matter how she tried to speed them up.

Her phone rang; it was Edward seeing if she was OK, again. She smiled and recalled his sheer horror when he thought that she was in some way losing their child. It really meant everything to him. She walked out of her office to get a better reception.

Although the call was no more than five minutes it was enough time for Eric to go into her room, unnoticed, to see what she was working on. He had to be quick, no names, nothing to give him too many clues, but he looked at the files open and memorised a few of the names that linked the case. He hoped that this was enough. He made a call and passed on the information he had as required.

The voice on the end of the phone sounded calm, cold and the call ended without a goodbye, or thank you, just a place to meet later that evening.

Sitting in his flat, the tall blonde-haired man filled another small piece of foil with the white powder. He mixed it with some more powder, his own special brand, something that gave the mix his own trademark. Allowing it to burn and turn to a liquid he quickly filled the syringe and placed a top over it. Placing another small amount on the table he carefully made lines with the back of a card and bent forwards to sniff it. He breathed in through his nose and then wiped his face with the back of his hand. Closing his eyes, he felt warmth run through his body with every beat of his heart. The substance relaxing and intoxicating him all in one smooth and warming motion.

Dropping back on his sofa, happy that no one else was in the house, he pushed his mind to the place where he knew he could see her. Beautiful, tall, and slender. He imagined he could feel her soft skin, kiss her lips, lick her mouth, suck her nipples, and fuck her so hard that she screamed. He could see her in the outfit from the club, tight and figure-hugging. He put his hand on his cock that was growing with his mind in his fantasy world. Coke made him hard, Leticia Dean made him horny, and his image of her made him unzip his trousers and release the member held inside.

Just filling his hand with his hot skin, he envisaged the image of her face. He pumped himself, in his crazed haze of pleasure, wondering how she would struggle when bound to his table, strapped to his bed, gagged and blindfolded under his body. He tugged at his dick, trying to make it longer, harder, knowing that she would expect something bigger than this, not his poor excuse of a cock he had in his hand. 'Come on you little fucker, grow!' he said out loud pushing his boxers lower down his legs as if this would help. He leant over, keeping himself in his hand and snorted another line of the white powder, waiting for the sensation to start again. As it did, he masturbated, shouting out her name as his final goal leaked his thick white semen over his stomach. 'Bitch, you can have that,' he said, rubbing himself as if he wanted to carry on, but the effect of the come down was obvious and his cock shrunk to its flaccid state all too quickly. 'Fucking come on.' He tugged at himself again, to no end.

Paranoia set in as he came further down from his high. 'Edward Dean has the biggest cock in the school!' he heard a voice say. 'Mini dick!' Another voice. 'Wanker, that's all you will ever be, could not satisfy a woman like Edward can.' A female voice popped up in his head with this last statement. The room felt as if it was shrinking around him and he needed to get out.

Throwing his hand off his body and pulling up his trousers, he kicked the table as he walked past putting the syringe into his pocket. 'Fuck you, Dean!' He made his way to his room and got changed and went out to the place he had arranged to meet his informant.

The park was dark as Eric sat on the bench. He was not sure he should be doing this, but he had noticed the CCTV cameras and tried to make himself visually seen by as many people as he could on his journey. But as he passed over the grass, the light from the street lamps faded and the seat was shaded by the trees. The promise of a fix drove him to sit tight. It felt like hours, but it was not that long until a person sat next to him.

'What have you got?' the voice asked, and Eric did not dare to look round.

Eric outlined what he had seen and was surprised when the person repeated, 'The death of Michael Dean, what about it?' He explained he did not know but looking at the DNA profile it looked like she was working on new cases as well as old ones.

'No names you say, you have not seen my name?'

'No,' Eric replied, resisting the urge to look in the man's direction. 'Can I have my stuff and go now?' he asked. A small packet was handed over to him and he thrust it into his pocket. The man stood up. Eric felt him pat him on the shoulder and he heard the words, 'Well done.'

It was the last thing he heard as he slipped into a coma. He had not felt the sharp pin-prick in the side of his neck, direct into his jugular. The high had been almost instant, dulling any pain, or any reaction he could make to fend his assailant off. Sat slumped to one side, Eric's body remained semi lifeless for several hours. Small breaths holding him in this world and the vomit from his stomach slowly started to block his airway. His heart was under pressure from attempting to process the limited oxygen it needed to keep working, until it gave out and finally stopped.

Out of breath from running most of the way back to his mother's house, Alex Girski closed the door and went to his rooms. His mother was out as usual for a Tuesday night. He quickly got changed, ordered a taxi and went into town. He needed a drink. All the way in the taxi he went over in his mind, 'If they don't have my name then I am OK, they will never find my name. I am more careful than that.' The devil on his shoulder spoke out, 'But what if she does find out your name? What then?' He paid the driver and went into the bar, and ordering a large whisky he sat and drank. He needed to know if she knew it was him. He needed to get close to her, ask. 'Don't be so stupid, she is not going to keep it to herself, is she?' the voice in his head said again, 'She has to go!'

A cold sweat came over him; although he wanted to take everything from Edward Dean, how could he take her away from him, without hurting her in some way? He was obsessed by her. He had never touched her, only had a few words exchanged with her, but he wanted her, for himself, not to hurt, but to adore, like he knew Edward did. Several more double whiskies soon took away some of the paranoid voices, all of which left him when the warm sensation of the coke hit his system a few hours later. 7am in the morning, this ridiculous time was nothing new for him to roll home as the taxi dropped him off outside the large, imposing house. He made his way in and slumped on the sofa, and there he stayed until the housekeeper woke him, and his mother once more scolded him for being a waste of space in her life.

'Lottie, can you come into the office?' the professor asked as he walked by, some time after 10am on the Wednesday morning. She did as she was asked after she closed the programme she was looking at. The toxicology results had come in and it had shown a match in the type of drugs she had been looking for. Todd had been able to find a trace of a substance that was not a usual mix, something that they thought the dealer was adding themselves to make a type of branding. It was this information he was working on in the US, trying to find if it had any gang links, or anything else that they could work with.

She closed the door as she looked at the older man sitting at his desk. He had not been in long, his light jacket still thrown on the couch in the corner of the room, and his lab coat still hanging on the coat stand by the door.

'I have some really bad news,' he said to her, offering his hand for her to take a seat opposite him. She looked at his face and it confirmed the news was going to be upsetting in some way even before he had told her.

'Eric,' he stopped himself, 'Eric was found dead this morning.' He came straight out with it as he thought it was a better way to break it to her.

'Oh my god, really?' she said in total disbelief. 'Where, how?' she carried on.

'In a park in town,' the professor continued, 'I was called out early this morning by the police as a routine post-mortem, but once I got there...' he paused. 'I realised straight away who it was. Early signs show some form of overdose. I never...' he stopped himself again and Lottie realised this had affected him more than he was letting on. 'I never knew he had a drug problem. He seemed such a bright young lad who really wanted to get on in this field. I was so wrong, and I feel responsible in some way as I did hire him.' There was a natural pause for them both to gather their thoughts.

'You are not to know everything about people and their private lives.' She tried to give him words to console him, but then had to ask. 'What are the police saying about it?'

'They were content with my first thoughts, but I wanted to look into it further, and, well, how would you feel about helping me? I know you knew him, but would you be able to work with me on this?' he asked her and although she knew it would be hard, she had to remain professional. 'His mother is coming in to identify him, formally, this afternoon.'

'Is he here?' Lottie asked.

'Yes, they brought him over as soon as I left, although the police are still looking over the area. I don't think they will spend much time on it, just another drug addict to them. I guess it will be in the papers, but again tomorrow's news after that. Such a waste of a young life.'

Lottie felt her stomach turn and ache at the thought of his relations having to come in and see their son, cold and lost to death so young. She felt a small tear in her eye; she had always thought there was something odd about Eric, but never wished this, or even thought he was capable of something like this, but then, not everyone was who they seem.

'Do you want me to meet them?' she asked.

'Would you mind, and then maybe tomorrow we could try to put some more pieces together as to why this happened?' The professor looked up from his computer, with his glasses halfway down his nose as normal. 'If it's too much for you, just say, Lottie, but my gut has a feeling, and if there is one thing I have learnt from you in the past few months it's that if something does not feel right, it usually is not!'

She smiled. He was right. Sadly, for her on several occasions in the past her gut feeling had turned out to be right. She was pleased that he thought so much of her that he had asked. The new pathologist, Todd's replacement, could have done this with him, but she felt duty bound, not just for Eric, but for the professor to see it through.

They chatted for a few more minutes and then Lottie returned to her desk. The first thing to do was to call Ed and let him know just in case he'd heard anything and panicked as usual. Pete always had his ear to the ground in the police world, and this sort of news would not take long to get back to Ed. She picked up her phone to make the call.

Eric's mother had been devastated. Lottie found it hard to compose herself, asking to leave the room so that she could cry out of sight. Her hormones were super-sensitive at the moment, and she needed to remain professional. She had made the excuse that would give her a moment alone, and it was not until she had composed herself that she went back into the sober chapel in the centre where family could come to wish their loved ones goodbye.

'I understand that you have to find out what happened,' Eric's stepfather said to Lottie out of earshot of his wife, who was still holding the boy's hand, and weeping softly. 'Does that mean you have to do tests?'

Lottie nodded in conformation, looking down to the floor to try to stop the tears once more. 'You will find out the truth, won't you?' he asked. 'Eric was always such a good boy, when we found out he had been asked to work here we were overjoyed. We were pleased that he was going to make something of his life.'

Lottie took his words and tried to think who it would have been in the centre that had found him the job. Was the prof related in some way to Eric; he had mentioned that he had a cousin, and was the prof that person? Is that why he was so upset? She wondered if she should ask. Was this the right time to ask questions, or should that be left for the police? Looking back at his mother, Lottie thought that today was not the time or place.

Tomorrow would be the day to ask questions, but first she had to speak to Ed and explain why she had to work on a Thursday. She was sure that he would understand.

Ed was not happy about her changing her days, but as she sat chatting to him over supper, she was able to strike a deal, saying she would take an extra day off the next week, or at least when they had finished looking into this.

The next day, Detective Sharpe sat in on the post-mortem. The professor took the lead and in casual conversation during the investigation, Lottie felt the need to ask the burning questions she had.

'So, you found nothing in his flat that could indicate anything?'

'Not really, just the usual stuff for a young single guy, ex-student. Not even evidence that drugs were his thing, or any dealers. His phone has a few missed calls, we have followed all of them, nothing really, friends and family mainly.'

'Anything from a cousin?' Lottie needed to know about this cousin. 'Contact or calls?' Lottie asked, looking at the professor to see if anything changed in his facial expressions. It did not.

'An ex-girlfriend. A pizza for that night, that he had eaten looking at what you have found. So that must mean he made his way to the dealer after nine. A small pack of coke, but nothing to OD on.' Lottie looked up at the detective and then back at the toxicology results.

'Do you have the pack?' She looked at the professor.

'Yes, the results are separate. I have not studied them yet.' The professor passed the paperwork to Lottie and she took a moment to study them. She wiped her face and then looked up towards the young man's lifeless body. She picked up the lab phone and asked for more details on the tests and as she put it down the detective asked her, 'What are you thinking, Mrs Dean?'

Should she say that she had seen this before, these results? Would this lead them to ask more questions and then suddenly open up all the problems that Ed and herself were going through?

'DC Sharpe, can I ask you to have a look into Eric's family? A connection or names of his cousins, those family members you said he called.'

'To what end, Lottie?' the professor asked, wiping his hands after washing them.

'Professor, who did you speak to about him starting here?' she asked him as the detective had left the room.

'An old friend of your husband's actually. I'm surprised he did not say anything. I can't remember his name, I would need to look in his files.' He sat in front of the lab computer and put in his password. Tapping a few keys, the staff files came up and he called her over.

Lottie looked at the name on the screen and felt her heart stop. Alex Girski.

'Edward knows him, they go back some time I believe.' The professor looked at Lottie and he blinked. 'Is this a problem?'

'No, no, Edward hasn't spoken to him for some time. I guess they have just lost touch, you know, busy lives,' she lied. Edward had not spoken to him for almost a year, not since the incident when he had to bail him out of some drugs thing with the Russians. If her gut feeling came together, she knew that she needed to see what he looked like. She had never met him but knew that if this was the person she recognised, the full pieces of the jigsaw had come together.

DC Sharpe called Lottie to say that the phone list was going to be sent to her email, and the final blood toxicity results would also be there for her the next day. Knowing that Ed would not take too kindly to her working another day in the office she packed her laptop to work from home. Before she left, she downloaded the photos from the autopsy, she just wanted to look through them all again. She was sure that the death of the girl and Eric's death had been caused by the same drug, she just now had to pull the pieces together.

As normal Lottie and Ed exchanged daily reports on their working life, her not lying, but omitting to lay all the facts out to Ed. She did not say anything about what she had been working on or her theory on who this person may be. Or why, if it was the same person, it all in some way related to them.

'Are we going to your mum's for Sunday lunch?' Lottie asked as they lay in bed, wrapped in each other's arms.

'We could. She hasn't said she is free, but I can call her. Why?' Ed asked, pulling away to look at Lottie's face.

'I just wondered,' she replied.

'Did you have anything else planned?' he asked back, trying to find out why she had suddenly asked.

'No, I just wanted to plan my day that was all, if we are going out for lunch, maybe I could get a bit of shopping in too!' She kissed his arm that was holding around her stomach.

'Oh, shopping sounds like it needs to be a girly thing. Maybe I could go to the gym? You could shop first and then I will join you for lunch?' He settled his head back onto the pillow.

'Ok I will call her tomorrow, see what she has planned.' Lottie tried to close her eyes, but her mind was working overtime. All the ends of the thread were pulling tighter, faster than she could process. Tomorrow she would sit down and mind map it all, and by Sunday she hoped she could put a final name in the last thought bubble and that would join this whole lot together. Then, well she was not quite sure what then.

'Oh, my feet!' was the cry as Lottie and Edward's mother walked into her house. 'My feet are killing me!' Mrs Dean Senior quickly jumped out of her shoes and left them on the floor where they fell. The large imposing hallway had a marble floor, and she was comforted by the cooling stone. 'Do you want a tea? I sure need some caffeine. That was some shopping trip.'

'I'll get the kettle,' Lottie said, showing Phil where to leave the bags. She had not really bought a lot. Ed's mother had found the whole experience invigorating and once the credit card had been out, it was out several more times in the same shop.

'Ed's going to love this.' His mother held up the sweetest yellow hat and boot set. 'I know you said not to get baby things, I just could not help it!'

Lottie had said before they even went into the shop that she was not getting anything for the nursery, or the baby yet, but it seemed that all they had been drawn to was prams, coats, boots, hats, and toys.

'Edward was a yellow baby for days before I got him into blue. It's not like you youngsters today being able to find out what you are having.' She held up another yellow and white outfit and Lottie rolled her eyes. It was a lost cause asking her not to shop for her first grandchild.

'We decided that we would not find out until the time,' Lottie said, putting coffee into the pot and a tea bag in a cup for herself.

'I am sure that pleased, Edward, not!' his mother said, 'I am surprised he did not want to know, he hates surprises and not being in control, although I guess you have sussed that one out for yourself?'

Lottie smiled, yes, she had on many occasions. 'I guess I am getting him better trained,' she remarked, and the two women laughed.

'What sort of a baby, was he?' Lottie asked. 'I have not seen any photos of when he was young or at school.' This was the lead that she had hoped she would be able to get in before he came to join them. Photos of Edwards school friends. The housekeeper came into the kitchen and busied herself with the start of lunch. She looked at Lottie, not happy that she had helped herself to the drinks; she would have happily made them if asked.

'Oh, I have some photos somewhere. Come to the spare room and let's have a look. He hates me showing anyone, and well,' she paused, 'any photos of Mitch seem to make him so sad. They all got put away after, you know.' Lottie gave her a loving smile and they made their way up the large Edwardian staircase.

They sat on the bed which was draped in white silk; the spare room was as everything else in the house, perfect. A mix of new and period features, making the house worth the millions she knew Edward had paid for it. Though it was such a big house for his mother to rattle around in alone with just Rosanna the housekeeper for company. But she did not seem to mind.

They sat for a while. Lottie was passed book after book of photos. For the first time Edward's father was on show, but there were very few complete family photos.

'Some old school reports, they make fun reading. Edward did not really like school!' She passed the bundle to Lottie and she skim-read a few.

'Yearbook.' She picked up the bound folder and opened it. 'His last year, oh my, he was so handsome.' She smiled at the photo lovingly. 'He still is to me,' she finished off before passing the book to Lottie.

Edward was dressed in a dinner suit, and although you needed to add another ten or so years onto his age, he really was just as stunning there as he was now. Strong board shoulders, wayward hair, striking eyes. 'All the girls must have loved him,' Lottie said, almost as acceptance that his mother could talk about old girlfriends and she would not get upset.

'They may have swooned over him, but he showed little interest in anything apart from making money, and his fascination for cars!'

'Boys toys,' Lottie said, knowing he still had that interest, and the making-money one.

'We never got to see many girls, even though he was never short of an escort. In fact, the amount of time he spent with some of his friends, Mitch used to say that he was maybe gay!' His mother pulled a face. 'Well, you hear such rumours these days, don't you!'

A sudden flash of sadness came over Lottie when she recalled all the issues Ed had talked about with regards to school. How he was bullied and picked on, how he had been abused and hounded, by older boys until he had met Alex. How he had promised that he would never let any child go through the same hate and hurt his school years had caused him.

'He had friends, though didn't he?' Lottie asked, noticing that none of the faces in the photos stood out for her yet.

'I am not sure if you'd class them as friends, as it has proven over the years that many of them have moved on, and not all kept in touch. I guess that is more because Ed has wanted to distance himself from them.' She carried on passing photos over to Lottie. School trips, holidays, and days out, all captured in colour and held in time.

Lottie carried on looking through the photos, laughing or asking occasional questions that came up from the images she viewed. The first they knew that Ed had arrived back was his footsteps on the top few stairs before he walked into the room.

'What are you two up to?' he asked immediately, coming in and kissing Lottie, and then kissing his mother on the cheek. He picked up one of the photos and quickly put it back in the pile.

'Really, reminiscing on old times?' he asked, not looking too impressed.

'We were just looking to see how sweet you were as a baby!' his mother said.

'Look at those chubby cheeks,' Lottie said, holding up one of the photos she had put to one side.

Ed laughed. 'What about them?' he asked with a fake smile.

'Let's hope Bump inherits those eyes, although the dimples?' she questioned, biting her bottom lip. He sat behind her and put his hands on her stomach.

'Don't listen to your mother, they have broken many a girl's heart!' he smirked back at her talking to his unborn child.

'And if Bump is a girl, would those dimples break every boy's heart?' Lottie asked.

'She will be locked up until she is 40 so we will never know. The first boy that even thinks of trying anything on with her will have me to deal with!'

They all laughed and continued to look through the photos. With the call that lunch was almost ready, they started tidying the photos together. One fell on the floor and Lottie bent down to pick it up. In doing this she twinged her back and gave a little yelp as she sat back up.

'Lottie, are you OK?' Ed quickly jumped back on the bed, sending all the photos flying once more.

'Yes, just pulled my back, I'm fine,' she protested as he tried to get her to lie down. 'Honestly Ed, it's nothing.'

'Stop fussing the poor girl, Edward, these next five months are going to be hard with you as a mother hen,' his mother said in a stern voice.

Edward looked at Lottie as if to ask her again if she was OK and she smiled at him, picking up another photo from the pile still on the bed. He snatched it from her as she laughed at his school uniform.

'How about this one?' His mother passed another large photo over. All lined in a row, a whole school photo, and she looked at the date on the bottom, along with a row of names of the boys who all stood in line.

Quickly she scanned the faces and as if her breath never went down her throat, she put her hand to her mouth.

There he was; the face, the person with the cruel eyes, blond hair and distinct features that were now somehow embedded in Lottie's mind. She scanned the names just before Ed took the photo from her hands.

'They are not that bad!' he said, looking at the photo for a split second, then looking back at his wife. 'Enough!' Ed said, 'Can we eat? I am starving.'

Lottie gave him a loving look, trying to cover up that her stomach was churning inside. The name went over and over in her mind. So much so that she could not face the food that had been left out for them in the kitchen. She tried to eat, but it was just getting stuck in her throat. She was caught between letting on she was in turmoil, or not saying anything until she had got her head around all the information, she tried to eat and was glad when she had been able to help herself so that her plate was not too full.

All the way home and on into the evening she tried to remain as normal as she could. Edward took a call, and then she found time to power up her laptop; she had a name and she wanted to see if anything else would come up, so she typed it in

Alex Girski.

Chapter 14

Late Saturday morning her phone rang. Lottie took the call and smiled at Ed as she walked outside on the balcony into the sunshine. More so that Ed would not hear the conversation she was about to have, than who she was having it with.

'Hi Todd, nice to hear from you,' she said, sitting down on the seat and resting her arm on the table. They had talked via email on the Friday. Lottie had sent him over all the details of what she had found so far and sent him a copy of her mind map, all leading to the same name.

'I can't conclude that he was involved this end, but the drug deal that went down last year can be linked to one of his associates, and he left the country the same day.' Todd paused for breath and Lottie let him continue. 'The LAPD have allowed me access to their DNA files, and I found something – it should come through to you on the work account. One thing that I have found on the body was the same brand of drug, but interesting something you picked up from the girl in the club is the injection mark, on the top of the neck.'

Lottie took in a breath and sighed.

'Is it the same as you thought for...?' He stopped and she said softly, 'Mitch, yes. I found something on the photos; the skin was so badly decomposed that I could not see, but the autopsy had picked it up.'

'Same MO, same DNA, it all looks like you are right,' he said. 'So how are you going to take it forward?'

'I want to meet him,' she said knowing that she had given it a lot of thought.

'No, Lottie why the hell would you do that? You have more than enough to open the case with the police and then let them deal with it.' She could tell by Todd's voice he was not impressed with her suggestion. 'What the hell would meeting him face to face prove?'

'I wanted to get some fresh DNA to be absolute,' she replied.

'Get the police to arrest him then they can swab him, and you will have it.' Todd almost pleaded with her.

'He never seems to get arrested. Someone else always seems to take the fall.' She had been looking up things online and the various police reports she could find but nothing. Although she knew that her own husband was one for evading the police with the scrapes that he had got into; it seems money can do that sort of thing.

'I could let the mob know where he was and then they would deal with him,' Todd remarked, knowing that people in New York were still not happy with the deal they had been spun, and the fact that he had made it away with over two million dollars from the drug deal that was intercepted by the police.

'I want to be sure so that I can give Edward and his mother a reason for Mitch's death, as well as the parents of the two innocent victims in all of this,' she remarked, looking towards the lounge where Ed was smiling through at her, unaware of the conversation.

'Oh, Lottie don't do anything stupid. If you are sure of the connection then say something – what does Ed think of your idea?' She was silent. 'Oh he doesn't know, I take it from the silence.'

'And you know why,' she said.

'And so, he bloody well should be worried, Lottie, because I am for you,' he said bluntly. 'Should I tell him, because I will if I think that you are going to do something stupid.'

'Hey, I trust you with this, so please trust me,' she said, getting quite upset now that he would stop her so close to getting the answers she needed. 'Anyway, I should let you go. I have taken so much of your time already.' She wanted to finish the conversation before it got out of hand, or she cried for whatever reason, as Ed was walking out to join her.

Todd gave her one final warning and she said she would email him later in the week, trying to make light of it now that Ed was in earshot. As she put down the phone, she smiled at Ed.

'Is he OK?' Ed asked, sitting by her side.

'Yes, he was just as shocked to hear about Eric, that's why I called him, to catch him up.' She was totally lying.

'Oh right, have you made any progress?' he asked, and she knew that she needed to lie again.

'The police have a few more enquires to make. The professor took the lead, so I will know on Monday if he has any doubts, or any leads he wants to follow.' She jumped up from the chair. 'Fancy a cuppa?' she asked, and he pulled her back down.

'I fancy you,' he said, kissing her. 'I still have not forgiven you for looking at all the photos while I was not around!' He smiled.

'You were such a cute baby, such chubby little cheeks.' She gently pinched one of his cheeks with her finger and thumb and he started to tickle her until she let go, giving out a scream for him to stop. 'Stop it,' she finally said, getting back up to make a drink. He flicked her backside as she walked off and she jumped to avoid his hand. She was not able to get away that fast and he ran in front of her, stopping her from going into the room.

'Oh, and I guess you have always been this beautiful?' he said, kissing her neck.

'Might have been,' she replied.

'Well, I don't think I can argue with that answer!' He kissed her again and she welcomed his arms around her.

Mrs B had already put on the kettle and they sat chatting after the drink had been made. It was some time before Ed changed the conversation back to work.

'Lottie, I hate to say this, and I am not quite sure how to say it but,' he paused, 'I need to go to Australia.' He looked up from his drink, knowing that she would say that she was not going with him. 'I don't want to leave you here and I know that you will say that you don't want to leave your work, so I am stuck as what to do.'

'Are you telling me you need me to come?' she asked, not quite sure what his angle was.

'No, I am debating losing the company if I don't go, but if you will not come then I am prepared to.'

'Why would you do that?' she asked.

'Because being with my family is more important than striking million-dollar deals,' he said as if he was only talking about a few hundred pounds.

'So, you are blackmailing me to come with you, my work or your business?' she asked.

'No that was not at all what I said. I was asking for your advice, and it is our business, not just mine.' He tried to keep her calm; he could see the reaction in her eyes.

'It did not sound like you needed advice, Edward, it felt like an ultimatum.' She took a sip of her tea and looked him in the eye.

'Well, then let me reword it. The Australian shipping business I bought four months ago has had an offer to buy it out. So if I don't go then I cash in, but I am fed up of losing so many people's jobs just by getting rid of companies at a whim. I have a buyer who wants to keep it running, wants me to be a silent partner and just fund and reward profit, but I must go over. The opposing buyer has put a clause down that the deal must be done in person or else they will fight to just take it. My team have tried everything, even getting them over here, but I have one month to settle it either way,' he paused. 'The only way I go over is with you.'

'And if the doctors say I cannot fly?' she said, making another reason not to go.

'Then it is a done deal. I don't go. That is non-negotiable and the 400 or so workers who lose their jobs will just have to know that my family came first. But, well, I sort of asked the doctor on the phone, and he said that as long as you are OK at this early stage, he could not see a reason.' He cringed at the thought that he had already looked into it without mentioning it to her, but she did not react. There was a pause for Lottie to think about her reply.

'So, I don't go, people lose out. Not fair to put that pressure onto me,' she said, slightly annoyed that he had.

'Cards on the table Lottie, no lies, no secrets. It is how it is, business is hard. When I struck the deal, I put in your name too, so not only do I have to sign, but you do too.' He took her hand. 'I have planned to compensate every worker, and totally understand that this is not fair, but I never thought the deal would turn like this. The company can ride the financial storm if I have to take the second option, we worked out about 6 million all told, but I wanted to start to build futures not just for us, and Bump,' the very word made the edges of his lips curl up in a smile, 'but also put some trust in the workers knowing that the Dean Incorporated brand was a job for life, or as long as they wanted it to be. Not how it was when, at the drop of a hat or literally in the past a turn of a gambling card, I made a decision that affected someone apart from me. I am growing up and facing my responsibility, finally and that is down to you, and I am sorry if that makes you feel pressured, but it is the truth.'

Wow, Lottie thought to herself, that really was a therapy session all rolled into one outburst. Put so well, how could she not go? He really had thought it through, checked out all his options, and now she had to make the final call.

'What happened to me being a silent partner?' she asked.

'Sorry, I guess I over-looked this one, or maybe before my situation changed, I did not care, but I just have a gut feeling.'

She interrupted him. 'A conscience?' she asked.

'Yes, maybe that now, as I know that family is the most important thing. If I lost it all, I would be devastated. A thing I have never considered when I buy people out, or meaningfully ruin them. I guess I never looked further than the bank balance for so many years. I lost any sight of that, if I ever had sight of it in the first place.' He smiled at her. 'I guess a lot of people have the right to be pissed off with me. You lose your job, you lose your wife and children. You lose everything.'

'So, I say that I am not going, and it turns me into the bad-ass businesswoman, the image of who you are trying to shake off?' She was not mad, just annoyed that she totally had his point.

They had a conversation about keeping aspects of the business, making things work for 'the good', like the hospital being for the service men and women and Lottie's trust fund set up for the music scholars. In a simple way her funding the fashion house; it was never going to make her rich, but would employ people and make them happy and make something for her to leave her children if nothing else.

'So, what is your plan?' she asked.

He held up his hands. 'I am totally looking to you for help and advice.'

She took a deep breath. This messed up what she wanted to do. It would take out at least a week if not more of her time. Time that she knew would allow things to go cold and now she had the strongest lead, a name, a face, something to finally put this to rest, she would have to put it to one side, again.

'Lottie, what are you thinking?' Ed asked, knowing that in her way she took all the information and turned it around in her head every way before she could give him an answer. He remembered her mind mapping, the way that she methodically worked things out. He asked if she needed any more information before she could make up her mind.

'I was wondering what time we could go to the doctors, to see if we can go, then I need to make up my mind.' She really did not want to go, but she almost felt that she had to. 'I guess then we take it from there. Do I have a week to sort out work?' she asked, knowing that she could not put her plan into action that fast without it going wrong.

'If we can go, I want to do it as soon as possible.' He smiled at her, holding her eyes with his.

'Which in real speak means the day after next,' she said with a pedantic grin.

'Or about three hours after you know it is ok to fly!' he responded holding his breath for her to come back at him.

'So, you have already booked it all?' She knew he had, she just wanted him to say it out loud. There was no way that he would not have wanted to dominate and control the decision, or the outcome.

'Sort of!' He winced again through his mind's eye.

'So, you convince me that your business morals are changing for the better, Mr Dean, but you still can't shrug off that controlling instinct that you have?' She smiled at him as confirmation that she was not angry, but she was wary of his tactics.

'Guess so!' was all he replied.

'Well then you had better let me know what is going to happen so I can rearrange my life if I can fly,' and she emphasised the 'if.'

Edward spoke to the professor on the way to their early morning appointment. Lottie tried to listen to the conversation to see how much information he gave Ed about Eric's death, but luckily he did not say anything. Even the gesture that Ed would boost the funds to help with the time that Lottie would be away as a sweetener did not allow him to break his professional code, which she took as a sign of relief. Anyway, what could he tell him, more than she had not? Every other thing she suspected, or had as fact, was in her head, or shared with Todd and no one else.

The more she thought about a week or so off, the more she hoped it would allow her to get a plan into place, give her real time to think about it. She could keep in touch via emails and phone if she had to; this modern world would allow her to work both for the centre and her charities no matter where she was.

Holding hands, they walked into the doctor's office. The young receptionist obviously was not used to being called in before 8am; she had blurry eyes and less make-up than normal, but when you pay the doctor's fees, ringing on a Sunday night to insist that they see you the next day seems to work, if you throw your cash at it. So, they went in and sat down.

'Well, Mrs Dean, everything seems to be progressing well. Flying carries risk to everyone, but I advise that you do not do the whole flight in one go, it is a long way. I advise you to break the journey at least once, if not more. Mr Dean, as you are flying privately, I am sure this can be arranged?' Ed nodded. He had already arranged for two stops, both for a few days and nights, that was why the trip was going to take two weeks, a fact Lottie was not too impressed with at first.

The doctor continued to give her a list of do and don'ts whilst flying. The long compression socks caused her to smile at Ed and when the doctor was not listening, she whispered, 'Very sexy!' and he smiled and replied, 'Could be if that is all you have on!'

'Shall we have a look at Junior, then see how we are? From the outside you're growing well, and a closer look will ensure that everything is perfect at this stage.' Lottie had noticed that in the last week she was developing a stomach, more than just a bump, and the last vain attempt to wear her jeans was now long down the line.

The gel was cool, and she lay relaxing, looking at the screen once more.

Ed joined her with as much enthusiasm as before; although he was now ready and aware of what he would see, it never stopped the lump in his throat and the tears from rising in his eyes.

The radiographer pointed to the screen. 'Bump is sucking its thumb,' and then she pointed to the heartbeat. 'Still not wanting to know about him or her?'

'No, unless you want to,' Ed said. Lottie shook her head, although she was sure she could see what she needed to as the ultra-sound passed quickly around the side of her stomach; it gave her a good view.

During years at Uni many aspects of pathology had led her to lectures of all sorts, although she wouldn't say she was by any means sure, she smiled and said to herself, 'Something in common with your father then.' She could not hold the laugh inside.

'What?' Edward said, 'What is so funny?'

'Nothing, just happy to see Bump is OK.' She smiled, and he kissed her forehead.

'It's awesome, can I upload the picture?' he asked, and the radiographer nodded replying, 'Of course.'

Ed left the room allowing Lottie to get dressed and she chatted to the nurse and the radiographer who asked, 'Dr Dean, I may have given the game away to you, with regards to the sex of your bump, I am sorry if I did.'

Lottie thought that she must have seen her face at the point and replied, 'I have a good idea, but I am happy not to have it confirmed.'

'I thought that you would, although I have to say, it was quite easy to identify!' She smiled at Lottie, getting her drift. 'Without sounding too crude, you have a fine healthy baby who is growing well in all aspects. You will notice in the next few weeks as you start to accommodate it,' she said, trying hard to avoid saying the gender.

'So here comes being fat!' Lottie smiled, doing up her final button on her crisp white blouse that was out over the top of her linen trousers.

'Blooming, I believe the term is, although it is important that you eat right. No matter how hard you try you will gain weight. I am sure that you do not need a healthy lifestyle guide from me. Just keep doing what you are doing, light exercise, although with flying away I would not recommend any high-risk sports Down Under such as surfing, rock climbing, cross country bush running or parachuting!'

'You have no fear of that, even if Bump was not with me!' Lottie replied as they walked out of the door to meet up with the doctor and Ed.

So that was it, they were off. If they had not packed it by the time the car was due to take them to the airport, they would have to 'buy it out there,' was the reply when Lottie said that she really did not know what to take, as none of her summer clothes would fit her. There was no time to shop now.

The Dean Incorporated jet was standing by and the next time their feet would land on soil they would be in Saudi Arabia. Two nights in a five-star hotel not far from the airport. The first stop consisted of a lot of sleeping and sitting in the sun for Lottie, Ed filled his time on the computer, phone, emails, or asking if she needed anything. Back up in the sky and they travelled to Malaysia. They had three days planned there, and nothing was stopping them from leaving earlier, apart from Ed had wanted to see some of the country and enjoy the time they had. Lottie found that she could not say anything to the contrary, as her need to be at home was something she was not sharing with anyone yet.

It was hot and muggy, hard to sleep even in the beautiful, air-conditioned room. Lottie lay on top of the bed after taking a cool shower just before they were due to go down to the hotel restaurant for a meal. She lay naked trying to cool down when she felt a small flutter in her stomach.

Not a pain but almost as if she had popcorn in her stomach. She rubbed her hand over the bump but nothing else came again. She held her breath to see if it was her breathing, but nothing. She knew that she was a bit early at 16 weeks to feel Bump move, or so the doctor had said, but she was sure something was moving around. She kept her hand in place and sat up to see if her movement spurred Bump on.

'You OK?' Ed asked, walking into the room with a towel wrapped round his waist, a look of concern seeing her holding her stomach.

'Um, I swear I felt Bump move.' She placed her hand on the area the movement had come from.

'You're not in pain?' Edward jumped to the conclusion again that something was wrong.

'No, quite the opposite, it was a weird feeling, knowing me it was just hunger pangs!' She placed her hand on her stomach again, but nothing. 'No, Bump must have gone back to sleep.' She rubbed her stomach and lay back down. Ed sat next to her on the bed and started to kiss her stomach.

'Maybe if I talk to your tummy that will wake Bump up?' He started to land gentle kisses on her stomach.

'And maybe if you kiss lower.' She pulled his towel loose to rub his upper thigh. 'Maybe he will wake up?' She insinuated towards Edward's dick, that almost jumped at the suggestion.

'Mrs Dean, you are just so incorrigible. We don't have the time!' He looked at the clock on the side table.

'Anyone would think that you don't want me?' she playfully said, knowing it would provoke a reply.

'Never.' He moved up her body to kiss her full lips. 'I find it hard to keep my hands off you all the time.' He kissed her neck and moved his body so that she could feel his growing desire pushing against her leg.

'They will hold the table for us!' She started to kiss his neck and rub herself into him, knowing the friction of her skin on the towel would stimulate him further. 'Or we could get room service?' she muttered in his ear.

She pulled the towel free from between their bodies and allowed her soft skin to rub on him. She rubbed her hands over his strong firm shoulders and down the centre of his back where she scratched her nails up his spine, not hard but enough for him to flare his nostrils.

'Really Lottie, you are persuasive in ways I cannot explain.' He ducked his head down and took her nipple in his mouth. He licked it with his tongue and gently blew air over it until it was pert and erect. The area around her nipple had grown darker in the last few weeks, another change in her body he could not resist, knowing she was carrying his child. Following the line of her hip he moved his hand down towards her sex, gently rubbing the neatly trimmed area, carrying on suckling her nipples one at a time.

Lottie pushed her head back in the pillow to enjoying the hot pulsing sensation that was travelling from her chest to her pubic bone. His strong but gentle fingers starting to rub inside her sex lips, finding the nub of her sex excited and aroused with the nerves feeling extra sensitive. She was wet, allowing his finger to gently slide into her without any objection. She parted her legs a little to give him better access and as a silent gesture that she wanted more; she wanted him deep inside her. Fluttering kisses down her stomach, he obliged and put another finger into her, following the stroking in and out of her. As he kissed along her stomach and hip line, he slightly speeded up his hand. Lottie tilted her hips again as she could feel each thrust getting deeper the wetter her sex became. Her breathing was speeding up, and she could feel her chest and neck start to burn with the increase of blood around her body from her quickening heartbeat.

Edward licked her open pussy, with one flick of his tongue allowing him to taste her. Wet and sweet, the smell of her fresh skin filled his lungs and he pulled out his fingers and licked them to get a better taste. She groaned slightly with the withdrawal of his thrusting digits, but they were soon replaced with his tongue mouth probing and thrusting into her. As he sucked her, the blood increased to the area, heightening her need for him to fill her. He put his hands under her arse to lift her, allowing him to go in as far as he could. He massaged her butt cheeks and gently circled her arsehole with his thumbs, gently dipping in and out of the delicate tissue every now and then.

The sensation of his mouth, with the heightened sensation of him touching the intimate area around her arse made her quickly grip the sheets; her orgasm was starting too soon for her, but she could not control it. She pulled in her stomach muscles to try to gain some composure, but with a wave of searing heat she gasped out and came deep inside. Timing it to perfection one of his thumbs intruded into her arse, reaching a sensitive spot he knew she had there.

It felt like the whole of her lower body was shaking, spasming violently as he continued to suck, lick, and penetrate her. Grabbing his head, not to stop him but to prolong the pulsing of her sphincter she cried out his name and pushed her hips up to him with the same rhythm he was using on her. She slowly came down from her high; he was just kissing her hips now, allowing her to languish in the afterglow of her climax. Moving slowly back up her body, he whispered in her ear, 'Mrs Dean, I believe you have come all over my face. You should taste it, you are so sweet,' and he kissed her, passing her own juices to her with the force of his mouth.

'Roll over,' he said, telling her to go onto her stomach. He pulled his body up to give her space to move and when she was on her front, he pulled her up onto all fours. 'Now let me show you how much I want you.' He parted her legs and positioned himself behind her, using his hand to spread her wet come over her entrance to ensure he did not hurt on his first thrust. Using one powerful arm to hold his weight off her and the other to keep her hips up he directed his cock into her, the pre-cum mixing with her juices to make his way easier.

Although a direct hit, it was only the swollen head of his cock she felt open her lips, and with a small rocking movement he pushed further forwards until she knew he was going to fill her in the next few seconds. He was rock hard, pulsing around her already-heightened nerves and muscles. From this position she knew he would not give her all his length, but his pace increased and she could feel his heavy ball sack hitting her backside.

'You have made me late for supper, Mrs Dean, and under any other circumstances you would be spanked for that,' he said, grunting out with the rhythm of his thrusting body. He had not showed her any acts of punishing sex since she had announced she was expecting. They had talked about it and Edward had shown a real concern for this type of rough sex. Although Lottie understood, she missed their games, but any sex was better than the abstinence he had shown before. She was content that he just lived out his virtual fantasy talking about it, although she secretly relished the day these acts would come back in a few months' time.

He raised up on both knees, holding her at the hips. Sweat dripped down his chest, joining the glistening skin on his wife's back below him.

Lottie tossed her hair back and it stuck to her in parts where she too was feeling the heat of the room and the passion that they were creating. Ed licked his lips. He watched as her pale skin slapped against him. The muscles in her back flexed and contracted as she moved with him, her low groans implicating that she was on her way to a climax again. He felt her tighten up around his cock that was as deep as he dared go into her.

'Don't you dare come again without me, Mrs Dean.' He leant over her and said in her ear, 'Control it, Lottie, just a few moments more.' He gritted his teeth, knowing he should follow his own advice as he was about to burst inside her.

'Oh, Ed I can't hold on,' Lottie gasped out as the heat surged between her legs and she closed her fists with a handful of silk sheets to try to take her mind away from it.

He lifted his hand, about to slap her backside out of instinct, carried away in the moment. He opened his eyes to bring him back to the present time just before it made contact. It took him off balance and he pushed all his weight into her. Her arms just held, but the deep thrust made her scream, and she fell onto her elbows.

'Shit, sorry,' he said, pulling back up. Control yourself for fucks sake, Dean, he said to himself.

'It's OK, please Ed, I need to, ohh...' She never got the words out, and she arched her back and shook as a second climax racked through her.

He could not help but speed up; her throbbing around him drove him insane and he had to release – he was desperate to. Holding her hips he furiously dictated her body backwards and forwards, impaled on his hard cock. Grunting with each push, urgent to the point that his balls hurt, he had to release before his lungs stopped working. His mind was in turmoil; he didn't want to hurt his beautiful wife, limp and helpless beneath him, but his carnal lust to pump her full and his selfish need for satisfaction only delayed his coming. Never before had he found it hard to release. He tried to clear his mind and almost as if she sensed his urgency, she shouted out to him, 'Give it to me, Mr Dean, come for me please, I beg you!' As if the invitation had been long-awaited, he obliged her request with a hard push. He exploded as come forced its way into her, so full it leaked back out and made her so wet he slipped out, directing his last few thrusts up her back. The thick white liquid spread out over her back and down her butt cheeks as he grasped himself to ease the last few drops out.

'Oh God, Lottie I'm sorry, I just...' He flopped down by her side. Unwrapping their legs, Lottie turned to face him. 'You just what, Mr Dean? Fucked your wife?' she smiled playfully with her words.

'Made love to her, Mrs Dean, for the record,' he corrected. 'Because I love you.' He kissed her.

'And it is because I love you that I want to be fucked by you!' she said. 'I will not break you know and you...' She ran her hand along his thick bicep, that was glistening with sweat. 'You should not forget that. The intimacy of making love to you only increases my desire and the passion to be occasionally fucked by you. You're not the only one who needs to be consumed by lust.'

'Yes, but I can be so rough when I get carried away.' He expressed concern as she wrapped her arms around him.

'And I will always tell you if you do.' She kissed his nose and he wrinkled it up.

'I love you, Mrs Dean.' He rubbed his hand over her shoulders and pulled her into his arms more. 'No one will ever understand just how much I love you.'

'I love you too, Mr Dean.' They lay for a few moments in their body heat. Ed closed his eyes, feeling truly relaxed. Lottie listened to his heart returning to a normal beat, safe and secure in the cocoon of his embrace.

'There!' She quickly jumped, and Ed almost bit his tongue he moved away so fast. 'Give me your hand.' She took it anyway without him even offering it. 'Did you feel it?' she asked, pressing his hand into her stomach.

'Shit, yes.' His smile filled his face as he looked at her. 'Yes, yes, I can. Do it again, Lottie?' he asked.

'It's not me doing anything, it's our bump!'

Once they arrived at Sydney airport, Lottie was pleased to get out and stretch her legs, but it was not for long as the car arrived to collect them and take them to the Sydney Hilton hotel. It was just Ed and herself on the trip; Phil and Pete had been left in the UK, a few weeks off she was sure they were pleased to take.

Liz had texted her several times asking how it was going, and she was sure it was for Phil's information more than her own, although Ed would be keeping up with Pete no question during one of his many phone calls.

They were rushed past check-in, and as Lottie walked through the entrance she marvelled at the hotel's plush surroundings. As always, the best rooms were on the top floor and this master king-size suite was no different. As they got into the glass lift the city came alive around them. Opening the door, they walked into the first room and continued to enjoy the panoramic views from every room they walked through. Lottie marvelled at the busy harbour; she could clearly see the Sydney Harbour Bridge and Ed informed her that in the other direction was Bondi Beach. She made her way through the dining area, past the marble table set with crystal glasses and gold-plated cutlery. The luxurious bathroom had a freestanding spa bath, much like the one in their apartment and it had a direct view overlooking the city and she smiled at the thought of lying there with Ed looking out onto the night sky.

'Like it?' he asked her as he plunged down onto the bed and relaxed, putting his arms behind the back of his head. She stopped looking around the room and focused on him.

'I Like what's on it!' she said, standing between his legs and then flopping down on top of him with a thud.

'Careful,' he said, catching her before she squashed her growing bump on his toned stomach that was half covered with a white polo shirt that had come loose from his casual dark brown linen trousers, showing his V line along his hip bones. She rolled her eyes as he lowered her to his side.

'The pool here is great, and the gym and spa will open whenever you want,' he said. He had stayed here several times in the past when on business before, but this was the first time he intended to actually see the city during his stay.

'Um, how many other women have you wined and dined in this room then?' She shuffled up the bed to get a better position, leaning with her hand under her head, fiddling with his top button and looking directly into his large blue eyes.

'Hundreds!' He smiled back at her and she playfully slapped his chest. 'None! That is the truth,' he added as a sweetener to put his joke to rest. He was not saying he'd been the height of chastity on previous trips, but he never took women back to any of his rooms unless he was in a long-term relationship with them, of which there had been very few, only Caroline to be exact. But he had never taken her on any business trips; no need to have done, she had been his toy not his partner.

'Hungry?' Lottie asked, looking over at the mini bar area.

'Maybe, are you?' he replied, rubbing her back and shoulders.

'What's on the menu?' she asked, undoing the next button down on his shirt and fluttering her eyelashes at him.

'My god, I have married a nymphomaniac!' He grabbed her hand.

'And your complaint is?' She asked him to make his point as he had never complained about the frequency and intimacy of their sex life.

'No complaints, baby girl, this is all yours.' He pointed to his body and she smiled biting her lip. 'And you get it faster when you bite that lip, you know it works on me every time!' He kissed her, and she straddled him, nuzzling into his neck.

The knock on the door interrupted her and he pulled her off to go to answer it. Lottie tutted loudly and said out loud as he walked off, 'Not this time obviously!'

She got off the bed and following him into the sitting room. He was talking to a man dressed in the hotel livery who was taking a large bottle of champagne, a fruit bowl and a huge bunch of flowers from a trolley he had pushed in.

'Mrs Dean.' The man nodded over to Lottie and she smiled. 'Compliments of the hotel, and if there is anything I can do during your stay with us then please let me know.' His deep Australian accent was warm and sincere. 'Mr Walker, hotel senior manager.' He put out his hand for Lottie to shake, which she did.

'Thank you,' Lottie said as the guy left the room, and he turned and smile to her. 'You're welcome,' was the reply as he closed the door behind him.

'Mmm, they smell divine.' She took a deep breath from the fragrant array of reds and pinks of the roses and various flowers that made up the display. She pulled off one small rose and placed it in her hair that was secured on top of her head.

'Still hungry?' Ed asked. 'For food,' he added in quickly as she walked towards him with a glint in her eye. She smiled and nodded.

'Shall we have a quick walk outside to see what is about? It's quite early for a formal dinner. I wanted to catch an hour in the gym before that any way, if you wanted to catch some sleep?'

'I'm not tired.' She had caught up on any lack of sleep that the time delay may have given her on the plane. It was only mid-morning according to their body clock, another good reason for stopping off in several places; it did not give them any jet lag, or seemed not to anyway. 'I could go to that swimming pool you were on about while you train,' she said, grabbing her bag and putting her flip flops back on then smoothing down her top that hung loosely over her knee-length shorts.

The city was alive and as they walked down the street from the hotel hand in hand, Lottie felt somehow free, no looking over your shoulder for someone, or having Pete or Phil walking a few steps behind. Although she had pleaded not to be away for so long, she could now see how Ed had been right, and that the break was something they both deserved, and unknowingly needed.

People went about their business, but as normal occasional women would look at Ed and smile. She had taken months to get use to this, but she could really see their point; he was drop-dead gorgeous so why not look? She looked down at his hand firmly in hers. After all, she thought, I am the one on the end of his arm.

Like a magpie to anything shiny, Lottie stopped outside an expensive jewellery shop admiring the glittering array of precious stones and metal.

'Like anything?' Ed asked. She knew she had to be careful to say yes as they would be in to buy it knowing him.

'No just looking,' she said. Everything was beautiful, she would be hard pressed to choose if she had to.

At the end of the road a cafe had chairs outside. Ed stopped to look at the menu and they decided to go in. A seat at the window allowed them to look at the life passing them by. Lottie had never really enjoyed eating on a street; it always made her rush her food and he remembered this when the young waiter asked if they wanted to sit outside.

Lottie sat back and put her napkin on the plate. Her salad had been light but had filled her. Ed had filled up on a large steak, something she said he would regret if he was going to train in a few hours, but nevertheless, he finished it off. Resisting the urge to have a pudding, although the ice cream did look so delicious, Lottie declined when asked. They casually sat and chatted over their tea and coffee. How normal was this? Ed thought as he smiled and laughed and loved looking at the woman who sat opposite him.

Momentarily their conversation turned to the meeting the following day and what they needed to do. One thing Lottie knew was that she needed a new suit, or something more professional than she had packed any way. None of her old office outfits fitted now, so she had not bothered to even bring them.

'Ed I can cope. You go to the gym and I will see you back in the pool in a couple of hours. I know where you are if I need you, OK?' she asked when she had suggested that she shop on her own for a while. He protested and she looked under her eyes. She was not a child, she would not beg, but did she ever need to. He gave in, outlining strict instructions that made her smile as if her mother were telling her to be back in time for tea.

The shopping mall was huge, every shop you could ever need, selling every item you could ever want, or buy, or clutter your life with. Lottie noticed mothers and fathers were pushing prams, young children being led by the hand, some laughing, most screaming but it all made her smile. Entering a lady's fashion shop, a young man sat on a stool playing a flute by the entrance. Lottie stopped to listen; he was good. He had his eyes half-closed, getting lost in his own music, a hand-written note on a card next to the instrument case intending to catch money said, 'spare me the change to go to university – or just a coffee to keep me playing – Thank you.'

Almost straightaway she went for her purse, then as if an apparition came over her Ed's voice said from his pre-shop lecture, 'Don't get your purse out in public!' But she wanted to give him something. She could put some money in her pocket and then when she came out, she could give it to him. Then she saw the coffee shop; she could give him both, coffee and money. She walked over and waited to be served. When she paid, she had very little of Australian money, but a bunch of US dollars, for some reason. Ed had said that many countries accept US currency more than their own. She quickly counted it out, not sure how much it was if it was converted to pounds, but anything she needed to buy would go on the card anyway if she gave away too much.

She walked back over to him and listened to him play for a few moments until he stopped.

'Well played,' she said, handing him the coffee.

'Gee, thank you miss, most kind of you.' His accent was not Australian but English.

'Are you from the UK?' she asked.

He nodded, taking a sip of the hot drink. 'Originally, my folks moved out here when I was nine, but...' he stopped short, not carrying on. 'You on holiday?' he asked, daring to take another drink as if he was so thirsty, he could not wait for it to cool.

'Sort of, some business too.' She smiled.

'What you do, it must be music, no one else stops to listen, they look as they walk by but only someone who likes music really stops,' he said, giving her a cheeky smile that instantly made her warm to him.

'I play the piano, not as a job but I enjoy working with youngsters who have talent.' She moved out of the way of people who were trying to get past her. 'Where did you live in the UK?' she asked, following on from his previous answer.

'Brighton. Still have an aunt there, she has a guest house on the sea front. I should really go back, but I wanted to give getting in to Uni here one more go first.' He was able to take a larger mouthful of coffee now.

'Do you have to pay to get in, does it work differently here than at home?' she asked, not sure how old he was, but he looked older than late teens.

'I dropped out when,' he paused again, 'my parents died in a car crash and I sort of lost it for a few months, so I have to try to get back in.'

Her heart felt suddenly sad, then Ed's voice came back again, like the ghost of Christmas present. 'Don't go taking to strangers on street corners either!'

'Sorry I don't know why I said that to you, I am not trying to make you feel sorry for me. I'm fine, please miss, thank you for the coffee. I should let you shop.' He smiled, put down the drink and picked up his flute, wiping his lips to carry on playing. He gave her one last smile and then the tune started to play. Lottie was not sure whether to put the money in his case, she did not want it to fly away, or be taken out by some street urchin as Ed had put it. She smiled back at him and went into the shop as she had first planned.

Browsing the racks, she could still hear him play. She had seen an outfit but needed to try it on; the skirt was slim-fitting, but she was sure a size larger would accommodate Bump for now. She was wrong, and disappointed that the skirt would not do up. The young assistant offered to help her. As they chatted Lottie mentioned the boy playing and the assistant replied, 'Paul, he is lovely, plays here as many days as he can. A part of me hopes he does not get the money to go to university so that we don't have to let him go, he has a CD with some things he recorded at home. I got one for my mom for her birthday.' She changed the subject and carried on with her intended work. 'Let me get you something that I think you will like, and it should fit, I have a few things in mind.' She took the garments from Lottie's hands and went off to another side of the shop.

Lottie sat on the couch and heard her phone bleep. She smiled, no guessing who that is. She replied she was in a shop just getting an outfit and she was fine and would not be long. Ed texted back a reply that she read and then put the phone back in her bag before the young girl arrived back.

Several dresses both for business and some evening wear too. Most of them fitted and Lottie was tempted to get them all. One of the dresses was drop-waist and pastel blue, short sleeves, but had a cropped top to go over it. It fitted all the right places but gave her room to move, and a few more weeks to expand! It felt light, nice and when she put it on, it made her look as the assistant quoted, 'Business yummy mummy to be!'

'I'll take it,' Lottie said, going back to take it off. 'In fact, I will have these other three as well.' The young girl smiled triumphantly and walked off with the items. In the privacy of the changing room, she quickly scribbled her name and the name of the hotel on her card that she had in her purse. 'I would love a CD if you have one spare,' she added at the bottom of the address. It was one of the Dean Charity cards Edward had made for her. 'Have you got a rubber band?' she asked as she handed the assistant the last dress at the counter.

'Sure do.' She took the dress ready to fold and put it in a bag. She gave Lottie the band and walked to the till, Lottie followed wrapping the band around a bundle of notes and her card. She paid for her clothes and took the bag from the girl, thanking her for her help.

Walking back out of the shop, Lottie noticed a few more coins in his case, but not much. She stood and got his attention for a moment and he stopped.

'Pleasure to have listened to you, Paul,' she said, and he looked at her with an enquiring face as to how she knew his name. He noticed the shop bag and must have put the two facts together, then he smiled and laughed.

'You have been talking to my girls!' he replied, and she nodded. 'They usually supply me with coffee if no one has been so kind as you...?' he said, with a question for her name.

'Lottie,' she informed him. 'Maybe I can get you another some time?' She handed him the bundle and walked away before he could say or do anything to follow her. If he wanted to get in touch then he could, if she could help him, then she knew she would. There must have been short of

$500 in his hand. He looked back up the street but the bustle of everyone had made her disappear out of view. He read her card.

She had asked that Edward be told she had arrived back and that she would go for a swim. Dutifully the receptionist called the gym where the staff would let him know.

After hanging up the clothes, she grabbed her bikini and covered up with the hotel dressing gown, which was the normal three sizes too big. Feeling silly in the lift she quickly made her way to the spa and dived into the changing rooms without too many people looking at her. The pool was surrounded by glass, some of which were doors opening out to let the Sydney breeze gently run through. The water was warm, and she slipped into the shallow end allowing her head to go under the water. As she came back up for air, she brushed her soaking hair away from her face and opened her eyes.

She held the side and allowed her feet to rise to the top; floating she took stock of the day, closing her eyes. She would tell Ed about Paul. He would go off on one for sure chatting to a stranger, but it was her cash after all, no harm done. He seemed genuine, unless he was in with the girls in the shop and that was their usual ploy to rob gullible tourists out of their money.

Opening her eyes, she could see a tall man walking along the far side of the pool in front of her. His hair was wet, freshly showered, and she remained still and admired him from a distance. His muscles rippled with every step and his smile was kind but alluring at the same time. Two young girls behind her who were lying on reclining chairs giggled, and she could only think that they were getting the same eye candy that she was.

He paused on the edge of the water and the splashing noise confirmed he had performed a perfect dive to get in. She continued to float, feeling the sudden movement of the water from the entrance of the Adonis at the deep end.

Using his powerful arms, Ed stayed under the water, swimming towards his prey. She had seen him, so he would not startle her. He had also noted the attention of the girls behind her, but they were not his quarry. Letting out some of the air from his lungs, he was only a few feet away when he reached out and grabbed her from underneath and round the waist. Although his ears were submerged he heard her laugh and give out a scream as the water covered her face.

'Edward, you rat!' she said as they both surfaced together. His watery lips sealed hers to prevent her from scolding him further as he kissed her. He used one hand to wipe his face, still supporting her in the water with the other. Lottie shook her head like a wet dog, splashing him and getting more water in his eyes. 'Got you, Mrs Dean!' he said. 'Rat, am I?' She confirmed it with a 'Yes!' and a flick of water back in his drying face. 'Hey!' he said in protest.

'Serves you right!' She laughed as he spun her round in the pool, and she noticed the look on the girls' faces now that they realised he had not been looking at them when he first arrived in the room.

They swam up and down several times. Lottie relished the gentle exercise but placed her arms around Edwards's neck as he towed her back to the shallow end one final time. She got out and used a large white towel to dry herself before sitting on one of the spare reclining chairs on poolside, laying back she put the towel over the back of the chair and watched Ed swim off. Within a second the waiter had asked her if she wanted a drink, and she ordered some juice.

As she rubbed the white absorbent cloth over her stomach, Ed's eyes welled up. Bump stuck far out over the top of her blue and pink bikini. She had worn that one the day after they got married; he remembered it well as the same night he had dived into the pool and come up under her and pulled the cords at the side relieving her of the clothing, before they made love in the water under cover of darkness. His dick twitched at the thought, and to be honest if they had not had an audience, he would have done it again today, but instead he had to swim off face down to hide the attention his member would have if he got out of the pool right now. He was rock hard.

He did four more lengths of the pool to make sure his dick was flaccid and still hiding in his shorts. He never used the steps to get out, he lifted his bulk out and jumped up in one full movement, creating another giggle from the girls sitting not too far away. He took the towel from the back of the chair and dried his hair, but not before he had dribbled some water onto Lottie's stomach.

'Pig!' she said, trying to reach out for him, but he moved too fast. He knelt by her side and wiped the water off her stomach.

'A rat and a pig, all in one day. I would like to think more lovable rouge!' He gently kissed her stomach once it was dry. 'What do you think, Bump?' he asked, looking down to where he had just kissed. He stood up to kiss her lips, making the girls behind them giggle once more.

'You have a fan base there!' Lottie said when his face was about an inch away from hers.

'I hope I have a fan base here.' He lifted her chin and kissed her again. She smiled and giggled not to mimic the girls but in response of the encapsulating blue pools of his eyes staring down at her.

'Sure do!' she said, and he winked at her, pulling up the chair next to her as close as he could to sit down.

'But not if you drink all that!' she said as he took her glass to his lips and finished the juice she had ordered.

'Sorry beautiful, I needed that.' He lifted his hand to the waiter to bring two more and reclined himself back in the chair, reaching out across to find Lottie's hand to hold. The drinks were deposited down by them and he thanked whoever brought them over; he never opened his eyes. Lottie gave it a moment and then used her free hand to carefully take the ice out of her glass. With precision she dropped it on his solid stomach, and he doubled up as an immediate reaction.

'Even Stevens now!' she said before he could do anything back at her. She passed him a napkin to dry off, but he just left it to slither down the side of his waist towards his shorts. 'You can lick it off later baby girl if you are good to me!' he said in a voice that was erotically suggestive and certainly not quiet. Lottie felt herself go red as an older lady had now joined the poolside group and heard his comment. She squeezed his hand hard, but he never flinched, relishing her embarrassment a little. Later, after their evening meal in the sanctity of their hotel room, she took him up on the offer.

Chapter 15

Whilst getting ready to go out to the meeting, Lottie had broached the subject of Paul, the young lad she had met the day before. She explained about the CD and just wanted the chance to get to know him. It would be easy to investigate him, something she was sure Pete would cope with if required.

They left the main city to the suburbs, where their meeting had been arranged. The shipping company had a large warehouse and storage port which took up a large part of the quayside. Lottie had looked over some papers that had been left at the hotel for them as they drove to their destination. She was not sure, other than to counter sign the documents that she needed to do today, or what details to read, but that was the whole point of the trip. For her to learn 'their' business.

The site manager was a red-faced stocky man in his late fifties. They had a tour of the yard with two more managers both younger in age and smaller in girth. Towards the end they were shown onto one of the large container ships. Lottie had not been keen to step on board but made no issue as she followed Edward up the gangplank a few yards behind. He had been engrossed in conversation, leaving Lottie to talk to one of the site foremen. He was pleasant, a keen surfer, tanned and blond, fit, and eager to make a good impression. He explained how his sister was expecting his first nephew, how his brother-in-law also worked at the dockyard, and keeping their jobs was so important at this time. She was not sure if he had guessed she too was expecting or if it was a silent thank you for the deal they were making today securing so many jobs.

It was a hot day, and her feet were hurting in her new shoes. She knew that although the size of the ship should have made the seasickness easier, it was not in her case. Within less than ten minutes she could feel the sweat running down her back and knew she had to leave. She started to breath quickly, keeping her nausea at bay, but she had to interrupt Edward. She was getting quite desperate to do so now but he had gone off into another room with Rory.

'Sorry Pip.' She interrupted him mid-conversation. He was talking about the crane system and how they got the containers off the ship to dry land. Lottie was not really paying any attention. 'I need to find Edward. Can I ask you to interrupt him for me?'

'Sure thing, Mrs Dean, you don't look so chipper.' He offered her a seat.

'Thanks, but I need to get off. I am not so good on the water.' She headed in the direction of the door to make her way back to the gang plank and off the boat. Pip gestured to another young man who had been following her to come over. 'Davie, see Mrs Dean to dock for me. I'll get Mr Dean.'

The sun beat down on her and she made her way back to the gangplank. It seemed to move more beneath her feet, only adding to the swimming in her head.

'Need a hand, Mrs Dean?' Davie put out an arm and she willingly took it.

'I feel so silly,' she said, trying to make light of the situation she found herself in.

'No worries, me mam gets it all the time. She was not sure how I got different sea legs meself!' His accent was strong, but the words just drifted past Lottie as her heels still clattered on the steel ramp. She felt like she was walking backwards not forwards.

Dry land and the covering shade of the warehouse helped. The ice water Davie had fetched for her was good, and momentarily soothed her throat, but the shock to her stomach had only made her need to rush to the washrooms worse. Luckily for her, the manager's toilets were close by and she had paid a visit when they had first arrived.

Edward did not need to be excused as he heard the first line of the message that Pip was relaying and he turned around on his heels. 'Gentlemen,' he said as he left the room. He overtook Pip even before they had reached the gangplank and made short work of getting back to the warehouse. Seeing she was not sitting in the room, he gathered where her location would be and opened the door without invitation. Lottie stood wiping her head with some damp paper towels at the basin.

'My God, baby, I forgot! I am so, so very sorry.' He walked behind her and wiped a tear from her eye.

'Don't panic, I should have said I would stop here. I did not think it would have this effect again. Whoever heard of someone owning a shipping company that gets so seasick!' She made light of how she felt to try to ease his mind.

'You need a chair,' he said, then shouted, 'Get a chair!' hoping that someone would have followed him and would hear. 'Fuck it,' he said, realising no one had followed them. He was so used to it at home, Pete, Phil or one of his team, they were never more than a meter behind, whatever the occasion. He opened the washroom door to shout again.

'Really Ed, I'm fine,' Lottie said.

'You collapsed last time, that I do remember.' He held the door, looking back at her.

'I had not eaten, and I was...' She stopped the words coming from her mouth and he finished the sentence for her.

'Pregnant.' He paused then raised his voice again, 'I need a chair!' Pip appeared around the office door, holding what he had called for.

Ed pushed it under her. 'See my point!' he asked her and she nodded knowing he was right.

'Pip, we are going to have to finish this at the hotel, make arrangements for you and the team to come over in an hour. I want Mrs Dean back there where she can rest.'

'Sure thing, boss,' he said, closing the door behind him leaving Ed and Lottie to their privacy.

'Don't ask if I am sure I am OK, apart from bringing up the contents of my stomach. Bump is fine, and I will be soon now I am back on dry land!' She pre-empted his question. 'I just feel so stupid and embarrassed.'

'Well don't.' He kissed her forehead, which was hot and clammy. 'If I mention seeing a doctor, you are going to jump down my throat, aren't you?' He looked at her and she rolled her eyes. 'Thought as much, but you will go back and rest for me?' She nodded; a lie-down would be welcome, although she was sad that she would not see Pip and his team again this visit.

As they got back to the hotel, Lottie made her way with Ed back to the lift. The receptionist called him over and handed him a package. It was a CD that had been hand-delivered and he looked at the name on the pack.

'From your busker,' he said, holding on to it until they got back in the suite.

She took off her shoes and made her way to the bedroom and flopped on the bed. Knowing that he could not get her anything else, he left water by the bed saying he was only a phone call away if she needed him. He placed the CD on the bedside table and Lottie rolled on to her side and closed her eyes. When the main door closed, she leant over and took the pack; it had a note inside which she started to read.

Mrs Dean,

For your kind donation I give my thanks. I have enclosed a CD of some of my works. I mainly play the flute, but you will hear several acoustic guitar solos and some of the pieces that I have written myself.

I have left my cell number, and an address, and a reference from my last tutor and mentor who has guided me these past years in the art of playing.

Sadly, he is blind, and would not be able to write to you, but I have passed on your details to him. He is willing to take a call, or indeed if you want me to meet up, I would be happy to bring him along. I know you are only passing through the city, but for someone to show an interest inspires me to work harder at achieving my goal.

Kind regards,

Paul Durrant

Lottie slid the CD from its case and sat up. She had seen a CD player in the lounge so she walked through to locate it. Pressing play the soft sound of his music filled the room and she sat on the sofa, looking out on to the busy streets below at everyone rushing around in their worlds, getting on with their lives. She felt the urge to play herself. She was inspired by his talent, but sadly, although there was everything else she could have ever needed in the room, there was no piano.

It was only after three pieces of music that she picked up her phone and called the number. No answer so she left a message for Paul, asking if he could call her back or pop into the hotel to meet her. Firing up her laptop she emailed Pete to see if he could research him at all, or even his aunt that he mentioned in Brighton. Just as another point of reference, something Ed would insist on if she was to show any more of an interest.

A low knock on the door made her get up, and looking through the security hole before opening the door (another thing Edward insisted on) she noticed the manager standing outside. She opened the door.

'Mrs Dean, Mr Dean asked me to check on you. I am sorry if I woke you, but I heard the music, so I was sure that you were awake, so I thought I would knock' he had been by told by Edward that if she did not answer to let myself in anyway and check on her. 'Is everything OK?'

She smiled and said yes. 'Mr Walker.' She had almost forgotten his name; luckily, he had a name badge on his lapel. 'Do you have a piano in the building, one that I could use?'

He pondered her question. 'The grand ballroom has one on the fourth floor. The room is being used at the moment, but it will be free after 3pm. I can arrange for you to have the area then if you wish.'

Lottie looked at her watch, it was over two hours away, she could hold on till then to flex her fingers, she was sure. She agreed and thanked him saying that she would come down to reception so someone could show her where to go.

Sitting back on the sofa, she looked at the laptop. Pete must work all hours as he had sent some information back. It looked like Paul was a genuine guy. His parting words to Lottie were to ask if she had discussed it with Edward. She quickly typed back that she had.

She fired off some more emails, one with some pictures attached to Agnes, and one to Gerald, who had received a laptop from herself the last time they were in Kent. He was teaching himself how to use it and getting quite good. She asked how he and Apollo were and expressed that he should do any jobs he needed to around the house, the new account for him to take money from was now set up. All he had to do was contact Agnes who would give him approval if it was over £1,000. She smiled at the fact that Edward, although he trusted Gerald, had said that all costs had to come from Agnes, if not them. Lottie found this hard to take in because they trusted him with their home. Lottie could see that he was truly grateful, and she had clearly stated that 'not everyone in life was out for a ride on the Dean wonder wagon!' Edward had laughed at her and the expression she had used, saying back to her, 'Over my business years, more people wanted to jump onto the wagon than were willing to keep the wagon rolling,' and with the light humour smashing the conversation. She had continued to negotiate the amount Gerald was able to spend without having to ask permission with Edward resulting in the usual way! She got her own way, and her man submitted to her body and soul.

Her stomach rumbled and she wondered if she dared eat something. The menu for room service was on the table and she looked through it. Everything sounded wonderful, so she took a punt on the chicken salad. She wanted to go for the seafood but thought she had had enough of the water for one day!

The knock on the door revealed Mr Walker with her food, and she wondered if every guest had his special attention, or just those spending a fortune in his hotel.

'Mr Walker, do you know what area of the city Maple Drive is located in?' she asked. This was the address Paul had put on his note.

'Yes, Mrs Dean, it is a quiet suburb to the east side, nice area. Quite close to the beach.' He stood hovering and she thanked him.

'I can arrange a cab if you wish to go,' he returned.

'No, no. I was just wondering.' She thought about it, but then held back knowing it would be a 'No' from her husband and she was supposed to be relaxing after all.

During her late lunch, her phone rang. It was Paul returning her call. She expressed an interest for them to meet and he said he could come straight over. He took it upon himself to pick Mr Chance, his tutor, up on the way.

Lottie had been directed to one of the conference suites by the porter, and she stopped outside, listening to the conversation. Holding her knuckle to the door she hesitated to knock. How embarrassing to walk into the room where they all were. Especially after her performance on the dockside earlier. She took a breath, closed her eyes and walked in. As predicted all eyes turned around to look at her and she smiled as best she could. Like a jack in a box, Edward jumped up and rushed to her side.

'Yes, before you ask, I am fine.' She got that in as quickly as she could. She felt like a schoolgirl explaining what she was doing there, so she just gave it to him before he could butt in.

'Mr Walker has kindly said that I can use the piano in the main ballroom for an hour. I just fancied relaxing. I can't really sleep so you know me. The music will help. I have spoken to Paul,' and before Edward had the chance to talk over her with some form of protest she continued, 'Pete has done some research before you ask. He is coming over here to meet me. I thought that was the safest thing, instead of me going back out on the street corner!'

'Oh, all planned out then?' Edward asked, relieved she was feeling herself again, but a bit annoyed that she was not taking her mind away from some sort of work.

'Just keeping you in the loop!' She smiled. 'Do I need to sign anything?' She remembered the whole point of her being on this side of the world.

'We have about an hour left, I will come and find you when we do.' He kissed her cheek. 'And Lottie...'

'Yes, I know. Call you if I need anything!' She rolled her eyes and he moved close to her so she could feel his breath, smell his male scent and his familiar aftershave.

'Actually, clever clogs, I was going to say, I love you Mrs Dean!' Ed rubbed his mouth on her ear, and she looked over his shoulder. Only one of the guys was looking in their direction. 'Get out of here!' he said, tenderly licking her ear. She smiled and bit down on her lower lip. 'I suggest now!' he said, looking at her bite down on the area of her body he knew that if he could, he would have sucked and bitten down on harder than she ever did. He took a breath to find some form of composure.

'Now gentleman, where were we before we were interrupted?' he announced back to the room as Lottie made her way to the door.

'What a very pleasant interruption,' Jon said, receiving a full Dean 'green monster' death stare for Ed for his sincerity and efforts. He quickly followed it with, 'To see Mrs Dean is feeling herself again, I mean.' Lottie smiled to herself as she walked out the door, well saved, she thought. She too had seen the look Edward gave his business associate so smiled at them all as she closed the door.

She was shown into a large, impressive room. Although the hotel was not a listed building by any means, the room had been decked out as if it was a 1920's ballroom. Sitting at the top of a raised area was a large white grand piano. Mr Walker took her over and lifted the lid for her.

'The room is free for another two hours, although the team will need to come and clear the tables. Is that a problem?' he enquired.

'No of course not. I just had the urge to play, and when my visitors arrive, could you show them where I am, and maybe bring some water or refreshments through?' she asked as she had already explained that Paul would be dropping by at some point.

'Yes of course I can, Mrs Dean. I will fetch a menu and you can choose what you would like.' He turned to dash off.

'Oh, just anything, cakes, fruit, don't go to much effort for just three of us,' she added, but knew that they would.

'No problem, Mrs Dean. I will see to it myself and do enjoy your playing.' He left the room.

She sat and put her hands on the keys, as if sensing the space around her. She closed her eyes and from anyone looking on, it would have looked strange, as if she were feeling for some sort of mystic guide, but Lottie was just getting a sense of the grandeur of the instrument. In her mind's eye she was trying to transport herself to the time the room was set out for, and how people would dance and enjoy the entertainment of that era.

It was not hard to know when to play as the notes always seemed to come from her fingers. She had not played for several weeks, even at home. The stress and busy work had just seemed to take her over, but the last few days had relaxed her, and seeing the enjoyment on Paul's face playing his flute reminded her of how lost you can become in music. After the first piece, she rubbed her hands together and wiggled her fingers as if that was an athletic warm up, and this was the stretch. She played a fast piece, then another all from memory. She had brought the iPad down and on her hard drive she had several spreads of sheet music. The problem here was that she could not turn the page by scrolling without removing her hands, but it gave her the opportunity to learn the sections page by page.

Several of the hotel staff had looked into the room, some stayed for a while to tend to tables and flowers, so she did not really notice when Paul and an older man on his arm walked into the room. At the end of the piece, they both clapped, and Lottie looked up and stood from her stool.

'Bravo!' the older man announced. 'Hardly a slur or stilled note, though I did catch a few.'

'Mrs Dean, good to see you again. Forgive my old friend, he has a very critical ear – that sounded fantastic.'

Paul led him over to where Lottie was now standing by the first table and the stage. 'Mrs Dean, Mr Rupert Chance, my mentor and guide, and my dear old friend.'

'Less of the old!' the middle-aged man said, holding out his hand towards the direction of Lottie. She wondered how he knew where she was standing if he was blind.

'Mr Chance, Paul, please call me Lottie, great to meet you.' She took his warm hand, and he placed his other over hers and smiled.

'I was wrong to criticize, these hands are warm and caring, and very talented, full of passion.' He pulled them closer to his face and kissed the back of her hand. Lottie smiled. Pete had said he was an ex-pat, educated at Eton and a scholar of music at Oxford in his quick emails research. He had been easy to find on a personal Google search as he had done several concerts in his time while at university, but then the loss of his sight in his late thirties due to a sudden illness had stopped him following his passion.

'Shall we sit?' Lottie offered the nearby chairs. 'And can I offer you any refreshments?' She pointed to the tray of drinks, delicate pastries, cakes, and fruit that Mr Walker had brought in some time after she had arrived. She helped herself to a glass of water and Paul passed one to Mr Chance.

'So, my dear, this young man said that you had been kind to him, crossing his palm with gold.' The conversation started. 'You must be a sucker for a lost cause?'

Lottie laughed. 'You could say that. My husband sure seems to think so.'

'Well, I have to say you are a long way from home, to offer the hand of friendship. Paul has never been so full of praise for a young lady, although I am sensing why.'

'I never told you as much, as we really did not have chance to talk.' Paul sipped his water, slightly embarrassed. 'Please excuse my friend, he does like to fantasize somewhat, although I have to say I am intrigued why you were so keen to talk.'

'I listened to your CD. It moved me.' Lottie continued to talk and explained a bit about her charity and how she strived to help those who had a passion for music, but a lack of funds. Something she felt should never stand in the way of playing at any level. She talked about the Music School in London, and the possibility that she would like to fund something for Paul if it was at all possible. Although the details as to how she could achieve this were somewhat sketchy to her at the moment.

'So not so much a bored, rich housewife looking for waifs and strays?' Mr Chance piped up in almost a rude manner.

'Rupert, don't be so cynical.' Paul admired his friend, he had been like an older brother to him over the last few years, but he hated the fact that he never held his tongue, and always said what was on his mind.

'Paul, your friend is right to be cynical. Many people do not believe that you get something in this world and people want nothing in return. I understand his concern,' Lottie interjected.

'And you see the good in everyone, something not many people do,' Mr Chance added. 'Another commendable attribute.'

'Mr Chance, I do nothing lightly, a trait I have learnt from my husband for business. I have done my homework, like yourself. Paul is not all that much of a lost cause, a little like yourself. Although not all of our parents were knights of the realm, being able to educate their only son at Eton and then follow them through a successful university career.' She added that last bit, so he knew she really had researched him.

'Touché, Mrs Dean!' he remarked.

'Well, you asked for that,' Paul added, with a dry smile on his face.

'So, what can I offer you, Paul?' She paused. 'I first must ask what is it that you want?'

He looked a little confused. 'I am not sure I follow you, Mrs... Lottie.' He changed her name as he remembered her introduction.

'I could set up a fund, something over here to see you through, or I could offer you a place in London, and a chance to go home if you really wanted.' She looked at Rupert and his face dropped. The thought of Paul leaving was what his harsh attitude was really all about, Lottie thought to herself.

'A scholarship here would need some careful planning, and a separate charity setting up, regular work for someone, whereas a place in the UK, well, all I would need to do is make the call. Either way I am prepared to take a bet on you making it somehow,' she finished.

There was an awkward silence and Lottie jumped back up to the piano. 'You have your flute. Will you play with me? I love Handel and you played him so well on the CD. Do you know the score by heart?' she asked, lightening the mood. She knew he did; he had played it the first time she heard him.

The music filled the room, and the only person in the audience sat fixed to his seat, face expressionless, sightless eyes closed and fingers resisting the urge to tap on the table.

Edward heard the music before he had even got to the room. The meeting had finished, and the only thing left to do was to sign the papers. Everything was in place for Dean Incorporated to keep the business and give it two years of total investment. It was not intended to make a fortune, but from today he was almost sure that with the team he had working for him, it would remain a profit-making scheme, and retain the original jobs, if not create some more for the local economy. Worst case scenario was that once a year he had to come over and have face to face input, but the trip had gone well. It was no different to his other holdings in the Far East or Asia, he could easily spend a few more weeks out here on holiday with Lottie and his family.

The group of men stood by the door as Edward hesitated to open it. He could already see her in his mind, sitting there playing, consumed, performing, a vision he would take with him to his grave and far beyond he hoped.

'Is Mrs Dean playing?' Jon asked. Edward nodded. 'Ripper,' he continued. 'Awesome sounds.'

They slipped into the back of the room, and Edward's face beamed seeing her there, focused on the young man he took to be Paul the busker. She, as always, was right; he was good. They complimented each other as if they had played together for years. His mind when back to his birthday the last time she had played for him in public. It always felt that she played for him, and him alone. He seemed to forget where he was; whether at home or in an open space his pride always came welling in his throat, which he cleared with a slight cough. Not to get her attention but to stop any form of tears leaking onto his face.

Lottie looked over and smiled. Paul put down his flute, sensing someone else was in the room. Mr Chance looked round. Jon started applauding, which the other men in the group joined in with.

'Edward,' she said standing, 'this is Paul, and his friend Mr Chance.' Edward had walked forwards and extended his hand to the young man and said hello to the older man who remained seated a few seats away from the stage. The email that Pete had sent Lottie had also been copied to Edward and once he knew they were meeting, he had ensured that he had read it through. Even during his own meeting he had taken the time to check what she was doing.

'Sorry we got a little carried away,' Lottie continued.

'Don't apologise.' Edward walked to her and helped her from the staged area. 'As ever you were beautiful.' He smiled at her and turned to Paul. 'But I do need to pull you away for a short time. Maybe you could join us tomorrow for lunch, Mr Durrant? I am sure whatever my wife has been discussing needs to be thought through. Although I totally understand that her powers of persuasion can be very precise, and once she has a mindset it is very difficult to refuse her anything.'

'You have a rare diamond, Mrs Dean, that is for sure.' The older man stood and held on to the table. Paul was quick to his side to assist him away from any obstacles. 'A real precious jewel, it was ever my very pleasure to meet.'

'Mr Chance, you must come tomorrow too if you can. I am sorry that I have to go now, can we say about...?' She looked at Edward to confirm a time, unsure of the schedule for the next day.

'1:30, here Unless you can recommend another venue?' Edward interjected.

'Here sounds great. Mrs Dean, thank you.' Paul turned to Lottie; he was not sure if kissing her cheek was appropriate, but she had done something to him. Watching her play next to him, he had never felt such a connection. He mostly played alone as he felt he had never found anyone to compliment him, but she just fitted. Lottie leaned in close and gently kissed both his cheeks.

Edward would never be happy with that gesture, not even to their close friends, let alone someone they really did not know. He hated the thought of her sharing her space, knowing they could feel her touch, smell her soft delicate skin. The hairs on his arms stood up, as he tried not to show this emotion that was still so very ingrained within him.

'Thank you for coming, I really enjoyed that.' Lottie smiled, and Paul felt his heart stop as the angelic face turned to him.

Oh My God, he thought to himself, I am infatuated with you. 'Mr Dean, thank you for your wife's time.' He could have choked on his words and then he smiled. He hoped no one could read minds as he thought 'you lucky bastard, she is a goddess.'

Lottie joined the men who had sat at a table while the goodbyes were exchanged and when Edward and herself joined them, she said that they should maybe go to the bar as the staff wanted to get into the room to set it up. As they walked to their destination compliments passed between them, and one mentioned that he had seen Paul before in the shopping centre.

Sitting around a table, Edward quickly went over the conclusions of the day, but Lottie was sure that he would not ask her to sign something that was not beneficial to them.

She occasionally smiled to herself and Edward looked at her when she did it for the third time with a questioning look.

'Well, let me sign and these good men can get home,' Lottie said. 'But I think we need to have a drink to celebrate.' She looked over to the barman who nodded and came over.

'Miss?' he asked.

'Mrs Dean.' Edward quickly corrected the young man holding his wife's gaze. The barman corrected himself with an apologetic stutter. 'Mrs Dean?' Lottie rolled her eyes at her husband trying not to shake her head at him too.

'A bottle of champagne and...' Lottie counted the number, 'six glasses, and an orange please,' she said.

Edward passed her a pen out of his pocket. 'Um very nice, Mr Dean,' she said quietly under her breath so only he heard. She put her name next to Edward's on the papers signing 'Dr Leticia Dean (Mrs)'.

'Six glasses?' Ed said as Jon popped the cork and started to pour.

'I was going to have a mouthful just to be social,' Lottie said.

No, Edward said with his eyes, but didn't take the glass from her. He was going to if she put it to her mouth. He swore he would.

'Dean Incorporated!' Jon held up his glass and the others joined in, including Lottie. She took the smallest sip and swallowed. It tasted awful, of which she was quite pleased as the last few weeks had killed her without a glass of wine. Putting her glass down, she picked up the orange and took a drink, hoping it would wash down the flavour.

'Don't get a taste for that, you really should not drink.' Edward could not help himself from saying something about the Champagne.

'Don't panic, it was horrid! And this little one needs something to calm...' she was about to say him as a slip of the tongue, then corrected herself, 'down. It may have been the music, or the fact that I have a good feeling about all of this, but,' she almost did it again, she almost said he, 'Bump is really active.' Without invitation Ed put his hand on her stomach trying to find the right spot but on queue Bump stopped playing.

Jon turned to the group of the newly-formed Dean International Shipping Company board and spoke quietly. 'Well, everyone was wrong about him. They said we never stood a chance of keeping the company going. Everyone said he would only come over to sell and break it all apart and kill off the dock without blinking. In fact, the point that we got him over here was almost a certainty that was what he intended to do, but look at him, bad-ass businessman, my own ass!'

Pip replied, making sure that they were not in direct ear shot, 'But look at her, don't you think that is the only real reason? We may have the other board member to thank for this deal, not the bad-ass businessman, but beautiful ass and every other inch of her body, businesswoman!' He raised his glass.

'Fuck it, Pip, don't let him hear you say that, or he would change his mind,' Jon added, aware of the visual roasting he had got for giving her compliments earlier, let alone comments about her body, although he had to agree she was truly stunning, from all angles.

'Well, whatever, she wears the trousers for sure and I tell you something, I bet there is nothing that he can resist giving to her.' He took another drink of his bubbles. 'And I am fucking jealous for sure! I love a dominant woman!' The men laughed but Lottie and Ed were so consumed with their own conversation, they took no notice.

The night soon came and Lottie lay back on the chest of her husband whilst they looked out over the city as the lights started to turn on. The water was warm and soothed her. Ed sat with one hand tucked around her waist resting on her stomach and one hand on the beer he had taken from the bar. They had not discussed her small sip of alcohol, but she had already stated the fact that she really did not mind him having a drink, so he helped himself before they got in the bath. They chatted about the day, and Edward had asked what she wanted to do about Paul. She outlined her options, both of which he said she should approach with caution, but he would back her. Of course, the fact that she would be funding it herself really gave him no cause to interfere, but she valued his opinion and advice. As a compromise, she had said to herself before the conversation even started.

Wrapped in a towel from the waist down, Ed sat at the table enjoying the room service. They had relaxed, knowing that neither of them wanted to go out for food, and as Lottie got into bed, she took a bowl of strawberries with her. They chatted into the night, no alarms were set for the next day and without a care in the world, they drifted to sleep in each other's arms.

Amazingly Lottie got up before Ed had even stirred. She had woken and looked over at the man left in her bed, so peaceful she did not want to disturb him. They only had today left here, then they would have to start the journey back home. They would not be back home for another six days, breaking the journey at the same destinations they had already visited, but she knew that Edward would not rest like he was now. She put the laptop on the table and started to look through the internet at music schools and Uni places in Sydney. She resisted the urge to open her emails but gave in after ten minutes. Todd had replied to her email from the other day, but it was nothing she did not know.

Her mind went back to her plan to get Alex Girski to confess to her. She was not sure she could pull it off without some help, but how could she keep that from Edward? Everyone she knew would tell him. Todd was her only hope so she asked him again if he would be prepared to come back for a week to help her. She would have to wait for his answer.

She flicked back to the internet and started to look at the Fashion House website. Liz had emailed to say it was up and running and it looked like Harrods was landing their first contract with them at the end of the month, another reason to get home. She quickly put some ideas down about her proposal to Paul and she was pleased the room had a printer, which she set working to get some sort of paperwork to give him when they met later.

The weeks seemed to be passing so quickly and she wondered how their life would soon change when the baby arrived. She had not really had time to give it much reflection and she sat back in the chair and looked at the bump that was resting below her dressing gown. She knew she would love him, but what if it changed her life too much? She had a sudden feeling of sadness that her mother was not around to talk to, to ask about the feelings she was starting to get. No sisters who had gone through the same, no cousins or close friends to ask.

Should she even have these feelings, did she have time to have these feelings? Edward had nothing but excitement, positive answers for her should she even approach the subject. Tomorrow they would go away she was sure they would, but what if they did not? Maybe she was just feeling homesick? She should not feel alone. She had Edward, what more did she want? Her mind was a mess and she needed to shake out of it. Concentrate on today. She got up and made a cup of tea.

She sat at the small breakfast bar and thought. Is this why Edward likes everything so organised, she asked herself. Being in control of everything so there was no doubt of failure? Oh god, what if she failed as a mother, was the next thought that crossed her mind. She took her tea and walked towards the window. The city below had not stopped and was still as hectic, so many lives, so many people with problems more than she had. She suddenly felt guilty. Life for her was protected, anything that she needed, or wanted was within her reach, but how could the money and the love of a good man make her a good mother, if she could not cope? And was having a child now really what she needed, just as things really were getting going again for her career-wise?

Shake it off, Lottie, she said to herself. She looked at her watch to see if it was too early to ring Agnes; she would know how to shake the thoughts away. It was too early. She took a deep breath and made her way to the bathroom. Turning on the shower, she slipped off the robe and stepped in. The water could wash it away for today, but she really needed to say something if she felt this way again. Controlling her hormones was something the water did not do, and the tears rolled down her face faster than the water could wash them away.

Ed rolled over and felt a cold space where she should be lying. He opened his eyes and the sound of the shower reassured him she was not far from his world. He got up and pulled on his boxers. Trying the bathroom door, he found it was locked.

'Lottie?' he asked, loud enough for her to hear. 'Lottie, you have locked the door?' Something they both never did. 'Lottie are you OK?' he asked, trying the handle again. Sudden panic struck him like an iron bar.

'Hang on.' She turned off the shower, grabbed the towel and put it round her. Glancing in the mirror at her face she was pleased to see that the water had helped and unless he had heard her, you could not tell she had been crying.

The lock released, and he opened the door faster than she could.

'Why did you lock the door?' he asked, a sense of urgency requiring her to answer.

'Sorry, I'm not sure why it flicked across.' She smiled at him and a reassuring kiss arrived on his lips.

'Sorry, did I wake you?' She tried to change the subject and his returned kiss confirmed he was happy she was OK.

'No but you should have woken me.' He yawned as he followed her into the bedroom.

'You were out for the count, catching up with you I guess.' She sat on the bed drying herself.

'I guess, you hungry?' He ran his hand through his hair.

'Um, I could eat but I'm not starved.' She stood in front of the wardrobe to choose what to wear. 'I've had some tea already.'

'And been working?' He looked through to see the laptop out on the table. 'Whatever time did you get up?' he asked.

'Hour or so ago, and I was just looking at the fashion house web site, it went live yesterday.' She continued to talk about the contract for Paul and it was as if she was suddenly Jekyll and Hyde. All feelings from earlier had gone. Maybe the crying helped? Maybe the fears would not come back? But for now, she had control again and once Edward had showered and dressed, they found themselves walking out of the hotel to a small deli for breakfast.

Their lunch was informal. Though Lottie noticed that Paul had put on a suit, with no tie and the jacket had been removed when they sat to eat. Both parties asked questions and made general small talk, and it was not until the final course, which Lottie had not ordered for herself, that she finally asked.

'Well, is there anything you want to ask?' She had given him the proposals and talked them through it. His first option was to accept a scholarship at his local Uni for two years, with very little return apart from if he left, he would have to fund any other projects himself. On completing Lottie was happy to back any possible record deals or attempts to make it in one of the large orchestras.

The second was to come to the UK and join the Music College for the same period. Both meant he would still be paying for his own accommodation, although there would be an option to live on campus making it a lot cheaper. The London option had another twist, for Mr Chance.

'Rupert, I know to ask you to move to the other side of the world seems so far out. I have no notion of the personal implications that this would have for you, apart from the fact that I want you to work at the Music College, for me.' She had not told this to Ed during their discussions either. In fact she had not thought of it until that morning, looking at how many places he had worked and the high standard his teaching and performing reviews got. 'I value your experience and your knowledge, and even your critical ear,' she added, noting the comments he had made towards her after hearing her first play the day before. 'I think you could bring so much to the college, open doors for other students who, perhaps, don't think they have what they need to make it. You would not need a visa as a UK resident, but I would happily do a temporary contract so that you could come back if you felt it was not working out.'

'Do you mean I could show others with a disability like mine that they are not useless?' Mr Chance asked in his usual abrupt manner and Ed thought to himself he was a 'to the point kind of guy, you asked for that Lottie! Not subtle!' He too thought that was what she was implying.

'I would not have put it like that, but I find so many people alienate anyone that is different. I have a good friend in a young, very talented boy with a real significant learning difficulty. When he plays, he is a true genius that the world cannot miss out on, and luckily the charity has been able to allow him to start to reach his potential, where others have just written him off. I cannot abide to see such skills wasted because of a difference in opinions with social snobs. No talent should be wasted. Everyone can achieve once people have been made to see through their social inadequacy, by themselves or others.'

The statement made all three men stop eating. Edward was blown away by the precision and calmness in her answer, as if she had been ready to give it throughout the whole meal. He had never been able to think on his feet like that, smart arse comments yes, but deep and poignant statements?

Paul was left trying to swallow his cream caramel, stuck by the intent in her voice and the content of the statement. He was sold, totally.

'Well, how can I reply to such an eloquent statement, Mrs Dean? I can see you are a force yourself that the world may not be ready for. You are right. There is much to consider, but in no way should my decision change your mind though, Paul.' He aimed his answer at the young man next to him who was transfixed on Lottie.

'So, have you considered anything, Paul?' Lottie thanked the waiter who passed her a cup of tea along with the drinks that the rest of the party had ordered.

'I was concerned for my dear friend, but he knows that this was my last chance to stay here. I had said that I wanted to go home if my attempts failed, in fact without your contribution this week, I would be packing right now.' This statement was true.

'I in no way want to rush you, but we are homeward bound tonight. I am happy to keep all the options open for the next few months, as term starts in September. We can talk, Skype or email, although I have to say I am not sure we will be back this side of the world for quite a few months. It is not impossible to arrange your scholarship over here from back home if that is what you wish, but I would love for the both of you to join the collage, purely from a selfish point of view in what I would gain.' She took a moment to drink her tea.

Jesus, negotiation! Where did you get that from, I'm dying here! This is my wife, but I would be under the table or out of the door and on the plane before you if you laid all that at my feet, Edward thought to himself almost spluttering on his coffee. He had remained quiet throughout all of this, knowing it really was her show.

'I'm in,' Paul said without a second thought. 'For the UK. I can't see any negatives.' He was hoping his friend would be so keen to reply.

'Oh, the anticipation of youth,' Rupert answered. 'Mrs Dean, your invite is a most fascinating idea, but an old soul cannot be so easily swayed.' He reached for his cup and with an unknown ability to find the drink, he took it to his lips.

'I understand that financial incentive is not the driving force for you, Mr Chance.' Part of her research revealed the fact that he was loaded, not that you could tell to look at him and the way he dressed, and it had been a thought why he had not sponsored Paul or helped him himself. 'But I know you have a passion that has only grown in your years of experience, something you are right no one younger would have the ability to possess and it is that very attribute of sensible thought and consideration that I have no intention of losing if it is at all possible. However, I respect your decision. I would be deeply disappointed but as I say I respect your hesitation, another attribute that inspires me.'

Bravo! Ed thought finding it hard to hold in his smile. *She has you, now you know how I feel when she has my balls in her hand!* He meant that both literally and physically as it seemed to be the same hold she possessed in everything. Luckily the latter was something he could truly hope no other man would feel!

'Your wife, Mr Dean, must drive you to distraction. She turns my inner self on its head, and I thankfully cannot even see her external beauty, for god alone knows how that must affect a man. I would not say I have reservations as such, more self-doubts.' Rupert could feel his heart start to race. 'Are you throwing me a final lifeline? One last encore before the curtain comes down?'

'No decision in life should be taken lightly. Everything should be done with the blessing of your inner soul to give you true peace and we all have self-doubts. It shows we are alive. I am offering you a chance to do what you set out to do a long time ago. To give the world, Mr Chance, the advantage of your true passion.' Lottie could see the colour rise in his face; he was thinking about it for sure.

Silence was welcomed and Ed asked for the bill.

'Paul. Before I go home, I will send you some information and if you are still as keen, when I get home, I will make the arrangements. You need to think about it further, but I hope that you will not change your mind. Mr Chance... Rupert,' she corrected herself but before she had time to finish, he looked in her direction.

'Mrs Dean, can I stop you?'

Oh, Lottie he is the fish that got away, accept it. You have met your match! Edward was pleased that he said it to himself, if only to prevent her from disappointment. The older man continued, 'Mrs Dean, to coin the phrase of my good friend sitting here.' He pointed to where Paul was still sitting. 'I'm in.'

Signed, sealed and delivered in one meal! Lottie, where have you been all my life? There is nothing I can teach you, but I have learnt so much just by sitting and watching, a true master. The silent voice in Edward Dean shouted out. He was so turned on by her masterful handling of the situation, he had dared not to stand, his growing arousal for such silent, intensive dominance was mind blowing, truly.

Chapter 16

With their flight from Malaysia being delayed and an extra night in Singapore, they arrived back in the UK fourteen days after leaving. Two weeks had seemed to go so fast and so much had been achieved. Lottie had carried on working out her new scholarship deal and the placement for Mr Chance. Both parties had not changed their minds and the correspondence between them had been exciting. Ed truly marvelled at her. After the meeting that night they had laid in bed and he openly admitted that he had not seen such a business deal go down so well.

The charity board had not been impressed with her decision-making, but again, the power of money and what seemed to be the backing of the Dean name had soon made them come around to the ideas and proposals she enforced upon them.

It was good news all round. This was the conclusion given to Mrs B when they arrived back, settling into the apartment. They both felt that it had been a successful trip, the only disappointment was that Todd had replied to Lottie and he was not able to get back to the UK until at least late July, three more weeks to wait. This disappointment she could not share with Ed as he would want to know why he was coming back, a reply for this reason she had not been able to concoct yet.

With fresh tea and coffee waiting for them, they put their bags down in the hall and went on through to the sitting room. Both Pete and Phil were waiting for them. They had chanced a taxi to get them back from the airport instead of asking for a car, showing how relaxed Edward had become.

'Well, my dear, whatever was in the water over there has done you well, you are positively blooming!' Mrs B said after hugging them both as a welcome home. 'Look at you.' She looked down at her stomach and Lottie flattened her top over Bump. She was surprised anyone noticed in such a short space of time, but she guessed it must be true. 'Four and a half months now,' Mrs B announced as if she was counting every day.

Ed had wandered off with Pete to the study, taking a large amount of post with him. There was not so much for Lottie and she just looked through, noting anything that took her eye that needed to be opened immediately. She put it down on the side and sat with Phil asking if there was anything she needed to catch up on. Their conversation soon turned to Liz and the fashion house. He was excited as soon as her name came up, and Lottie could clearly see that he had spent time with her since they had been away, and it had only strengthened their relationship. She was pleased for them both.

For a Saturday, the city below was quiet, but it was a hot summer's day and Lottie welcomed the breeze as she walked out on to the balcony a few hours later. Ed had emerged a few times from the study, but Lottie really did not mind the peace and quiet, winding down from the travelling. She sat with a soft drink on her knee and closed her eyes.

'Hello, you.' She pressed her hand on her stomach. 'You've been quiet for a few days.' She said it out loud, but no one was listening; or had Ed been right that Bump was listening? He had taken to talking to her stomach on more than one occasion to try to get a reaction.

She did not feel tired but guessed the heat and the relaxation of closing her eyes had made her sleepy. She got back up and took her phone into the bedroom. She texted Agnes to say they were home and that she would call tomorrow. The text back was one to let her know she was out shopping with

Jane and wanted to catch up with Lottie and when were they next coming down?

Lottie replied saying she was not sure yet but would let her know tomorrow. She lay back on the bed and closed her eyes again. Without any warning sleep took over her and she found herself giving in to it without a fight. She murmured as Edward took off her clothes and wrapped her in the light summer silk sheets, but never hesitated to find her dreams again soon after. He sat stroking her hair gently, looking at her changing form, as she did seem to be blooming. He sat holding the image in his head. He was sure that he could see his very future lying in front of him. He caught his breath; he felt again in a place he was so unsure of, but so very happy with. The gentle sound of her breath seemed to soothe him, but he did not want to lay next to her yet, to wake her. He sat for some time longer before he pulled himself away to clear out some work.

Monday was always fast to creep up, and even more unwelcome after being away. There had been several new cases that the centre had taken which the professor was keen for Lottie to look into. She was only interested in one case, and when the professor said that Detective Sharpe had not got any other leads, she knew that without sharing her evidence with anyone, this chance could be missed. She had to bide her time.

Wednesday took her to meetings and lunch with Liz, who thankfully had been working on a range of clothes for Lottie. She was sick of wearing unflattering clothes and the new items she had brought home were eagerly shown to Ed in his own fashion parade that night.

She was looking at the dress that she had chosen to wear at the charity event for the summer ball on Saturday. This would be the time that the media picked up on the soon-to-arrive new member of the Dean clan, so the dress was the all-important choice. Donning the dark blue silk dress made him smile as she did a usual twirl for approval. She liked to know what she was wearing and prepare for things before the day itself, just in case of a last-minute change of plan.

'You can't hide bump forever,' he said as she fidgeted with the front material of the A line, full-length gown.

'I know but I don't want people to think I just look fat,' Lottie said.

'I heard a woman talk to someone about self-doubt not so long ago; it can be overcome by anyone!' He quoted her.

'I know but I feel so in-between.' She pulled a face, still looking at her reflection, holding her hair up or down as if she was also undecided about how to wear it. He beckoned her over to the edge of the bed where he was sitting.

'You. And you,' he kissed her stomach, 'look amazing. Let the world know that. Now take it off and come to bed and stop worrying.' He wanted to reassure her of how beautiful she was and did so by slowly worshiping her until she reached her climax, and then again, this time joining their bodies so he could fulfil his own.

As Saturday arrived, it came with all the glitz and glamour of a red-carpet event. One to put any Hollywood event to shame. Edward helped Lottie out of the car as Pete dropped them off outside the Park Lane Hotel. Daring to walk in the high-heeled shoes, she was for once as tall as he was. Holding her arm they walked into the room with smiles, and even a pose for the cameras standing at the large double doors.

Lottie was pleased that the event, although paid for by Edward, was organised by an event company and she had really taken a back seat in the arrangements for this one. His mother had done most of the hard work. Orange juice in hand they started to mingle, and it was obvious that there was only one topic of conversation; their bump. She at first clung to Ed like a limpet, but before they sat down to eat, she had to go it alone to the ladies. She battled the comments and conversation from almost every female in the room asking questions about her pregnancy. In the sanctity of the toilet, she was glad to get away from everyone. She washed her hands and the water splashed over her dress, so she had to use the dryer to remove the marks on the front, cursing herself for being clumsy.

Aware that she had been longer in the toilet due to the water incident and knowing that most people would be sitting down she hurried herself back. A young waiter stopped her and gave her a note, handwritten. She quickly opened it up and read the words.

> Congratulations Mrs Dean, I would say this in person but the fractured relationship with your husband prevents me from doing so, however I am watching you and I wait in anticipation of blessing your new arrival.

She quickly looked around but no one except the hotel staff were walking about. The note was not signed by anyone, but a cold shiver went up her body. Who was invited that Ed did not get on with? If he saw Alex Girski here, Pete would be instructed to get him out. Even Alex's mother was not invited to such events, much to Ed's mum's disappointment as they had become good friends as the boys grew up together. After that fateful day, Ed had insisted that they all break ties with them and his mother had dutifully obliged, not really knowing why, but doing as she was asked for the sake of her son.

Lottie pushed the note in her bag; every second she was away would make Edward nervous, so she hurried her way back, seeing the relief on his face as she got back to the table where they were just about to eat. It was not uncommon for them not to sit together at such functions, and the vast size of the tables meant that he was looking directly at her, but he had no chance to speak as she took her place.

To her right she had an older man. He was a film director and had some interesting stories which made the table laugh from time to time. On her left she had a very glamorous lady, who Lottie found to be interesting, if a little deaf, having to repeat herself on more than one occasion. The night seemed to go well, but every now and then Lottie turned her mind to the note. Where had he seen them, arriving, or had he been in the room? She was sure that his name would not be on the guest list. Pete had closely studied it, and the amount of protection officers in the room was the most she had ever seen, as the dinner invitation had been extended to two royal visitors, albeit very minor ones and two very famous film stars, though she felt slightly out of touch as she had only ever seen one in a film a few years ago.

Periodic smiles and silent gestures from Ed were made to ensure that she was OK. Another friendly face was located on the table in Joe although Sarah was not able to make the event, as she had been away at a race meet where several of their horses were running. Lottie took the opportunity to find Edward's mother as soon as they had finished eating.

'You look amazing, my dear.' She greeted her for the second time tonight with a kiss on each cheek. 'Good event?'

'Yes, well done you, and thank you for taking over the organising of it.' Lottie smiled as she was genuinely grateful. 'Were you able to sneak some friends in on the guest list? It is so nice to have a few friendly faces around at these sorts of things,' she said, noticing that she had been talking to many groups during the night.

'A few of the bridge club, and I was amazed that one old friend asked to come. I really wish that Edward would sort out his differences with Alex, as his mother is a dear friend. Don't say anything but I do still meet her for lunch every now and then and have a good old catch up.' Lottie was amazed that she shared the information with her and was taken aback by the statement. 'The poor boy did wrong, but they were such pals, friends like that are important. God alone knows that my boys are not angels. Edward should give him a break.'

'I am sure that Ed has his reasons, after all, Alex caused a lot of problems for him and...' she stopped, not sure if Edward had ever gone into the details with his mother.

'Oh, the money to bail him out was long forgotten, and his mother says he is off the drugs now. Maybe you could talk to him about it?' she asked, and Lottie looked over at her husband deep in conversation with another group of donors.

'I,' she stumbled, 'I am not sure I want to face that challenge. He can be quite determined.' She paused again.

'Bloody minded and stubborn, you can admit he has faults to me. I am his mother and I love him anyway, a feeling you will soon have for yourself, unconditional love.' She smiled at Lottie just before she was interrupted by an older gentleman asking her to dance. Lottie had not even noticed that the music had started in the room next door, and the two women agreed to catch up later.

Maybe this could be the excuse to meet up with the elusive Alex Girski that Lottie was looking for? But first she would have to tackle the question, not tonight. Maybe the letter was some sort of request for her to meet up with him, although she was not sure of what his motives were if it was him.

'So why don't you tell Pete then? Get him on board, Lottie,' Todd expressed as they spoke on the phone later the Sunday evening.

'Because he will go straight to Ed and then, well you know why,' she replied quietly. Ed was only in the room next door attempting to make their evening meal.

'If you have your reservations then you must know it is wrong. Lottie, do not do anything stupid until I can get there in a few weeks, will you?' She grunted at his request, more because she did not want to have to wait that long to finally get to the conclusion of this case.

'Lottie, promise me,' he said, and she grunted again. She could not promise as she had the letter tucked into her back pocket and needed to share it with Ed at some point. The longer she left it the madder he would be that she had not shown him it earlier, but if it was from Alex, any chance of reconciliation would be further out of the question and she had been fully tempted to throw it in the bin.

She turned the food around the plate, not that she was not hungry as her stomach churned. She built up the courage to say something, then it went away, then again, she almost got the words out, and it went to a different conversation. Finally, she saw the opportunity when Ed noted it was nice to see his mother having a good time the night before.

'She looked so relaxed, and with a few friends there, although I am not sure I like the attentions of, who was it, some colonel or someone.'

'Captain Brewer,' Lottie corrected him. 'He was sweet. I understand he is often your mum's afternoon tea companion.' She smiled knowing the disapproving son look Edward was giving her.

'I am going to ask Pete to look into him. I don't want some gold digger upsetting her.' He took another mouthful of food.

'Oh Ed, don't be so hard on your mother. It's not fair to dictate who she can be friends with or not, she is a big girl and can look after herself.'

'I don't tell her who she can see,' he defended himself.

'Oh, no?' Lottie asked. 'I know that she misses Mrs Girski.' Lottie just came out with it and hoped for the best. The silence that followed was a surprise. 'Just because her son pissed you off, your mother did not have to lose out!'

'Has she said that?' he asked.

'Yes, in fact she said it last night,' Lottie commented back.

'Has this conversation been rigged so that you can talk to me about her?' Ed asked, putting down his fork.

'No, you started talking about your mother's friends,' Lottie pointed out, glad that he had as it had saved her trying to get there in the end and open up the discussion painlessly.

'But you were quick to interject!' he came back at her.

'Well, she did only mention it last night, that's the truth. She misses her old friend, and if the truth be known, I am sure that at some points over the last twelve months you have missed your old friend too!'

'You are so wrong,' Ed said, getting up to move his plate from the table. 'He was a fucking idiot, and no one treats me like that.'

'So, tell me who you really wanted as your best man?' she asked, knowing that before they fell out Alex would have been his first and only choice. 'You were thick as thieves before I came along, so be honest, if he had not got you mixed up with shelling out a lot of money to save his skin, would you still have him as one of your closest friends?'

'Yes, but as one of my closest friends, you do not take the piss and land me in trouble that could have had significant repercussions on me, you, or my family. That is what it boils down to, his behaviour put you at risk.'

'Has he tried to make contact since or was the warning off Pete gave him enough to keep him away?' she asked, honestly wanting to know.

'He apologised enough, after it was safe for him to surface again. He never even had the backbone to show his face for a few months. It was not just me he had pissed off. Going underground for a bit of time avoided the beating I am sure he deserved. The mob never take too kindly to being pissed off, less than I do,' he answered, sitting back down. 'Anyway, why are you asking? It seems more than just for my mother to keep her cliquey friendship group going. You have never even met the guy, remember? So much of a good friend that he never even showed up when he was invited to meet you.'

'Just asking.' Lottie skimmed over the facts.

'Is the subject closed then?' he asked.

'If you want it to be, but I hate to think that you are not friends now, just because of me. I mean, if all this had happened and I was not around, you would have forgiven him?' she said. 'If it is the fact that he put your family, me, at risk I mean.'

'Maybe, but my life is so different now, we would have grown apart anyway. I have grown out of the things we did; places we would go. I hated the drug taking and it seemed he would get us into more trouble every time we did anything. I was sure he was depressed or had some mental illness. He was so changeable, his moods were unpredictable and, knowing him, he would not have stuck around very long once he knew you were around to stay.'

'Is that what he did with other girlfriends, warn them off?' Lottie asked.

Edward gave a dry laugh. 'At the time I was not willing to give that behaviour up either, although you know I disapprove of drugs in every way. When it looked like I was becoming a distant friend because of business or a woman he usually put pay to me seeing them again or messing up the deal in some way.' He made the comment but did not explain, so she had to ask.

'How?'

'How do you think?' He still left her to ask again as she was not on the same wavelength yet.

'Edward, I don't know, that's why I asked.' She had a fair idea but wanted him to say it.

'He was always jealous of me. If it looked like I was going on a second date, he would try to muscle in, although for most of them he did me a favour by getting rid of them. If they were so fickle to be tempted by him, he was welcome to them.' He stood up and walked to get a drink from the fridge. Except Caroline. He had been gutted when Alex announced his triumph with her. Although Edward had never seen her as 'the one' he did have feelings for her of some sort. But when she tried to get him back, being sorry for her behaviour, he knew that the feelings he had then were of only hate and resentment. Although she soon scurried back to Girski for a short time, then she went off the scene; no one knew where she had gone to. He had been told that she had tried to commit suicide but nothing else seemed to have been said.

'You mean he slept with them to prove a point?' Lottie asked.

'Yes,' Edward answered sharply, 'and now I have finished the conversation.' But Lottie had not.

'So, you took a risk by asking him to meet me?' Lottie asked and Edward did not answer. 'Or did you want me to meet him to see if I could be trusted not to be using you for what I could gain?'

'Underhand and unfair question, that was not the case at all, and you know it,' he replied quite sharply.

'But we had seen each other several times before you asked if we could meet up,' she replied.

'And that in itself should answer your question. You know I was smitten by you after our first meeting, I did not want to run the risk that you would–' He stopped talking.

'Be so fickle and fall under his spell and not yours?' She finished it for him with a sarcastic tone.

'Yes, if that makes you feel better. I could not take that chance because I had fallen for you and you were the one thing that I wanted for myself.'

She was almost on the verge of blowing this out of the water, expressing to Ed why he could not see who the person was sending messages through the post, advising him to be careful. Now she had to show him the note and let him in on all the details, but something still made her hold back.

She took a deep sigh, and opened her mouth to start to explain, just as Pete put his head in the doorway to say good night. The two of them walked into Ed's study and left Lottie sitting at the kitchen table, pondering her next move. She was sure that this conversation was not fully over, but by his reaction, it obviously was for him now.

Lottie was just getting changed after helping the professor on another autopsy. Quite a clear case, so she was surprised to see Detective Sharpe waiting for her in her office. She looked at her watch: 4:30 on Wednesday afternoon. She knew the car would be waiting for her without fail at 5 so she rushed putting on her lab coat.

'Detective Sharpe, can I help you?' She shook the tall man's hand and offered him a seat.

'Mrs Dean, I have been looking into the case notes for Eric's death and I wanted your opinion.' He took out a file and placed it on her desk. She looked at him with questioning eyes. 'Something in my gut says there is something I am missing, and I wanted to ask if you had found anything off the record?' He emphasised the off the record part, although in her experience, a policeman never slept, a bit like her in that respect she mused to herself.

'I don't follow.' She tried to act as if she did not, but it must have been her body language that somehow, he was the one now with the questioning eyes.

'We looked around his flat, in fact I went back several times and well, I found this.' He handed Lottie a photo of herself and Edward. It had been taken when he had been to the centre to pick her up. 'I wondered why Eric would have it in his possession; it is hardly the sort of thing that is shared with a colleague, not like office party photos?'

Her heart sank as she turned it over and written on the back in handwriting she had seen before, it said, tell me all you find out!

She looked at the detective, knowing that to lie now was futile, and was he the person she needed to have on her side to pull all the bits together.

'I guess by the look on your face that there is a little more for me to know, and I guess as you are a very intelligent woman, I don't need to put you under arrest, do I? I need to be sure that you are clever enough that you will not hold it back.' His words were not threatening, but direct and to the point.

'Detective Sharpe, I will not insult your intelligence, but I need to ask you for a favour on this. I will tell you everything you need to know. If I can explain fully without you leaping to any conclusions or taking any actions before you hear my proposal. I must warn you, this goes back a few years and is linked to, well I think it is linked to, several more cases. I am not asking that a potential murderer walk free. I am asking that a plan is put together to make sure that everyone involved gets it right without any doubt of the facts to ensure this person is caught and justice is done.' She paused to look at her watch.

'I know that you are a creature of habit, Mrs Dean and your driver will be waiting for you, but to be able to do as you ask, I would need to know tonight so that I too can ensure that the law is followed,' he replied. 'I understand that both your husband and you require a certain amount of anonymity, and of that you can be assured. I trust you fully as there must be good reasoning to your concerns. Can you spare a little time for me now?' he asked.

'May I call my husband? I would not want to discuss this here. Maybe we could find a quiet place?' she asked not wanting to talk about it anywhere that they may be overheard.

'For sure, how about I meet you in the park at the docks in about half an hour?' She nodded and said that she would taking out her phone from her pocket to make the requested call to Ed.

'Sorry to ask but I just need to meet up with the police on a case, they need some answers tonight so I will be late. Phil is here and I will ask him to take me to the meeting place, somewhere on the docks. I think that is where the accident happened, and he can hang around until I am finished,' she explained to Ed and although he was not happy about the delay in her getting home, he knew that Phil was not far away and that if he did not say yes, she would go and meet them on her days off anyway, so he agreed.

She walked across the gardens with her laptop bag and files under her arms. She noticed the man sitting at the bench looking at the children playing opposite on the swings. He had two coffees waiting. He offered her one, but she declined.

'This all must seem very cloak and dagger, but as you have suspected there are some personal implications here, and so I must have your complete discretion, but in no way will I intend to, as you, prevent the course of justice on this. I just ask that you hear my case and then keep an open mind and view on how you want to take this further.' He nodded and said that he would as far as he saw fit.

She began to explain, starting at the beginning with the incident in Monaco, then she outlined the break-in at her flat, and the car incident. She took a breath while the detective looked through the relevant files of information to what she had carefully explained and then she contributed.

'And here is where it becomes more personal.' She handed him Mitch's files. 'My husband's brother died in a car crash, something that has not settled well with him. For no other reason than the DNA found at the scene which showed as a match, I looked at it again. Although this person could have been in the car weeks before the accident, it made me wonder if there was a form of connection. Even though this is not enough to go on to place someone at the scene or accuse them of any crime...' She again passed over some files and carried on explaining. 'He was not into drugs, although a heavy dose was found in his system at the time and after the autopsy on the young girl, who I also think was not a regular drug user, well coke anyway, I suddenly clicked.' She outlined the possible connection and found herself becoming increasing embarrassed explaining the connection between the girl, the club, and the person she had bumped into there.

'I had the same notion for Eric, although his toxicity levels were higher, suggesting he did do drugs on a more regular basis, but the fatal dose was the same both structurally and amount to the other two. Looking at the connection, the phone records, why he was there at that time of night? I have a conclusion.' She allowed Detective Sharpe to read the evidence and he then replied, 'Your conclusion is?'

'The guy at the club the same night that the girl died. I am sure I met him; I remember these.' She passed a photo of the cuff links. 'Eric's relation, cousin I think he called, and the guy who I suspect I met is the same person. Eric was on the phone to him hours before his death. The same person is,' she corrected herself, 'was a family friend and knew Mitch and has a motive to send letters to my husband and I.' Again she passed over some samples and the latest letter she'd received at the ball.

'So, you have a name?' he asked, resting all the documents on his knee.

'I do, but any good lawyer could pull the evidence apart. Even though the DNA is a positive match, it could be proved all circumstantial. I think the only way to have solid evidence is to have a confession to any one of the deaths, which would be conclusive.'

'Well, Mrs Dean, can you give me the name?' the detective asked.

'Before I do, please hear the rest of my idea to achieve the latter. I want to befriend him and then get a confession,' she said.

'And your husband knows about this?' he asked almost in surprise.

'No, Edward and Pete are aware of 80% of the case notes. The rest I wanted to follow through myself to get a result, not for the glory of the conviction as Todd put it, but to give my family and others a reason why and case closure.' She informed him of the start of her plan that she had discussed with Todd.

'This Todd used to work with you and knows it all?' Sharpe asked.

'Yes, he is coming back to the UK in a few weeks and I hope by then I will have made some progress,' she announced.

'So, Mrs Dean, the name of this person, or do I have to go and find it out for myself from the information that you have given me?' Sharpe asked, quite matter of fact. 'I am not in anyone's inform, if that is what you are worried about.'

'It is not that. I don't want you go and arrest him, question him, give him a chance to cover up and go to ground,' she explained.

'I get that, and against my better judgment, I want to nail him, as much as you. I am not sure I agree with whatever plan you are hatching, but I am prepared to work with you on this. However, I can't let anyone else get hurt so I must give you a timeline of three weeks. Then we do it my way, although I want to be in on anything you plan to help anyway I can.' His request did seem quite genuine and so Lottie exposed the assailant's name to him.

'We will talk soon, Mrs Dean. I understand your need to go home. I must express that anything we plan, such as a sting or a trap also must be fool-proof, we cannot be seen to be manipulating the law or any form of entrapment. And I have to insist that your husband is fully behind you, in your condition. I am not willing to take any risks. If all of this is right, and I suspect from my first glances at your case notes it is, this person is a calculated, deluded killer and will stop at nothing to get what he wants, and that, I am afraid, does seem to be your husband in some way.' The detective smiled at her and for the first time Lottie actually saw some warmth in his eyes. 'Can I take these to do more research, and get further up to speed? There is a lot to take on board.'

'Yes, but the files are sensitive, so I need you to sign for them, as I am not back at the centre until Monday. Can I email you the document and then get them securely delivered to your office for your attention, or I can hand deliver them tomorrow?'

'I understand. I am on shift after 2pm, so maybe you could call by then?' he replied, knowing that she was sticking to some procedures if only in a small way.

The two of them parted and Lottie made her way back to the car where Phil had dutifully been waiting.

'Sorry,' she said, apologising for taking up another hour of his day.

'No worries. Mr Dean has asked me to take you to the office. I think he took the time to catch up a little too.' She smiled at his reply knowing that Ed would not ask too many questions if he had been occupied while she was away.

The security guard on the door greeted them and they took the lift. Phil walked over to the small office on the right where Pete usually hung out and Lottie walked over to Ed's door; the blinds were up and she could see him talking to two men around their own age, well-dressed.

She smiled at him through the glass and he jumped up to open the door. She reached it before he got there and let herself in. He greeted her with the usual kiss on the cheek and introduced the two men as local estate agents. Lottie was quite surprised as she was not aware he was going to take the thought of looking for a house seriously. She held out her hand and both men stood and shook the outstretched limb in turn, introducing themselves to her.

'I know it was only a thought, but I wanted the guys to get out there looking for us, to see what is on the market.' Ed spoke directly to Lottie as if the two men had left the room. He offered her his chair, but she chose to perch on the edge of his desk, her usual space she often took while in his office.

Ed smiled, looking at her in the light chiffon top and baggie black trousers. The position she was sitting in made their bump stand out, as well as the fact that her shapely backside was only half an inch away from his hand and the fabric showed off her new curves. He was tempted to stroke her lower back, to touch her, but he refrained as one of the young men spoke.

'Mrs Dean, we wanted to get an idea of what your needs are.' The other one interjected, 'Any area you would like, room sizes that sort of thing.'

'Price?' Lottie asked, looking at Edward.

'Immaterial, really, Lottie you know that if it is what you, we want.' He looked over at the men. 'Though that is not a free reign to go mad by any means gentlemen!'

Lottie sat and thought about it for a moment. 'I guess within easy reach of here and the centre, nothing more than half an hour in the car really for us both.' She thought again. 'I guess I would like some green space, of my own, visiting the park is all well and good, but to open the doors and feel safe is important. I guess that is why I love the apartment so much. It is so city life, and even though the green is from the balcony plants, the outside space is really generous but can be so very private.' She paused again. 'Open living space, with offices, large kitchen, and dining room, and of course room for the piano. Four bedrooms is a must, and a large bathroom just like what I have now, as well as a shower room, and then, oh!' She stopped. 'Ed what about Mrs B, would she want to move from the apartment block, and Pete, they all live so close? Are you sure that moving is a good idea really?' She looked at the two men, who she had almost forgotten were in on the conversation.

'Sorry gentlemen, I don't want to put you out of a job!' She smiled at them and they smiled back saying, 'That's OK' in a salesmen way where the client is always right.

'Gentleman, as you can see my wife does need some more time, but please arrange for a valuation on the apartment with Pete and at least we can have some more time to give it some serious thought. In the meantime, anything that you feel is worth a look, with the remit my wife has already noted we will be willing to look at online. Maybe if we see what we don't want, we will have a better idea of what we do want.'

'If that makes sense,' Lottie said, working out his word play in her head trying to understand it.

As they left, Lottie nipped to the bathroom and joined Ed again who was gathering some papers together.

'Dinner out, Mrs Dean?' he asked and Lottie looked at the time. It was late. With the summer nights being long it was easy to lose track of time. He walked over to her as she looked out at the city.

'How have you two been today?' he asked, sliding his hands around her waist to her stomach and kissing her neck. She closed her eyes to absorb his closeness, take in his smell, feeling his radiating heat. She relaxed her head back on his shoulder and she said, 'Good, fine,' then she said, 'Sorry about being late, I just needed to get some more bits to one of the detectives.'

'And I guess as a doctor/client confidentiality thing, you will not go into any more details?' he asked as he always did to show an interest in her work, even if he did not want her to be working at all. He was right as she changed the subject quickly.

'So apart from selling my home from underneath me, how has your day been?' She giggled as he pulled her around to face him and she held onto his dark pink silk tie with both hands, caressing the material in a suggestive sort of way. She bit down on her lip. 'Made any millions?' she asked. Bump did do one thing, it made it hard for Lottie to rub against him when he was this close. Something she often did to tease him, he reacted so quickly to her touch.

'Potentially. I lose count after the first few mil before 9am!' He smirked, joking with her. 'Can you stop that?' he asked as he was now feeling her kiss along his collar line and around his ear.

'Why, Mr Dean, can you not think about holding a conversation and be distracted?' She carried on, rubbing her chest on his hard torso, and sliding her hand along his hip towards his inner thigh.

'I can think fine, but only of one thing!' he replied.

'My point! An inability to multi-task!'

'How do you know I was not going to say my stomach? I have not eaten since lunch!' he said, thinking he was giving a smart reply.

'You may have been going to say your stomach, but I am guessing this has other ideas.' She placed her hand on his groin and rubbed down the hard member straining against the layer of material. Then she loosened the zip, replying, 'Maybe I should have a quick taste of the menu?' She released him without effort, and her cool slender fingers gripped him hard, sending more blood to the already swelling end.

'Lottie, the blinds!' he exclaimed, noting that anyone walking past the outside the office could still see in.

'Close the door after you then,' she said, walking into the room off to the side that was his executive bedroom.

The sheets were cool against his now-naked back as she pushed him down in the centre of the bed. The scattered clothes led a trail to her sitting astride him, so that just her bra and panties remained. She had continued to suck him off while he undressed himself, until the urgency for her forced him to surrender to what she wanted.

'Um, is that the taste of things to cum?' she giggled, licking his pre-cum from her lips.

'Oh God, yes, if you keep doing that!'

She bit down onto his nipple and then lovingly kissed it. She tossed her hair over him as she worked back down to his stomach. She was always drawn to the V-shape that framed his manhood so perfectly. She licked her way down as if it showed her the way to his throbbing dick. She took him again deep into her mouth and flicked her tongue over the purple end on her upward stroke. Rubbing her chest into his thighs, not just for his enjoyment, but because it arose the burning deep inside herself. Her breasts were so sensitive to touch, even the rubbing of the silk bra on his skin felt like it was sandpaper, but it was a deeply enjoyable pleasure, not pain.

She worked him in and out of her mouth, round and round on his end, took him so far that she felt herself gag and needed to take more breath on her upward stroke. She used her hand to massage his balls, they withdrew and dropped back at her touch, indicating he was close to release.

'Let me have you, Lottie,' Ed gasped, wanting to feel her warmth, and still have time to get her to climax with him. He pulled her hair as an indicator to get her face off him, but she sucked him harder forcing him to let her slide her lips back down the stem of his prick.

'Christ, woman, do you ever do as you are told!' he gasped out again, this time using his hand to hold her head down on him; he was about to blow. The sudden rise of his balls showed her he was at his moment and extend her sexual teasing she pulled off him, crawling to his side on all fours.

'Fucking hell!' he said as his internal muscles spasmed but her timing left him without release. He pulled her back, quickly standing up at the edge of the bed, leaving her ass up in the air. He ripped at the delicate lace on her gusset, taking it to one side and exposing her sex, placing her directly in front of his cock, which was almost reaching his stomach, and as strong and hard as a rod of iron.

'You teasing little...' he held his word.

'Would that be 'bitch', Mr Dean?' she asked.

'Yes, it fucking well would be. Now get on this.' He pulled her onto him in one movement, not caring if she was ready for him or not. He was soon aware of how wet she was, and he had no problems with absorbing his full length into her in a matter of seconds.

'Oh!' She flew her head back with the impregnating shock of him in her. Her knees almost losing grip on the edge of the bed, she clenched her thighs, which made her close her legs slightly, intensifying his size in her and tightening her grip on him.

Sweat glistened off his chest as he tried to slow himself down, but Lottie was still in control of the speed and she pushed back on him as much as the silk bedding would allow her to in order to get traction. He had to keep control. At any other time, he would have been hitting that peach soft skin on her arse until it was blood red. He wanted to grip her around the throat to slow her down. He had found it worked – the less they can breathe, the less they squirm and wriggle on the end of your cock! A sudden voice came into his head as he remembered conversations about rough sex in his younger years.

Control yourself, Dean, for Christ's sake, the other voice in his head kicked in. Lottie gave out another moan and it brought him back into the room. She had collapsed onto her elbows, her face now on the sheets, gasping in pleasure and excitement.

'What do you need, Mrs Dean?' he asked, falling on top of her, but still holding all his weight.

'Oh, I need... I need to come!' she spat out, her nerve endings almost like electric shocks in her sex.

'What as much as I did a moment ago when you denied me?' Now who was in charge as he whispered in her ear.

'Yes!' she said. 'Yes!'

'Yes, what Mrs Dean?' he asked, wanting her to say it.

'Yes, please.' She gave in as she did not want to be without the ultimate climax that was building.

Thank God! Edward thought to himself. He was never going to hold on any longer, and she had only to get the word 'please' out before he reached underneath her and pulled at one of her tits, rubbing the nipple as hard as he could from this angle. He burst inside her like a pulsating beacon. Still wary of how deep he was inside her he tried to slow down, her muscles contracting around him as she sobbed out her orgasm. He still had more to give her but could feel her going weaker under his arms.

'Greedy!' he said. 'You had your fun and your fill?' He pulled out of her and rolled her over, with his cock still spilling his thick white gel over her chest. She pushed up to take him back in her mouth and finished off the last few thrusts, taking his come down her throat.

'Now I have, Mr Dean!' she said as his knees shook and he rubbed his hands through his hair in pure exultation as the very last drop of him was extracted by her mouth.

'I have totally died.' He slumped by her side and held her in his arms. He kissed the back of her neck, tasting the salt on her skin and she closed her eyes, totally exhausted from their lovemaking. She still had her bra and panties on, but he was naked, exposed for the entire world, and they held the pose until they had both regained their breath. Lottie was so relaxed that for a moment she may have been asleep. Edward surely was out as his breathing had slowed right down and his mind was devoid of any other thoughts except the bliss that surrounded him.

She opened her eyes slowly and moved his hand over her hip to her bump, and he stirred in his position at her touch moving him.

'Someone is not sleeping,' she said, kissing his shoulder as it reached over her. He sat up to get in a better position, little flutters on her skin pressed into his hand. He smiled, then he started to grin which turned into a laugh, as he followed the movement over her. As quickly as it started it stopped, and he kissed her, moving the hair from her face.

'I love you, Mrs Dean,' he said, then planting a kiss on her stomach. 'And you too Bump!'

They finally made it for a meal out, but it was way past 10:30 pm after their delayed office meeting.

Chapter 17

As promised Lottie took the paperwork round to Detective Sharpe the following day. They had sat and had a hot drink in his room and chatted for longer than they had intended. Not just about how this would pan out, but Lottie explained a lot about how normal it was to have a driver, and the detective expressed how hard it must be to have a shadow.

'It takes some getting used to,' she had explained, and it had been for her. 'But now I just see them as part of life. Paid staff as some might see it, I just see it as friends who help out,' but her explanation had still been a marvel to the detective, who she had found out was married and had two sons, one still at school and the other about to leave for university.

The conversation had got around to some of the other cases Lottie had worked on, and to her surprise he had heard of a few in the police circles.

'Well, Mrs Dean, it is a small world, but one I can see causes you some problems at the moment, so we need to get this right. I agree that we need to tread carefully, but to contradict that we do need to act fast!' He smiled at her. 'Your plan, getting to meet this guy and befriending him into a confession. I am not quite seeing how it will work, and we may have to finalise and agree on the finer details, that is what is going to take some time. You say your friend is coming back from America in a few weeks, how does he fit in?'

Lottie explained how she wanted to use Todd as a decoy to get her back into the club. God knows how she was going to persuade Ed to let her out with him, or get into her outfit, or not to have a driver, but she would have to think of something. Hoping that once there, Alex would talk to her and she would arrange to meet him somewhere more private, explain how she wanted to pave the way for him to get back in touch with Edward, then, and again these details were sketchy, get him alone and broach the subject. This was the part that would take some careful planning too as she could not just come out to accuse him, and the detective knew this would be the part where she was going to need his back up.

'So, we get him to the point of admitting it, you're wired up and he turns on you, what then Mrs Dean?' he asked.

Lottie was not sure she could answer him. 'You come to my rescue?' she tried to joke.

'I don't like it, there is too much doubt, too many areas where this could go wrong. I still think that arresting him and getting him here is the best way forwards.'

'What do you arrest him for?' she asked.

'Anything. Breathing if that is all it takes.' Sharpe was genuinely concerned that the plan had more holes than he dared to think about. 'We need to talk a lot in the two weeks before Mr Carter comes back, maybe he can think of a better way.'

'I cannot see one at the moment,' she replied, pushing her cup of tea to the side.

'And you insist that Mr Dean is no part of this plan why?' he asked, offering her another drink, but she declined.

'I have a gut feeling that he will just blow and then, well I have to say I don't know what will happen. Alex could just disappear, and we lose him or,' she paused, 'Edward does something stupid and one of them gets hurt, or he, well I have seen his temper, anything could happen. If he harms him, or worse, he will lose everything.'

'And if you get hurt, he loses everything anyway. I have my reservations, and as you can tell they are great. I will make a deal with you. We try your way, and if I feel there is any danger of anything getting out of hand I step in and do it my way.' He tapped the pile of papers. 'I am sure that there is enough here to get him to go down for a long time.'

'But that is not the whole point, I need Edward to have closure on his question of why Mitch died, and only Alex knows why he did it.' She took a deep breath.

They chatted for only a few more moments and then her phone rang. Phil reminded her that she had an appointment at the Music Collage and that the traffic was getting bad so they would need to leave.

'I will give it a lot more thought,' Sharpe said as she stood up, explaining that she needed to go, and they agreed to meet the following Monday at her office.

'Just make sure you keep me in the loop with anything, as you insist on the business as usual. I will try to continue to build the case; he sounds clever, but everyone messes up at some point.' The detective shook her hand and followed her out to the waiting car.

So, it was very much business as usual for the next two and half weeks. Lottie sealed the placements at the collage for Paul although it had been a struggle; in fact she had at one point threatened to pull her funding until the board agreed that the placement for Mr Chance was also the only option they had. They would arrive in time for the September term, a little over a month to go. She Skyped Paul and was pleased to see that he was already making plans to be back in the UK. His aunt had offered them a place for a few weeks to get them back in the country giving them time to find a place to stay, although Lottie had already had her letting agents pick out some flats that were much better than the student digs the collage could offer. Ed had suggested they buy somewhere as an investment, then maybe it could become part of the collage accommodation when Paul left after his course, like a package. She jumped at the chance as it made him feel like he had the idea, and he was part of the process too. She did not tell him she had already made some accommodation enquiries.

The fashion house was really taking off and she showed Mrs B the spread they had advertised in the *Sunday Times* magazine outlining new business in the city. Lottie had tried hard to keep her name out of it but had to give in when Liz said she did not want to take all the credit, and as soon as the Dean name was mentioned it made good reading for some. The fashion house had employed more staff and had to start to think about bigger business premises. Towards the end of the first week Lottie felt that all she did was look at letting agent's emails and possible houses, factories, and homes. Ed had given her a few places in the city that he was suggesting for their new home, all of which were overpriced and needed a lot of work, which did not bother him, but stressed her out even more. They kept their social diary busy as ever and Lottie was starting to feel the effects of taking on too much all in one go.

Sitting at the breakfast bar she had woken early, her mind in turmoil with everything she was taking on board. It was the first week of August and Todd was due to land in from America the next day; she hoped things would settle with someone else to talk to. She looked at her emails as she sat in the darkness of the kitchen, waiting for the kettle to boil. She had slipped out of bed. Ed was used to her getting up in the night to go to the toilet and found it easier to go back to sleep if she had woken him now, so her escape to the kitchen had not been hard.

Her head pounded, and she hoped the drink would ease the pains she felt. She leant on the side of the counter waiting for the water to boil for a flavoured tea and looked out at the gloom of the wet August morning. Then she looked down at her bare feet on the marble floor, and she wiggled her toes. At least I can still see them, she thought although she was making good progress at growing outwards, noticing that the customary shirt, one of Ed's old ones now struggled to do up in front of her. She smiled and patted her stomach; today she had four months left, and the time was just going so quickly she had not even noticed it. She took a breath as she carried her drink to the lounge and sat in the dark, enjoying the 'me time' she had so long forgotten existed. The room was so silent she could hear the ticking of the mantle clock. She put her drink on the arm of the chair, but it missed, and she spilled tea all over the floor. Cursing under her breath she got up and turned on the light, rushing to the kitchen and taking a handful of paper towels back to the room. She almost jumped as she was greeted by Pete picking up the cup, which had fallen to the floor also.

'Mrs Dean! Whatever are you doing, it's only just five?' he asked just as surprised to see her, but something had woken him from his joint accommodation.

Lottie pulled the shirt around her to cover her thighs.

'Here let me.' He held out his hand to take the absorbent material and started to wipe up the spill.

'I couldn't sleep,' she said, walking off to get some more cloth as the first lot was not enough to cope with the accident.

'Too much on your mind at a guess,' he said, taking the second lot she handed him on her return.

'Maybe, although if I admitted it, Ed would have me stop the lot, so I was just trying to get some time to myself,' she replied, smiling as he took the towels to the bin.

'Everything seems to have gone quiet now with your case and the notes though, hasn't it?' he asked as if he knew something.

'Seems that way,' Lottie lied. She had not said anything about her meetings with DC Sharpe.

'Maybe when Todd comes over you can ask Mr Dean if you could have the weekend in Kent?' Pete asked.

'Maybe.' Although that was the last place she wanted to be as she wanted to make up the excuse to meet with Alex Girski, somehow.

'Well, if you are OK, then I will go and shower.' Pete looked at her, she was sure that he was on to her, but she simply replied with a 'Thanks'.

He closed the door quietly and she returned to the sofa. She picked up the last email of houses – maybe this was the excuse to meet him. Ed had not found the time to visit every one and she was sure he would not quibble if she said she had another viewing. It would be an easier cover than meeting at the club. She felt the laptop slipping from her knees and her eyes closed. She pushed it to the side as she put her head back on the sofa. Maybe she was tired after all and she should go back to bed.

'Hey,' Edward said, sitting on the floor with his back against the sofa, the paper in his hands, fully-dressed and hair almost dry from his morning shower. Lottie almost jumped, seeing the daylight come in through the window. She pushed herself up, feeling the sheet laying over her.

'Pete came to get me when he noticed you had gone back to sleep. I did not have the heart to wake you.' He planted a kiss on her head. 'Not sure why you got up so early as you clearly are tired,' he said, resisting to ask if she was OK. It seemed that was all he ever asked her, and he had made a mental note to stop it.

'I just woke up and could not get to sleep. I came out for a drink but...' she started to explain.

'Pete said you spilt it. Mrs B has been desperate to come in and make a better job of cleaning it up. I will give her a shout as she has been beside herself the past three hours!' he smiled.

'Oh, what's the time now?' Lottie asked, noticing that if Mrs B had been in for that long she must have been asleep for ages. She looked at the large grandfather clock sitting in the corner of the room. It was just before 10 am; she had been asleep for hours.

'You should have woken me,' she said instantly to Ed.

'Why, it's not a workday.' He turned around and rested his head close to her bump.

'No, but I need to get on with a few things,' she said.

'Like what?' he asked.

'Todd's coming tonight, have you forgotten?'

'Hardly!' Edward said under his breath. Although he knew she was excited he also knew that he had to share her again with him and the thought of him being in their apartment for a few days really did annoy him. Having him across the other side of the pond really had made him feel better, but he had to conclude that if Lottie missed him and wanted to see him, he had to let her.

'He is one of my best friends, Ed. I know that you don't want him to be here, but I want him to be.' She pushed the sheet off, and it revealed a little more of her legs than she wanted. Edward rubbed his hands up her thighs.

'I know but...' he started kissing her knees, working his way up. His breath was warm, and his touch was like velvet to her. She took a long breath in, looking quickly around to see if anyone else was able to see into the room. Although she could hear Pete and Mrs B, they were safely behind the kitchen door, which was closed.

'But what?' she asked. 'He will take my undivided attention from you for a few days?' she giggled as his kisses went further up her legs and she covered her sex over with her hand to try to stop him progressing too far, although the gesture was futile as he unbuttoned his own shirt she was wearing and kissed her stomach.

'No,' he said in between the feather-like kisses.

'Yes,' she said. 'It's only for a few weeks,' she added, still enjoying his touch, but he stopped and looked up.

'The deal was days, Mrs Dean, when did that game plan change?' he asked, trying to recall when she had mentioned it.

'Well, I can't ask him to do a flying visit, he may not be back for some time and he has a lot of family that he needs to catch up with,' she replied, putting her hands on his face and drawing him up towards her.

'He could stay with them and then he wouldn't need to do so much catching up!' Ed retorted, trying not to put his weight onto her, holding himself above her with his strong muscular arms.

'I want him to be able to stay with me, it will help fill my days and time when you are working,' she replied back. 'I thought that we might spend a few days in Kent, and you could join us for the weekend.'

The expression on his face must have changed to give away the thought that was in his mind. '*You alone with him, not an option*' he said inwardly, but Lottie must have read it as she replied out loud.

'The green-eyed monster appears at the very thought of me being alone with him, doesn't it?' She took a breath. 'Don't you trust me by now?' She was not mad or showing any emotion in her voice, but she was slightly perplexed that he would not think her faithful after all this time, even with the growing evidence in her belly that she was truly committed to her husband.

'I do trust you,' he said. It was Todd he was never sure of. 'I am a little envious of you being free to get some time off, that's all. It's so busy at the office.'

'So, having him around to keep me safe in the country is the perfect solution. It will even free up Pete and Phil who will not need to be around,' she exclaimed as if she had won the debate.

'I would not go that far.' Ed lovingly pressed her nose with a delicate fingertip and kissed the place it left.

'Oh, really Ed, the boys would like a break I'm sure, they don't want to sit around doing nothing but listen to two old friends drivel on about stuff. Apart from maybe visiting Agnes, a pub lunch or two and long walks with the dog, what trouble am I going to get up to?' She smiled at him.

'I dread to think!' He backed off her. 'But I'm in a losing battle I can feel it in the conversation, so OK, Mrs Dean, you win. Fail to answer your phone once and I will come to Kent myself and spank you!'

'Promise?' she said with a slight raise of an eyebrow, and she grabbed his arm as he was about to walk off. She stood up on the sofa, so she became taller than he was, and she pulled him close to her. His face met her bust line, and he rubbed her arse with his hand linked around her as she wobbled on the leather beneath her feet.

'Promise,' he said, still rubbing his hand and giving it a sharp slap as advanced warning. He shifted his pose as his inevitable erection twitched in his trousers.

'Um, I like the sound of that, how naughty do I have to be?' Lottie bounced on the sofa knowing her unsupported tits were wiggling close to his lips, and she could feel his breath through the light material of his shirt. 'This naughty?' She lifted her foot to reach his groin, knowing that he would be easy to tease through the lightweight material. As if guided by a sat-nav, she hit the spot straight away, rubbing him. 'This naughty?' She lent forwards and licked his ear kissing around his earlobe and down his neck. The reaction of her foot and the kisses worked as predicted and his dick shot up in delight. She undid the buttons on her shirt, and she put her hand under the loose material and rubbed at her own breast, allowing her nipple to be pushed up, tantalisingly close to his mouth. He looked at her with a grin, shaking his head as if he knew he would resist her – really!

'What happened to not having enough time?' he asked, attempting to suck the hard-dark mound on display in front of his face, but she pulled back.

'Good point!' she giggled, pulling away to cover herself over.

'Like hell,' he said, pulling her back and taking her weight in both arms, encouraging her to wrap her legs around him. He lifted her in one movement, and she squealed. 'You started this!' he said, using all his strength to carry her with a full hard-on, battling with the door to the corridor to make sure that it did not hit her before he opened it.

'And somehow, Mr Dean, I can see you are going to finish it!' She flung her head over his shoulder and kissed his neck again.

'Too damn right I am, Mrs Dean!' He made short work of the distance between the sofa in the lounge and their bedroom, the door closing with a slam of his foot as he reached the destination. He sat her on the edge of the bed and undid his trousers, revealing his large, engorged dick. He had woken with a hard-on and suppressed the feeling, now it was back and was not going to rest until he had reached his end goal.

'Fucking suck this.' He held himself in his hand, his purple head protruding far away from his palm due to his size and he started to stroke himself. 'Then I can tell you how naughty you must be, and currently you are pretty close!'

She shifted closer to him, smelling his skin, and his soft, musky personal smell that had set her own senses on fire so many times before. She opened her mouth and took him, slowly at first to ensure that she did not gag, but his hand soon came around the back of her head and increased her speed, pushing her face onto him. It was seconds before his seed spilt the first few drops of salty liquid into her mouth and she sucked harder, holding her mouth, gently grazing her teeth along his shaft. Taking a moment to catch her breath, but licking around the top of his head, then in the ultimate move to make his legs weaken she licked his balls, sucking each one in turn.

'How can you do that?' he asked, daring to open his eyes to look at her. She could make him vulnerable and weak, as she had his most sensitive areas in her mouth. 'Lottie, I have to warn you, this may not last long!' His voice rose slightly as she took another assault on his member.

'Stop,' he said. 'Turn around, I have to have you.' As if she was a limpet, he had to prise her off him and physically turn her around. Since she had grown, she found it uncomfortable to lie on her back, and so taking her from behind made him feel more comfortable to ensure that he did not hurt her. Although he was sure that she enjoyed it more this way anyway. One problem for him was whenever her bare arse was in his view, he had to hit it. An act he found hard to restrain from.

With his trousers still around his knees Lottie turned, the shirt still on her shoulders and covering her skin on her back. She put her knees on the edge of the bed and lent up to him. He drew towards her, aiming his erection like an arrow at her sex, and placing a direct hit between her legs he thrust into her, pushing her forwards and making her yelp out in shock of his size. He put his hands on her hips to steady her, and she flicked her hair over her back. He was too far away to kiss her, and if he lent forwards, he would lose his timing, and would not be able to take his own weight. He wanted to smell her skin, bite her tender white flesh. He pulled out of her and she gave a disappointed sigh.

'Lay on the bed, on your side, I want to feel you next to me.' She did as he asked, and he spooned in behind her. Lifting one leg up he was able to reposition his cock back to the place he wanted it to rest. Now he was close, he could hold her in his arms and kiss the flesh that he lusted over. She reached her hand over behind her to him and he kissed it. Extending her arm made her breast lift and tighten and he cupped the plump mound that was now noticeably full in anticipation of her motherhood. His gut turned and the pure excitement of the gift she had inside her overwhelmed him.

They were co-joined, coupled in love-making now. He felt that the first position was more for sex, fucking as she had put it, but like this, his world was safe with her and his child encapsulated in his arms.

She gave out pleasurable noises as he slowly pumped and grinded into her from behind. She took his hand from her waist and kissed it, licking at his fingers, as if to gesture that this was his member she had taken in her mouth moments ago.

'Bloody hell, Lottie, I was trying to make this last, but you just have this way. That unforgiving mouth of yours!' He felt her grind herself further back into him and he held her leg more so he could get further into her. It worked as she took another deep breath.

'Edward, I love you,' she said out of the blue, in a deep sexual voice.

He pulled her hair away from her neck and kissed it. 'I love you too, Lottie. More than ever before if that is humanly possible.' He really did not know that it could be. She started to silently shake in his arms as her body was wracked with her climax, her core muscles contracting and spasming as he slowly pushed in and out.

She closed her eyes as the heat rose from deep within her upper legs to fill over her whole body. She could not feel more joined to him, protected by him than at any other point. She held her weight on the sheets with one arm to prevent him pushing her over, as his moves became faster; she knew he had held out for her, but now she would take him all. He pushed his head into her shoulders and gritted his teeth as he felt the explosion from his dick into her. Slowing the pace so that each thrust could drain the juice out of him and fill her, he thrust his upper body with gentle ease. Once he had no more to give, he looked back up and gently kissed the nape of her neck.

'I didn't want that to stop, ever,' he said in a low, exhausted voice.

'I know.' She smiled although he could not see it, and she pulled his arms around her as if to try to get them to be one physical body. 'I know,' she repeated, closing her eyes. He moved his hand to include her bump into the family circle and nuzzled back into her, a small tear falling down his face. The pure emotion of how he felt at this moment and what they had just done came over him and he smiled and took in her smell. As if she intoxicated him, he fell into a light sleep. Their partially clad bodies lay on the bed for several hours, with only one attempt to pull over the sheets to keep Lottie warm, and they savoured their moment together.

'Lottie, we'll be late!' he shouted to her, waiting by the door with the car keys in his hand. He was going to drive her to the airport to meet Todd; he just wanted to get more time alone with her.

'Alright,' she shouted back, 'I can't find my phone.' She was sure that she had left it in her pocket. 'Is it in the living room?' She asked for someone else to have a look around.

'Why do you need it, you will be with me,' he said in a bid to hurry her along.

She emerged out of the bedroom in a tight-fitting top, and leggings that really showed off her expectant size and her new fuller bust.

'I know but it keeps losing its charge and I wanted to make sure I left it charging while we were out.' She continued to look in a panicked way around the room. Ed walked to her and stopped her still.

'Stop clucking like a mother hen, calm down. Mrs B can have a look for it and then charge it up for you. Now come on!' He kissed her on the cheek; she was hot and flushed from dashing about. 'Think about your blood pressure!'

'Panic not, Mrs Dean, I have it.' Mrs B walked from the kitchen with it in her hand. 'I will get it charged up for you while you are gone.'

Lottie mouthed a 'Thank you' to Mrs B as she grabbed her handbag from the counter and made her way to the lift door that Ed was holding open.

'You should get the phone changed if it is causing an issue,' Ed mentioned in passing as they stood holding hands in the lift making their way to the underground garage.

'I will,' Lottie replied with a smile, feeling the cool breeze hit her as the door opened and they made their way over to the Bentley, parked next to the array of shiny cars that belonged to Ed. Not his first car of choice to drive – he would take the Audi R8 – but Todd would hate him even more when trying to get in the non-existent back seats.

They had parked and walked over to arrivals, the flight was in and all they had to do was wait until he made it through customs. Lottie stood with the crowd anticipating the people as a few faces started to appear around the corner of the corridor. Several squeals of joy could be heard as they and others awaited their loved ones. All of them willing to catch the first sight of the arriving passengers. Ed stood behind her, one hand on her waist and the other browsing over his emails. She gave a sudden shriek of joy as she saw Todd. Tall, proud, really tanned and looking good. She quickly ran towards him, making Edward lift his head as he saw his wife launch herself into another man's arms.

Todd froze to the spot. He had seen her face, and had beamed at first, but then the realisation hit him as the crowds had parted and he got a full glance of her whole body. She had never once in their conversations mentioned that she was carrying Edwards's child! And by the look of it she had been keeping it from him for months.

'Todd, oh god it's good to see you!' she said, wrapping her arms around him, but then she could sense from his body language that he was not sharing the same experience. Ed remained a few paces back from the old friends, hating the emotion she was giving to another man, another man who had touched her and kissed her, and he closed his eyes to remove the image of them together.

'Todd, what's wrong?' She pulled herself back and looked at his face.

'Well, that is a welcome home, I take it from both of you.' He directed his eyes towards her stomach, and she felt the pain now in his words and the meaning of the statement.

'Sorry, I guess it never came up in conversation,' she said. Really, she had not told him as she knew that there would be no way he would let her put herself at risk with whatever she was planning, and telling him she was pregnant could have caused him to refuse to come back to the UK at all. That for sure would be one way she would not be able to follow through on her plans.

'Jesus, Lottie, "it never came up in conversation" is the understatement of the year. Hitting me in the face with a brick would have been an easier blow to take.' Todd picked up the handle to his suitcase to move as they were standing in the way of other passengers. They walked away from where Ed was standing, the crowd putting up a natural barrier between them.

'Why is it a big deal? I thought you would be pleased to see me?' she asked, now feeling slightly rejected.

'I am, Lotts, I am, but a bit of warning would have been good,' he said looking at her face, knowing he had changed the smiles to sadness, and it melted his heart straight away.

Months away from her and he finally felt he was moving on. He had even started to see a girl, for more than a few dates. But thirty seconds with her, looking so bloody beautiful and he was back to square one again. Years ago, he had had the aspiration that one day he would be the one she had a family with. He would be the one to stand next to her, with all his male pride on show, as this blooming angel stood by his side.

Edward Bloody Dean had bagged the love of his life, and now he had well and truly stamped his mark, Todd thought to himself. He had a sudden pang of guilt as he pecked Lottie finally on the cheek as a 'hello' and 'I am really pleased to see you' gesture. He almost said the following statement out loud: *I love you so much, if he makes you happy then I guess I must live with it.* For that very fact, that you are happy is not nearly enough, but will satisfy me that you are OK.

'Sorry Lotts, it is good to be back.' He gave her a smile and a quick hug and she instantly smiled back, and she bit down on her lip.

'Forgive me?' she said, looking all puppy-dog like with her eyes.

'Of course,' he said pressing his finger to her lip. The fucking lip, but yes, he had to wake up to the fact that he was the dickhead that had let her go in the first place. So he had to live with it, but he would never get over her, he knew that was a fact.

Edward caught the last part of their greeting and now knew he had to break them up. He knew that look melted polar ice caps in seconds and if you loved her, it did more to your male genitals than at times was required! He quickly walked over to them and put his guarding arm around his, yes Todd, *his* wife's shoulders. As if a dog marking his ground, he nodded to

Todd and stuttered out a welcome. Todd mumbled the same greeting back, taking every note in their mannerisms and body language that the two men were, if not physically calling each other out, mentally on the same page of dominance showing just who had the upper hand. Sadly, for Todd, it was Edward Dean every time.

No one mentioned anything else in the car on the way home apart from what it was like to work in New York. Todd had been slow to start off, but soon found his well-oiled voice once Lottie sat in the back with him for the journey home.

Todd could have laughed to himself noting that Edward had looked in the rear mirror maybe every second to see what was going on. In fact, he was surprised they had not crashed as he must be spending more time looking in the back than looking at the road ahead.

Lottie was oblivious to all of this, never caught a thing, but it was obvious to the men that they were still ever much in competition with each other, but with only one prize.

They both arrived at the centre on the Monday morning. Lottie had given him a chance to catch up on some sleep and settle into the guest suite when they had got back. Todd had a lot of catching up to do and was keen to see his family.

So nothing was said until the next day on the Tuesday morning, when Lottie sat at her desk and the door was closed; they were alone.

'So, your real reason for not telling me about Bump was you were worried I would not come over and carry out your ridiculous plan?' Bump was Edward and Lottie's general term of endearment and it had rubbed off on him.

'Why don't you just say what is on your mind?' she replied, knowing that he knew her so well, and yes it really was what she should have said.

'You won't admit it then?' he asked, looking at his computer screen.

'And if I do, would that change your mind?' she replied, walking to his desk to sit in front of him to get his attention.

'Well, I had better know the full plan, and then I'll see, but be warned Lottie, this is one of the stupidest things you have ever wanted to do. You are risking so much and for what, just so Edward gets peace of mind. I am sure that faced with losing you or you being harmed or him getting his peace of mind'. He paused 'Well, I know he would sooner just give it over to the police, now. Like you would do on any other case.' She had his attention and he held her eye to show that he was serious.

He had to use all his strength not to stand up, take her face in his hands and kiss her. Taste her lips, which held such devoted memories for him. He wanted to put his hand on her knee that was so close to him, but he knew that the temptation to then follow the line up her thigh would kill him even more.

'It's not just another case, it's personal,' she said.

'And that is where the problem is, you are too involved.' He couldn't help it, he stood and pushed the hair that was covering her face out of the way. 'I can't see you hurt, just as I know he does not want you harmed.'

She knew that she should have resisted his touch, but she could not recoil from him. In fact, she welcomed the thought that he still wanted to be close to her, no matter how that may look wrong in some people's eyes.

She took his hand in her own and held it.

'I know, and that is why I have asked for your help, I trust you.'

'And not Edward?' Todd asked, all matter of fact.

'To be blunt, no, not with this. I think that he would not go to the police. I think he would have an underhand way of getting Alex out of the equation, which may come back to bite him in some way, if not now but later down the line. I do not want that for him, me or our baby.'

Todd stood back. 'You mean get him bumped off?' She never said the words but just nodded.

'Well come on then, spill the plan, let's meet this DC Sharpe bloke and get it going.' She smiled at him and stood, catching his eye she leant to kiss his cheek and whispered, 'Thank you.'

His heart would never recover, never and she would never know that it was breaking in two and had stopped for anyone else, forever.

The dockside cafe was not busy, and Lottie, Todd and the detective chose to sit outside. With no one around them they knew that they could talk. The vantage point was a good one from the other side of the water, and although he could not see what was being said, he could watch her, observe her. The way she was with her friend must have driven Edward wild with envy, he said to himself as it was driving him insane. He knew that he could not even dream to be that close to her. He drew deep on the cigar poised at his lips as he sat in the car with the window wound down, the binoculars in his hand.

'So, Saturday afternoon it is, Mrs Dean.' DC Sharpe confirmed the plan. 'I will have as many staff as I can get around without sparking off any questions. Mr Carter, I wish that you would choose to be armed, I can arrange for training and the relevant licences to be in place. It would make me feel better,' the policeman added.

'It would make me feel more nervous and then more likely to blow an innocent person away!' Todd was no way having a gun; even if he thought it would protect Lottie, there was no way he was carrying.

As the policeman walked off Todd moved his chair closer to Lottie. She smiled at him.

'You know that just because I have said that I will do this, in no way am I happy about it!' He finished off his drink and looked out of the window.

'I know,' Lottie said in a low, compassionate voice. She held out her hand and touched his to get his attention back. 'Thank you, Todd. It means so much to me to know that we have such a close friendship.' She gave his hand a squeeze to get him to turn to her, and it was then that she noticed the wetness on his eyes.

'Hey,' she said, 'Todd, what is it?'

He took in a deep breath causing his shoulders to rise and then he looked at her.

'Lottie, I...' he paused. 'You know how I feel about you. You know how I have always felt about you.'

She smiled at him. Yes, she did know how much in love they had been in the first few months they were together. They had shared some amazing moments. Their lives had taken different paths and a future as lovers was not to be. She had loved him, she still did. But she was not 'in love' with him. Nothing like her feelings for Edward, which consumed her.

'I need you to do this for me, Todd,' she said, trying to get him to look her in the eye.

'I know you do, and I feel like it is emotional blackmail. I have no way of saying no to you, even though with every bone in my body I know I should.'

He leant over so he could smell her skin, feel her breath on his face. She held his eye, and with the slowest movement he moved in to kiss her. She didn't back away or move. She somehow knew that she had to kiss him. This was not how friends would kiss, even though the passion and need were not stirring in her.

He took her lips as if they were made of paper, that would dissolve at his touch. His heart was beating so fast that he was sure he would burst. The fact that she was allowing him to take her lips made the hair on his arms stand up. Somehow, though, she felt different, distant; she felt like she belonged to Edward Dean. That was the plain and simple.

As he pulled away from her pink lips, he wanted to say that he was sorry, but he was not. Lottie had her eyes closed and as she felt the flutter of his skin leave hers, she opened them.

'I know,' she said to Todd, without him asking a question. 'I know.' She knew he loved her in a way that she would never be able to give back to him again.

The person watching them was pleased he had held off for a few moments more before leaving his long-distance vantage point. He inwardly laughed as he observed the couple kiss on the lips and linger in that attitude for more than friends maybe should. This was because he knew the assignation would be something Mr perfect fucking Dean would explode over. For him it just gave him another wish that he could be the lucky bastard sitting in front of her once more.

'Ed, I'm going to see your mom after work. When I said Todd was over, she asked how he was, and I said I would pop in to see her. I also guess there are more items to arrive for the nursery too, judging by her excitement!' This was no lie as luck would have it. Alice had called Lottie just to see how she was doing. She rang Edward and luckily, he had not said he would go with them. The first part of the plan was complete.

Greetings over and gifts for the bump exchanged, Lottie came out with it, saying how good it must be for Alice to occasionally see her old friend and it was such a shame that Edward was not budging on wanted to rebuild old bridges towards Alex in the same way.

'Lottie, why don't you meet with Alex and his mother, tell them why you want him to meet Ed, maybe they could suggest something. I could call her now?' She went to pick up the phone.

Todd felt awful; part of any plan was not to have doubts, but he really did. This would never work, it was so false, so set up.

'Do you have Alex's number? Maybe I will ring him, and not get his mother involved for now. One step at a time?' she questioned as a phone number was written down on a slip of paper.

'Whatever you think best, you know how Edward is going to react to these underhand tactics don't you? Do you think you can face that?' There was an air of concern in her voice.

'I'm sure I can cope with him. We have chatted about it,' Lottie replied.

Again, not a lie, just not the complete truth of the matter. Ed had been more than adamant that he was never, the expression was 'while he had a hole in his arse going to talk to the twat again', let alone make up with him.

'Are you texting him now?' Todd asked as they sat in the back of the car on the way back to the apartment.

'Can't see why not,' she said as her fingers worked the keys.

Alex

I hope that you do not mind me contacting you out of the blue, but I wanted to finally get the opportunity to formally meet you. Edward and I have been talking and I feel that it is time that we tried to make amends. I have an old friend over from America and it has shown me just how important such people are in our lives and I would like to try to bring you and Edward back together. I wanted to meet up first with you, before meeting with Edward to see if this is at all possible. It has been too long, and this is long overdue. We are going through a rough time and his friends around him, I am sure would be welcome.

I would like to ask you for a drink at lunchtime, about 12:30 Saturday at the Kensington, if you are free. I would very much like to get together, just the two of us.

With hopeful regards,
Lottie Dean.

'There it's done,' Lottie said, and Phil looked at her in the mirror. She held the device in her hand and waited to see if a reply came back instantly. Much to her disgust the phone turned off as the battery died once more.

'Problem, Mrs Dean?' Phil asked.

'No, my phone keeps cutting out, it just needs a charge.' She pushed it back in her bag ensuring that it was the first thing that she did when they got back. Phil instantly dialled Pete just to let him know that if Mr Dean needed to call her, she was in the car and would have to use the speaker phone as her own had gone down.

Like a well-oiled machine, Edward knew this information before they even arrived back to the apartment.

'Pete. Get Mrs Dean a new phone for Monday. I'm not sure why it keeps cutting out, but I want it sorted please,' he instructed as he walked back to the kitchen with a beer in his hand.

'Sure thing, I'm on it. I think it could be the new tracker, they seem to take more out of the battery,' he commented. 'Does yours have the same issues?' he enquired and they carried on talking until Lottie, Todd and Phil arrived.

The reply to her text had arrived soon after her phone died, but she did not pick it up until the next morning when the phone had charged. She quickly read it and forwarded it to DC Sharpe. His reply came back that he would call her on Friday to make sure things were still on. When the time arrived, Lottie texted back and said, 'yes they are'.

'I don't see why you have to go now. You'll be really early,' Edward said to Lottie as she picked up her overnight bag ready to make their way down to Kent. Edward took it straight from her hands and shook his head.

'Ed, the bag's not heavy,' Lottie replied, knowing why he had taken it from her. 'I want to catch some shops first.'

'Pete can drop you in town.' He tried again to get at least one member of his staff to be with them.

'No changing the plan now. I'll drive, I am still very able, and at least I still can reach the steering wheel, for now.' She patted her ever-growing stomach and smiled as Bump was quite awake today. She was not sure if it was him, or the butterflies of nerves or anticipation that she hoped today would go alright, but her smile fooled Edward as he put his hand on hers, smiling as well and feeling the gentle movement. 'Pete is on leave anyway.' She finished the conversation, walking to the bedroom door.

'He is always on call,' Ed reminded her; paid staff never really had time to themselves.

'He is with his family; you are soon going to know how important that is.' She grabbed her handbag, pushing her phone in her pocket.

'All the more reason for me to come with you.' She rolled her eyes, not wanting this discussion to go on.

'Ok!' He held up his hands. 'I give in.'

'Good!' She kissed him on the lips, and he held on to her, making it last longer than she had anticipated. The gentle cough behind them reminded Lottie that Todd was waiting for her. The male pride in Edward just made him hold her for a few moments more.

As they walked to the car Edward was giving them both final instructions. Todd elected to stay quiet; he was sure he was going to burst, keeping this plan secret for any longer. He had woken several times in the night, even contemplated going into Edward's office when he saw the light on to blow Lottie's plan out of the water and tell him, but he had not. He watched as they kissed once more, knowing how he would feel if she was with him, not wanting to let her go. She looked fantastic in a light summer dress and jacket, clearly pregnant and looking so healthy.

Finally, they were on their way. Lottie put the phone onto speaker as she called the detective and they both listened to the plan once more. As they pulled up at the Kensington, the valet took her keys and they walked to the lounge. When the detective arrived, they went to the reception and Lottie got the room key. The same room she had stayed in several times and they all went up together.

'So, my guy will be in the bedroom,' he said as Lottie and a policewoman were in the bathroom next door fixing the wire to Lottie's bra strap. 'Mr Carter and I will be downstairs and we'll follow you up and wait outside until we hear you give the word.'

'Safe word,' Lottie said, smiling at the meaning, but inside she was now really nervous.

'Which is?' the detective asked.

'Kent,' she replied. 'We are heading to Kent,' she repeated.

'Good.' The detective put his hand to his ear. 'I got that. Jo, just check the recoding is clear.' The young policewoman rewound the tape she had on a hand-held tablet and Lottie's voice could he heard repeating the words. 'Good. Let's go downstairs and wait.'

The group moved out. Todd looked at his watch. They had half an hour to spare and he really thought he was going to give the game away. Although he was trying to read a paper and drink a coffee, he constantly kept looking from the door to his friend, then to the detective. Lottie sat on her own, with Todd a few seats away and the detective and young policewoman, who were dressed in casual clothes, sitting in a corner by the main door. His phone buzzed, he looked at the text. Oh God, he thought, it was from Edward.

I know you guys may be driving that is why I have texted you, Todd, just checking everything is OK?

He took a breath and replied

No issues traffic is light. Lottie is fine, nice car by the way!

A reply came back saying he would text again in an hour and he put his phone back in his pocket. The distraction had moved his eyes away for only a second, but he had missed the arrival of the man they had all been waiting for. He was sure that he had also walked in with a woman but could not be clarify this as his heart jumped into his mouth and his brain fogged when he noticed the tall figure walking towards Lottie. He clenched his fist, thinking that he was going to get up and do something, but as he saw her stand with her hand outstretched, he did not. A fleeting glance at the detective assured him they were all covered.

Lottie stood, but felt her knees give way. She faked her smile as the blond-haired man walked towards her. She almost felt bile in her throat, and she knew her hand was shaking as she held it out for him to take. The touch of his skin made her recoil and she told herself over and over in her head to keep calm.

'Mrs Dean, finally the pleasure I have been waiting for.' To her surprise he lifted her hand to his lips and kissed it. Lottie wanted to scream but had to stay composed. 'You look amazing. I have to give my congratulations to you and Edward, you are positively glowing.'

'Please call me Lottie.' She held her nerve and cast her eyes very quickly to Todd for some reassurance. Her guest noted the gesture and was tempted to follow her gaze, but he could not take his eyes from her for a second, his skin still smouldering at her touch.

'I have to say, this is all very out of the blue, Lottie.' He exaggerated her name and again she recoiled. 'So, tell me how did you get away from that control freak? What web of lies have you spun him to get here?'

'He thinks we are shopping,' was her short reply, her not noticing her mistake.

'We?' Alex Girski asked with a quizzical brow.

'We, yes sorry, the bump and me, we.' She hoped that she'd quickly recovered her mistake, thinking she had as the man smirked at the reply.

'How sweet!' he replied but he really wanted to spit the words back. Fucking Edward Dean, once more had it all! 'Dean has been tamed at last. Well, I sure can see why, you are the very vision of true beauty.'

Lottie felt uncomfortable, once more looking towards Todd, but this time Girski caught her gaze and noticed the man. He felt a fleeting moment of confusion; the face he recognised. He quickly glanced around the rest of the room and another face came to his notice; the three of them had met a few days before at the cafe, now they were all here. His brain tried to compute what was going on and Lottie noticed a bead of sweat on his brow.

'Alex, please order us some drinks, tea for me. I need to use the rest room, sorry!' This was not in the plan, but she really did need to get out; she felt sick.

'Sure,' he said, waiting for her to get up and as she walked away, he also noticed the young woman with the dark-haired guy he recognised going in the same direction as her.

Todd had to find out what was happening, so he walked to the detective, taking his eyes off Girski.

'Sit back down!' the detective spat out, trying to keep calm, but it was too late. Girski stood and quickly made his way to the female washroom. He forced his way through the door when he noticed Lottie walking back out. Not talking to anyone, and the young woman was nowhere to be seen. Maybe he had been wrong, and she was on her own after all.

'Oh,' Lottie noted as she saw him, surprised that he was here. She knew the female PC had followed her and gone into one of the cubicles.

'I wanted to make sure you were OK?' he lied. 'It's a bit warm in there, is it not?' He watched as she nervously nodded. 'Maybe we should go for a walk and talk about why I am really here, Mrs Dean.' He used her full name again and as he did, he took her arm, making her jump at his touch. 'I have this feeling I am not really here to talk about getting back a long-lost friendship.'

He pushed her towards the fire exit door, and she soon found her feet going along a back corridor. Lottie was trying to get back on plan, but saying the safe word was so far from her mind she could not get it out even if she wanted to. But she needed to do something.

'We can go to the penthouse. I have the key,' she stuttered.

'And why would I do that?' His sinister voice was cold, and she was aware that they were moving out of the hotel towards the back-service yard.

'Alex, please let me go, you are hurting me,' she pleaded.

'Mrs Dean. Trust me, I am capable of hurting you more.' He was flippant with his words.

Without thinking, she just blurted it out. 'Like you did Mitch!'

As if a knife hit his chest he stopped in his tracks and dragged her round to his face. She felt the putrid smell of alcohol on his breath; she had not been that close before now to notice.

'Oh, I see. Tell me, Mrs Dean, wherever did that statement come from?' He continued to walk her out to the car park. 'What is your little plan here?

I see you have some back-up waiting for me in the entrance hall, so I think we will leave this way, don't you?'

She quickly kicked out at him, landing her foot in his shin, allowing her the second she needed as he let go for her to make her way to the fire exit.

'What the fuck is going on, why can't you hear them anymore? Where have they gone?' Todd was trying to get an answer from the detective who was talking into the walkie-talkie and trying to move in the direction that Lottie and that sick bastard had headed. 'Fuck!' he shouted, getting the attention of some guests. He pulled his phone from his pocket and dialled.

The detective asked for the officer from the penthouse to join them and they went out towards the car park. He had made the mistake of going down in the main lift, leaving the apartment empty.

Lottie felt her lungs burning. She had made her way up the fire escape as fast as she could, checking that no one was behind her. Her phone started to buzz but she was not wasting the time to get it out to see who was calling. She had to stop; she was out of breath and feeling dizzy. She looked over the banister again, relieved that no one was behind her. She started the climb again, taking off her shoes to make sure they were not going to hinder her. Dragging her key card out of the bag she did not notice that her phone had fallen out with the fumbled action. Finally, at the back fire escape to the penthouse, she scanned the card which unlocked the door and closed it shut behind her.

Out of breath, clutching her chest, she shouted out for the officer, getting no reply. She pulled herself from the door and went to the bedroom to find that there was no one there. Reaching in her bag she found that she had not got her phone. She swore under her breath.

'They never came out this way!' Todd shouted to the detective who had by now been joined by the other two officers. 'The car is still here. We need to split up. I'm going to go back to the penthouse, she could have made it up there.' He tried her phone again, but it was dead.

Other guests and hotel staff were now starting to pay attention, and as he jumped into the lift the manager came over to him asking what was wrong. Todd explained that he needed to find Lottie and was going to need access to the penthouse. Rifling through his pocket the manager produced a key card. Todd felt a sign of relief, hoping that she was there. He almost ran from the lift door, encouraging the manager to hurry to open the large wooden doors to the apartment.

Lottie heard voices at the front door, so she stayed in the bedroom, locking the small door behind her. As the people burst into the room, she heard her name being shouted and could have cried when she heard Todd. She quickly opened the door and ran to him.

'Oh god, Todd it's all gone wrong. I'm such a fool, I should have listened to you.' She snuggled into his arms and he held her. Feeling her fast breathing and hot skin, he rubbed her hair out of her face.

'It's OK, I'm here now,' he said, gently kissing the top of her head.

'I should have just done what you all said and let the police deal with it,' she almost sobbed, still encased in his arms.

'Shh, it's OK,' he said, still cherishing her touch and need for him.

'It's not. I must have been mad to think I could get him to open up. To admit why he did it, the girl at the club, his cousin. What had they done to him, what had Mitch even done?' Lottie was mumbling into his chest.

They had not noticed the figures approaching the room from the service elevator. The male was breathing fast, laboured but quiet. The female was smiling, almost laughing, as the man pushed her out of the way.

'Hey, Lotts, it's OK, you're safe here with me.' He almost did not want to say it, but he had to let her know. 'Edward is on his way, Sharpe has called him, he will be here soon and I am sure that the detective will catch up with the mad son of a bitch!'

'Well, well, well,' a deep voice said, making them both turn around. Lottie gasped and caught her breath. Todd pulled her closer as if to shield her from the man who had arrived at the room.

'I am sure that Mr Edward Dean will enjoy walking in on this happy, loved-up scene.' He glanced behind him as if he were looking for someone, but the female figure had vanished from sight.

Todd took a step forwards and Lottie pulled him back as Alex Girski drew out a gun from his back pocket. 'Or has he given into his possessive ways?' There was a smutty laugh, and Lottie thought she could also hear a female laugh too as the door closed to the apartment. 'I don't think so. Mr Dean does not share anything, let alone his women. And one so beautiful, but hey, who would blame him?' He sat in the chair that was close to him. 'Maybe we should wait around for him, see how he reacts. I guess he thinks he can trust you both, but this little plan of yours, Lottie, maybe he will find out that he cannot trust you after all. A failing in the perfect Mr Dean; just goes to show that he can't have it all.' He grinned again at Lottie; Todd was still holding her close to him.

'So, explain this little plan you have just mentioned, why am I really here?' Alex directed the question and the gun at Todd. 'Speak, Lottie, your friend here may just be the next one to experience my madness, as I am not a son of a bitch as he put it!'

Her voice was silent, and Todd squeezed her arm as if for her not to say anything. 'Come on, don't be shy, what do you want to hear?' He raised an eyebrow. 'How I was driven to kill his brother because I hate the man so much?' He took a breath. 'How I broke into your flat because I knew you were getting information on me?' He tapped the chair next to him. 'Come here, Lottie sit next to me.' He pulled at the safety catch and continued to aim the gun towards Todd. 'Move!' he yelled in an impatient way and Lottie jumped, pulling away as a reluctant Todd tried to make her stay.

'You sit there.' He looked at Todd and pointed to another chair in the room. Lottie approached and sat as far away on the two seated chair as she dared without falling off.

'Now, Lottie, tell me. Why do you think Mr Edward Dean took an interest in you? Was it because of what you do for a living? He was hoping that you would reveal the answers no one else would about his brother, but the stupid fool had to go and fall in love with you. He had to have it all. Once more in his life there is nothing that Edward Dean cannot have, all that power and money, and luckily for you he did not have to buy your services to get the results he wanted. It seems that you are hell bent on getting to the bottom of it yourself for some reason. What is that reason, Lottie, what do you want out of this conversation?'

She remained quiet and then whispered, 'I don't know.'

'Oh, I'm sure that you do. It's not just because you are a brilliant forensic scientist, and you want to prove yet again how fantastic you are.' He moved closer to her and Todd started to stand in his seat. 'Sit, fuckwit!' He pointed the gun at Lottie this time. 'Sit!' He almost foamed at the mouth repeating the demand. 'I would hate to get anyone hurt, Lottie, on your account, after all we are all here for you. It seems we all love you, doesn't it, Todd?'

Lottie felt sick. The thought that she had put them all in the room together and soon, oh god, she hoped soon Edward would arrive, but not to this. Maybe if she answered him, he would go and she could bargain with him.

'What do you want, Alex?' she asked.

'I want to know why you have done this, why did you have to dig into the past, bring up old shit?'

'I wanted Edward to know what happened, and why.' It was the truth. 'I wanted closure so that he could rest, sleep at night with some form of peace.'

'I bet he does not sleep at night, but not for the reasons of worrying about how his brother left this sad little world.' He moved close to her again; this time she could feel the heat of his skin and he rubbed the gun along her thigh from her knee up and then he stopped. 'I bet he gets no peace at all with you around. This soft skin to rub against, that smell, so sweet and seductive.' Todd gripped the side of the chair almost exploding and Alex noticed his anger.

'Would you like to touch this skin, Todd? Oh, I bet you have, and before him at a guess and now he has what you want. Does that not piss you off? It pisses me off. Knowing that someone you want so very badly to love you wants and loves another. Knowing that even if or when they came back to you, they would still think about another man. Think enough about the other person so that in the end they do not want you at all, not even as a friend!'

Lottie quickly spoke. 'Is that what you want?'

'You will have to be more precise Lottie,' Alex said with a smile that sent a shiver down her spine. 'Is it you that is on offer? Can I finally get what he has, something that he owns becomes mine?' He paused. 'I don't think so, that's not how he works.' He licked his bottom lip. 'Although if you are offering, I am sure your friend over there would not mind watching, maybe even joining in, just to get back at Dean. What do you say, Lottie, should we give him a little sex show, here and now?' He pushed his face to hers and licked the side of her face, rubbing his hand along her thigh towards her sex. She jumped, pushing away his hand.

Todd could not stop himself and he jumped out of the chair. As a lighting reaction, Alex swung the gun around and a shot fired.

As if a ten-gun cannon salute had gone off in the room Lottie felt her ears ring, and it seemed as if the world had stopped and was spinning slowly as she watched her friend clutch his shoulder and hit the floor. She screamed out, 'Todd!' She felt the restraining arm of Alex next to her reach out to prevent her from moving. Todd lay on the floor pressing hard onto his shoulder, red lifeblood leaving his body, silent in his pain.

'Please let me see him.' She pleaded with her assailant, sure she would just do it anyway, get up and cradle her friend, stop the bleeding. What was the worse he could do, shoot her? But then she had a thought; it was not just her. Bump. Through all this madness she had not thought about her own safety, but it was not just her. She came back to earth with a significant bang realising the magnitude of her stupidity. Maybe he was right, maybe she had wanted to prove to Edward how very good she was at her job. But to what ends or possible cost?

'Well, Mrs Dean, this death is not on me. See what you made me do, just like Edward made me kill his brother for the things he had done to me and to her.'

He stood still facing Lottie. 'You look confused?' he said as if there was no one else in the room, no one struggling for life in front of them.

'I don't understand, tell me.' She tried to sound as needy as possible.

'Oh yes, explain to you why I had to show Dean that you can't have it all. Is that what you want to hear? His perfect life came at a cost, just as mine had when he started to become so very rich. Oh, he needed me when he was at school, shared everything, became my brother, and then after I helped him, well he just started to forget where he had originally come from. Got all serious and protective, forgot who his real friends were. I lost him as a brother, and I wanted him to know how that felt. When I did find something I wanted, something of my own, he took that too.'

'So, you killed Mitch?' Lottie could hardly ask but she had to. She also had to hope that the detective would come back soon and that he was hearing this, if it was still being recorded. Alex just lifted his eyebrows and replied.

'Car crash, Mrs Dean. The boy was on drugs.' He walked away from where Todd was laying on the floor. His eyes were still open, but he clung to his shoulder as if it was the only thing he could do. Lottie wanted to reach for him, but Alex turned around again to her. 'Accident,' Alex continued.

'Hardly,' Lottie said, knowing otherwise but not giving it away.

'Really, do tell me Mrs Detective.' He sat in the chair that Todd had occupied before his outburst. He leaned forwards and put the gun to Todd's head. Lottie looked at his pale face, beads of clammy sweat on his brow; he really was losing too much blood. Alex tapped the gun on Todd's head to spur her on and continue her explanation.

'You gave him those drugs; they have your brand, that unique marker.' She continued to explain how they had matched the drugs and those to a batch in New York which had somehow gone missing.

'Aha, so the ex-lover here,' he tapped the gun on Todd's head once more, 'was spying on me in New York. Not just keeping away from the one he loves.' He pointed to Lottie and nodded his head. 'Yes, the one he loves and cannot let go of.' Then he turned back to look at Todd, kicking his other shoulder. 'So that you could try to pick up the pieces of your sad, shattered little life. Maybe a bullet in the head would be better for you, as I can see it has not mended your broken heart being miles away from her. You poor little shit!' He tapped the gun on Todd's head, this time making it bleed, and Lottie screamed out again.

'No!' She stood. 'Take it out on me.' She pushed towards him. 'If you are going to.' She stopped in her tracks as the gun was turned.

'Feisty.' He licked his lips. 'I like that in a woman, another reason for Dean to fall for you, the list seems to be endless. So, what would he do if he lost you too?' He stood and they faced each other, just an injured man at their feet dividing them. 'So fucking what to everyone who has had to suffer? If he lost you, it would finish him for sure. I win, he loses, and we all move on. Of course, not you two,' he corrected himself looking at her stomach. 'You three! Just more casualties for the formidable Mr Dean to live with I guess.' He chuckled and turned away.

Lottie saw her chance and launched towards him as the gun seemed to lower. Todd must have seen what she was going to do, and he grabbed out at her foot. The split second that it took for the gun to go off once more was timed to perfection as the main door to the apartment burst open and three figures made them all look up. The smell of gunpowder overwhelmed Lottie as the searing pain ripped through her thigh. She dropped to the floor alongside her best friend and with what seemed to be her last few breaths she held his body, and he pulled her close.

The ringing in her ears seemed to go on forever. The pain in her leg intensified as the noises continued and then she felt the heavy lump slump beside her.

Out of the noise came a deep voice, almost foreign to her at first, but the arms and the touch were unmistakable.

'Fucking hell Lottie, oh fucking hell! Pete get an ambulance here now. Help me.' He pulled her to him and the blood from her leg covered him in seconds. The other figure in the room, Lottie could make out as the detective was kneeling at Todd's side pressing on his shoulder, seemingly talking to him but she could not hear anything, just the gunshots still ringing through her brain and the pain in her leg.

'Lottie, speak to me, please, what the fuck is going on?' She looked at Edward's face, and she burned inside as she felt the guilt of why they were there, why her friend was laying dead – was he dead? She wanted to ask but the words would not come out of her mouth. She pressed her hand to her stomach and looked at her leg. She now realised why it felt hot and wet. She raised her eyes to Edward. She felt the hot pain take over her body and her head swooned.

'I'm so sorry, Edward.' She gasped for a breath.

'Lottie, baby. Stay with me, look at me.' He was desperately trying to hold her, shake her without hurting her. 'Stay with me Lottie, fucking hold on!'

'I never meant to hurt him, or Todd,' she whimpered, 'I am sorry for hurting him.'

'Who Lottie, hurting who' Edward was sure she was not taking about Alex Girski, who was for sure dead. No one could take six rounds direct to chest and survive. Pete had not even bothered to confirm it, not even gone to hover over him to confirm that the three of them had all fired into him and it had not completed the task. The fucker was dead that was all that mattered, and now his only focus in his life was to keep Lottie in his arms.

'I never meant to hurt him,' she said again, and Edward was still confused until she took his hand in her own and placed it on her stomach. 'I am so sorry if I hurt him,' she repeated and as if a coin fell into a hole in Edward's head he understood.

'Oh, baby girl, he, you, you both...' He could not hold back his tears now. They were running down his face.

How could this moment of compete carnage render him so breathless? The joy that once overwhelmed him to know they were having a child had taken hold of him again, but her muttered words, a boy, had blown that out of the water a thousand times more. He felt as if his heart would burst and he looked at Pete who was wrapping a dressing tighter around Lottie's leg. Edward put his hand to his face and wiped away the tears and snot from his nose, like a five-year-old child.

'Lottie, baby girl, hold on for me please. It will be OK, you, you both will be OK!'

A blackness fell over her eyes and she tried to mouth the words 'I love you,' making Edward lean closer to her.

'Lottie, keep talking to me please.' He gave her another hug as if to encourage her to talk and she tried but the black cloud descended and she lost all sense of everything, except the pain in her leg and then after a few seconds even that was gone.

Chapter 18

Edward paced the white corridor floor, running his hand through his hair. Although the detective had tried to answer his questions, he was still at a loss as to how the hell this had all happened.

The ambulance had arrived quickly, but not soon enough for Edward and he had tried to control his emotions all the way to the city A&E. Several times getting in the way of the crew who were trying to treat Lottie. Todd had also been taken in by a second ambulance, and though he had been conscious, he had not been able to answer any questions. He had taken a shot to his shoulder, but the muscle took most of the impact, and lucky for him it hadn't been lower. Both of them had been rushed to surgery and ever since Edward had been banished to the lone corridor all he could do was pace.

Pete had been on the phone and the rest of the security team had arrived at the hospital. However, with Girski confirmed dead at the scene there seemed to be no threat to anyone anymore. Mrs B had arrived, flask in hand, but Edward would not sit and talk, he walked up and down, trying to make light of the madness. The doors at the end of the corridor opened and he looked up. DC Sharpe walked towards him looking as if the weight of the world was on his shoulders. Another man in uniform walked alongside him and at first glance it was apparent that he was of a very senior rank. The men walked up to Edward, and he stopped pacing to greet them.

'Mr Dean. Commissioner and Chief of Police for the Met.' The older man put out his hand, which Edward took in greeting. 'DC Sharpe has filled me in on the situation and I understand that you asked to see someone with authority, so I have come along to try to assist with this in any way that I can.'

Edward looked at the older man, well-dressed, well-placed and at the very top of his organisation. Edward almost laughed, wondering if every victim of a shooting in the capital would be dealt with by the top brass. He doubted it but the threats he had made on the way into the hospital about the negligence of DC Sharpe to have taken this on without formal awareness must have got the Metropolitan police on high alert.

'I understand that Mrs Dean is in surgery?'

'No thanks to this prick.' He looked at Sharpe who lowered his head, unable to speak. Edward had already got him up against the wall in the penthouse, demanding to know what the hell had happened. He was so angry, frustrated and lost he didn't have the energy to do it again, although he wanted to. The older man spoke, and Edward just shot him a glance with no words. In an authoritative voice the commissioner asked, 'Can we go somewhere to talk?'

She was somewhere beyond the doors he had been walking past, so not a chance was he leaving once they brought her out or gave him any news. He had to be here on this very spot.

'Here is fine.' He continued to look through the glass panel in the door which never gave him any other view except the blank corridor beyond. 'Unless you want my lawyers present?' There was a hint of sarcasm in his voice.

'Mr Dean, it seems that your wife had found out information that should have been passed to us some months ago, but she chose to keep it to herself.'

Edward felt his blood boil. 'Don't you even think about blaming Lottie for this fuck up! You!' He jabbed a finger at the detective who continued to remain silent, almost in shock from the situation. 'You should have said something the moment she approached you.'

'Mr Dean,' the older man interjected again as if DC Sharpe had been put on silent for a reason. 'I have some questions, with regards to the shots fired and the responsibility of the death which includes the recovery of your gun and that of your security detail.' There was a pause and Edward's sharp face shot him a glance that almost made the older man sweat. 'DC Sharpe has explained the basics; he was working the case and, well it seems your wife was very persuasive in asking him to go along with her plan.'

Edward knew he himself could not hold out on any request from his wife, so he knew the effect she had on most men. However, he still could not give any sympathy for the broken man in front of him. Edwards blood-soaked shirt still evidence of the event just a few hours before.

'We have been able to get the recording of the events as Mrs Dean had a wire.' If the news should have made him feel better, it just dug into Edward deeper knowing that she had planned this with such detail and betrayed his trust to share it with him. 'I think that you should hear it.'

Edward looked up and held the man's gaze. 'I think it will make it clear as to the reasons why your wife went to such lengths.' There now seemed a warmth in the older man's voice and Edward knew he had to hear what they were talking about. But first he had to know how she was before he went anywhere.

'Mr Dean?' A familiar voice behind him made him turn and Pete walked towards him. Edward nodded as a silent request for him to speak. 'Your mother has arrived. She is with Mr Carter's sister in the relative's room. Please go to see her as she is distressed. I will stay here and come to you the moment there is any news.' He took a breath, hoping his calm voice would assist in moving his shattered boss. 'Mr Carter is out of surgery. He is in recovery doing well.' His final statement did make Edward smile slightly. 'Please Edward, go to your mother.' The term of endearment using his first name now made the situation less formal. 'And I have these for you.' He lifted a bag where a new tee shirt and jacket lay neatly folded. 'She does not need to see you like that.'

Edward looked at himself; the fact that he had spent hours walking around with the blood on him from his wife sent a shiver down his spine.

Edward rubbed his temple with his hand to try to clear a path in his mind. 'Pete, the moment...' Before he could finish his request, Pete replied, 'The very second Mr Dean,' and the two men understood.

'And the questions from the commissioner, about the firearms?' He nodded his head into the direction of the two police officers.

'Leave it with me, now go!' Pete lightly patted his shoulder as the young man turned and walked away towards the small room, too far away from her, but he now had to console his mother. Although he did not have the answers he knew she would be asking.

After what felt like an eternity to Edward, Pete returned with the detective, almost filling the small room. DC Shape stuttered his way through every detail of what happened, how Lottie had first contacted him and how the events had unfolded.

On more than one occasion Edwards's mother gasped and held her breath. She twice grasped out at her dear son's hand for moral support more than anything. The part where he played the tape to them both had the room fall to silence, until the confession and the mention of Edward's youngest brother.

Unsure if it was rage or emotion, he punched at the arm of the chair. The crack from the wood could have been mistaken for the bones in his hand all crunching together. The slow sobs that filled the room came from his mother, now overcome with the emotion. Edward sat forward his head in his hands, silently shaking his head as if the words would not go in.

'Mr Dean. I can only say it again. I am so sorry. Mrs Dean,' he said, looking at Edwards's reaction as if he dared to speak her name, 'She really wanted you to have closure. I am just sorry that it came at this cost.'

'Oh Edward. His poor mother!' Alice Dean seemed not to care for her own loss of a son.

'Mother, I know she was your best friend but please, really? You have fucking compassion for him, after you heard that? And your daughter-in-law shot and for all we know...' He could not say the word 'dying' and he finally stood and paced the room.

'Edward, I know how it is to lose a son, to love unconditionally regardless, and she wouldn't have known what he was really like. He was such a sweet child.' She mopped her eyes trying to keep her mascara intact whilst watching him pace the floor.

'Please, Mother!' He recalled to her the mess he got himself into with the Russians and how Edward had to bail him out, the reason the friendship had ended.

'Well, I still need to make sure she is OK. She has no one else, you know that.' She gave a smile to the detective who was remaining silent.

'Her husband was a cheating bastard. Her son was a fucking mad man. She is better off without them, but I am sure she has more friends to rely on than just you.' Edward looked out of the window; the words seemed to settle in his head and he felt a sudden sick feeling in his stomach.

'I know you're hurt, Edward, but as soon as I know that Lottie is OK I am going to go and see her. Do you know if she has been informed of any of this?' Alice turned to the detective, referring to Mrs Girski, and he nodded. Edward turned to see the silent reply to his mother's question.

'We love our children, Detective, but we cannot be held responsible for their actions as adults.' She smiled. 'Something you will find out for yourself Edward sooner than you wish as time moves on so very quickly.' She stood and joined him at the window. She looked at him and could see that the wet tear in his eye was threatening to fall, but he would not show his weakness with someone else in the room. He knew that if he opened his mouth the lone trickle of water would surely grace his cheek. She pulled him close, although he towered over her and she kissed his hand as she held it to her mouth. He continued to stare hopelessly out of the window.

'Let me leave you two. Mr Dean, if you have any more questions, I will leave my details with your man outside.' Edward nodded his head in a reply and quietly the door closed.

It was only a moment before he turned to his mother. The soft skin of her face, the half-smile on her mouth was the driver for the tears to begin to flow.

'I nearly lost her, Mum.' His words were quiet and sobbed. 'And I, I as good as killed Mitch too.' He sat back down on the chair. She pulled him to her stomach, soothing his hair as he continued to say the same words over and over.

'Shhhhh, darling boy. Shush now, that's not true.' She kissed his hair, and she could have had the small child back in her arms that she had just referred to. The boy who sobbed like this every time she returned him back to school, or his father had scolded him. The little boy, her darling boy still needed his mother right now. In this private room away from the prying, judging world she knew he had to get this out, so she let him cry.

The gentle knock on the door could have almost been missed, but Alice looked at the face at the window and beckoned him in. Edward had fallen to sleep on the sofa only a half an hour before and the silent foot fall of the person coming into the room allowed him to get a few moments more.

'Mrs Dean has been moved from surgery. Everything has gone OK; it seems it was a deep tissue wound. Nothing major hit and the bullet left no trace. She is fine and recovering.' The whispered words filled her heart as if they had been shouted from a loudspeaker. 'She should wake within an hour. Mr Carter is already awake and his sister is in with him now. Can I get you or Mr Dean anything?'

'No thank you, Pete,' her soft voice came back. 'I will let him sleep some more, but then I would like to get a ride into town. Can you arrange that?'

The nod confirmed it and she mouthed a 'thank you' and again they were left alone. She gently sat by the side of the make-shift bed and brushed a stray hair from his face. He wrinkled his nose, but it was the only movement that he made.

'Edward.' The faint voice came into his mind. 'Edward, sweetheart.' He moved his head, and the voice became clearer. 'Edward,' the voice came again and as he opened his eyes, he immediately recognised his mother's face.

The here and now rushed back to him like a force nine gale blowing in his brain.

'Lottie, is she, are they...?'

'Yes, darling. They are fine, she has been awake for a while.' The reply made him jump up.

'Mum, how long? Christ, where is Pete? He was supposed to!' He rushed to get up.

'He did but I sent him away.' She stood and collected her bag 'There was no need to jump straight in. The doctors needed some time.' She picked up his jacket and he brushed his hand through his hair. 'And you needed some rest before you go to see her – them,' she corrected herself.

For the first time in several hours, he smiled. He kissed his mother on the cheek. 'Now go!' she said, pushing him towards the door and as it opened Pete stood up from the chair that was stationed outside.

'Sorry, Mr Dean, your mother...' Pete tried to apologise for not waking him up as first requested.

Ed put up his hand as if it was all forgotten. Most importantly now, he had to go to her with a clear head.

'Mrs Dean, your very handsome husband is desperate to come in and see you. Are you feeling up to it?' The middle-aged nurse had been fussing around Lottie since the doctors left her. Her full face and attractive smile made Lottie feel at ease, although her mind was racing with everything that had happened.

She was not in pain, mainly due to the light sedative she was still feeling the effects of and the other drugs that the doctors had assured her had not harmed the baby. Lottie knew that this was going to be hard. As the nurse had walked around checking charts and flattening the bed, she had explained that Mr Dean had been made fully aware of what had happened in the hours leading up to the accident.

It was no accident! It was all her doing. She knew he would be seething mad and she knew he had every right to be. She had been so blind, wanting to make it all right for him, and she had never for one moment wanted anyone to get hurt. Even with hate in her heart for Alex, him dying was not want she had aimed to achieve. Laying in her bed she did wonder what her aim was after all.

'Mrs Dean?' the sweet voice came again as the knock on the door continued.

Lottie snapped out of her thoughts. Of course, she wanted to see him. God yes, she was desperate to feel the heat of his skin, the touch of his lips on hers, everything as good as it had been 24 hours earlier when he had held her in his arms, preparing for her to go away for a few days. But the guilt of her own actions was hard even for her to forgive herself, so how and why should he?

'Lottie?' The strong, impatient voice came around the half-open door. And without a chance for her to reply, the tall handsome figure would not have let an elephant stop him from almost running to the side of her bed.

'Baby girl!' Within an instant the strength of his arms was enfolding her. 'Thank god, oh baby girl I thought I had lost you!' His hot mouth pressed on her cheek, on her forehead, covering her skin with kisses as he looked deep into her eyes.

A wave of sickness came over her and the heat that instantly travelled up from her heart to her face made her feel as if she were going to pass out. The usual head rush of his touch was nothing compared to the heat of her guilt and shame that she felt. She turned away, not being able to hold his besotted eyes.

'I'm sorry.' The words floated out of her mouth as if they had been whispered by a mouse in the corner of the room, and then again. The words drifted from her lips, and with the third release of the words the tears from her eyes streamed once more down her face.

'Hey.' He put his hand gently on her face and turned her back to look at him. 'Hey, whatever these are for, stop them.' He referred to her tears. 'You, Bump, Todd are all fine, you hear me?' He used his thumb on her skin to try to wipe away the flow, but it was like a tidal wave that just continued to batter in a storm.

Knowing that she would not be able to turn away from his powerful grip, she still could not bear him to look at her, so she closed her eyes. 'I'm sorry,' the words came again. This time it was a press on her lips from his own that silenced her. She tried to talk, to say sorry again but he applied more pressure as if to gag her. She opened her eyes as if it were the only way to breath and it was only this need that made her pull away from him. The silence that fell seemed to be forever, as Edward pulled the chair as close as he could and sat down with his face still on a level with her own. The nurse had only just left and they both watched as the door closed behind her.

Lottie opened her mouth to speak, but the words failed to leave.

'If you say sorry one more time, Mrs Dean, I will walk out the room and not come back in!' Of course, he would not. Yes, he was seething because she had held this from him. He was furious that she had felt she had to lie to him over the last few days, maybe even weeks. Yes, he was really pissed off that she had felt that she had to do this for him, but all this anger outweighed the fact that he was so fucking glad to the point of not caring about anything. She and the baby were OK. They were going to recover, no matter how long it took. He was not giving thoughts to anything else right now.

'But I am,' Lottie managed to get out and he rolled his eyes at her.

Technically it was not the words again and he had to smile at her tenacity.

'I know, but now I want you and my boy to get better and out of here.' He smiled at her, remembering that she had let it slip that Bump was in fact a boy, although his smiled faded as the picture of her face at the time he was informed of the perfect news was blood-stained.

A joyous moment he had been holding in until now all the same. 'And then we will talk about it, if there is anything left to talk about. Yes, I am hopping mad. I thought we said no secrets, and this was one big fucking secret, but I really don't give a damn to reasons why just now, got it?' He asked as sternly as he could, fighting the will to just pick her up in his arms and cradle her. He was sure that he was not letting her out of his sight again and one thing that would be discussed was that she was not working any more. Whatever defence she gave him to keep working at that place, he would ensure that the professor sacked her if he had to.

'You know it is a he?' She looked quizzically at him.

'You mentioned it before.' He stopped. 'Before you passed out.' He put his hand on her arm, smiling.

'Another thing to be sorry for!' She almost gritted her teeth as she said the words and as she did his eyebrows drew close together as if to scold her again. 'I know, I know.' She almost held up her hand. 'Something else I have kept from you, but I sort of spotted the difference for myself! The nurse did not tell me, and I did not ask but...'

'Like father like son I guess!' He smiled and winked now trying to make light of what had been a goddamn awful 12 hours of his life. Lottie smiled. 'Mr Dean, I love you,' she said, putting her hand over his.

'Mrs Dean, you drive me to distraction and back again in every way, but I love you more!' He stood and kissed her on the lips and moved his head down to her stomach that was covered with a thin hospital blanket.

'And you too, Mini-Me!' Placing his lips to her make her giggle and as the door opened, they both looked up to see Todd's sister, who flushed with embarrassment at the intimate moment she had caught them in. She almost turned away.

'Come in, please.' Lottie instantly recalled Todd. 'How is Todd? Is he OK, can I see him?'

Edward raised his eyebrows at the last question as she was going nowhere, and it silenced her from asking again.

'He is fine, up and awake and asking if you are OK so I said I would come and see.' She moved closer to the bed and Edward sat on the other chair to make room. They generally chatted, nothing of the last few hour's events was mentioned and as the nurse came in again to see to Lottie, the visiting friend made her own exit to leave them alone.

There were moments of silence in the next few hours, during some of which Lottie knew she should be trying to explain to Edward her reasons why she had tried to take the situation into her own hands, but she somehow could not find the words to do so. His physical contact never left her, as his hand held her, or he placed his head and hands on her stomach silencing her until she questioned her own actions, knowing that she could not justify them to Edward at all.

In confusion, her mind played out the events, and although she tried to sleep she found that she only dozed, waking up in a panic, to still find that he was there holding her in some way.

Although her physical scars would heal, she was not sure if the mental ones of the day would go away so quickly. She was not sure at what time sleep did come to her, and she was not sure if Edward had been in the room all the time, but when she woke the sun outside was shining and he was now sitting in the chair opposite with his laptop open, looking studious at work. She took a moment to peek at him, admiring his face, his perfect blue eyes, and just hand-brushed hair.

He must have left at some point as he had changed into different clothes from yesterday, and the beautiful face that she longed to kiss was shaven clean. His suit jacket was draped over the chair and the crisp white shirt had a tie that was not quite secure at his neck, allowing his top button to be open, revealing a tantalising peek at the golden skin below. She moved to pull herself up in the bed, and this movement made him raise his eyes to meet hers.

'Hey you!' she said, smiling at him. With the speed of an eagle, he put down the computer and leapt to her side, helping her sit up.

'Hey to you two!' He placed his hand on her stomach while kissing her softly on the lips. His eyes looking bright and somehow alive again.

'Working?' she asked.

'Just a few emails that could not wait, nothing to worry about.' He gritted his teeth, but she could see that was not the true fact. Whatever it was, it had worried him.

'Oh.' She was not sure to ask, 'Just work?' There was a pause. 'Are you going in?' She paused again. 'To the office?'

'No, but I do have to go out for a time.' He sat on the edge of the bed. Edward did not want to expand; it was easy to see in his reaction. Lottie was not sure if she should push him, hoping that the information would come freely. To his relief, as if on cue the nurse walked in and greeted them both. Edward stepped back to allow her to carry out the checks that they had now both become accustomed to and while Lottie answered the medic's questions, he picked up his phone to summon Pete.

'Now, Mrs Dean, I don't want you to get too excited but how does a shower sound?' The nurse smiled, looking in the direction of Edward as if seeking permission for something. Lottie seemed to do the same thing, although she was not sure why. The bathroom was off the same room she was in so technically she was not going anywhere really.

'Good?' the nurse asked again. Lottie nodded. 'Right then I will be back in a few moments.' She looked towards Edward, clearly taken in by his powerful elegant body that was now formally dressed, tie in place and a jacket on his toned shoulders. He moved to the bed, flashing his perfect white teeth at her and she blushed.

'Pete has some fresh clothes. I've asked him to come up.' He looked back at Lottie and took her hand and kissed it. 'I am hoping to persuade them to let you out by the end of the day, but only if you are feeling up to it.' He smiled. 'How does that sound?'

'Good, I think. Is there a but?' Lottie replied, knowing that something was playing on his mind.

'I have to go out for a few hours.' He shifted on the bed. He was not sure if she needed to know where he was going, or about the news reports and the awaiting paparazzi outside. 'But I will be back before you know it!' He kissed the end of her nose and then lovingly tapped it with his finger. They held each other's eyes, and he placed a final soft kiss on her mouth.

Lottie breathed him in, that sweet, musky smell that she loved, that fresh clean husband smell that was hers.

The barrage of questions hit Edward as he left the building. Hand in the air, the words 'no comment' was the reply to the number of reporters that had been drawn by the state of events. He said to Pete as they got into the car that he must arrange for Lottie to leave another way if she was going to be let out today. He knew that she would not want to face the papers, and the reality of his next destination would, for sure, make the news. He had been asked to attend the police station where he knew that avoiding an arrest would be hard even for his legal team this time.

Entering the police station, he was shown into a room, and under caution was questioned about the events of the day. There was no denying that the bullets that had been retrieved from the body of their tormentor had come from his and Pete's private handguns. But he was not aware that the detective had also fired off rounds.

As he was asked questions, his lawyer answered on his behalf, and all that could go through Edward's mind was the detective. Torn that he should have said something to his superiors, and now suspended for the shooting did not bode well for the DC. Edward needed to think fast, but now had to focus on the charge he was facing. This was a charge of murder. He faced losing them both all over again.

As they walked out of the building, Edward turned to his lawyer. Pete was under the same caution in another room.

'What do you think?'

'Mr Dean. I am not sure that we can cover this – my only defence is the incompetence of the officer, therefore you and Pete had to take your action. By default, the fact that you are licensed to carry a firearm does not in the eyes of the law allow it to be used to kill someone, as it was not self-defence. Technically Pete has his firearm for your protection, but it still does not mitigate him.'

'And my wife's protection – that's what he was doing,' Edward exclaimed, knowing that it was going to take more than money for him to get out of this without some repercussions.

'We need to find out who the judge is, and stay away from the press as much as possible. I am on to the latter, but there are whispers already out there so it may be that we have to run to ground for now.'

Edward stopped. 'And Pete, how do we defend him?' The lawyer smiled. 'He knows the drill,' was his reply.

'And the detective? They said it was not in the line of duty as it was not official. What about his family? Especially if we try to get me off with him as my defence plea?' He took in a large sigh, knowing that Lottie would be beside herself if she knew what trouble they were all in.

'Christ, if only she had said something to me. This could have all been avoided!' Ed ran his hand through his hair.

'I am sure that we can work this out. At the end of the day, they are both safe, Mr Dean.' The middle-aged man tried to steady his voice to add an element of calm.

'I don't even want to think about the fact that the police need to speak to her; perverting the course of justice is no simple allegation. How long can I put that off for?' he asked, knowing they had already tried to get a statement from her in the hospital but had been warned off by Pete and the hospital staff under Edward's request.

'I would say get it over and done with and then take off to Kent, let the team and I get to work on this. Take some time out to recover, both of you.'

'It's bad, isn't it?' Lottie asked as she sat in the chair by the window. She may have looked brighter and refreshed but her heart sank when she saw the news reporters outside and she'd been advised by the doctor not to go to the shop where she had wanted to get a magazine after her shower. 'I never thought about how this could have panned out, and now...' She paused. 'I have landed so many people in trouble; you, Pete and poor Detective Sharpe. Edward, I cannot see a way out of this.' She could have sobbed but somehow the tears had dried up.

'Shush, Lottie. I don't want you to worry, really you must rest.' He rubbed her hand as he knelt on the floor to the side of her, looking up into her eyes. The dagger in his heart was twisting with each of her silent breaths, killing him because he could see into her soul, he could see the turmoil in her and could not seem to sooth it.

'How can I rest? It's bad, and you haven't even said how you got on. Edward, don't deny it. I know where you have been.'

He smiled at her and rubbed her good leg another time as a soothing gesture. Even if he could lie, she would know and with the ever-present press interest the best thing that he could do was keep her up to speed. Keep the story together so that the facts could not be missed. Edward looked at his phone as it buzzed. 'Pete,' he said to Lottie as she gave him an enquiring look.

'Is he OK?' she asked.

'Yep, and I am sure this is the news that you wanted to hear. We can get you back to the apartment by the time Mrs B can prepare some supper.' He smiled and kissed her nose as he stood up, putting the gadget to his ear to take the call.

He had been right; they made it back to the apartment, via the back of the hospital and under the cover of the blacked-out SUV, which Pete was driving. Although pleased to see her, Lottie had avoided the arms of Mrs B as she had arrived, needing to go to the toilet as soon as they stepped foot inside the doors. The wound on her leg slowed her down. She had refused the crutches to assist her walking, almost as a penance.

Forewarned by Edward not to fuss the housekeeper just went about her business making food and keeping as quiet as she could. Her police interview had taken place hours before, giving a statement to her side of the events which was nothing. As she was so shocked at the whole event, it was not hard for the young female officer to take her quick statement and then leave the flat.

Although the aroma of the food smelt good, Lottie played with the small helping she had on her plate. The usual ginger tea was even hard to swallow, and Edward was also finding eating difficult.

'Let's get them in now if they want my full statement. Let's do it now before I have time to work my insides up to a point where I am going to burst.' Lottie blurted the words out knowing that Edward and Pete had been talking about the request, only for Edward to silence him that he did not want it happening this soon.

'Edward please. I need to do this now. I am not going to rest, or sleep until I have done so. To be honest if you don't call them in, I am going to get to the station myself.' She paused. 'Somehow,' she added, knowing that if he did not want her to go out then none of the staff would let her have keys to any of the vehicles sitting in the downstairs garage, let alone get out of the door without physically being restrained.

He looked at her, his face dark and his eyes pleading for her not to ask this of him.

'Don't, don't say no. Edward, this is all down to me and I have to do this now. I know you don't want me to, but I want to and if you really do, as much as I know you do, love me...' She waited for a reaction. It was not a question of his love it was an understanding that she knew why he did not want her to do this now. 'Then please, make the call.'

He held his tongue. He wanted to scream it is too late, you need to rest, but he fell foul to her eyes once more, holding him so deep that she once more convinced him to submit to her.

His study was full. His legal team had no place to complain about the hour in which they had been called out, and the two police officers, although in plain clothes very much made their presence felt. Lottie had held the room with her statement. She had started at the very beginning and he at times was struck not by the information that she was giving, but the convincing way in which she outlined her reasons, her findings, and her suspicions. Even though the female officer at times questioned her, Lottie never faltered. Edward was sure this was from years of her going to court, handling information that the police needed, but this time it could be not to convince someone else but could incriminate the person he held most dear to him. Lottie, this time, was the one on the line as well as the detective, Pete, and himself. He was prepared to do anything to make sure Lottie was not affected, even to the point of him taking the rap for it all if that was possible.

The information had flowed from her. Files, documents, and evidence most of which Edward was unaware of, all passed over from Lottie to the awaiting pen-pushing policeman, and the lawyer who sat fixed on Lottie as she spoke. The only break they took until the early hours of the morning was for Lottie to go to the bathroom, and Mrs B to replenish the hot drinks.

Although the officers had asked that she be on her own with the Dean Incorporated lawyer, Edward had only agreed to this if he was in the room. His presence did not make any difference; Lottie held her own in every way possible until the very end of the questions and the meeting ended.

Pleasantries done the door was finally closed and Lottie took a breath. It was at this point she must have crumbled because as Edward returned, she was leaning against the arm of the chair in his study, having been told to stay sitting down and that he would see everyone out.

'You should have not pushed for this, Lottie, it has exhausted you,' he said, rushing to her side.

'It's done – now we wait.' She looked up at him with a faint hint of a tear on her cheek. 'And if they...' she stopped, knowing that she could be facing a criminal prosecution. 'And if needs be, I'll take the outcome.'

He interjected, 'We take it, Lottie. This is not just you.'

'I know that and for that I am truly sorry. I will never keep things from you again, a lesson learnt too late. DC Sharpe will lose everything in more ways than one. I can't see how he can stay working for the police even if they don't take him down for gross misconduct.' Her stomach turned and she was not sure if it was Bump, or bile rising at the thought.

'He will be fine; it will be fine.' Edward held her as tight as he dared.

'I wish that were true; no amount of money can save the day this time. We can't just throw money at this and hope it goes away,' she said, and Edward remembered someone else saying that to him once. His smart comment had been that it had always worked in the past, but even he, too, was having some doubts.

Chapter 19

Lottie looked out of the window. The day felt grey and it reflected her mood. Edward had left early in the morning. Kissing her head as she dozed, he'd left her laying in the safety of their bed. Pete and the house staff were under the strict instruction not to wake her, and to call if she wanted anything. As she heard the main door close, she got up anyway. She was not sleeping much, her head in a turmoil. The pain in her leg a continuing reminder of the events.

The one thing that Lottie did want was to go out, get a change of scene, but every time she had tried to do this in the week that had followed the police interview, the press had stampeded her. Even leaving via the underground garage would only see them running after her car. She had asked if they could go to Kent, get away from it, but Edward had to stay in the city for the next few weeks; he too was under police caution not to go anywhere.

Lottie opened the door to the penthouse terrace and hobbled out. She had given into the crutches after a few stumbles, but she often just used furniture for support. The high-up open space was the limit to the fresh air that she could have, and although 30 floors up from the hustle of the city streets, she still felt stifled.

She looked down at her phone as it vibrated into life. Ed again asking if she was OK. She smiled. She had replied to his last text while eating her breakfast – well, attempting to. Although the morning sickness had gone, her loss of appetite this time was due to the stress.

After her fingers had typed the reply, she again looked at the list of other callers who had sent her messages. She smiled as the picture of Gerald and the new canine houseguest appeared, another reminder that she wanted to be in the house in Kent more than where she was.

Agnes had sent several messages and despite the constant invitation to come, she was too busy with looking after her business and the grandchildren.

Todd had stayed with his sister since returning from hospital, and although he called her every day, he too was a face that she really wanted to see. He had been grilled by the police the same day that Lottie had been interviewed. And the only good thing from this was that he was on the road to recovery and that no formal charges would be brought against him, even though he was going to be charged for withholding information, they were not going to take it any further.

As for Ed and herself, it seemed that the lawyers were hard at work as she had not heard anything for the last few days. Or at least that was what she was being told by Ed and Pete when she had asked last night. She smiled to herself as they both said not to worry, but the very fact that she knew they were not telling her everything made her worry more.

The phone vibrated with the reply from Ed and she had a sudden need to hear his voice. She pressed the call button and knew that no matter what he would be doing it would not ring for long, and on cue the voice, always tinged with a hint of worry when she called, started the greeting with 'Lottie, are you OK?' She smiled again as if she felt the warmth of his voice as she sat in the sun.

'I am now, I just needed to hear your voice.' She turned to see the housekeeper bringing her a drink of water she had not asked for but welcomed it, mouthing the words 'thank you' as the ice clinked and the glass touched the table.

'I won't be too late. Do you want to go out for a late lunch?' Ed asked. It would be nice to get some time together. He had tried to stop the press, tried to get the police to move them on. Even Pete had failed in his attempt to get them moved, and he had even hired several additional members of security staff during the day to ensure that they did not get into the building, but he knew that Lottie would still be a focus for their attention, so she was not going out.

'Um, suppose, although I'm not hungry,' she said, and Edward took in a breath. He had noticed her lacklustre attitude towards food and the more he mentioned it, the more he noticed that she was really starting to look withdrawn. He was keen for her to go back to the doctors to check that she and Bump were ok, but again Lottie insisted that she was fine. Maybe he would just ask for a house call instead. He mentally made a note to do that as soon as he put down the phone.

A low cough in the background made Lottie realise that Ed was not alone; he was at work and she had interrupted him.

'Sorry, you need to get on,' she said, really not wanting to go back to being on her own but knowing that things had to get back to some sort of normal. The very thought of what that was seemed to bring a small tear to her eye.

'It's ok, sweetheart, I have all the time for you if you need me, you know that.' Edward smiled at the man sitting across the desk from him. He had taken the hint that the police detective and the lawyers were all still in the room as he took the call from his wife.

Lottie finished the water and slowly moved back into the apartment. The TV was on and she sat and flicked the channels, but nothing seemed to interest her.

'Mrs Dean?' Mrs B asked as she passed the room. 'Do you need me for anything? I just need to go out to the shop. Mr Dean wants dinner in, so I have to pop out to get a few things.'

Lottie gave a smile. Edward must had phoned her after she told him she did not want to go out to eat, but he was still determined to try to feed her up. 'Can I get you anything special?' the housekeeper asked, bringing her attention back to the room.

'Some of that chocolate ice cream.' She smiled. 'And maybe the toffee one too, Bump seems to like that one, although so does his dad and we missed out on the last tub.' Both of the ladies giggled and Mrs B was pleased to see her smile, but it was short-lived. Her face once more became sad.

As she left the building, Lottie could hear on the two-way radio report that Mrs B had been troubled by the press and Graham, the new security detail had intervened and needed back-up from the young man who seemed to be cemented at the front internal door to the penthouse. Lottie had only seen him move once and had only spoken to him on the one occasion when she had tried to stretch her legs by going down to the lobby. She wondered if he got as bored as she was.

She smiled to herself as a warm feeling came over her. Bump had been quiet for the best part of the day, but now he seemed restless. She had to move as he seemed to favour sitting on her bladder. She hobbled to the bathroom. While washing her hands she looked at her face and fixed on her own reflection. She felt fat, frumpy, and wondered why, even though Ed told her every day how beautiful she was, she felt at such a low ebb. Bump kicked again and she put her hands on him.

'Slow down you. I am not a rugby pitch.' She dried her hands and straightened the towel and as she started to move again, he did as she had asked. As soon as she sat down, he started again, kicking and pressing on her. She stood up, walking to the window and outside. He became quiet. Sitting back in the seat she had already occupied once today he started again. 'You are as bored as me,' she said, hand on her stomach. 'We just need to get out of here and expel some energy, don't we?' She stood back up, wondering if a quick swim would calm him down.

The building had a pool in the basement. It was for the exclusive use of the penthouse. As Lottie felt the warm water hit her skin, she pushed forwards and took a few strokes to propel her in the water. Ducking under, wetting her hair, she dived deeper and then broke the surface, blowing out what air she had left.

After only a few moments the water was doing what she had hoped. Resting her head on the edge of the pool she floated. Bump was the first to surface and she watched as the shape of her body came into view on the mirror above.

Strictly speaking, she was banned from the pool. Her leg had healed but she was still instructed to keep it as dry as possible and always covered. The pressure tights had been a passion killer, she recalled as Ed helped to put them on the first few days after she returned from the hospital. The more she looked at her refection the more she could see the angry wound on her thigh. With a sudden pang of guilt, she became overwhelmed by tears and found she was gasping for breath. The anxiety and panic caused her heart to race and her breathing increased. Like a child having a crying episode, she could not control her emotions and had to stand up. Her flailing arms and legs took the directions for her brain and could not seem to get her to keep her head above the water. She panicked more and felt as if the world was helping the water to envelop her. She felt like she was drowning.

The realisation she was swimming alone shot through her head and sudden pain in her chest from hyperventilating cleared her mind in a flash. She reached out for the side of the pool and pulled herself up. Her tiptoes just touched the bottom to keep her head above the water line. Clinging to the side she focused on a spot on the wall, trying to get back to a place of normality. Her breathing slowly returned as she counted her way through the panic attack, and she found the strength to drag herself to the shallower end and use the large stone steps to get out.

The room was hot, humid, and once the support of the water had gone, she felt the weight of her body, and her knees seemed to give way. The panic attack had left her legs with pins and needles, due to the imbalance of air that should normally course through her veins. The lounger was only a few paces away and she made it to the soft cushion, unaware or without a care that she would get it wet.

As if she were having an out-of-body experience, she could see an image of Edward scolding her for swimming alone. No one from the penthouse had seen her leave or would have known where she was. An image of herself standing next to him was scolding herself for not being able to get a grip on her emotions. She could hear Edward's voice, concerned but continuing to ask why she put herself at risk so often.

Like in a dream, without any warning, her thoughts jumped to the scene in the hotel room. The last time she had felt this panicked. The last time that she could not control her tears. She could feel the hot wetness on her face, and it was as if she were there again. In that same room, seeing his cold hard face, watching his every move as if in slow motion as he took control. She pressed her eyes shut, trying to rid herself of the memory. She pushed her hands up to her face, trying to shove the image of Alex Girski out of her mind's eye. It felt real; she could smell him, she could feel the heat of Todd's body against her trying to protect her until he had been forced to move. She so wanted to forget the next bit because she knew what was to come, but then a small sound flashed through her overloaded brain. It was the sound of a woman, a woman laughing.

She started to move her body as if on autopilot, to the lift to get back to the flat. Her eyes were closed. It was the only way that she could keep the images there. She was desperately trying to reach the side of her brain that had heard the laugh. Could she also see a face?

Mrs Dean,' came the soft but enquiring voice of Mrs B, 'Mrs Dean, are you all right dear?'

Lottie was deep in gathering her thoughts and without drying, had dressed in the towel robe and got back to the penthouse. Drips of water had alerted the housekeeper when she had arrived back and when she followed them, they led her to the bedroom door. She had not passed the security detail they were still downstairs now dealing with the police that had been called to deal with the incident. Lottie grabbed a towel to wrap her hair and stepped carefully from the shower.

'I'm in the shower, Mrs B,' she shouted out, knowing that there was little chance of the sweet lady hearing her in the room without opening the door. She put her hand on the handle and opened it to find Mrs B, still with shopping bags in her hand, halfway across the bedroom.

'My dear, what on earth, there are wet footprints everywhere! Do we have a leak? How has the water got from the bathroom to the entrance hall?' Mrs B turned around to give Lottie some private space to pull the new crisp white towel around her expanding waist. Lottie smiled.

'No, sorry. I went to the pool and forgot the towel.' The white lie came out so fast that she never thought about the admittance of the fact she had gone alone and as it clicked the housekeeper confirmed the scolding she had already taken in her mind's eye from her over-concerned husband.

'Mrs Dean, Edward would blow a fuse if he knew you had.' She was cut short by Lottie.

'Mrs B, I know but, well, I was going mad in here. No one was around. Oh, please don't tell him.' She smiled at her as she now had turned back round so they could have a face-to-face conversation.

'Are you sure everything is all right?' The question came again, and Lottie was sure that this sweet lady knew her inner self better than she did. She had some superpower to see inside her.

'Yes. I feel much better,' Lottie said, now letting on that there was something wrong in the first place. 'I mean, nothing was wrong, but just to see different walls has made me feel better.' As if to reassure her she placed her hand over her now quiet Bump. 'He was a bit restless, but the swim has worn him out too!' She smiled. This bit was true.

'Shall we have some tea?' The question came as the older woman started to leave the room, stepping over the still damp areas of the floor. 'I'll get a cloth and have a wipe around too. Watch your step, don't want you slipping!' The last part of her sentence was a trail of her voice as she went from the room along the corridor in the direction of the kitchen.

Lottie smiled to herself. Mrs B thought a cup of tea was the answer to all ills! If only that were true.

Lottie dressed and sat opposite the housekeeper, watching her start dinner. The tea was a pleasant, light ginger flavour that was refreshing. Mrs B was humming along in between the chatter, but Lottie was distracted. She had tried to call Todd from the office but had got no reply. On calling his sister, she was content that he was OK – he was sleeping. She had left a message to ask him to call, saying it was not urgent but she had to ask him – she needed to know if he had heard the woman's voice too.

Her mobile was sitting on the breakfast bar charging as she had run out of battery earlier. It had died just before she decided to go for a swim. Both females jumped as it rang into life. Looking at the caller ID, Lottie smiled. Picked it up and welcomed the caller. Before she could get another word out, his voice penetrated with an anger she had heard before.

'What were you bloody thinking?' There was no real pause for her to reply as he screamed down the phone. 'I have just seen something that I never want to see again.'

By the noise in the background she guessed he was driving, and at some speed which was incredible seeing as he was driving across London. 'Jesus, Lottie. It looked like you were drowning.' He took a breath. 'For fuck's sake, Lottie, I got this sent to me on my phone when I was in a meeting and… shit!' The curse came down the phone and Lottie could hear the scream of a car horn in the distance followed by a 'Fuck you, arsehole!'

She had to say something before the caller crashed.

'Edward, I am fine. I'm sitting in the kitchen with Mrs B.' Lottie tried to get her attention to say something so that she could confirm to him that this was the truth. Mrs B looked up but, the conversation remained one sided: he was only moments away and did none of the phones in the building work? Or could no one hear the office phone ringing, and where was the security team? His forced requirement was that she had better not move an inch. She guessed by the fact that they were cut off seconds later he had arrived in the garage; phone reception was always bad down there. She also wondered if she had not put the office phone down correctly, as she had not heard it ringing. She braced herself for what was to come. How had he found out? Mrs B had not been out of her sight. She wanted to jump up from the stool and check the phone, but then knew that she would not have time.

On cue the lift doors opened, and the crashing sound confirmed to them both that Edward Dean had arrived. Mrs B looked through her glasses at Lottie and said kindly, 'Take a breath, Edward, we are all fine!' He had not even walked into the room, but he heard the statement.

'Mrs B, you are wrong, we are not all fine. I am far from fine.' He glared at his wife, who was red in her cheeks. He pulled his phone out of his pocket and thrust it towards Lottie.

She saw a clear picture of the pool; she could see herself relaxing and then, as if the water were boiling, she could see her lone figure struggling to stand, to catch their breath. It was CCTV footage of her.

'See what my head security manager sent me? Oh, he may be on a day off but thank god he just can't stop watching what is going on.' He had both hands on the worktop, trying to control his breathing. 'And no one answering their phones this end. What's that all about?' He looked to see where his housekeeper had gone for a reply but, like a silent angel, she had left the room. 'He started to call me about the issue with the fucking press.' The word made Lottie look up, his tone still indicating that he was more than angry, and maybe not just with her. He continued, 'When he looked at the CCTV he flicked through and noticed...' There was a pause. 'Well, you've seen it.'

Lottie could not dispute that to the unknowing eye it looked almost as if the swimmer suffered some form of attack, or seizure.

'I am sorry, Edward.' She had said this more than too often to him of late, but it was all she could muster as words to reply. She looked up, but failed in her attempt to appease him with her smile, and her cheeks were now burning.

'No, no, no!' he shouted as if to emphasise this. He slammed his fist down on the counter. Lottie winced. 'In whose world do you think that swimming on your own is right? Lottie, in what existence do you think swimming on your own, while you are heavily pregnant and having just suffered one of the most horrific times of your life, is okay?' He stopped. Mrs B was standing in the doorway. Without knowing, Lottie had found the tears that she thought she had shed enough of today; in fact, she was sure that she had lost control of her tear ducts and they just worked on their own without normal stimulus from her brain.

'Mr Dean,' the housekeeper started, using his formal name to get his full attention. 'The poor girl is beside herself, locked away in this ivory tower. I knew she was swimming, and I am to blame. I popped to the shops as you requested, and I fully forgot to go and sit with her. And the house phone – I made a call and must have not put the receiver back correctly. You know that office phone can be a bit temperamental in these old hands.' She smiled sweetly, but never showed any other emotion in her face. Lottie had to think hard and fast about saying anything else that would then make Mrs B the one who was not telling the truth. She was sure that although the loyal and honest woman had worked for her husband tirelessly for years, that would count for nothing. In this mood she would be sacked on the spot.

'Look at it!' He now picked up the phone and thrust it towards the older lady, playing the footage again. Lottie felt her heart break as she locked eyes with her ally. 'Look at it!'

'Edward please, enough!' Lottie held her stomach as she pushed herself off the stool, not in pain, or for any other reason than she found she was getting so large she felt that she would over balance. 'Please!' Her legs found the strength to move as she headed out of the door, bound for the bedroom, or anywhere to gain some sanity.

He followed although there was total silence and she didn't attempt to close the bedroom door when she reached her destination. She knew he was only a pace behind her.

'I know, I get it,' she said as she sat on the bed pushing up to the cushions. 'But Mrs B is right. I am going out of my mind. As you saw from the footage, enough to have a panic attack, and yes, before you say it again the swimming pool was not the place to do that but...' She stopped to make sure that she worded this right. She was not going to lie. 'I had a flash back, it has not happened before and...' She paused. 'I am sure that there is something else, something that we are missing in this.'

She looked at his face. He was now on his knees at the side of the bed, level with her. His eyes were still ablaze with anger, although his facial features were softer. She could see he still needed time to cool down. 'I'm not the only one who is uneasy.' She put her hand on her stomach again, taking an internal kicking. She reached for Ed and took his hand, placing it on the area where Bump was really active.

She smiled as the colour of his eyes changed as it always did when he made this connection. 'I just want this to be over. We should be enjoying ourselves but, and you may find this hard to hear but I am going to say it anyway.' She took a breath. 'I think someone put him up to it. All of it.'

The pause gave him time to look up at her, now with a question in his eyes.

'I know you have said you will deal with everything, the legal thing and what is going to happen. I am not to worry, to just get on with it. I cannot change anything that has happened but the more I think of this, the more I know I am not going mad. I keep hearing a woman's voice, her laughter just before the shots. Someone was in that room and I think it was all overlooked. I have this feeling in my gut and, well to be blunt, a feeling in my gut was the whole reason I started all this.'

Ed stood up and took the chair from the dresser, placing it back on the spot he had just left. He sat, all his actions in silence. Placing his elbows on his knees, he dipped his head and ran his hands through his hair. Pulling at his tie, he loosened up his top button.

'Ok,' he started, and it sounded like a final statement. Lottie sat up more, moving to get a comfortable position. He held up his hand. 'The swimming thing, it's not gone away.' He clenched his teeth. 'But I am all ears for this new information. Explain to me what your gut thinks.' He wanted to also add, 'It is either I ask and listen, or you do it behind my back anyway,' but he never vocalised this.

'I don't have any evidence, any facts but...' She paused. 'I wanted to speak to Todd, to see if he remembered a woman, either at the hotel or when we got to the room. Not in the room with us but behind the door. I thought it was the police, but obviously not.'

'But you haven't spoken to him?' he asked.

'No. The flashback as I said only happened the once, but the more I play it over in my head, the more I know it is not the first time I have heard the laugh. But where, and who, I don't know.' She stopped. 'I want to ask the professor for the crime scene info to see if there is anything.'

'No, Lottie, even if that were possible you would never be able to, neither would Todd before you say it. I do not want you stressing over this. No, that is final. No.' He had another stern look on his face.

'I know but just to ask the prof, to see if he knows anyone. Pete has connections. They said that the hotel was on lockdown as soon as it happened. If someone else was there, they may be able to find a witness or something.'

He took a deep breath. 'To what end? The prosecution and the case that is currently happening will not change.'

She tried to read his face because she knew that he had been with the legal team that morning, but he remained poker-faced. He rubbed his hand through his hair, the way he did when thinking, or troubled.

'We could be on the edge of losing it, all of this,' he paused, 'and each other.'

She could have sobbed at the last words, but she held her voice. 'My only intention was closure. Why, why did it all happen? Everything happens for a reason and it's just...' She held her hands up. 'Why did this all happen to you, your family – my family?' she swiftly added as if the addition would give extra weight to how committed she was to him. 'I just have this feeling and if I don't ask now I may not get the chance again. I can't help it, it's in my blood. You make money, run the business world to the max. Me, I solve crime cases, give closure to people, explain why things happen and for what reason. There is always a reason, it's simple physics.'

He stood and moved to her side, bending to reach for her. Placing his hand on the side of her face, she pushed into it as a way to get closer. She smiled and held his eyes.

'If I say yes or if I say no, I have the same worry. You. Both of you and how this is going to stress you even more.' He kissed her cheek. 'But it is stressing you anyway, so I am stuck, powerless and out of control. You never said about being stuck in here, you never told me. We can go away. I can solve that. I have been able to get the legal team to agree that we can go to Kent, take a few days to go up north to visit the hospital if you want first. This I can do, but I can do nothing that will stop your gut instinct other than say yes and help you.' Every bone in his body was regretting saying the word yes, but he could never say no and truly mean it. When she looked like she did, her eyes melted him. Whatever his future was, it was hidden in her soul, behind her eyes and in her breath.

He looked at Lottie and she smiled. Not in triumph but to acknowledge that this was a big thing for him. He had promised her that he would always listen, do anything in his power to help as long as she was honest. He had also said that he would never stop caring, worrying for her, and never let her be put in harm's way alone again. So, the earlier outburst was not forgotten and potentially justified not to be. She understood why he had reacted that way.

'Thank you. And I am sorry you had to come over in such a panic, really, I never thought of any consequences. I would love a few days away, but can we call the professor, get him over, and talk to Pete while it is all still so fresh?' She moved over to give him room to sit on the bed next to her.

'And set some ground rules?' he asked, pulling her to him.

'Yes, ground rules.' She smiled. 'The first...' He looked at her as if to say 'hold on a moment'. 'The first is to kiss me and say that you are not mad with Mrs B or me for earlier. You will not punish her?'

He lent into her and hovered his lips over her mouth. His hot breath aroused her like a heatwave and she closed her eyes, waiting for the searing contact of what she expected to follow. But on not feeling the contact she opened her eyes, immediately seeing the blue pools she knew were back from the angry grey.

'The kiss, yes Mrs Dean, I will kiss you, and yes I will forgive Mrs B. You, however... I have a way I can make you remember why I was so mad and to ensure that you do not do it again.' He ran his hand along the line of her knee and up towards her thigh. Their faces were still millimetres apart and she opened her lips to let a slow sigh out. Not stopping his hand movements, he touched her on the outside of the light trousers she was wearing, and her sex clenched. His hand ran over her stomach and he circled her heavy baby-primed breast and gently squeezed the erect nipple that had developed from the moment his hand had started its journey. She gasped; she knew that pain, she knew that feeling of pleasure that very often followed and, as he hovered above her, she longed for it again.

Their eyes had not once left the other's while he caressed her, and another of his hot breaths on her skin made Lottie push up, impatient to taste him. He pulled away. Not allowing her what she wanted, she pushed up more.

He put his hand over her mouth. 'Not a chance,' he whispered in her ear, kissing her neck. The kiss he had promised, and she had hoped for she had not been intended to be on her neck. 'And at this very moment will you remember why I was mad?' he asked, pulling back from her more.

She screwed up her nose and looked to the bulge in his trousers. He followed her eyes and, as if to tempt her, he rubbed himself. 'Remember that if you ever do that again...' He stood up now, adjusting himself as much for the release of the pain his trousers were causing on his member as to draw her eyes to him. 'Remember this very moment, Lottie.' He gave her a cheeky but stern smile. 'I will give up anything to ensure that you are safe, so next time, just think of what you are missing now before you put yourself in harm's way and know that I would give up everything for you, go without everything to make sure you are safe.'

He turned his back on her; he had to. Every fibre of his being wanted to jump her, touch her, take her, have her in ways he had dreamt of over the last week. He had tried not to be aroused because she was still recovering. He'd fended her off more than once to make sure she rested. He desperately wanted to slap her arse, to leave it hot and red to remind her of what not thinking about her safety did to him. But he kept his composure because he meant every word. He would help her because he knew he had too, but she had to know it was not easy for him. At least he was trying.

She slapped the bed sheet, holding up her hands. 'I get it!' she said, like a child. She stood and made her way slowly towards the toilet. As the door closed to the bathroom, she said it again, 'OK I get it or not,' under her breath.

Chapter 20

Lottie looked over at Edward and smiled. The rain had eased as they left the city and although they had departed before 6am, she felt awake and alive. They were heading to the hospital to see how the charity was getting along and then they had a day at the stables. Lottie loved the new car, and as they reached the open countryside she was feeling more at home. Observing the surrounding scenery of this green and pleasant land started to make her mind settle, as much as it could. Things had not gone away and the thought that they all could be separated by the law did still loom as a silent cloud above their every move. At least for now there was room to breathe some clean air.

Edward rubbed her leg, making her turn her attention back to him. She smiled to confirm the question he had already asked every five minutes of the two-hour journey so far. She was alright. She was pleased that they had spent the last nine days working on a plan and sorting through everything that she had needed to ensure that the few days away could go as well as expected.

She had spoken to Edward about how he felt about it all. She had not really given much thought about him and how the fact that he shot his old friend may be affecting his state of mind. It had to be. She was shocked at first that he even had a gun, and that he was capable of using it. He was reluctant to share his feelings on this subject with her at first. She expressed that they had to talk, share this; they had agreed never to keep secrets. Loving someone as they did meant that you share the good and the bad. It had to happen that way. So, they had sat, for what turned out to be a few hours, talking it through from Edward's side, although he was still not totally admitting that he was at ease with taking a life, a life he had once been so very dependent on and that it had taken its mental toll.

'You can put your front up to the world, Ed, but not me,' Lottie said, holding his arm and hugging him. 'Please remember that.' Since then the subject had been closed.

The only thing that was still looming from the whole sorry event was the court hearing, due for the following Monday. But until then, four days away, she hoped they would recharge their batteries for the battles ahead. She tried not to think of any of it, to do as Edward had said and relax, but she could not help but think of the things they had arranged and set in motion before they had left in case it did.

The first thing was the press injunction. That could not come too soon for everyone. At least they could leave the building without having to look over their shoulders. The fact that no story or pictures could be sold or released had soon made the scavengers move onto the next poor soul who made the news.

Next was that Todd was doing OK. The three of them had had a meal out without any interruptions. Only towards the end did Lottie ask him if he knew any more about the day. Sadly, for him the whole event was a blur, and he could not recall anyone else around, only the possibility that a woman had been with Alex as he had arrived. Neither Edward nor Lottie had prompted this information, but they both knew that there was a possibility of it as Pete had acquired the CCTV footage. No questions had been asked about where he had been able to access it. Pete and Edward had first viewed it and there was without doubt a slight possibility that Alex had been holding someone's hand as he entered the building, and they let go just before the camera picked him up entering the main reception area.

Pete was still on the case for more footage from outside, maybe the parking lot. Nothing had come to light from the corridor to the penthouse. For the privacy of the guests the footage stopped at the lift, so it was clear that if there had been someone else and Lottie had heard a woman laughing, she had not got in that way – but then another entry would have been easy because Lottie and Alex had arrived via the fire escape, and they did not appear on any footage either.

Lottie had watched the footage over and over to the point that Edward had turned it off, worried that she would recall at some point the horrific scene, and sure that this was why twice now she had been crying in her sleep. Lottie could not account for why she had been, when he asked, and was very honest about not having nightmares when questioned the following morning by Edward. She even reassured the doctor Edward had insisted she saw before they took the trip, just to make sure everything was OK. And it was. A few more months to go and all would be well. Lottie knew this and was sure that although predicted to be over 7lbs, Dean Junior would come out with football boots at the ready and more like 7 stone.

The professor was very pleased to see them when they arrived the day after meeting with Todd. In the car Lottie had bantered ideas about what they should be looking for, although the hotel room had been cleaned out and would not be worth another look. The evidence had to be. It was a good thing, although Lottie had not mentioned this, that Alex had not yet been released from the morgue. A fact that they knew from Edward's mother, as she was still visiting the bereaved Mrs Girski. Although not pushed for the information, she had also noted that a young woman had been visiting Alex's mother. Mrs Dean had not seen her for herself. This information was worth pursuing.

Still having the body made Lottie think that maybe he had someone else's DNA on him. Again, she only shared this with Todd and the professor, once she had him on her own.

Todd and Edward were looking through the first lot of papers. According to the professor he did not have access to them, so was in no way assisting in anything illegal. The large payment to the foundation had in no way been made to buy any papers or the professor's time but because Edward and the Dean corporation often gave to the good cause.

The documents had just been left in an inbox and the professor had picked them up and taken them home.

Lottie was scanning some electronic copies of the police reports and needed to stretch her legs so offered to go to the kitchen to make tea. The professor took the time to show her where the supplies were, as if she had forgotten, and both saw this as an opportunity to chat.

'We think he had someone with him when he arrived. I wondered if he had any additional DNA, other than...' She stopped and poured the hot water into the cups.

'I will look at the autopsy report. I have to say I have not read any of it.' He too stopped as if this was a touchy subject.

Lottie took a breath.

'I guess it was a bit grim for the first porter. I mean he took some fire power by all accounts.'

'Lottie, my dear, I have to be honest. It is all a bit close to home for you and in your condition. Do you not think that you should be leaving this one to the others? I know you and how so very consumed you can become, no, correction you do become in such cases, but this one... well, it is so very different.' He gave her a knowing smile, as someone who cared for the young woman soon to be a mother in the room with him now.

'Prof.' She put down the cup and put her hand on his arm, and he rolled his eyes at her pet name for him. Something she had always done, and he had always shown that he did not approve of, although the term of endearment was actually something he secretly loved, but only allowed her to use.

'I am touched by your concern and thank you for understanding, and caring so much, but I do this with the same passion and concern for the truth as I would for any other case. Yes, this has a very personal meaning for me, Edward, but it does not calm my need to know why? Why has this happened and for how long has it been going on? Who else is involved and...' This is where she stopped and, without knowing, instinctively rubbed Bump. 'What consequences could, would or will be had on others that we love if we do not get that answer? It has to be concluded, there has to be an end.'

The professor had set to work and better than just looking at the paperwork alone, he had assured Lottie that he would, by whatever means, take another look at the body. On the night before they left the rule was made – one last catch-up with everyone and then that was it. No mention, but when the car stereo changed to the ringing tone of Lottie's phone, she looked at the caller ID to see that it was the professor and as it was connected to the Bluetooth system, she was going to have to take the call on speaker. Edward beat her to it as the controls were on the steering wheel.

'Professor,' he said. It was his intention to let the caller know he was with Lottie and they had asked not to be disturbed unless it was critical. 'You are on speaker with us both, how can we help?'

The pause in the caller's voice was one that made Lottie momentarily panic. She was not sure if she wanted Edward to hear what the prof had to say as he was still not aware of the request to look at the body again. Then again why hide it?

'Mr Dean, Lottie, my dear, I am sorry to disturb you but, well I had a thought about some of the things we talked about and I wondered if there was any mileage in a re-examination?' He paused, and Lottie let out her breath. He had covered and made it look like he'd had the thought about it and not that she had asked. 'I never mentioned this as I was not sure if I would be granted access, you know with the case still ongoing, complications and access rights with the family etc.' Another pause. 'Anyway, strings pulled and well, I am sending you some emails. I do not wish to offend your intelligence, Mr Dean, but I am sure that once you get to have a look through, Lottie will be able to agree with my conclusion. Indeed, there is some evidence that was overlooked and that I think you may want to take a little further.'

'Thank you, Prof,' Lottie said, already reaching into her bag to get the device out.

'Yes, thanks Professor.' Edward emphasized the name, looking at his wife, knowing the irritation the older man showed if anyone else called him that. 'I am sure my wife will be all over it, even if I am insisting she takes a break for the next few days.'

There was a laugh down the phone as if knowing it was not possible that she would wait, and that Lottie would be scrolling through her inbox as they spoke.

'Good luck with that, Mr Dean, and have a safe trip.'

'Lottie really, can you not wait? I will stop, we can eat somewhere.' Edward looked at her seconds after terminating the call. 'Then we can have a look.'

'Ed, I'll just take a quick look now,' she said back as if it were life and death. Edward looked at the sat-nav to try to find the next turn for a possible village, hotel, or a basic café. He had to admit he too wanted to know more. 'I can cut through the boring stuff and just get to the...' She stopped and flung her head back, smiling like a cat that got the cream. 'Yes! I knew it, I knew it would.'

'You knew what would what, Lottie? Please I need to pull over.' Edward braked as the car in front of him did the same.

'I knew a fresh look...' Her inner voice had to word this first, so she slowed down to allow her brain to compute. 'I knew a fresh look at everything would show something. And ta-dah! DNA from an unknown female under his fingers, in his hair and, well, let's just say a few hours before I met him, they slept together and thank god for us, he was a dirty bastard in more ways than one. He had not bothered to take a shower.'

'OK, too much information. Now put it down and let me stop.' Edward looked at her, trying to pull the phone from her hands. 'I'm not joking, Lottie. Put it down, be as smug as you like now you know the basics but put it down and let's stop and eat.'

She did as he asked, but the smile remained on her face. They pulled off the main road and found a small, beautiful old hotel. They were informed it did not offer breakfast to non-residents, but this was soon changed when the manager was called for and he found out that their financial circumstances would benefit from saying yes just this once.

'The window is very private. I am sure that you will be well seated here for the view of this fine morning in the beautiful Derbyshire countryside.'

Edward's face said it all as if he just wanted him to go away. The advantage of showing your cash very often got you what you wanted but on the other side when some people knew you had the cash, they sucked up to you, and in this case, it was over the top. Lottie let him suffer; he had pushed for food and he had got them it.

'Very impressive. Tell me how old is the house? It is so beautiful, it must have a history, you must tell us.' She smirked at Edward who was looking for a menu, but the table was without one. As the man started to speak, Lottie interrupted, 'Oh. Sorry – baby! I need to use the ladies.' She stood and held her stomach. 'Long car journey. I won't be a moment.' She grinned at Edward. He knew what she was doing.

She returned and Edward was sitting with a steaming coffee in front of him.

'So how old is the house?' Lottie had been impressed with the internal décor as she had navigated her way to the toilet. So different from the plush furnishings of the London apartment, and even the house in Kent did not compare to this splendour. This was her idea of what she thought a country house should be like. 'It must have been a special place in the mid-Victorian period, a great family house.' She had noted the date above the door when she walked in, so she was only mocking Edward as she asked him. She had also noted the coat of arms, which meant that it had been a single residence at some time. But she suspected like most houses at the end of the 1900s or during the wars, families could no longer afford them, or whole families were lost with no one to take them on.

'I ordered you some food, was not sure what, so I just went for one of everything I know you like.' Edward did not react to her question he just retorted, 'He was very interested in his workplace, shows dedication to his employer!' He locked eyes with Lottie, pursing his lips as he knew she was mocking him, but she just looked so beautiful he almost needed to hold his breath. 'He scooted off to find you some ginger tea,' he said, but then knew he had to ask. 'Go on then, fill me in with the details.' He knew her well; she had looked again at the pages of the report sent through.

The hospital staff had not been expecting to see the Deans, with the recent hassle from the press. Edward felt it best not to publish where they were going too much. Lottie became involved in walking around and meeting people while Edward went off to look at some paperwork that needed to be signed off.

Waiting for him she walked out into the garden and sat on a seat. The sun was very welcome on her face and she closed her eyes for a moment.

It was not long before her mind fogged up again with the information and she opened her eyes and crossed her arms over her bump to contemplate. The DNA had no trace, so how could they find out more? Although it proved something, it gave them nothing more and this was annoying.

She was sure she had dozed off once they got back in the 4x4 because the welcome face of Sarah was soon waving at them from the entrance to the stable yard. The next three days were at times hectic with the hustle of the working yard, and the small baby in the house. Lottie had laughed as Edward had insisted on doing a nappy duty even though Joe had warned him it was not as easy as it looked, admitting he got out of it as often as he could. As she lay in the queen-size bed in the guest room, she listened for the shower to stop, knowing that he would emerge at any moment. Towel in hand, rubbing his hair, he smiled and walked towards her.

'Like what you see, Mrs Dean?' he asked. Did she ever. She was hiding her bump and increased body size under the covers, ashamed almost of how out of shape she felt, but she marvelled at his toned, chiselled body and wondered how he kept it so. He ate well and in the past few days, with the exception of walking and one ride out with Joe and Lottie's Pride, he had not been to the gym or any of the classes which he usually did, giving the trainer an ass-kicking as he called it on his return.

'Would be better under here.' She pointed to the covers and gave him a smile that she hoped would persuade him. She longed for him to be intimate. Ever since she had come home from the hospital, the closest she got to being passionate was kissing and being held while she slept. He said that he did not want to hurt her even though she insisted that she was fine. But she needed to be consumed by him, she wanted him more than she had felt before. He stood at the side of the bed, the towel showing off all his curves, just tucked in around his waist showing her favourite place. The 'lickie V' which outlined the muscles on his hips down to his thighs and most of all to his manhood. While he was still drying his hair, taking his eyes away from her for a moment Lottie pulled at the towel. On all fours she pushed closer and kissed his hip, ensuring her tongue licked a slight line down towards the growing bulge she wanted to aim for. He jumped slightly, taking the towel from his head.

The covers had fallen from her and the small, black, lacy baby doll nightdress was fully showing her backside and legs. Her hair covered her shoulders and back with a few strands falling down her face. He felt it brush his skin, making his own body hair stand up. 'Lottie,' he said as a protest, as a warning. His voice may have been a warning not to, but his body was showing it was a lie. She kissed him again, this time lower so her face was in his pubic hair. He heard her breath in deep, as she took in the scent of him, fresh and washed.

God, he needed her, he worshiped her and knew there was nothing he would not do to have her. He had tortured himself the past few weeks trying to hold back from her. Even resorting to self-gratification at work in the shower room to try to reduce the lust he had. The more she bloomed, and grew, the more it seemed to attract him, and the sight of her now was killing him.

He felt her hot lips surrounding his dick, making it pulse and throb as if thunder were running from his gut to his growing erection. 'Lottie,' he said again, and he heard her say 'Shush' before she took him again, this time deeper into her mouth, making him gasp for the next breath. He closed his eyes, putting his head back and knowing he could not fight the burning sensation in his balls.

Clasping her hands around his backside, Lottie pulled him closer, so she could feel him deeper. With increased speed, she moved him in and out, knowing that she was affecting him, but also aware of her own need that was sending vibrations to her sex. On her knees the pressure from the bump was removed, but the weight of her heavy breasts rubbed the bed cover as she moved with Ed's now-increased rhythm. This itself was stimulating her, sending messages that were directed to her core.

Ed placed his hand on her shoulder, and she looked up at him; she could feel how close he was. She could take him all the way but the selfish need growing in her was preying on her mind now and she desperately wanted to feel him inside her in other ways. Scratching her nail along his back made him jerk and the first taste of the salty seed entered her mouth followed by another low, slow grown. He pulled her hair, making her look at him again, to slow her down as he was close.

She stopped and pushed up on her knees. She licked him all the way up to his face and kissed his mouth, smiling as he still had his eyes closed and a grin on his face that she loved. She pushed her tongue deep into his mouth, mixing his own juice around and tasting him once more.

He pulled away 'Jesus, Lottie, I love you,' he said as she kissed around his ear, feeling the dampness on his hair, 'But you are killing me, woman, I need you so much.' He let his hand wander over her shoulders and down her back. She was so close that Bump was pushing up against him and he pulled his hands around to cup both of her breasts, amazed at how dark and hard both nipples were, standing proud to greet him. She ran her hand down his body to his pulsing dick, clear liquid flowing from him as she used it to massage him further. 'No Lottie, I can't hold back if you do that.'

She whispered in his ear. 'Give in to me. Why hold back?' she asked.

'Because I want this to last. You are amazing and how I feel right now, nothing in existence could be better and I will submit to you completely.' He gasped again as she squeezed him.

'Nothing?' she asked. She took his hand and with simple ease that even impressed her she turned her back on him and lent forwards, again on all fours, like a bitch on heat begging for her mate. She managed to get his hand to cup her sex. She was so very wet, even the smallest touch from him made her start to quiver.

'I can't hurt you, Lottie.' Edward knew what she was asking and like a moth to a flame he found himself leaning over her, pushing his member to the entrance of her cleft that was so proudly on show for him.

Like a well-fitting glove as if it honed to her core, his purple, bulbous head pushed the first folds of her private skin, and she gripped the sheets in her fists. 'Please, Edward,' she whimpered, sending him into mental turmoil. He had to drive into her, thrust and pump into her to make her come hard. It was the only way this was going to end, but he had to be gentle, he had to take back some control. 'Please,' she pleaded again, and his gut knotted with a surge of blood to his cock. Holding all his weight on one arm slightly to the side of her he fully covered her back, pushing his face to her neck. 'I will stop if I hurt you, Lottie, promise me.' He felt her slick cunt soothing his hot skin and she was so wet that his change of position had allowed him further in. 'Lottie?' He was desperate for her reply now because he was about to blow, he was sure. She grabbed out at his arm. 'Please Ed, yes!' She gasped as if the light touch around her soft flesh was also driving her to the edge.

He did not have to move much as she bent her back and with one smooth motion, he pushed up to her. She stretched round him as he filled her and with just one push he was there. Her eyes were closed, and she smiled, dipping her head down. She could feel every inch of him, as if he were sending electrical sparks to her, she pulsed, and with a slow long drag he pulled almost out of her. She felt the loss and pushed back as if defiant to lose him. He pushed in again, each time the rhythm faster, the shocks in her sharper and the pure lust in her veins swamping her brain. She pushed back to him, this time flicking her head back, her hair wiping her back, and she moaned under her breath. The gentle rubbing of the sheets on her tender breasts was now to the point of painful, but she was not stopping until she got where she needed to be.

With his free hand he held her hip, he felt her need and increased the speed of him in her. He had to slow her down, he had to, but the more he felt the need to protect her, the more he had to thrust, burst inside her. 'Fuck it,' he said, feeling his balls tighten and then his head spin. On the first pulse of his cock spilling into her, Lottie felt his depth hitting the very core of her and she tried to pull back, he was too deep, but he pulsed and ground her once more forcing his weight down and his shaft in. She struggled to hold herself on her arms but almost buried her face in the bedding as she yelped out when her own wave of pleasure tightened her inner muscles around him. The shear reaction of her spasm and his pulsing sent them both into a suspended climax, one which once they had come down from left Lottie desperately clinging to the sheets as he pulled out. She felt sore, tight, but fulfilled.

Ed pushed away, leaning on his side and slipping his arm around her to pull her close, wiping the hair away from her neck he kissed. 'Woman, what have you done to me?' He paused to breath. 'Are you?'

'More than,' she replied, stopping him from asking. 'Pull up the sheets?' she asked, not because she was cold; the opposite was true, she was so hot from the exertion.

'Can't I see you? You are so beautiful,' he asked, leaning up onto one hand, pushing the final lock of hair from her warm, red face. 'Glowing,' he said.

'Fat,' she retorted pulling for the sheets herself, 'I look fat.'

'Pregnant with my child, and not that I ever thought it possible but more beautiful that I could ever imagine. Now rest and say no more.' He planted a kiss on her shoulder and helped with the final tugging of the sheets over them both.

Ed closed his eyes, waiting to come back down from the high he was having. Submitting to her every time, her every need was his life mission. It was not long before a reality check hit him; if this all went wrong, and they were all prosecuted he would never feel this for a long time, years maybe. His heart started to beat fast again with the thought of not seeing his son grow, his wife become the most fantastic mother he knew she would be. He pulled her closer, as if that would remove the thought, to the fact that it could be so.

Sleep never came for him, but while they were wrapped in his arms, he alone could have them and keep them safe. At this moment in time, he was in control; that was soon going to change.

One final look at her dress in the mirror and then she moved her eyes over and watched Edward in the reflection pacing up and down the apartment floor with his phone to his ear. They had been in court yesterday but after only twenty minutes the judge had asked to adjourn, and today they were due back as instructed.

Any relaxation of the past few days had gone, and Lottie had another restless night with her mind playing too many reconstructions and theories of the whole situation.

Nothing still from the professor, or Pete from the DNA. The only thing that was pleasing was today Todd had to also be at court and she would get to see him.

Still talking to the caller, Edward moved closer to her and stood behind her, moving her hair to the side to gently kiss at her neck. 'Yes, Mum, I will say hi to Lottie. She is here if you want to talk?' The reply must have been yes as he handed over the phone and mouthed 'Mother'. Lottie took the call and repeated the same information Edward had said several times – not to worry and to take it easy. After the call, Lottie joined Edward and Pete at the door and they left as a group.

In the entrance to the court Lottie had dashed with joy to her friend who was waiting with his sister. She had released the hold of Edward and jogged as fast as her Prada shoes, injured leg and Bump would let her into the arms of the man who had shared the ordeal first-hand.

Edward was uneasy with the reciprocal embrace, and Pete noticed his manner which instantly changed as the couple held on to each other and they only broke off once the whole party had come together.

'Todd, you look really well,' Lottie said, holding him at arm's length. 'Oh god I am so pleased to see you.'

'We spoke yesterday Lotts, it's not been that long,' he said, still holding her as Edward moved to the side of his wife, placing a very positive arm around her waist. Todd noticed and put his hand out to shake the spare one Edward had. The greeting was made. They all greeted Todd's sister too and with a roll of Edward's eyes, Lottie had the conversation going instantly with Todd about the professor and the information. The chat was only broken as the group were called in by the young court clerk.

Thankfully for all parties the court was a closed hearing. Press had been outside, but they had been easily averted as the injunction still stood. As they walked into the court, Lottie hesitated. Something made her turn round, not so much as a voice but just an uneasy feeling. There were other people in the hall, voices echoed and came and went, but as she looked back up to reply to Edward's question if she was OK, and to come in, she heard a laugh and a voice that she knew was the one.

Pete had the door open and Lottie had almost touched Ed's outstretched hand when she fully turned to look to see if she could follow the laugh. Even the court clerk who should have been the last one to enter the room moved aside because she was aiming back out of the room.

'Miss?' 'Lottie?' Both the voices of the clerk and Edward came at the same time.

She put her hand up. 'One minute,' she said, trying to speed away because the voice had gone, and no one seemed to be in sight now. 'Lottie?' The stern voice said again, and it was now Edward who moved out of the room. 'What the hell?' Without turning around Lottie said, 'That laugh, the voice with the laugh. She is here somewhere.'

Causing a commotion in a courtroom is never an advisable fact. This information was ringing in Lottie's ears once she had been persuaded to come back in. No one could be found, and she sat motionless as she was being scolded by the young lawyer sitting to her side. Her cheeks red, not from embarrassment, but from anger that she had been practically dragged back to the room without been allowed a proper look. On protest Edward had sent Pete out to look for any females, but without him knowing what or who he was looking for Lottie felt it was paid lip service. With the judge in session, Lottie whispered something to Edward.

'I know Lottie, but we need to be here and everything we have worked for will, if this team are as good as they say and cost, get some form of result and then, well we can carry on with whatever you think it is that this voice is relevant to.'

She retorted back. 'So, you don't believe me!' She kept her head down as their defence team was talking and she did not want to distract anyone.

'I said I did.' He turned to her now, taking her hand. There was a 'shush' that came from the clerk sitting to the other side of them. 'Sorry,' Edward mouthed. There was only a small moment of silence from her, then she whispered back.

'There has to be a connection,' Lottie carried on as if the request to stay quiet had not even penetrated her ears, 'Something we are missing.' Another shush came but this time loud enough for the judge to hear and he interjected.

'I am sorry, Mrs Dean, but is there something that you need to say?' In a flash all eyes now fell to Lottie and even Edward was staring at her as if she had two heads. She had to think fast on her feet, and knowing that she had to create a diversion she used her female assets and rubbed her stomach.

'Your honour, I'm sorry but I am uncomfortable.' She stretched as if trying to get a better position. 'I am sorry.' She smiled and bit down on her lip, directly holding his eyes.

As if he had been sucked into her somehow with an invisible power, he gave her a smile. 'Maybe we can get you a glass of water?' He looked at the clerk who jumped to assist.

She quickly interjected. 'I think it is because I have had too much water!' Lottie wiggled in her seat again with the insinuation that she had a full bladder. Edward gave her a questioning 'Are you OK?' and she quickly nodded.

'I see,' said the judge, getting her meaning. 'We could spare you for a moment I am sure, shall we adjourn?'

'No, I'm sorry to cause a fuss, please I am fine,' she insisted giving everyone her best smile to convince them otherwise. Her plan worked.

'Mrs Dean, please I am happy for you to leave us for now. My wife was very much the same with our first. Clerk, please see Mrs Dean out for a moment.' He gave her a smile, and Edward stood as she started to move off the chair. The judge added, 'Mr Dean, I rather feel that you should stay since we are close to the conclusion.'

He wanted to go, but also wanted to stay. He said very sternly to the clerk while pressing buttons on his phone, 'Find my CPO. He is outside, tell him to go with Mrs Dean, and then wait for me outside.' Looking at his wife he was not happy not to be going and he made sure Lottie knew. 'Wait with Pete,' he said, and she nodded. 'Lottie wait!' he said to repeat his request.

She got outside and thanked the clerk. Pete was waiting as instructed by Edward. Sometimes she was amazed how fast the two of them communicated and she was sure that they just used one-word codes.

'This way.' Pete pointed to the female rest room, but Lottie stood in front of him.

'Pete, I just wanted to see for myself. I am sure that whoever it is has an interest in the outcome today and will still be around.'

'Mrs Dean!' He scratched his head, but the complaint was futile as she was already walking off down the stairs to the ground floor, away from the toilet area.

'Only five minutes, I am not lying to him, I don't need to go as badly now I am standing!' She smiled but Pete knew this was her plan all along. 'You are here. We will not be able to go back in until they have finished so we may as well be proactive.' She gave him another smile and he shook his head, and finally nodded. Lottie scooted off before the giant of a man had chance to change his mind.

From the side of the vast hallway, the female onlooker watched the attractive woman that she loathed more than any other walk away from the court room with the older well-dressed man. She knew Pete; she had met him with Edward many times. She sniffed and wiped her nose. The powder that she had used to take away some of the pain had lost its effect over an hour ago. Her brain once again was clear that Edward had to change his mind and see how much she loved him and what she had and would do to have him.

Her whole existence for the past five years had been a mess because he had dumped her. Everything he had, they had was not enough. He'd still wanted more; he had told her she was not good enough to share it with him. His brother had found out that she had been unfaithful to Edward, but she never thought that Edward would abandon her like he did for just one stupid night. They had done everything with sex, dominating, rough, experimental so she was sure that her sleeping with someone else would not bother him. But it did. Once his brother had told Edward, she was out. Her livid revenge was to hurt Ed in the same way, and so Mitch had had to go.

The goal of making Edward want her again had been moved further away now Lottie was on the scene. Her plan to stay close to Edward failed once again when Alex had fallen out with him, and this last mess once more because of Edward Dean wanting someone else, more than her, had meant that she had lost the only other person that she could rely on to help her get back to him.

She looked at the woman again and felt a tear in her eye but instead of crying, she laughed. Something she was glad the drugs seemed to do. Stopped the tears and made her laugh. She put her hand to her mouth, and with another thought said out loud she should be having his child, not her. Why had she not been the one to have his child, to win him and live happily ever after?

The woman and the man she knew as Edwards COP stopped walking and she fell silent, hiding behind a large stone pillar. It was only when the silence fell that they moved towards the door and out onto the street. She turned around and left the building by the side door.

The celebrations at the apartment were obvious. The case, for whatever reasons Lottie would never know, had been dropped. Pete was never in question. He had a licence and although he was on the manslaughter charge, it was passed that it was self-defence and part of his employment code. The fact that Edward had also fired a gun took more accounting for and a heavy fine was taken, along with a suspended sentence. He had a criminal record but nothing that could not get lost or would make any difference to his financial or business life.

For DC Sharpe he had sadly been found guilty of perverting the course of justice, lost his job and had a large fine and a suspended two-year sentence. Lottie, in her absence along with Todd had been deemed to have suffered enough and all charges had been dropped. The judge gave no reason for this other than the previous good works that the centre had done, and what both Todd and Lottie had achieved in their professional lives, had sent many other people to prison and solved many cases.

Mrs B was busy filling up the glasses of everyone who had been asked back to the penthouse. Lottie had tea and was sitting in the living room when she noticed someone being escorted into Edward's office. She excused herself from Edward's mother and went to the door. As she looked in, she felt her skin heat up. She was so sorry for what had happened to the man standing by her husband's side. She pushed the door and they both looked up.

'DC Sharpe, I am so very sorry. Everything has been my fault.' She was really sorry that the long-earned career of this well-established man had been lost on her say so and actions.

'Mrs Dean, it's not DC anymore, but please, it's OK,' he said, putting out a friendly hand to shake hers.

'Darling, meet your new CPO. Mr Isaac Sharpe has agreed to join the team.' Edward smiled at her. 'I have insisted as a bonus for starting work that the fine has been paid off too, so Mr Sharpe can assure his good lady that this job is genuine and that we will welcome him to our team, if he accepts.'

'Sounds like a bribe to me,' Lottie said, very sceptical.

'Sounds like a life-line to me, Mrs Dean. I would do it again, just maybe next time share it with your husband sooner.' Sharpe smiled as if to allay any concerns Lottie had.

'There will be no next time! I am looking at you both, but mostly my wife there, Mr Sharpe. Nothing happens without me knowing. Pete will be very clear with that when you start your training, but for now please with my blessing and thanks, whatever you did at HQ, whoever you managed to talk to about the charges and the case, thank you. I hope that you have a great few weeks in France, and please use the villa as your own. I am sure that you and your family will love it. Pay for nothing and ensure that I get every bill from any local places you shop.'

The older man nodded and thanked Edward as another glass of champagne was put in his hand from Mrs B. Edward wandered over to his wife and kissed her cheek.

'The man who can fix it all?' she said sipping at her tea. 'And remind me just how is it going to stay out of the papers, and what will Mrs Girski say about the verdict, being shot is no accident in my eyes,' Lottie said, trying to keep the sarcasm in her voice down to a low whisper.

'I don't care is the honest answer, we need to put this behind us now and move on.' He pushed a lock of her hair back over her shoulder. 'I want to take a few days in Kent, just to see how Gerald is getting on, and of course Agnes.' He changed the subject to one that he knew would please Lottie.

'Nicely avoided, Mr Dean, although I have to say I would love to.' She smiled at the thought of seeing her dear friend and took in a deep breath. She really did want to get away again. She had felt so much better even after the few days they had just had, and as much as she knew there was still things to do, answers to find, this was one huge weight off her mind.

She should take Mrs B's advice and not worry about how they got the result that allowed the whole affair to go away. Just take it and move on, after all in a few months their lives would change once more. As always, Lottie had listened but it meant there were only two months to answer the remaining question of that woman, whoever, wherever and whatever the connection was, because she was sure there was one.

They had driven down the day after the court hearing. Even Pete had some time off, although they still had one of the team staying in the house. Edward had still worked every day, usually when Lottie was out walking, or with Agnes, or resting, as she was now starting to feel the last few weeks of her pregnancy taking their toll. She had still been able to find time to log on to emails and ring the professor for any updates, but it seemed that everything was quiet. Mr Sharpe had called to say all was well in France and he was staying in London on his return. Even though she had tried to ask him to do more digging, he really was taking his new boss' word for it and reported straight back to Edward that she had made the request. Luckily for her she had mentioned it at their evening meal before he took the phone call from the CPO.

'I know you were just checking, but nothing has changed. I said that we were still looking into it, but Lottie, it seems there is nothing really to look into,' Edward said as they sat on the sofa huddled in each other's arms watching a nature program.

So, three weeks had passed and today was the first day that Lottie was on her own in the house in Kent. The silence was somehow warming her, so she sat on the old piano stool. Gerald was out at the shop. Edward had asked him to wait until Agnes had arrived, but she was not due for another hour and Lottie really could not see the point of him having to wait around. Edward had kissed her goodbye and said he would be back for their planned evening meal. Once more giving her the order not to do anything and call if she needed anything, anything at all. She had rolled her eyes at the word anything, and he raised his eyebrows stating for her not to look at him like that. Playfully she stuck out her tongue as he turned to leave the room.

She lifted the polished cover and looked down at the keys as they shone back at her in their black and white glory. The musical instrument was not as grand as the one in the apartment, and maybe was not as old, but it made her smile when she thought about its own history in her life. Her fingers sprang to action as if they had never left it.

She stopped playing as she felt the soft fur rub against her leg, an indication that Gerald was back from shopping. She stood up knowing that the reward for him going out was ice cream.

Closing the door to the living room behind him, Edward placed his briefcase on the breakfast bar.

'How has she been?' He directed his question to Gerald, who was washing plates.

'All good, Mr Dean, sir. Mrs Dean played for us, well, Apollo who looked fixedly at her. 'Twas like the music mesmerised him. All good. Mrs Agnes came, and they had tea outside, we ate ice cream and then we had a walk, not too far mind!' The housekeeper was now walking to the fridge in anticipation of the next question. 'Mr Dean, sir, you want a beer?'

Edward nodded and sat at the bar and smiled, knowing that it had been some time since Lottie had played, and she must have felt relaxed to do so. He looked over to a pile of post. Gerald caught his eye. 'All for you sir. Mrs Dean, she had her post.' Edward thanked him as the cold bottle was opened and placed in front of him.

'Has she been asleep for long?' He loosened his tie and took a grateful mouthful of the alcohol. London had been hot and busy.

'No sir, just dozing in front on the TV. Apollo has his eye on her.' Gerald smiled, Apollo had more than his eye on her when he had looked into the room. Lottie and the dog looked like one as they were twined around each other on the sofa.

Sitting with the laptop open, Edward put his attention back to the post noticing one that looked as if it had been eaten by the dog. He pushed back and lent over. Gerald was about to serve his dinner as he had been informed Lottie had already eaten and did not want any more as she was still feeling full from eating two large tubs of Ben and Jerry's.

He looked at the hand-written address, but then noticed no post mark. He pulled it open and out fell a paper clipping of the trial, and a note typed on a computer stating, 'You will pay Edward Dean for everything.'

He pulled the note out further to make sure that he was reading it right. The paper clip had been highlighted on the bit where it stated that Mrs Dean had played a key part in finding out other unsolved cases and again the words of accidental death had been marked as if for special attention. He pushed it back in the envelope as Gerald placed a hot plate of food in front of him.

'When did this come?' Edward asked, lifting the envelope to identify what he was asking.

''Bout an hour before the post, sir,' Gerald replied, looking at what he was holding before he started to clean the oven.

'Did you see who it was?' Edward asked, keen to ensure he did not see the contents.

'No, sir.' Gerald stopped for a moment.

'Mrs Dean, did she not see?' Edward sounded slightly panicked now and the housekeeper looked up with more concentration. 'No, sir, is everything OK?' As he asked a small noise from behind them made them both look round.

'Hey you, you should have woken me.' Lottie padded in and her bare feet made a noise on the cold stone floor. The tapping of the claws indicated that Apollo had also walked in to see everyone. Lottie leant over and kissed her husband; he responded, making sure that the package was not in her line of sight. 'Busy day?' she asked, pushing around to try to sit on him and he had to push back to give her some room and he quickly put the package into his case.

'Sort of,' he said, trying not to indicate that something had disturbed him. 'All good though. Pete's on his way back so we have a few days to ourselves.' Edward stopped as she kissed him again.

'Good, got you all to myself.' She pinched a potato from his plate and Gerald noticed.

'Mrs Dean, are you hungry now?' She shook her head. 'Stealing food tastes better.' She took another and jumped from his knee to get some water, beating Gerald to the fridge. He scowled at her and she laughed. 'So, if I have you all to myself, you had better finish that lot.' She pointed to the papers and post. 'And hurry, I need you to come and rub my back, I'm going to run a bath.' She blew him a kiss and left the room.

Pete and Edward had their faces firmly fixed on the PC monitor.

'It was a woman, definitely a woman, but you cannot see her face, and she has so many clothes on you cannot make out her figure.' Pete leaned closer to the screen as he sat in Edward's office on the Monday morning. They had returned from Kent three days after the mystery post person had been and not a word had been spoken to Lottie about the document that had arrived.

'What was the point of the CCTV if it does not give us any clues to who this is?' Edward stood up and went to the window. He had seen the footage as many times now as Pete and he was still none the wiser. 'Sharpe does know not to let Lottie out of his sight no matter what?'

'Yes, Edward.' The use of his first name may have been to try to defuse the anger that was rising in the younger man's voice, or maybe it was frustration of not having control of the situation.

'And your man at the yard, the CCTV expert, what did he say?' He turned around to look at the CPO, who was stood still stopping and returning to look as the unsub, as he called her delivering the letter.

'Not sure if it is a wig, but there is a mask of some form over her face, and well, to hazard a guess, the designer shoes cannot be something you get off the shelf. Most criminals don't have that sort of taste in clothes.' The attempt at humour did not lighten Edward's mood.

'If I could get out of this meeting today, I would not leave her. I just have a bad feeling about this, I fucking don't like it. Throw everything you have at this, and get Claude glued on the front door.' His phone rang on his desk and he rushed to look at who was calling. The reception informed him the clients he was seeing had arrived and he asked what time his next appointment was before putting down the phone.

Lottie could tell that something was not right. She thought that she was used to being escorted but this morning the two men working in their white shirts, black tie and jet-black suits seemed to pen her in as she walked from the building to the car.

'Is everything OK?' she asked as the door was closed behind her. Sharpe turned around and replied to her.

'Mrs Dean, everything is good. Your last appointment now, you must be getting excited?' He had avoided the question which only made Lottie more suspicious, but she responded to his question that yes, with four weeks left, this was the last normal appointment at the doctors. Maybe she was just nervous, making her more aware that something was wrong and that she should be focusing on the birth of their child. She sat in the back seat as the car made its way to Harley Street and took the call on speaker from Edward, who was apologising as he would be a little bit late but was in the car ready to go. She smiled as she could picture him swearing at the cars in front to move out of his way, although she did wonder why Pete was not driving him.

The buildings loomed over her as she got out of the car which was parked directly in front of the door to the surgery. Getting out of the car was now quite a task as Bump had made her heavy at the front, so she held onto the door to get out. Leaning back into reach her bag, she smiled at Sharpe who was almost by her side.

'I can manage thanks, well just about!' she said as he assisted her, leaving him to close the door.

As she stood up away from the car a young woman walked past, and Lottie turned as she heard her name.

'Mrs Dean?' There was a very short pause. 'Mrs Dean, Edward's wife?' Lottie struggled to recall who it was that was addressing her, but she smiled politely and replied 'yes.'

'I'm Caroline. I'm sure that Edward must have mentioned me. We have met each other before at a few of his charity functions.'

The name was very distant to Lottie, but yes, she could remember her. 'Hi,' she said again more from good manners than wanting to strike up a conversation.

'Not long now then?' The bleached-blond woman stared, looking at Bump who no longer hid under anything Lottie wore. 'You must be so excited?' As a gesture that only friends would do the young woman placed her hand on Lottie's arm.

Sharpe was alongside Lottie in an instant after this and he added, 'Mrs Dean', gesturing towards the door which was now opening with a face Lottie knew as the receptionist.

'Yes, last month now.' She smiled, noting everyone seemed to want to get her inside, but she focused on the place where the young woman had now taken her hand from.

'Ed must be thrilled.' The blond licked her lips. 'His own little family.'

Her last comment made Lottie raise an eyebrow as the woman was now being quite personal. She smiled again.

'I am sorry to dash but I am a little late.' Lottie pulled her bag from under her arm. 'It was nice to meet you,' she said, again as a call of manners.

'Remember me to Ed then,' was the last word from the woman who was not moving, but watching the two people take the steps and be greeted by the private care staff. 'Take care of his little family.' And she laughed.

Lottie froze as the door closed behind her. She must have gone quite pale because the receptionist and Sharpe both said together, 'Mrs Dean?'

Lottie felt the need to turn around, but the door had been closed. There was no mistake; it was the laugh that had chilled her bones for days now, and she had just heard it again.

'Mrs Dean?' The voice came again and this time she got Lottie's attention. 'Here sit down.' She was helped down into the chair and the young woman went to put her hand on Lottie's arm. She quickly shouted, 'No!'

The receptionist was shocked by the reaction and Sharpe was now almost on his knees by her side. 'Don't touch my arm!'

'Mrs Dean, whatever is the matter?' He was stopped by the request Lottie verbally made to the receptionist that could have been made by a two headed monster from the look he gave her once she stopped talking.

The young girl replied, 'Mrs Dean, Sellotape? I am not sure I...' She had been about to offer water but the request for the sticky tape was a million miles away from what she had thought her patient would want.

'Or some cling film?' Lottie asked and now Sharpe had a questioning face and he had one hand on his top pocket to get out his phone.

'Mrs Dean, what is it?' he asked again.

'I need to take a sample,' Lottie stated, knowing that from the outside world this may look mad, and this was why several other people now had started to look over. She put her hand over her mouth and took in a breath. 'That laugh.' She paused just as the door was opened and Edward walked in.

Noticing the fuss around his wife, he dashed over to her and she stood, resisting his embrace. 'Edward, stay away from me, just for a moment please.' His face was the inevitable picture she knew it would be. 'Please don't ask, not yet, please I need to just...' The young girl had been to the reception and brought a roll of the tape Lottie had asked for.

Lottie dropped her bag and pulled at the tape. 'Let me just do this and I will explain but I need to make sure I get this.'

Edward looked at Sharpe who gave over the information of the previous events without even being asked. 'A woman? Jesus, Lottie, what the hell!' He looked at his wife and she was carefully folding the ends of the tape that she had strategically placed over the lightweight material on her arm.

'There, got it.' She looked up at the on-looking crowd, triumphant in her mission. She looked again to the receptionist. 'Sorry – another request. Have you got an envelope?' The young girl gave a silent nod and walked off to complete her mission.

Without any prompting, she turned to Edward. 'That laugh. I know who she is.' She started to speak just as the door opened and her doctor walked out to greet her. Edward said 'Hello' without taking his eyes from his wife and then with a gesture of his hand asked the man to wait a moment. The offence on the doctor's face was obvious but Edward insisted that Lottie carried on. He had to ask more. 'Who, Lottie, who is she?'

Lottie did not have to go into details. She had told Edward about the laugh that she was so sure she had heard that day. In fact, she had told him several times because she had woken suddenly in the night hearing her in many of her dreams. They had nothing at all to say anyone else had been in the apartment during the shooting but Lottie knew she was not losing her mind or having baby brain as Todd had first stated. The voice was very real.

'Caroline. Edward, it is Caroline, Alex Girski's girlfriend.'

Edward pulled out his phone to contact Pete.

If she had been on the streets, then she had gone to ground. Pete worked on it for the coming days. They had checked her address and another address outside of town. He had called in favour after favour and no one seemed to know where she was. Footage from the CCTV had shown her in the street and the meeting was witnessed again as they sat watching it. Lottie even managed to convince Edward to let her go to the Phoenix a few days later to do the DNA test herself. It proved nothing except that she did not have a criminal record. All of which the professor had told her the day after the sample had been taken in.

Lottie had been up for a while. She felt hot and restless and had found that walking eased the pain in her lower back. She had not mentioned that it had been getting worse for the past few hours; her mind was still focusing on what the connection could be as for the second time this week she had been having the same dream with the same laugh. She wandered into the kitchen, following the smell of food, although when she was offered some of it she declined and just took some milk. She pulled the trousers of her jogging bottoms up, in fear of tripping over them as she wandered to the window to look out at the bright day.

'Is he busy today?' The question was directed to Pete.

'This morning he is, Mrs Dean.' She turned and smiled to the man who had now stood up. 'Anything on your mind?' he asked.

'Yes, there must be something, something that I am missing. I wish I could just have something to compare the DNA.' She took another mouthful of cool, white liquid. A sudden twinge in her side made her swallow quickly.

'Nothing came back from the letter then?' Pete stood to walk closer to her to hold the conversation.

'Sorry Pete, what letter?' Lottie asked.

'Mr Dean had a letter, it arrived last month when you were in Kent. He said he took it to the lab for tests to see if there was any DNA match.' Now it was his turn to look in the dark, and on cue Edward walked in pushing up his tie.

'What did I miss?' he asked, smiling at Lottie and reaching for the coffee.

'Edward, a letter?' Lottie asked and Pete stayed quiet. 'A letter that you got in Kent? Any time about now would be a good time to tell me about it.'

She held her breath as a pain in her stomach shot to her side. She breathed out slowly, trying not to let anyone notice.

'Mrs Dean, sorry, but I thought Edward had told you this.' The CPO looked angry at his own boss, shaking his head. 'I thought he'd shared it with you and that you knew.'

'Obviously not.' She walked to the bar to lean on it, hoping that the now distinct pain in her groin would ease a little.

Edward moved closer to her and she raised her eyebrows. 'Go on then, preach to me about secrets and then you hold this one in?' She bit down on her lip, for no other reason than she needed to gasp in pain but had to hear what he had to say first.

'I did take it to the professor, and he could not pull anything from it, so I did not see the point.' He finished his drink and put down the cup. He held Lottie in his gaze and shrugged his shoulders. 'We had nothing, and I totally forgot.'

'Now we have DNA we can see if there is a match!' Lottie exclaimed, amazed that he was so flippant. 'And the prof would not know what to look for, there are so many more tests that you can do when you know what you are looking for!' She stopped, and falling to her knees she gave out a scream that felt as if it came from her soul.

Four arms were instantly holding her as she opened her eyes aware, that she had not hit the floor and was being suspended by the strength of her husband and Pete.

'Lottie, your waters!' Edward exclaimed. 'My god, shit! Shit! Lottie? Pete, quick. Get Mrs B, and the car and the bag and the hospital and, and an ambulance!'

Lottie came back to reality after the sudden pain had gone, although having felt discomfort for the past four hours she knew that this was labour, and it was time.

She clutched at Edward's hand and almost used his tie to pull herself up. 'This does not mean that the conversation about the letter is over Mr Dean!'

She almost gasped each word out and took another deep breath as the pain started to come again. She started to pant out the words 'I, will,' she took a breath, 'take this up after.' She gave out a loud scream and Edward felt as if his hand was being ripped off as she dug into him.

Mrs B had been hurried into the room, Lottie's bag in hand. She stood behind her and rubbed her lower back, smiling.

'You got about two minutes between them?' Mrs B asked Lottie, as if she had been noticing her all morning. Lottie nodded, still concentrating on her breathing. 'Well then, Peter. Ambulance will be no good it's too slow, the car it is. The hospital is aware I called them about an hour ago!' Lottie smiled but soon grasped out to Edward who had turned a shade of white that had Pete following him more closely than he was Lottie.

'You kept this quiet, then?' He aimed his question to his housekeeper as his arm took another crushing motion from his wife in the confines of the lift. Her breathing and shrill scream almost deafened them in the small space.

The housekeeper shrugged her shoulders as she pressed the button again as if it would make the descent any quicker. Lottie gave her a look to say that she was sorry Edward had scolded her and she was greeted by a warm smile as she felt the pain shooting again. She was now really sorry herself that she had not said anything earlier, as the thought of giving birth in the lift was not appealing to her at all, but it seemed it could be a reality if the doors did not soon open.

'Christ, Pete!' Edward exclaimed as the car took another corner at high speed. Pete gave him a look in the rear-view mirror. He knew the cargo was precious, he had already been told three times, but he was the last one who wanted Dean Junior to be born in the back of the Bentley. He gave a sigh of relief when the hospital came into view. Edward took another when he noticed the welcoming party, and thanked god under his breath. He was not sure how much more he could stand. The thought of the pain Lottie was in had never crossed his mind until now, and he was powerless to say or help her in any way. He had tried to stay calm, comforted her, kissed her, rubbed her, but all she seemed to do was zone him out, as if he were not there at all.

Apart from breathing, puffing, or screaming in the car she had not responded to any of his attentions and it took kind words from the housekeeper to reassure Edward as they rushed Lottie through the doors in a wheelchair that this was normal.

The hospital staff worked like ants around Lottie and soon she was in the private labour room, hooked up to all sorts of machines. Edward looked over at the doctor and the midwife who had worried faces. He pulled away from Lottie who was still concentrating on her breathing; she had seemed calmer now that she had some gas and air. Edward had smiled to himself when friends had mentioned that when this time came, he should also try some, as it would calm him down too, but Lottie held the mouthpiece so intently she would not have let it go for her life. He walked to the medical team feeling his own heart race a little faster at the words he heard.

'The baby is in crisis; he has to come out soon,' the female said as quietly as she could, and the doctor nodded. 'I agree.'

'What do you mean, crisis?' Edward asked, getting their attention.

'Mr Dean, your wife is close to delivery but her body is not yet fully ready. She is not dilated enough for this and the baby is getting very stressed. I am not worrying you, but for a first-time birth this is happening quickly. Mrs Dean is not physically showing us that the birth will be natural at this rate, and she has started to show signs of bleeding that, well, I am concerned about. We cannot take the chance of this for much longer and, well, I need to ask you about a C-section.'

Edward rubbed his hands through his hair, and looked around at his wife. She had been flushed and sweating but was now pale and quiet as if she too were having the life taken from her, all energy gone. 'Your doctor will have spoken about the birth I am sure, the possibility that if it was required, this may be the case. Mrs Dean had time after the miscarriage and seemed to make a good recovery, but internally sometimes the body is not strong and there has not been enough time even going to almost full term as Mrs Dean is.' There was a pause in the explanation. 'We have to take precautions.'

Edward looked back round, and his heart seemed to stab at the word miscarriage. The distant memory of seeing Lottie in such pain. He did recall the conversation, but Lottie had dismissed it, she was sure that a natural birth was what she wanted. In fact they had taken days to convince her that a home birth was the wrong idea, and that although they could set up a room to fully cope, if anything did go wrong the best place was in the hospital. It was a place where the royal family had had babies, with the best staff in the country, and now Edward was glad she had finally come around to it as it seemed if what they were telling him was true, she was going to need them.

'Does Lottie know?' he asked.

'We need to tell her. Mr Dean, I am only talking minutes here, will you or should...' He was stopped mid-sentence as one of the machines beeped at a higher level with a constant tone. All eyes turned to face Lottie and to his horror Edward knew there was no decision to be made.

'She's going, Doctor,' the midwife said.

His voice boomed out as he rushed to the bedside. 'Mr Dean, your wife has become unconscious, with or without her knowing this *is* happening. Prep for surgery.' The doctor rushed through the doors and the team started to move the bed as he had asked, machines and all, heading in the same direction he had gone. One of the nurses said as she passed, 'Mr Dean, if you are coming in, then I suggest you follow me to get scrubbed up.' Her words seemed like a whisper as his eyes followed the moving bed.

He clearly heard the words, 'I am not losing them both,' ringing in his ears. This was all he needed to be spurred on, even though his feet felt as if they were encased in lead and refusing to move. Was he sure he could do this again, wait by her bedside, useless to help? Grinding to a stop he was not sure he could, he closed his eyes and pressed the memory of her in what only seemed weeks ago out of his head. 'Shake it off, Dean, man up, go, move your goddamn feet.' All the voices of Pete, Mrs B and even his mother rang through him and he found the energy to open his eyes and do as the nurse had asked and followed her into the side room.

'How long now?' Edward asked as he gently and almost motionlessly moved across the floor of the pure white room once more to his sleeping wife, his shoes making the tiniest noise and feet being placed as he walked as if on eggshells.

'We would think about an hour. Don't worry, it was as the doctor has told you, all good. Mrs Dean is doing really well and this little one...' The midwife pulled the crisp soft blanket away from the red screwed-up face that was swaddled in what seemed to be a giant's arms. 'This little one is beautiful.'

Edward had not released his son since he had been handed him a little under half an hour ago. His hand shook and his eyes stung from the tears that had rained down his cheeks since the moment he heard the first blast of air leave the little lungs, proclaiming that Bump had now become Dean Junior, his son. All he knew was that Lottie was OK and this wrapped gift had arrived in his grasp and he was never letting either of them go.

He held the bundle in his arms so gently and it was only the undying need to be next to his wife that had given his legs the strength to finally allow him to stand up and go to the room next door where she had been taken to recover.

He felt as if his heart was too big and his chest had expanded somehow, making him hold this jewel out at arm's length, but as he looked down at the little nose taking in air, he knew it was real and almost the opposite. Was he holding him too tight, pulling him too close? He watched again for another breath, and as it came, he too inhaled. He gently placed a kiss on the hot little forehead; the closed eyelids squeezed tighter in response, but he did not wake.

Edward watched as the next breath came, and another, and another and it must have been hours, or at least it seemed it before his concentration had been broken by a voice, soft and at peace from behind him.

'Edward.' She blinked again to fully see the image in front of her. The powerful shoulders she would know anywhere, and her brain sprang into action wanting to know what had happened. The next mention of his name was a more a hurried panicked one. He turned and to her joy the strong frame of his dark blue shirt showed an image of a tiny white package and a smile on his face that in itself lit the room more than the afternoon sun that was flooding in from the window.

'Hey you.' He effortlessly moved to her. 'Hey, look Junior, your clever mommy is awake,' he said, pushing the blanket back so that, although his eyes were closed, his son could see his mother for the first time.

Lottie cried and reached out. 'Edward, please?' As if she had to ask, but it seemed that he could not let him go. It should have felt the most natural thing to do, pass a new-born baby to its mother but as she received him into her arms, he instantly felt a loss. As if she had reached into his chest and pulled out his heart.

Seeing the tears fall from her eyes, he reached to kiss her. She looked up and he caught her on the lips. She tasted the same, but somehow different. She looked the same, but somehow different. Her eyes shone as before but somehow different. Then, as he glanced at the small face, he could see that his tiny dark eyes had opened, and it was the reflection of him that was making his beautiful wife different. He never conceived it could be possible but at that moment in time he loved her more. The heat from his cheeks stung as the salty tears streamed down his face. Nothing else in the world mattered to him now.

Pete smiled at Mrs B as they looked in through the window of the door. 'Edwards's mother has requested that we collect her, so I sent a car. They have just arrived, so do you need a lift back?' he asked.

'Yes, I am sure my time for a hold will come but for now let us leave them to it.' She picked up the bag at her side and wiped another tear away from her face with the already-drenched hankie that she had been holding for the past three hours. An excited Alice Dean rushed past them, with an arm full of flowers and a smile that filled the corridor more than the poor driver behind armed with balloons, teddy bears and another bag of gifts.

'Oh, Mrs B, Pete, sorry, how are they?' Mrs Dean exclaimed as she turned, missing them in the rush.

'See for yourself.' Mrs B finished wiping another stray tear and pointed to the next door on the right. Mrs Dean turned around and rushed to the door, opening it so fast that the rush of air moved her flowing skirt.

Being told to stay in hospital for four days had been the last thing that Lottie wanted. Although everything had gone well so far with her recovery, she had to rest and once the painkillers had subsided, she got to understand how her body had been mutilated during the operation.

Dean Junior had found his lungs and the ability to make what Lottie knew as painful nipples even worse. Edward had stayed overnight for her first night but had to pull himself away because even Lottie said not eating or showering was no good for any of them. So, when they both slept, he found the opportunity to drag himself away.

Stepping back into the apartment the high smell of flowers hit him and looking on the parlour table a mountain of cards awaited his attention. His phone buzzed for what felt like the hundredth time that day and as he looked at the display, he knew that as much as he wanted to put work on hold, he had to face some of these calls.

America was having some sort of financial meltdown, and the last message had been the director of the Australian shipyard stating that a storm had caused so much damage, staff had gone in and been hurt trying to make the area safe.

Clean from his shower, Mrs B hovered around until he took her offer of food and a hot drink. The questions as to names and how Lottie and Junior were seemed to never end. He had to focus, but even the news of the new arrival had reached the other side of the world and although he was focusing on the damage and injuries, he could not help but find himself talking about his son to his employee. After he put down the phone, he said out loud, 'My son,' and he smiled. 'My son,' he said again as if to someone in the room.

The door opened and Pete walked in.

'I have sorted the main issues. New York are on hold and we need to get the German Ambassador the main points for the meeting next week. He sends his regards and congratulations, but I tried to say that Banks or Mollor would be going in your place. He seems to want to have no other conversation about the deal than with you. He declined my offer to come over here all expenses paid. You will have to call him yourself.'

'OK,' Edward said looking at his phone. Not for the number to call the ambassador but at the screen saver of his wife and their son. Pete broke his train of thought. 'Mr Dean, the call?'

'How can something be so small?' He turned the screen to show Pete the photo that he had already seen several times before and continued to say how he was so scared to hold him in case he crushed him or dropped him. Pete smiled; he knew how it felt to be a father. He knew that the hole in your chest never stopped hurting until they were back in your arms. He had to learn over the years to mask the pain, cover the hole. Working and daily life had a habit of making you have to do this, as much as you did not want to. It was a necessary evil, but the feelings never went away, even when they got older and less dependent on you.

'So, will it be Junior forever, or does he have a name?' Pete put a pile of papers on the desk. 'Although I have to say Junior is an improvement on Bump!' Edward laughed and scrolled through a few more photos.

'Today's post.' Pete gesticulated to the assortment of paper, but Edward just carried on.

'We have narrowed it down – well, I thought that we had but that was before he was born. Lottie has a few more ideas. One of the calls was from the media team saying we need to make a statement but looking at that lot out there most people already know about him and his arrival. I could go public with Junior; I like that, but I think we have decided on Charles, after Lottie's grandfather. I don't think he looks like a Charles, but Charles Michael Dean I think it will be.' He smiled again. 'Charlie.'

It did go to the press once they had both come home, which after a day longer than Lottie had wanted, felt like a sad occasion. In that time Edward had tried his hardest to be with them, but the work thing was not going away. He even had his financial director emailing, noting that shares in several of the companies had gone down as there was word on the street that Edward Dean was downsizing and dropping his game due to the new arrival. So, he had to do as much as he could to keep the CEO post as active as possible.

Standard paternity leave was not going to cut it with the German embassy though, and much to his disgust the next day he had to take the private jet that sat at the airport, leaving Lottie in the hands of Mrs B and his mother.

Staying in bed was hard, although she was still in discomfort from the operation. She got the 'no lifting' and 'no overdoing it' bits of the reminder she had been given several times by her husband but sitting at the computer would be easy.

With the excuse of emails and keeping in touch, Edward did give into her on this. It was another means for him to keep up with them, to check they were safe, so he had to give in to her having access to the laptop or tablet. In between feeds there was no shortage of people to smother Charlie with love and hugs and so Lottie sat in the study on the end of the phone.

'Todd, I just know it was her. I don't know why but we need to find out.' The line went quiet.

'Lotts, please let it rest, or get Sharpe or Pete on to it; look how it went last time, did we not lose enough?' He gave out a sigh, knowing that Lottie would not rest until it was fully closed. In fact, it was this attention to detail and pride in her work that he loved about her, amongst other things, and he knew he was not going to sway her from this crusade.

Caroline was not hard to look up using today's media technology; she was a social girl and was always at some event or another. The connection to Edward was obvious, and to Alex Girski, but what was missing? Lottie only had a limited access to the files that she had already gone through before the shooting, but she wanted more. Edward needed to know there was no getting out of it, so she had made up her mind that she was going to speak to him when he returned that night.

'He smells so baby clean,' Edward said, holding Charlie in his arms. He had arrived back looking worn out but fully intent on holding him before climbing into bed besides his wife, much to Lottie's dismay as she had fed him and put him down a few hours ago and managed to get into bed herself before 11 pm.

'Ed, please don't wake him. He will be up soon enough for more food.' She knew this not only from the time of night but the way her breasts felt; heavy and full.

'He is sleeping soundly.' He kissed the little head showing through the blue fluffy blanket and took him to the edge of the bed and sat at her side. She winced slightly as she sat up, ensuring that Edward did not notice. He was so intent on the bundle in his arms she was sure he was not even listening to her. The mangled muscles in her stomach were taking their time to heal, and according to the midwife she would be like this for several weeks. The thought that she was going to be so housebound only made her want to research her lead with Caroline more, but after today's work she had to get more information and only one place would provide this.

'I thought I might pop to see the professor tomorrow.' She quickly added, 'Show Charlie the place I work!' It got a reaction, one that made Edward look straight into her eyes. Suddenly he was in the room and the power behind the single word reply almost echoed. 'NO!'

'Edward, he has been to your offices, why ever should I not go to show him to my friends and colleagues?'

He was not sure if the word 'no' had been for the fact that she wanted to take him out, or the fact that he did not think she was well enough to go anywhere, or the fact, and possibly more to the point, that she still considered that she would at some point return to the place of work.

He stood back up as he was aware that his arms had started to shake. Placing his precious package back into the cot that had been arranged in their room, he pulled the light cotton sheet back around his son's waist, kissed his fingers and gently placed them on his forehead, almost as if a priest were blessing a parishioner.

He straightened and faced her, pulling at the tie still around his neck and threw it to the floor. He started to unbutton his shirt, pulling it loose from his belted waist band. There was a silence, which was growing in volume. He paced to the washroom and lent over the sink looking into the mirror at his reflection. The only thing that the centre reminded him of was death, destruction, and pain. He had contemplated withdrawing his donations from them after the accident, as a sure-fire way that she would not return. He had then thought of the wider good the staff and the professor had done and would continue to do only with large donations from people like himself.

In what seemed like an age to her, he finally returned to the bedroom. She had heard the shower, water falling over his body and she smiled at the view in her mind's eye which must be in the reflection of the large glass enclosure. A warm feeling spread through her, making her breasts more attentive and what seemed like a distant tingle between her legs reminded her of how he had the ability to turn her on, even though her damaged body was not capable of following any of her desires or carnal needs that were now coursing through her.

Towel firmly around his waist, his hair damp, he remained silent until he was dry and had put on his night boxers and checked first on his sleeping infant and then second on his phone, turning it to silent. She moved as he pulled the sheet to get in besides her and as she took a breath, he stopped her before the words could escape her mouth.

'Lottie.' He held his arms out as if to beckon her to come close to him. He was still hot from the water and the scent of his shower gel filled her head with even more memories of his touch and manliness. 'Please, I am exhausted, I don't...' He corrected himself, 'I won't get into this conversation now.' He had lowered his tone and gently kissed her hair as she placed her head on his chest, wrapping her arms around his waist. 'I have to work tomorrow, I can do this from home for a few hours, maybe then we could have some family time?'

She stayed silent but kissed his chest. She looked over to the cot, mulling his words through her brain. What did he mean by 'this conversation?' The more she thought about it the more she knew that she would have it, whatever it was he was insinuating by 'this conversation', but maybe not now. By the slowing of his breathing and the gentle thud of his heart she knew he had found sleep, but her eyes remained open, computing her own thoughts.

The whimper of their son did not need to wake her; she had almost sensed it as she slid from the bed to him and walked to the silence of the open lounge. Closing all the doors as she went to keep any crying away from her sleeping husband she sat and nursed her feeding child, looking through the large glass windows out over the city sky. It would soon be another day, and from the clear dawn sky and cool start it would surely result in a crisp sunrise, throwing light onto the now-sleeping mother and baby, encased in the large sofa and white throw that she had pulled around them less than an hour ago.

He had woken with a start. Feeling the cold space next to him and then the sight of a missing child, he forwent putting on more clothes and left the room as fast as his feet would carry him. When he opened the lounge door the light from the windows was pouring in, shining so bright onto the beloved sight of the bodies lying on the large sofa that he for once in his life almost felt religious. It was as if the very image of the holy Mother Mary was in his very living space, holding the Lord's child. It was almost a surreal sight, but he smiled, content. For a moment he stood motionless.

How could he not give her what she wanted, how could he ever say no and really mean no to her? The mother of his child, the very gift that he knew had changed his life. He had sat on the private jet on the way to his meeting knowing that if he wanted, he could just say no to everything, stop all his businesses and sell, and they would still have a life that was better than anything other people could only dream of.

He had worked it all out in his head, dissolving assets without any damage to anyone working for him, and it was on this he had stopped. It was not going to be possible in every case. He knew that loss would occur and that fathers like himself would be out on the street, and now knowing how important this was, it was the paternal instinct in him, one that he had never had before, the feeling in his guts that would not go away that made him rethink. The hard-ass businessman had been put on his backside by a small bundle of flesh, a living breathing reproduction of his wife and he knew that, against his better wishes, she would go tomorrow to the centre and see the professor. He knew that when the time came to have the conversation he would cave in and she would go back to work. She dominated him in every way and he freely submitted.

They had spent an hour at the centre the next day. Junior had been shown off to everyone, Mrs B had gone with them and Lottie had managed to access what she wanted. Concealing the memory stick in her pocket as she returned, she smiled as the other females in the group had forcefully prized him from Mrs B; she was the one clucking more as a mother hen than the rest. She smiled again, satisfied that her work here was done, for now.

Chapter Twenty-One

The hot breath on her neck felt warmer than the water passing down her body, and she fell back into the enclosure of the secure arms she loved. Closing her eyes, the scent of the shower gel filled her nose and she smiled as his hands gently cupped her hardened nipples.

Two months had passed since she had given birth and as much as she had begged, Edward had not been this intimate. After relaxing and putting Junior to bed, she had left him on the sofa to suffer his own torment and now she knew he had given in, joining her in the shower.

Leaning up against him she felt his hard shaft pushing into her back. She licked her lips. They had been lying on the sofa not half an hour before. Their passionate kiss had started her brain and her body wanted him. The feeling was reciprocated and although the shower had been more to cool her off, the gleam in his eye as he had offered to wash her back was one she knew well enough and when the bathroom door had opened moments after she had stepped into the flowing water, she knew that he also had a need.

The kissing turned into a gentle nip of her earlobe, the stinging sensation went to the throbbing place between her legs and she was sure she let out a small moan of pleasure. He followed the flow of the suds slowly over her body; the pink scar neatly sitting across her lower stomach was healing well, although he avoided it to reach his goal. Without effort his hand cupped her sex and smoothly his finger parted the soft folds of skin that protected the delicate area.

Suddenly feeling the heat rise in her cheeks, maybe from the fact that over the past few months she had not paid too much attention to shaving herself as she would have, his palm pushed hard against her pubic bone, and she felt the increased penetration of his finger into her. His other hand steadied her but also took the time to rub at her swollen breast. Now she did let out a moan as the pleasure built in her and needed to be released. She tried to reach behind her, seeking out the hard penetration that was now burning in her back. She found her prize and gently massaged him, instantly feeling his response in both his throbbing dick and the intensity with which he penetrated her. She gasped again, knowing that it wouldn't be long before this ended. She needed him inside her as her climax built, so she tried to turn around.

Edward second-guessed her and assisted, pulling her close to him, the water still streaming over them both. Mouths clenched, they gasped as breathing, kissing, and avoiding the water was all heading in the mix of the passions rising in them. He pulled her off her feet and took her in his arms. Dripping across the floor and without a care he pushed open the bedroom door and before she knew it she was spread across the bed, soaking the sheets. Neither of them was bothered by this at all as they were focused on each other.

'I need to see you,' he said, standing back slightly running his hands along her body. He quickly took his eyes off the areas on her that showed recent damage, but she was just as perfect as she had ever been. He licked some of the water that was running down her stomach to her bellybutton and she instantly pushed his head down willing him to replace his fingers with his tongue. 'In a rush, Mrs Dean?' he asked as she purred at his touch when he reached the spot she wanted him to. She murmured and he replied, 'I asked you a question?'

'Yes,' she said louder so he could hear. 'Yes,' she said again as his mouth covered her clit and he sucked.

God, he was going to come over the sheets like a teenage boy. His mind was so full of his need for her that even though the thought of hurting her had flashed past, he had to take her, make them one and be as close as he could. She was wet, not just the shower water, but ready for him. Her breathing was fast, her thighs tightened around his head and she bucked her hips into his face as the assault on her continued. She smelt and tasted as he remembered her, the irresistible force that she held over him in every way dragged at his core and he knew he could not wait. Slowly he moved up her body and she grabbed out at his head. 'Edward please,' she begged, and he almost exploded at the sheer need in her voice. She tried to kiss him, but he knew that would defiantly do it; he had to hold on for a few seconds at least. Level with her face she thrust her hands between then grabbing out at his shaft as the seed leaked from him, she aimed him to the spot that she desperately had to have him.

With one smooth push he was in, at least halfway down his throbbing dick and she felt every inch of his length. Lottie pushed her wet hair back into the pillow and grabbed out at the sheets, knowing that the next push was going to fill her. He was slow and she looked at his face, knowing he was holding back. She did not want him to, so she grasped her hand around his backside, and pulled him in to her. Shifting her hips to take him, he eased out and she pulled him back into her quicker than he had wanted.

'Shit, Lottie, I can't hold on for you.' He closed his eyes as if trying to be somewhere else to take his mind of the fact that he was about to come.

'I don't want you to Edward, please baby.' She grabbed him again and he pushed deeper and harder, and again.

He could not touch her nipples although he wanted to bite them, he could not kiss her but he wanted to take her mouth and make her taste her own juice. He felt her tighten around him as he thrust into her faster, her hands digging her nails into his skin and he knew this was her reaching her place. 'Fuck!' he gasped as he knew his seed was now pulsing into her and he could not stop it. He could not breathe as the heat from his body condensed itself in his dick, bursting with months of need. He had to slow down because he could not breathe, but he knew she was still on the edge. She pushed him into her again and then held him.

The pulsing of him on her soft tender sweet spot was building and just by this tiny feeling she came. The pressure on her clit and the him filling her made her orgasm so deep that she had to open her eyes to know she was still alive. The forced rattled through her body and she shook. The slight movement of him pulling out only increased her contracting muscles and she held him in place again until the overwhelming feeling slowed, but only slightly.

Slowly he pulled from her, his arms burning from holding himself in place; he too was shaking. Flat on his back for the first time he felt a welcome breeze across him, realising that they were wet, more so now with sweat than the shower water. He guessed that she must be cold and so pulled her over onto his chest, clutching the damp sheet as she rolled over to him.

'Wow!' he said, 'I guess I am still alive?'

She put her fingers to his neck and then kissed the bounding pulse that was visible. 'I can confirm that,' she said back at him. 'I would say that your recovery rate is slower than normal.' She put her chin on him as her head moved with the rise and fall of his chest.

'So, Dr Dean, what do you recommend?' He dragged at the pillow to push his head up to see her face. Her damp hair clung to her forehead. He used his hand to push it away. Her large pools gazed back at him and he had a flashback to the very first time he had seen her. Her eyes had fixated him as she glanced up at him then. It seemed a lifetime ago now, but the result was the same. His dick, although shot and flaccid, twitched and he was not sure that was possible after that performance, but the pain in his gut was real just the same. She smiled. 'I recommend more exercise, Mr Dean!'

'Oh, do you now?!' He pulled at her to try to tickle her ribs.

'Yes!' She giggled as she resisted him, almost sitting up. 'Edward, stop!' She almost squealed the plea. They both drew their attention to the slight whimper making the reality of the moment hit them. The little man who had been asleep in the room stirred. Silence fell almost instantly, only the breathing of the two adults could now be heard and she lowered her voice, 'But not now.' She pulled the sheets around her. 'You have killed me, and I need to sleep before someone else wakes for sure.' She smiled, putting her head back on his chest.

'The sheets are wet.' Edward tried to find a dry bit but was not able to.

'I don't care,' Lottie said fighting him as he pulled her off. 'Edward, where are you going?'

He had shot up and as quickly as he went, he had returned with a clean quilt, pulling the other one back he rolled her over and then threw the damp one to the floor. Lottie felt the warmth of his body return to her only seconds later, and wrapped in his arms they both found what would turn out to be only a few hours' sleep.

'Is everyone out, sir?' the young police officer asked Pete. Pete nodded as he looked across at Sharpe driving off in the large range rover, his boss, wife, son, and the housekeeper on board.

'Do we know what it was?' Pete asked, turning his attention back to the older man who was also stood close to the group that had now gathered some way away from the building.

'Bomb threat, so we cannot go back in for some time I am afraid, having to wait for the bomb squad to do their thing.' The officer's radio sparked into life and Pete listened as much as he could. He was sure that he heard the words letter and penthouse so without thinking he raised his mobile to his ear and dialled.

'Pete, that is all I have. I am sending you a scan of the letter, not sure what good it will do you but yes mate, it does state the penthouse, that's where you are, I am guessing.' The voice on the other end of the phone was one of Pete's many friends in high places. Ex-service men, police chiefs, gangsters, he seemed to have a few on speed dial for most occasions. 'And you just want me to hold this for how long? I have to say, mate, it's a bit hot, questions are being asked and it is on the news. Not sure I am going to be able to do that.'

'Just try for at least another five minutes so I can get hold of Mr Dean,' he pleaded back down the phone.

'Five is all and hey, big guy, you owe me.' There as a short pause. 'Again!'

Pete held his phone up to see the promised scan. It said 'for the attention of the penthouse' on the envelope, and the letter inside said: *I can get to you even in your ivory tower.*

His phone buzzed and he looked at the caller ID; as predicted it was Edward.

His boss' voice came down the phone, knowing that he was not alone in the car that was by now several miles away. 'What was it?'

'Another letter, addressed to the penthouse, and a suspect package left at the reception. Peterson the night guy raised the alarm when he noticed the woman walking around outside with the bag, and then saw the same bag just left at the reception.' Pete kept his voice quiet just in case Edward had not got his phone glued to his ear and the words leached out.

'Fire alarm, I got that.' Edward tried to keep his voice calm. 'Fire in the bin store, well we may as well carry on now for a few days in Kent while they have a clean-up then?'

'Yes,' Pete replied, getting why he was saying this and not the facts. However, he could speak the truth because no one was listening his end. 'A few days will be good. I have notified the rest of the team and we will look at the office and a few of the other Dean buildings just to make sure. I am going to stay here, but I will come over tomorrow. I am going to forward you the scan of the note, not that it tells us much, but the woman is a lead. Although I suspect anyone would do anything for a price so at this moment, I don't have a clue. I guess even if I had the real letter, it would not help.'

'Right yes, and the Fire service are sure that it is only the power to the flat that is out, nothing else damaged.' Edward carried on the conversation as if having it with himself. 'I guess they will do a full investigation and let us know?'

'I will send off to the lab, but I don't think we will get anything from it. I will keep Sharpe in the loop and email things through so you can pull them on the laptop. The bomb squad are here now, and I am guessing that they are going to have to blow it. I do not think you should encourage anyone to listen to the radio or the news, the place is starting to get a bit busy. Do you need me to bring anything over tomorrow?'

'No Pete, that's great, you get off to your sister's and just keep me in the loop.' Edward put down the phone and looked over to his wife. Their sleeping son was tucked into her arms, but her eyes were pleading with him for information as to why they had been whisked from their sleep and were now heading out of the city faster than she knew was safe.

The bin fire lie seemed to settle her, and even Mrs B relaxed and found her head bobbing off as she fought the sleep that she too had been woken from. It was dawn before they reached the house in Kent. Edward had to wake Lottie. He had also had the time to look at the scanned document and was desperate to fire up the laptop to look at any further information that had been sent his way.

Gerald had also been texted and the few hours it had taken from them to arrive had allowed him and Apollo to supply a full welcoming party.

Greetings and pleasantries all-round as the sleepy group made their way into the kitchen, where Mrs B turned her nose up at the offer of the breakfast that had been prepared. As if the faint smell of bacon had awakened him,

Charlie needed feeding and so the ladies left the two men to chat alone in the room.

'I fully understand, Mr Dean, yes. Pete has spoken to me and yes Apollo and I will keep you safe.' Gerald's face was full of concern as his boss had shared his worries and the reasons they had come so quickly. 'This place is safe as houses.' Gerald smiled and Edward could not help but smile back. He did have to agree there was something about the place that did make him feel relaxed and at ease, no matter what the crazy world outside was throwing at them.

Later the next day Lottie was pleased to see her friend as Agnes had arrived over an hour ago. Pete had arrived a short time after and Edward and he had gone off to the office leaving her slightly redundant with all the ladies' attention on Charlie.

'You know you should get out and get some air,' Mrs B said, clearing the cups up. 'I am sure that Apollo would love a walk.'

Lottie did think that she should get some 'her' time. She had given little thought to the Caroline issue with leaving London so quickly and she grabbed her phone knowing that she could give Todd a call. She went upstairs to change into her jogging bottoms and filled her purse with some money. A walk to the shop, not that they needed anything, but it would be nice to stop off and see the old faces.

Coming back down she looked towards the office and pushed open the door, her intention being to say where she was going to Edward. Both men were crowded over the desk, the laptop open and several papers in front of them. She would not have thought anything of them working away if it wasn't for the look of guilt and the fact that Pete had tried to swipe the papers up into a pile and pull them off the desk, but he was too slow so she had noticed.

'Everything OK?' Edward moved from the desk as if the tactic were to divert her eyes.

'Yes.' It was more a question than an answer.

'Good.' He continued to walk towards her, but she was able to go the other side of the large chair that was the opposite side of the desk.

'Is that information about last night?' she asked, still aware that Pete had hold of the items they had been looking at and she noticed that the plastic bag that a document was in was something she had seen many times before. An evidence bag. She held out her hand and never asked; she just beckoned with her fingers. 'Please,' she said as the document seemed glued to him.

'It's nothing, Lottie,' Edward said, now in front of her. She still held out her hand, now aware that the writing on the paper was cut out letters.

'Well then, let me see nothing.' She was close enough to snatch it from the fully-grown man if need be.

It was not offered but he did let go as the document dropped into her hands and silence fell as she read the page. Aware that there were several similar ones in the bag she pulled the seal and took all the pages out. All had the same type of letters, cut from a newspaper or a magazine, and on the final one a picture of her and Charlie while they had been out walking in the park. First, she looked at the Close Protection Officer's face, then to her husband. Both men stood in silence. She looked again at the desk and open on the laptop was a scan of a similar letter, and her eyes fell over the word 'Penthouse'. The clouds in her brain joined all the dots and she then opened her mouth to speak.

'And so, this was going to be shared with me when?' She did not give either of the men time to answer her question. 'This shit.' She slammed the papers down on the desk. 'Edward, I am insulted that you have kept this from me. This shit has put my son in danger, and you have not shared this with me.' She pulled the photo back out. 'This was weeks ago.'

'Lottie, please.' She silenced him by putting her hand up almost in his face.

'Mrs Dean,' Pete tried to explain, and he got a stare that would freeze water.

'If you even think that you are going to lie to me, then go ahead. I tell you one thing, both of you. I will pick my son out of my best friend's arms and walk away. Try me if you are not quite sure I will.' She threw another of the letters on the desk. She took a deep breath, tears in her eyes more for rage than anything else.

'You knew someone was threatening us and you just kept it quiet?' She looked at her husband, but it was the older man who dared to speak. 'No, Pete, he needs to explain clearly why the fact that this psycho, who has been sending these for...' She hesitated as she looked quickly through them again. Neatly written on the top of each one was a hand-written date. Pete's writing and then a location that it had been left at or sent to. She carried on, 'four weeks has not been shared with me.' Once more her questioning eyes fell to her husband. 'In fact, Pete please leave us, I want his side of the story and then you can tell me yours and I will see which one of you is the better liar.' She was almost shaking with her rage.

Pete looked at Edward and she could see her husband take a breath. He swallowed and wiped his chin with his hand.

'Pete, stay. Lottie will have questions, and I am sure that you will be able to answer them better than I can.'

She sat as if he was going to read her a bedtime story. She held on to the arm of the chair as she was feeling the rise of the blood to her head left her legs without strength to support her.

She was amazed at how easy he explained when and where the letters had been received and at the end of it, he looked back to the floor. 'Pete asked me to share this with you several times, but I was sure I would be able to find out what was going on. Last night the woman dropping the last one it seems also left the package – that was a real bomb.'

Lottie took the information with her arms firmly crossed on her chest, as if in defence, or maybe for protection and at last the world came back to slap her.

'Woman?' she asked, 'You said woman?' Edward simply nodded. 'And this lot was a woman too?' She then looked at Pete for the clarification as she held the bundle that had first arrived.

Oh god. She had raved at them both for withholding this, but then she was just as guilty and now going to have to explain she had also been holding things back from them. She had to eat humble pie because this had to stop now.

'It's Caroline,' she almost said the name into her hand as she looked down, rubbing her forehead. 'This whole thing, before me, everything it's her.'

Both men looked in amazement and she clarified this to Edward, 'Your crazy ex, Caroline was behind all the deaths and she still wants to carry it on. To get you back.' She looked at Edward. 'The woman laughing when the shots rang out, I know because when I met her the other week, she had that same laugh, the one I cannot get out of my head.'

'Mrs Dean.' Pete broke the silence. She was sure that Edwards's eyes would pop out of his head with the information, she had just relayed to him. He was leaning on the table so close to her that she could feel the heat from his skin, the hairs on his arms standing on end. 'How can you be so sure?'

'Because...' She got up and walked out of the room. She had left her handbag in the living room and she stopped Edward walking out after her. 'I need to get something to show you.' In a short moment she returned with the small hard drive and placed it onto the side of the laptop. The machine hummed as she typed in her pass code and then the screen lit up with a graph and numbers. 'Because I tested for her DNA and, well at first got a blank but, then pulling the old files tried another search and well there it is. She was there that day, outside the room when the shots were fired, but she had been in there hours before, with...' She paused as the thought of the man's face who fired the shots came as clear to her mind. As if he was standing in the very same room. 'Alex,' she said, quietly but both men heard her. 'And this one.' She clicked again, and a similar page came up. 'This shows that she had been with Mitch, hours before...' Now she did stop her sentence short. The look on her husband's face was painful.

What was he thinking? She knew this was hurting enough. She had accused him of the very thing she had done. After everything they had promised that they would not keep anything from each other they were both as guilty as the other. It had drawn them to this very place that was clearly putting their lives and those of the people that they loved at risk.

'This is too fucked up to be true!' Edward looked at Pete as anger then poured out from him. 'If she,' implying his wife from the direction of his finger that was being jabbed out, 'can work this out, why the fuck didn't you?'

Lottie was taken aback by his tone and the way he had addressed her. Could she blame him though? He was being kind to her by not going off the handle as she had thought he would, or was he waiting for that? 'It makes sense in a sick sort of way.' Edward walked off to look out of the window. 'After he died, she said they had become close just before, and the bitch admitted that they had slept together. He was with someone, but she had to dangle the temptation in his face.' He looked up, as did the other occupants of the room as the door opened. The crying sound was for food and there was only one-way to stop it.

'Sorry, my dear,' Mrs B said, noting the tension, 'I was not sure if a bottle had been made up.'

'That's fine, Mrs B.' Edward held out his arms to take his son, just as Lottie did the same. She sat back down to let him take him. 'Shush!' He continued the rocking motion, with a small kiss to the youngster's brow. 'Let's go and find what Mummy has left in the fridge.' He kissed him again and moved towards the door without a word to anyone else. He pulled the door to as he walked out.

'Anyone going to spill?' Mrs B looked Pete. She may have come across as a kind housekeeper but that look scared the pants off many people, and she had over the years shared everything in Edwards's life. Lottie started to explain, and the room filled with her voice. Mrs B was the first to speak.

'I saw her hanging around a week or so ago. I spoke to her, but she just walked past. I was at the shop on the corner getting Edward's favourite ham, you know the one?' she asked as if this conversation belonged with the other. 'You know just after Mitch' Mrs B paused. 'She did call round a lot, almost pestered Edward. Became friends with his mother, through Girski's mother, I think. Edward tried to dismiss her; he was in a bad place and I think that we all suffered knowing how much space he needed. I guess really, she only left the scene when,' Mrs B paused and looked at Lottie, 'when you, my dear, came into our lives.'

Lottie felt her stomach lurch. She was trying to get the full picture, join all the dots together.

'We need to stop this.' Pete pulled out his phone. 'Let's get her arrested and see what she has to say for herself.' He started to punch the numbers.

'No,' Lottie said, 'There's not enough here, a good lawyer could talk his way around all this, it will not stick.'

'So, your plan?' Mrs B asked.

'Get her to admit it.' Lottie spoke the words that she knew she had said before, but to a different crowd. It was if it was all happening again.

Pete was on her wavelength and followed up with a closing comment just as Edward walked in. 'Get a confession?'

Edward spoke up, 'And we know how badly that finished, don't we, Pete? Make the call.' He walked back to the desk and sat down. Lottie's face must have asked the same question as Mrs B's.

'Gerald and Agnes have taken him for a walk, he was settling.' The comment was not directed to anyone, it was just to state the facts.

'Edward, no, she will confess, I know it. As it is, with no other convictions, nothing like murder will stick and a claim of insanity may not even mean she gets locked away.' Lottie stood to walk over to him and sat on the arm of the chair he was sitting in. She instantly wanted to touch him. The gentle smell of her freshly washed son lingered along with his own distinct smell of sandalwood shower gel. Filling her nose she took in a deep breath. 'There will be a way we can work this out, and if you are going to bring this up now, I have said sorry for the way I tried to solve this last time, but this time, everyone knows. Pete, Sharpe, your whole team. We will be able to take her down.'

Pete put down his phone and everyone's eyes rested on Edward's face.

'It's me,' he said, reaching into his pocket. 'It's me she wants.' He pressed a few buttons and put the phone on the desk. Pete was the first one to reach it and after looking at the words he passed it to Lottie, only first getting the nod from Edward.

'So, you got this last week?' Pete was clearly angry with his boss. The reply was visual more than verbal as he screwed his face up and nodded. Lottie put down the phone and Mrs B picked it up.

'And you did not want to take it seriously?' Pete continued. 'Fuck, Edward, what were you thinking?'

'I don't know. I did not know who it was from, or how they got the personal number so I thought it may have been for someone else!' He looked at Lottie and she smiled.

'Oh my God!' Mrs B exclaimed. 'Edward Dean you are supposed to be highly intelligent and you failed to see this as intended for you?' She showed him the screen as if he had not seen it before and then read out the message.

'"*Leave her or she will die. Delay and your son will die too!*" Mr Dean, how could you not see, or think that you are not the intended recipient?'

'Well said Mrs B!' Pete ran his hand through his hair and shook his head. There was an awkward silence then the voice sitting opposite the desk spoke up.

'So, leave me!' she said and all heads turned. 'Pack your bags, get out of our lives and leave.' Edward's mouth shot open, but nothing came out. Lottie stood up and focused straight on his face. 'If you don't then I will leave you, simple, whichever way it will be the most public thing you have ever done.'

'Lottie?' he asked, walking towards her and she stepped back.

'I mean it, Edward. How could you continue to put my son's life at risk knowing this information? I have been stupid in the past few months granted, but never to this level.'

'Lottie, baby, what are you saying?' He walked towards her and she turned her back. The other two people in the room were wishing they could get out, but they would both have to walk past Lottie who never changed the expression on her face.

'I am saying do it, go, get the hell out of my house!' Then she turned to face him; he was so close they almost touched lips. She pushed her hands up to his face. 'Make it as public as you need to that we are over!'

Edward was as white as a ghost and she could feel him physically shaking.

'No! Fuck it, never, no,' he said.

'Yes,' she replied and pushed him backwards, so he was seated on the desk. She let go of his face and again turned her back as if to walk out.

He jumped to his feet knowing she was heading to the door. 'For fuck's sake Lottie, what are you saying?'

She stopped dead and turned. She smiled and they met eye to eye.

'I am saying protect the people that you love, so do what she wants and leave us.' She then walked back to him and without hesitating reached onto her toes and forced herself forwards. She pressed her lips hard onto his. Once the hold was broken, she gasped, 'In everyone else's eyes leave us, run to her and make her think she has won. When a predator is content, they become weak. Then we strike and truly put this monster where she belongs.'

As if the air had been lifted by a crane, everyone seemed to take a breath. Edward pulled her close again to him and took her mouth just as hard as she had his. 'I will never leave you,' he said going back in for another kiss. 'You know that, don't you?' She held his eyes as they burned into her soul.

'Yes,' she said. 'Nor I you,' she whispered in his ear and the cough from the security detail reminded them they were not alone in the room. 'I am just very convincing when I need to be!' she almost giggled as they moved apart slightly.

'Sure had me fooled,' Mrs B said, tutting and shaking her head.

'I don't like it,' Pete stated.

'Neither do I, not one little bit. Lottie has a point and well, babe I am not having a go at you when I say this!' He thought he had to get that in and looked at Lottie as apologetic as he could. 'Knowing my wife, she is going to do something stupid anyway to try to get to the bottom of this, and to be honest if the most stupid thing is that I pretend to leave. For the record it is a stupid thought, then that is the way it will be. On one condition.' She nodded as the request went to her. 'It does not take long and no matter what pictures you see, whatever you hear, there is only you that has me?'

'Who says you will be the only one photo'd with someone else?' She smiled and he shot back up.

'I do!' he said, 'Second condition and no way negotiated.' She walked back into his arms and once more without a flinch whispered in his ear, biting the lobe as she left her words ringing around in his head.

'We will see, Mr Dean, we will see!'

Even Gerald was not in on the truth. Lottie smiled at Apollo as herself, Edward and Pete had sat until the early hours of the morning planning the 'break up' as it had become called by them all. When the words were mentioned, she was sure his eyes looked sadder and his ears dropped more. He was at her side, head in her lap as they planned the next few weeks. 'It's only pretending,' she whispered in his hairy soft ear and ruffled the fur around his neck, making his collar rattle on his name tag. She gave him a little kiss on his muzzle, and he gave a little whine as if he still did not understand but her words had seemed to make it better somehow.

'Too right it is!' Edward patted the dog on his head as he walked past to get another drink from the sideboard, stooping and kissing Lottie on her head. 'Anyone else? Lottie, water?' He held up the whisky decanter to Pete before he poured his own. Both declined but he needed another drink just to be able to stomach the plan, let alone start it off.

'So,' Pete started, 'Sharpe will only be informed when we have left for London, and the others will be none the wiser until the last stage.' They both nodded. 'Your invite to the charity dinner has already been sent in so everyone knows you are going. I am not sure how your mother is going to take this – maybe she should know?'

'Pete, it is really important that the information gets back to Girski's mother as quickly as possible and my mother is the quickest route, God help us.' He took a sip. 'Worse than jungle drums sometimes the way the women can gossip!' Lottie smiled but the CPO never broke a smile, he just frowned and continued.

'So, at lunch tomorrow it will start; we pack up as planned but go separately.' He continued to talk them through the methods of communications and places that Edward would be staying in. The Kensington had been mentioned as a place to stay for him, but Lottie really did not want to go there again if she could help it.

The last-minute renting of a fully-furnished apartment would also help it look very spur of the moment. The only part that Edward had faltered on was the reason that they were going to fall out. The part where Lottie was going to get upset in public and the reason, totally untrue, that during his last trip he had been seen with a 'woman of the night 'and had been unfaithful.

'But it gives good reading and all the other crap they usually put in the papers might have happened,' Pete said.

'And she will think that if you are unfaithful once, the chances are, you will be again with her,' Lottie said earning her a scowl from her husband.

'Yes, but I am still not sure about it,' he said. 'People who really know me will know how much-' She cut him short.

'Yes, I know, how much you love me, and that is why we are doing this. End of! Now fetch your son because he has woken up.' She lifted the baby monitor up to her ear. 'And any minute now...' There he was on cue, he started to cry.

'How do you know, just like that?' Edward said, walking towards her, taking the monitor out of her hand and kissing the side of her face as their skin brushed.

'Because I know my men!' She smiled back, raising an eyebrow with a cheeky grin. 'And I trust them.'

The few other diners in the pub had been shocked to hear Lottie raise her voice to Edward. Living in the village as neighbours, their faces had been seen several times before, and everyone would have only ever seen them joined at the hip, kissing, holding each other. The reaction of Pete as she yelled at him from outside was worthy of an Oscar.

'My goodness Lottie, whatever is it?' Agnes had followed her out of the pub when Lottie had shot up, grabbed Junior out of his carry case, and walked to the side of the car where she was now standing.

'Oh God, I don't know where to start!' Lottie cradled her child in her arms as the shock was also apparent to him too. 'Apparently he was with someone, on a recent trip, said she was something to do with work, but she keeps texting him and he keeps replying.'

'Edward is always on the phone to God knows who from work,' Agnes said trying to appease the young woman in front of her, her adopted daughter almost.

'Yes, but how many times does he take the text in the middle of the night? Hide his phone from me and then when I do see the text, it says he misses her too, a lot!' She felt herself almost wanting to laugh as Edward came out of the pub, Pete in tow. 'He got another just then before he got up to go the toilet.'

'Lottie please, I can explain,' he said, not being able to make eye contact with her.

'Pete, can we please go back, I want to go home.' She was still trying to quieten her son who was now in full screaming mode. This made Edward look even more fraught.

'Let me take him,' he said in a still and calm manner.

'Not on your life,' Lottie spat out, 'I said to leave me alone, and that goes for him too!' She was still well in character and this scared Edward more and more, how easy this was for her. She was acting, but her son was not and was genuinely distressed.

'Lottie, he is getting stressed.' Again Edward wanted to take him, but she pulled back.

'Stressed, stressed to know his father was sleeping with someone while he was still waiting to come into the world. Yes, that would stress me too. To know that you were with someone else no matter how much you have said you can't wait for me to be here and that you loved US!' She opened the door that Pete had unlocked.

'Lottie, it was nothing like that, please.' He looked at Pete who knew he was to drive off as requested, but not before he got in.

'Lottie, my dear God.' Agnes was holding her mouth. Lottie looked up back at her.

'I am so sorry to have ruined you day, can you get home?' she asked, knowing that Ed had to get in as they would not be able to keep this going in the back of the car if there was someone else in there with them.

'Yes, but I am not sure I should let you go in this state,' she said, almost in tears and Lottie could not look at her because not only was Charlie upset, but Agnes too was also starting to cry.

'It will be fine. I want to go home.' She put her hand on her son's head to protect him getting in the car. 'I will call you,' she said. Lottie smiled as she pulled the door shut and Edward slammed his, just to get an effect, or because he was more than pissed with the whole situation. The car pulled off.

'Shit, that was horrid,' he said, reaching out for her hand. 'I'm not going to be able to keep this up. Lottie, look at the two of you!' The noise that their son was making was adding to his terror of how this was going to be over the next few days, well, Lottie had said weeks, but he was going to have to put a stop to this sooner. He could not see them distressed for nothing.

'I'm going to pull the plug on this, Lottie,' he said as the car pulled into the drive. Charlie had settled and was almost asleep.

'We have to keep going, it is the only way,' she said, still clinging to the bundle in her arms.

'Like fuck it is, there are other ways, and you know it,' he said back, both remaining in the car even though the engine had stopped, and Pete had got out.

'How, I don't see one.' She still could not hold his eyes because if she did, she would also admit that she could not carry on for long with this pretence.

'Take it all to the police or something,' Edward pushed close to her, 'I know people who can.'

'No,' Lottie said, 'I need to know why, not just for Mitch, but the others.'

'She is psycho, that's why!' He ran his hand through his hair. 'I can't lie any more Lottie. I don't have it in me, not where you and my son are concerned.'

'So, you have her, let's say "bumped off", and it comes back to you. We lose everything because of her and she wins again.' She did take his hand now as he placed it on the side of her arm whilst she still held their son. 'She threatened him, me and you. As much as I want this done, we have to do it right.'

'And this is right? In whose world is this fucking right?' he expressed.

'Ours for now,' she said, opening the door. 'We need to go, but I do need to go back on one thing, I need to tell Gerald so that he can go to see Agnes – she was so hurt and confused. So, I guess that we need to also tell your mom.'

'Straying from the plan, it's not going to go well,' Pete said when Lottie was downstairs telling Gerald the story from the start. 'And Sharpe, is he still going to be in the dark?'

'No. We are going to do this differently. No big public fights. I am going to go to Caroline, tomorrow night. I will be able to get her out for a drink as a way to get my mom and his mother back together. I am sure they will come for dinner. Lottie can stay down here where she will be safe, and Phil can come and keep her company.'

'Ok so when did this change so quickly?' Pete almost scratched his head.

'From now,' Edward said, putting a few bits in his bag.

'And Mrs Dean knows this?' Pete was sure he already knew the answer.

'No, I am going to tell her once I have packed.' He never looked up to hear the 'Good Luck' mouthed from the CPO's mouth as he left the room.

It was dark and Charlie had settled. Edward walked into his room, where a soft lullaby was playing. He was being watched by Lottie as he softly took each breath.

She looked up. 'I know, Pete told me.' Edward shook his head. 'Well I listened to his conversation with Sharpe to be honest.' She smiled. 'Plan sounded good until it came to playing it off?' She stood up. 'I was never going to be able to keep that up.' Edward sighed, pleased with her answer and that it was not just him who was the one to give in so soon.

'Neither was I.' He held out his arms as he admitted it to her. 'So what now?'

'I need to be back in town. Paul and Mr Chance are due to meet me and we have the charity dinner, so staying here for me is not an option. I want to go back.' She stopped and looked at him. 'There will be a way. I know you want me to stay here, and you, well you meet with her as planned but I don't want to be that far away from you.' He bent to kiss her forehead. He smiled and nodded as if he echoed her thoughts.

'Edward, well that is a shock,' Alice Dean replied to her son once he had given over some information of the last few weeks. 'And well, I am not sure that I can take all this information in. I never liked that girl but what you are saying is truly horrid. Your father...' she stopped herself from saying that his father had gotten into bigger circles of evil people, but found that holding her tongue was easier than getting Edward to speak of him. 'I'm not sure how I can play my part, and well, the police should be in on this.'

Edward continued to explain and when he had finished she finally spoke in reply.

'Don't you think poor Gail has suffered enough, without trying to honey trap this person into a confession? They are good friends.' She referred to how close Mrs Girski had gotten with Caroline of late.

They all had connections to each other's families from way back. Once more she would not explain this to Edward as it involved his father and hers. They all kept the same underworld connections, along with several Russian names that escaped her, that is where the Girskis had first come in and it was through Edward's connection from school that Alice and Gail had become friends, and their husbands' business links increased.

Edward continued to talk to his mother as they sat in the living room at her home.

'So, she needs to know what type of a friend she is, and to be honest, I am sure that once she knows all the facts, she will be able to accept them.' He cleared his throat as if it did not really matter what the older woman thought; he wanted this over, concluded and to move on. 'Will you help?' he finally asked, and the reply was yes, yes of course she would, he was her son, this was her family.

The meeting was set. The restaurant lobby was full, but Edward could see the two women at the table and as he got closer the younger woman also came into eyeshot. His skin moved under his crisp white shirt and he almost felt a shudder.

He forced a smile as the woman spotted him straight away and he almost cursed under his breath as he walked towards the table.

'Ladies, I am so sorry I am late.' He kissed his mother on the cheek and nodded to Mrs Girski and Caroline. He took his jacket off and he could feel her eyes follow every detail of his shoulders and his arms as he consciously tucked his shirt into the back of his fitted trousers. He swallowed and took a breath. As requested, the chair next to his mother and Caroline had been kept free so he had to sit next to her.

They made small talk while the food order was taken and then he turned to the young woman. He almost had to look through her because all he felt now was abhorrence for a murderer. He had to admit he'd once felt something; she was stunning on his arm, and had been fun mainly in the bedroom. It pleased him to dominate her and she was a very willing submissive for him. He noticed that the years had not been too kind of late and the bags under her eyes were heavily masked by makeup.

'You look well.' He was hoping that the lie was as easy to believe as it had been to say it. 'It's good to see you.'

'Thank you, Ed, you look fine as always,' she replied with a smile that was sickly sweet.

As his mother had been primed with information before he had arrived, he was only late to make sure that she had passed on the information that Edward and his new wife were struggling and that he was staying at work more to keep out of the way. The bait to try to get Caroline to show her true colours as quickly as possible.

The meal continued, although Ed found it hard to stomach much of the fine food he was served with. On several occasions he silenced his phone.

'Edward, darling, if you need to take the call, we do not mind,' his mother said, giving him a glance and a smile although very tentative.

'My wife can wait,' was his reply and he gave a smile to Caroline who had looked up from her food. His phone then beeped alerting to a text, he took it out of his pocket again and then opened the device. Laying it on the table so that Caroline could see he stood and said, 'Ladies, excuse me.' He got up and walked towards the men's room. He gave a wry smile as he looked back; she was leaning over enough to look at the words.

On his return, it did not take long for the meal to be over. Although this was very staged, Alice did genuinely feel at ease that she was once again with at least one of her friends, who she had missed in the recent months, but as she kissed her son goodbye, she whispered in his ear, 'Be careful Edward, please, she is an evil woman.'

He was going to the bar for a drink and Caroline was the last to get up and go. Almost flexing his fingers in preparation to touch her he reached out to pull her back from the departing group. Fighting the bile in this throat he said as sweetly as he could, 'Want to stay for a drink?' and of course she accepted without a second thought. So, the pre-arranged, well planned sting had begun..

It would have been hard for him to be able to carry out the plan to get her drunk, take her home and then get the confession if every drink he ordered was a strong bourbon, but lucky for him the bartender had complied with the request made to him the day before from Pete to only serve the lady the hard stuff – Edward's drink was a mix of cold tea and ice. He needed to keep his wits about him throughout this. He needed a clear mind and to be always one step ahead of her.

With the wine at the meal and the large brandies that kept coming after an hour sat at the bar, Edward seized his moment.

'What you say we get out of here? I could do with something a little more mind-blowing than this.' He sniffed, wiping his nose and raising his eyebrows. 'And I have to say I am right out.' He tapped his top pocket.

He had never done drugs in his life, but he had been around enough people, mainly Alex, to note the mannerisms and the body language that someone who uses regularly displayed.

'Edward Dean!' It was a stern but definitely slurred statement. 'Never a man alive I would have thought liked a bit of coke.' She lowered her voice for the last sentence.

'Never would I have known being married would be so...' God, he did not want to say this next bit... 'Fucking boring and, well I have never regretted anything in my past, but this.' He looked down at his wedding ring and gave it a turn. Again, he paused and was grateful that it looked like it was to focus from the drink more than curse himself for having to do this. 'Being shackled, married to her, this I,' he held out for the last word as it struggled to leave his lips, 'regret.'

If a normal person had confessed this personal dismay, one would hope that the person being told their sorrows would show sympathy, and concern. But Caroline was just the opposite. This was like music to her ears and she beamed a smile which never moved the lines on her face due to too much surgery.

'Well, Mr Dean. I think I have the just the thing for you at home.' She paused. 'Care to join me?' she asked almost stumbling off her stool. Edwards's reaction to catch her would have been the same for anyone, but he knew he had to do this as it gave him the opening to get close to her, for his next comment.

'I take it back, there may be one other regret!' He left the comment open as he planted a kiss on her mouth. 'You.'

Calling a cab gave him the chance to pull the fresh air to his lungs. The limpet clinging to him made his flesh crawl and he felt nothing but distaste for her long, witchy fingers groping his body. He felt no reaction to her, other than to slap her to stop the desperate fondling. He closed his eyes, trying to envisage Lottie being safe at home not having to see any of this. His rage only increased knowing that if she did, he could not blame her for being upset, mad as she had been when he outlined his plan to her.

Getting in the cab only seemed to increase her attention on him and he found her hand slipping to his groin. She held his eyes, although hers were almost closed and she rubbed him.

'Edward, I see marriage has made you hard work. This I feel, we need to fix. It never took so much to persuade you.' She rubbed him again but still the hate and distaste was better than any chemicals you could get on the black market to keep your dick down. Edward could have laughed as he just wanted to say, it's you, that is the effect you have on me. But he just went along with the game.

The front door to the imposing house had hardly shut when she tried to rid him of his jacket. His face now had stains of red where her painted lips had assaulted him, and as he glanced in the side mirror on the wall, he thought that he would never be able to wash it off.

'Hang on,' he said, 'let's do some and see if that makes the moment down there more interested!' She giggled.

'OK.' She pulled at his tie, 'Follow me.' She started to take the stairs, kicking off her shoes as she went.

'Got any whiskey?' he asked. She nodded and pointed to the door that they had just walked past. 'Start without me, I will be up in a moment.' He pulled at her and after a final kiss on his lips she let go. He went through the closed door to find a room that was empty of the plush furniture he had expected in a house like this to find just a small chair, a TV and the drinks bar, stocked with every kind of alcohol you could imagine.

He looked at the bottles and pulled the cheap whiskey and brandy out. He then checked his jacket pocket for the small device and put it into his trousers. He had more chance of being able to control these when he got upstairs. He knew he would have to take off his jacket, but he prayed to God that this would be over before he lost his lower garments. Slowly he took the stairs, and he could instantly see her in the bedroom, her head over the glass tabletop doing the lines of powder that she had neatly placed out in front. Her hair obscured the view. She lifted her head quickly as he walked in and she wiped her face.

'I left you some.' She pointed to the last line on the table. 'It's good stuff, the best and a bit of something added to give you that little bit more!' She smiled laying back like a rag doll. He sat beside her, but she never moved. He took off his jacket and instantly she started to rub his arms as if the promise of him removing his clothes had awoken her. He smiled and licked his finger, placing it in the white powder and then just like a mother bird feeding her young he held the digit to her mouth to suck it off. She obliged, licking his finger suggestively holding her eyes, she pulled him close to kiss him and he quickly turned away to get more of the powder. With her facing away he was able to wipe the table clean and use the other finger so that when he placed it to his mouth to the rest of the world it looked like he had taken the drug.

'Good, huh?' She rolled her eyes, not able to focus, but her hand shot to his groin and she fumbled with the buckle.

'Drink?' he asked, aware that he sounded as sober as he was, so he started to kiss her neck. She said yes, and he reached over to pour the liquid in to the two glasses. He did not want to but felt the need to at least have one hard drink to get him through this. Knocking it back, she noticed and said, 'Someone is eager!' She picked up her own glass. 'Just like your brother.' Although it was said in a low voice, he had heard it.

His heart rate shot up and his face instantly became red. He thought he would not be able to control himself at the sound of her saying his brother's name. She did not deserve to speak his name ever, let alone around him. She continued, 'Look at you all hot and flustered, let's take this off.'

He let her start to disrobe him but not without him asking, 'Do you miss Mitch?' She never moved her head to try to focus on him, but she replied, 'I do,' and he fumbled into his trouser pocket to move the recorder to make sure it was on.

'Why do you bring him up?' she asked, still working on his belt. Edward was grateful he had put this on in anticipation that she would struggle, and it would buy him some time.

'I just wondered, and well, I wish maybe you and I had been closer then. Things could have been different maybe and I should not have pushed you away.' He was fully aware that he was pushing the conversation in a direction. Was it too fast? She pulled back to look at him and he met her cold eyes. 'You did push me away Edward, to someone who was more than grateful to share my pain.' He felt her dig her nails into his thighs and he knew he had to get away from her; it was as if she had somehow turned into another person in front of his eyes.

'I'm here now,' he said, trying to soothe her.

'And do you want me now?' she asked, starting to unbutton her own top. He tried to smile and took her hands, slowing her down by taking over the job and unbuttoning her top for her. Even with the hatred he had, he still had to look at her body. Her breasts rounder than they should be now from the surgery she had had, the nipples out of line. Nothing could have turned him off more until she pushed forwards to kiss him.

After a few minutes more he found that she had succeeded with his trousers and making an excuse to lay them on the floor and get more coke, he left the room under her direction of where to find it. The bathroom cabinet was full of every type of medication you could need for any illness you would suffer, and he found the small packet wrapped at the back by the needles and sharps box.

On re-entering the room, he immediately noticed that she had managed to lay herself naked across the bed. He had already opened the packet and tipped some away, walking back in the room rubbing his dry finger on his teeth and licking his lips.

'That's really good stuff. Where is it from?' he asked, slowly walking to the bed.

'Our dear departed friend.' She smiled. 'But be warned it has a kick and too much could just finish you off.'

She beckoned him with one of her thin fingers. 'Get over here Ed and let me see the effects.' She put her hand under the sheets and brought out a whip and hand cuffs. 'I remembered how you like to play.' She reached and took the small plastic bag from him and licked her own finger in the way that she had licked Ed's a moment or two ago.

In one movement, he flicked her over onto her chest, thankful that he did not have to look her in the face. 'Still like it rough?' he asked, slapping her backside hard. She yelped. As she did not answer he did it again and she shot her head back. 'You bastard,' she said, 'Yes, you know I do.'

'Good girl, let me just have some more and then I will show you how rough I like it.' He tipped some of the powder onto her back just so she could feel it and he let the bag trickle down further so she would think he was taking a long line.

'You men, you love to do this, don't you?' She laughed, reaching her hands up to the bed head. He made a sniffing noise and then slapped her backside again.

'Who else liked it like this, Caroline, tell me you dirty bitch?' She mumbled and then after another slap she said, 'Alex.'

'Who?' he said again, making her say the name louder and then she finished with 'until her.'

Edward came to instantly. 'Who?' he asked, taking one of her hands and attaching it to the cuff already on the bed.

'Your whore of a wife,' she spat out. 'But I guess that you know she does not like it rough and that's why you've found yourself with me again.'

'Explain. I don't understand.' He quickly shackled the other hand knowing now that no matter what happened she was not getting away and he would be able to keep some of his clothes on.

With her face down on the sheets she started to speak, and Edward could hear every word.

'That weak cunt.' She paused. 'He always wanted what you had, tried everything to get close to her. Even when you fucking married the bitch, he still wanked off over her, followed her places. Even when he was straddling me, fucking me, he would say her name.' She tried to turn to speak to him. 'But I'm the one laughing now. I have you and she will never get you back.'

The look of horror on his face would have given the game away and she wriggled around. 'Take me, Edward, take me like your wife will not let you have her.'

'Does this make it better?' he asked, straining himself to kiss her shoulders. When she did not reply, he used the whip on her upper thigh, so she spat the acknowledgment out. 'Tell me why it has been so bad, how I can make it better?' he asked again, kissing her shoulders.

'Fuck me, Edward, take me and never leave me again. You left me and I had to do bad things. I had to make him do bad things for me. Things that would make you see that I wanted you, you were mine from all that time ago and you will always be mine.' She gasped as he hit her again.

'What have you done?' He paused. 'Caroline, what have you done to deserve me to come back?' He was now playing the game. Their sex life had been just that, sex, hard rough sex. He was forceful, dominant and she submitted to him every time. Not for self-gratification now but for instant answers; he still did not know how far this was going to go but he knew the drugs, the drink, and the relationship they had had would bring out the real woman laying beneath him and he was getting it all recorded.

A quick eye on the red LED on the small machine on the far table told him that much. He had left it there once his trousers came off and he returned with the drugs. He placed his hand on her inner thigh and ran a finger up.

'How can I make it better if you don't tell me how bad you have been?' He felt spit in his mouth, and he knew he would be sick soon.

'I would do anything for you,' she said almost breathless, maybe from the sexual kick she was getting or the fact he was putting his weight on her shoulders and she was gasping for breath. He put his hand on her throat.

'This?' he asked and she bucked her hips, thrashing her hands against the chains. He released her so she could speak.

'Yes,' she said, 'I would fucking kill for you, Edward, take me, I need you.' He used the whip to part her legs and ran the material onto her bare cheeks, allowing the tip to reach towards the sheets where he knew it would hit her intimate lips. It did and she whimpered. 'I would kill her too if you ask.'

He closed his eyes, and breathing fast he held in the sick that was in his throat.

'I asked him to do it, but he fucked it up, the prick. When he was faced with her, he could not see past his fucking infatuation and he fucked it up.' She sniggered. 'He did not want to do it like he did the others. They went quick, fast with the right dose.' She paused. 'No, he wanted to have her. That was where he went wrong. I had to find a way to do it myself.' She was still wiggling beneath him. 'But now I don't have to, you took my advice in those letters and left her for me.'

That was it. He could take no more and he pulled himself clear off the bed. He retched to the pit of his stomach and vomited on the floor.

'Edward, what the fuck?' she asked, still prostrate on the bed unable to turn back round. Shouting now for him like a rabid vixen. He had picked up his phone and sent the pre fixed text. He slammed the door and jammed it with a chair from the other room; he needed to make sure that she was not getting out and that he had it all recorded.

He was going to be sick again when he played the last few seconds back. Totally disorientated he opened the door to his left; it was not the bathroom he had first been in and he was sick on the carpet as he fell to his knees, still only dressed in his boxer shorts. Wiping his face, he slowly looked up and tried to focus on the vision in front of him. The room was dark, the wooden blinds pulled together only allowing a slither of light from the street.

He slowly stood up, making more sense of the walls around him. As his focus cleared, he could see pictures of him, pictures of Lottie, pictures of them both. Venues they had been to, and through the windows of the house in Kent. Newspaper clippings from charity events. He moved closer. Clippings of the death of his brother. The red marker that had been scrolled over to another picture of Alex, red marker over pictures of Lottie, spelling the words 'Bitch'.

He felt sick again, and knowing he had nothing left in his stomach he retched, holding his mouth as he carried on looking around. The club, the dead girl, the young guy from Lottie's work, even the professor and Todd with Lottie eating out at what looked like lunchtime. Paper spread on the desk, jumbled as if a mad man had been looking for something. Then as he flicked through there was a photo of Lottie and him, on their wedding day.

'How the hell did she get this?' he asked himself, but as he looked closer Lottie's face had been cut out and a picture of Caroline had been put in. Vomit rose to his mouth once more and he had to move his feet before he fell over; the room was swimming, and he was sure he was going to faint and get trapped in this hell hole he had found.

He thought to himself, shit how the hell did she get all of this? The banging on the front door woke him from his coma-like state and he rushed down to the lobby just as the door was broken in.

Pete, Phil, and Sharpe all rushed in. 'Thank fuck you're here.' He moved to the side as they were followed by the police. Pete automatically put out his arms to defend Edward, who realised he was still almost naked, and the door was fully open. Although a quiet street, people were walking past, drawn by the sirens and police cars that were still pulling up and Pete took off his jacket and gave it to him.

'Fuck, Pete that was...' He was dumbstruck.

'I know,' Pete said, 'Get in the car, Mr Dean. The police will deal with it now, Sharpe has this.'

'Lottie,' was his next thought. 'Where is she?'

'At the apartment as planned.'

‘Alone?’ he said, still not worried about the people staring as he took the first step out of the front door half naked.

‘No, Phil brought Liz round, and your mother came straight over as soon as they left the meal.’ He handed him his phone. ‘Call her.’

Edward then realised that his phone was still in the room, with his other clothes. Telling Pete the information he was hurriedly shown to the car and told not to worry about his stuff; he just needed to get home.

The call made the connection and he sat in the car and cried to the person on the other end. The gentle sobs could be heard from the driver’s seat and the privacy screen was raised.

Even the second shower and the boiling hot water could not rid him of the ordeal he had just been through. Minutes before, their embrace had been long and he held his wife as if she were the only thing left in the world. He would have held his son, but he was soundly sleeping, and Lottie had insisted he went for a shower before he tried to explain what had just gone on to clear his mind.

‘I’m so sorry,’ he sobbed over and over in her arms and she recalled how many times she had said this to him after the last encounter.

‘Shhhhh.’ She kissed his head, rocking him as she did her son to sooth him to sleep, still sure she could smell the stench of a woman’s perfume on him, not the usual sandalwood and musk. ‘Take a shower and then you can eat,’ she said but instead he shook his head and took the second large whiskey that was handed to him by his mother. She asked him again, knowing that the water would only wash away a bit of the day, the memories would take longer, but she knew he had to take the time to reflect. She needed the time too, now she knew he was back safely.

Once the last of the amber liquid was taken, she asked him again, ‘Go, Ed, I will come in and wash your back. Let me just check on Junior,’ she whispered and smiled, almost having to prise herself from his arms and finally he gave in as if the last fight had gone out of him. As if they did not need any asking, both his mother and Liz got their belongings and left the apartment.

The water continued to flush over him. He had already got out of the shower, but went back in knowing the smell of her was still in his nostrils. He was glad as this time he heard the low humming of his wife and as he looked through the steamed-up glass of the shower he could see her naked form walking towards him. He closed his eyes, hoping that this image would fight off the one of the other woman's body that seemed to still be burning in his head. Her hands were already warm, and once the water hit her body her smell filled the cubical, with a gentle hit of clean baby too. He smiled to himself as the hands worked along his shoulders, down his back and round to his stomach and he felt a weight starting to move from above him.

As her body brushed with his backside, she reached around to take a firm grip of him, and the water was no longer able to get in between the two of them. She reached past him for the shower gel and with expert practice she filled her hands without being able to see and started to lather the areas of him she could reach from this angle.

Guilt flashed through his brain from the last hands that had touched him, but as every bubble of the fragrant gel burst and washed away down the brass plughole, her hands created another emotion in him. One he knew all too well and was never going to be able to control. He felt his stomach lurch this time with the electrical pulse that shot to his groin as the blood flowed to his dick, now almost fully erect. He took in a deep breath, his nostrils flared and she reached around to find the member pulsing as her nails gently grazed him and he instantly needed to turn to her. With speed he did, pushing her up against the wall. She gasped as the cold tiles touched her wet skin, but within a second the air from her lungs was being replaced with the breath from his kiss.

Passion raised through their lips and the urgency to feel her, be deep in her made him force his weight forwards. Grasping for her backside he pulled her off her feet and she clamped her legs around him to hold on, clinging to his shoulders with their mouths still locked as their tongues swirled and thrust at each other.

Water dripping down their faces made them both come up for short pauses of air, and then they locked again.

Lottie felt the steel of his erection pushing at her pubic bone and she tried to wriggle to get him to move so that she could encase it with her sex. She was swollen with need and the gesture was enough for him to take his own action. He used the strength in his shoulders to hold her whilst he guided himself to her soft spot. There was no delay once he was in the desired place, he held her again and thrust straight into her, forcing her tight lips open to take his full length.

Her eyes shot open at the hot pain of herself expanding to his size and she gasped out, grabbing at his hair as within an instant he withdrew and thrust again almost within the same motion. She again had to gasp as she pushed her head to the wall, accepting him, but still needing to expand to take him fully. She tilted her hips and the third push filled her. She felt his balls hit her and the thrusts continued to come. With each push he grunted either into her neck where he was kissing her or her mouth, as he bit her lip. No words passed between, only the animal noises of the sexual act.

He was close to release, too fast for him. He wanted it to last but the burning in his stomach and the aching in his balls told him that no matter what he did he was going to fill her. He tried to slow down but she dug her nails into his shoulders, the pleasurable pain only made him squeeze his arse cheeks harder and thrust again.

'Oh god, Lottie I can't.' He did not get the words out before he felt her tighten around his dick, as if she were swallowing him; she pulsed her inner muscles, suffocating his manhood as if willing him to release, her calf muscles digging into his waist as if she were hanging on to him for her life. Her face was buried in his shoulder, her soaking hair hanging down his back and she gave a whimper, and he felt her teeth gently graze the skin on his neck as if she were trying to hide her climax. He pulled her hair back so that she had to move to look at him, her eyes closed with a smile on her face that only he knew was for him.

Her chest expanded with the speedy breaths she was taking in, still silent in her high state. Feeling her still surrounding him internally he started to thrust harder again, her tits moving up with each thrust. The ripe nipple that was close to his face was far too tempting, so he caught it in his mouth and bit down, hard.

'Jesus!' She finally spoke, 'Edward!' It was not a statement to stop, it was the disbelief that she was going to climax again. As if she had not been greedy enough the first time she pulsated around his thick head, and this time the noise was too much to keep inside as she screamed out his name.

He had to steady her because the next push was him done too. He moved her back to the wall even more and used his other hand to hold the slippery tiles the best he could. His legs could have given way; he had to use all the strength he had because he burst inside her, thrusting as hard as he could, his eyes so tightly closed he thought he saw stars. 'Fuck it, yes!' he said, quiet at first. 'Fuck, Lottie.' He could feel her trying to resist him pushing back into him and he opened his eyes, knowing he was heavy on her but, as if the eight inches of hard muscle had replaced his brain for those few moments, he could not stop drilling her to the wall. She dropped her head onto his shoulder and he could feel her breathing fast trying to increase the oxygen in her lungs. He closed his eyes so that the movement of her body reverberated through him and he leaned into her, almost resting his head on the wall.

'I love you,' he said into the soaking wet hair that dripped around him. 'I love you so much,' he said again, not because she did not hear him, but because he needed her to know. 'So, fucking much it hurts.'

Lottie turned her head and she placed her lips close to his ear. 'I love you too,' she said almost in a sleepy voice, grateful now that she could breathe. She released the hold with her legs and Edward knew he was not going to be able to hold her; his arms had taken the weight and the sexual power and need was diminishing and as he came down from his natural high, they started to throb, so he lowered her to the floor.

'You OK?' he asked as he felt himself slide out of the warmth of her sex. She gave a faint reply, but the smile confirmed it.

Silence fell over them as they dried each other and slipped into the bedclothes.

It was sometime later as Lottie watched her husband through the reflection of the mirror. She had got out from the bed and was finally drying her hair. Their son had woken, and Edward had moved to retrieve him, walking back into their room, and sitting on the bed cradling him in his strong arms. She smiled as she watched the face of the man she loved glow in response to the small smile, chubby cheeks and glowing blue eyes that stared back up at him. She never wanted another day like this one, and she was so glad it was almost at an end. She knew there were still things to be said, but she also knew that there was an end in sight and that normality, whatever that would be for them as a family, would soon return.

Chapter Twenty-Two

The court room had been full. Though the reporters had been asked to stay away the case that was being heard was one that over the last eight weeks had made the headlines several times. Starting with the events on the day of her arrest and knowing that Caroline the 'high society chick' as the reporters had documented it, she had then been admitted to hospital, under guard as a stalker and was being cared for in a psychiatric unit until the final sentencing was concluded. As if she had to have the last say she had tried to commit suicide only days later, hitting the headlines again. Even though Lottie did not want anyone else to suffer from this whole nightmare, at least now they knew the whole story. It would be final for them all if she was out of the picture for good, but her attempt to take her life had failed.

During the long wait for the sentencing date Lottie had been into work but had found it hard to concentrate on other cases. The taste for the dead had finally, she felt, been rested. As if the answers she had found with this last, very personal case, was enough. Edward had been to work and had very reluctantly travelled abroad twice leaving her at home. His absence made up her mind that she wanted to be at home more and concentrate on the charity work, the fashion house, and the music foundation. When they talked about it, she could almost see the relief in his eyes, although he never pushed or said anything, only that he would go with whatever she wanted to do and if he could help in any way he would, and if they knew each other's plans he would be happy. He had talked the talk, but could he walk the walk when it came to it if she changed her mind? He would have to wait and see, but he had not just said this to appease her, he could see that she really did want to do this.

Pete had called in while they were both sat in the office to inform him that Caroline had been taken ill and the trial date had been adjourned, putting them back another week and the conversation followed about how they would all sleep better when the outcome came.

Winter was soon going to be setting in and plans were being made for Christmas parties. Lottie sat in the office reflecting at the year and how, without her noticing, the time was flying by. This set back would put them into October and as she looked at the grey day from the office window, she also looked at the photo on her desk of her young son, whom she knew was sound asleep at home with Mrs B. She had called only moments ago, the third call within the day and again she knew that she just longed to be at home.

The door between their offices had been closed all morning as Edward had meetings and Lottie looked back again to see he was still busy. She was tired. Today had just seemed to make her feel lethargic and unable to concentrate. She moved to the soft sofa, and pushing back into the soft cushions, she put her head back on the rest. She closed her eyes, pulling her jumper across her. The room was not cold, but it made her feel protected as the soft mohair covered her skin.

'Hey, Lottie.' The gentle whisper disturbed her, and she opened her eyes. Meeting hers were the blue pools she recognised and the smile that sent a shiver of passion through her on every occasion. She smiled back.

'Sleeping on the job, don't let the boss catch you!' The gentle kiss on her forehead made her close her eyes again as she smelt the subtle sandalwood shower gel she had helped apply that very morning in the shower.

'Busted!' she said, keeping her eyes closed now and feeling the warmth of his body settling next to her. She switched sides for her headrest, finding his shoulder to replace the cream fabric.

'You should get more sleep at night!' He wiped a strand of hair away from her face and she opened her eyes at his touch.

'Then so should you!' She walked her fingers playfully up his chest, resting on his chin and pulling at it.

'Don't blame me!' He took her finger in his own hand and kissed it, 'I have an irresistible wife.' This made Lottie giggle, showing her dimples.

'And a son who does like a night-time snack!' she finished off, referencing the night feeds she was still carrying out, not her husband worshiping her at every opportunity he got and preventing her slumber.

'Well, when he sees the menu who can blame him?' He ran his own finger now playfully down the blouse to the top button and cupped her breast firmly. Lottie quickly looked around to the glass door as if checking who was around although with their back to the world it was only anyone who was also 20 stories up in the city who could see them.

'Mr Dean,' she mockingly protested, but noted how tender his touch was.

They were interrupted by a very loud and staged cough, both looking up to see Pete by the door.

'Time to go?' he asked, looking into her eyes. 'You.' He kissed her lips. 'You go home, I will only be another few hours.' He pushed up from the sofa. 'Boss's orders!'

'Ok.' She smiled but not before she sat back at her desk, looking through the phone book and calling the number that she required.

Later in the week Lottie had several appointments all of which she was driven to by Phil. The last one for the day required her to meet with Edward. Phil had dropped her off earlier and she was waiting inside by the window. As the car came into view, she smiled and went outside. As the car pulled up, she knew he was not alone. After parking he walked around the back of the large SUV and pulled out the child seat with ease.

The little sobs confirmed that Charlie had been whimpering all the way to his first check up and the small beads of sweat on Edwards's brow confirmed he had been stressed at hearing his son's protests and the amount of traffic he had just faced.

'Oh, baby boy, Daddy's driving is not so bad.' She reached and took him out of the cot as her husband pulled a face, still holding the now-empty receptacle. Within a moment of her touch Charlie was stilled, and she smiled at Edward, raising her eyebrows.

'What?' Edward smirked. 'Do you have a point?'

'Nope!' She grinned, kissing her son's little head. 'Not at all, ready to do this?' she asked, walking through the large white door, he dutifully nodded and followed. She was still grinning.

As they sat at the breakfast bar, Edward was on the phone. Lottie was already dressed in her suit; today was the day in court and the sick feeling she had was not going away. Mrs B had left out breakfast and coffee and had gone into Charlie's room to tidy. Lottie could not help but grin at the fact it was spotless in there – really, she just wanted a cuddle. Lottie poured a cup of boiled water and put in a tea bag. Anything in her stomach would for sure make her feel worse; she never did like having to go in and face the families, let alone going in with Edward and his mother today. She sipped her tea and smiled as she caught Edwards's eye. His face remained glum and she smiled to try to lighten his mood. He walked over to the window, still listening to the person on the other end of the call. He looked out at the day, which seemed to reflect the atmosphere and she joined him. He reached out for her hand and she put the cup down on the table and went to his side.

She tried to mouth 'are you ok?' but knew he was not. She could not hear any of the conversation and would have to wait for the information. Finally, he put down the phone and he rubbed his neck.

'Edward?' she enquired.

'She did it,' was his reply. She was confused but knew she needed to give him time to continue, which he did.

'Somehow she managed to get enough pills to kill herself, last night.' He paused, leaving Lottie stunned. 'I suppose one piece of good news is they found a full written confession, pages and pages of reasons why she did what she did.' He took in a deep breath. Lottie had to speak now, to say that surely this was a good thing, and closure is what they all needed.

'I suppose it is,' he replied, 'But not if you are me.' He paused and turned to her 'You see she constantly blames me, said it was me that drove her to it, pages and pages of blaming me!'

'Edward, really. You did not make her do anything.' She tilted her head as if questioning that he even though he was to blame.

'Well, according to her lawyer, her family will not rest until I have paid for it all, as they seem to blame me too.'

'Rubbish,' she shot in. 'They have nothing, nothing at all that would mean you had anything to do with this, the facts are plain to see.' She paused to breathe and then continued as he did not seem to want to reply. 'She was clearly not of sound mind, even before you and she were an item.'

'Her family have connections; they can make life hard, and not just in business.' He looked up as Pete walked into the kitchen.

'Let them try,' he said, clearly hearing the conversation and going to the coffee pot to get a drink. 'Anyone else?' He held up the pot. Edward nodded a yes, and Lottie bent down to pick up her tea.

'Maybe I am just getting too old for this cutthroat world, and I don't have the fight anymore. I just want to be left alone with my own family, is that so bad?' It was a statement that stayed in his head; he wanted to say it, he wanted to shout it, but he just walked to the stool and took the drink that was passed to him.

Light feet pattered back into the room, and Lottie could not help but smile at the lady standing there with a bundle in her arms. She knew she would not resist and that the room cleaning, even if it needed to be done, would wait.

'He was awake, Mrs Dean.' Mrs B looked to her and Lottie nodded with a smile. He had not been awake when she looked in on him and as if anyone could forget the child intercom was on the worktop, so the one-sided conversation had been heard about not telling mommy that you want to go to see daddy really!

'So, what do we do now?' Pete asked.

Lottie answered. 'We go to court, hear what they have to say.' She took a sip of the drink, her eyes fixed on the giggling bundle. 'And then we move on, end of.'

As predicted Edward's name had been slammed all over the newspapers the following day.

The story, depending on which one you read ranged from the stalker who could not live without her lover, to the lover who killed his stalker in revenge for several incidents and previous killings.

Another caught the fact that the Russian mafia had been involved with the local businessman and they had bumped her off. This one did get the Dean legal teams' attention and Edward laughed at the final settlement amount that the paper handed over for the fictitious news, which he promptly gave to charity, and the written retraction that they gave the very next day.

News is only news when people are interested, and waves of information filtered back through the Dean businesses, none being affected any more than the statement that Edwards's team had sent out, both to the business world and their friends.

So, within two weeks the storms had blown over. Normality hit Lottie and Edward once more with the diary of events slowly increasing day to day.

Lottie looked across the office and smiled; she found that she did this a lot of late, even with the nagging sick feeling and increasing need for sleep. Charlie had been awake for several nights; he had a cold and would not settle. Edward had taken it on himself last night to ensure she finally got some sleep, so he had sat with him in the nursery.

She had been so sound asleep that she had missed him creeping into their room and kissing her good night. By the time she was up, and almost to her horror, both of her boys had gone.

Mrs B allayed her fear by saying Edward had taken him to work, stopping off at the doctor's first thing to make sure he was OK. Lottie was sure that he was, but she still phoned just to check. As ever Edward had tried to make her life easy and had instructed her during the conversation to take it easy. So, on that advice, shopping was the order of the day. Phil waited for her in the car outside, smiling and almost ecstatic as he opened the door for her and bid her good morning. He was happy with the change of plan for the day and the request to drive because the companion for the day was Liz, and once they had walked around several stores they were dropped off at Harrods where they made their way the food halls for some lunch.

'Wine?' Liz said with the menu in her hand.

'No, I'm good, going to the office after so I will keep a clear head,' Lottie replied. She noticed her friend looking at her phone; this was the second time since they had sat down.

'Everything OK?' she asked, closing her menu knowing that a sandwich and a cup of tea was all she would manage.

'Yes.' It was almost a giggle and then her face went red. Looking at Lottie she noticed the questioning face. 'What?'

'Spill whatever it is, I'm not blind. You two are as thick as thieves – what's going on?' She gave a nod to the waiter and he came over.

'Not sure I can,' Liz replied, changing her attention to look again at the list in front of her. Lottie tutted and picked up her phone, pushing the keys and then returning it to the table.

They ordered but then were disrupted by a commotion in the doorway. There, dressed in a suit, was Phil, hurrying past the shoppers and making his way to them. Urgency on his face.

'Mrs Dean, is there a problem, are you both OK?' He was almost puffed out, unusual for him as he was so fit, but Lottie guessed it was a long way from the car park where he would have been sitting awaiting instructions. And the instructions in the prefixed text that Edward and Pete had insisted that she have in her phone was 'Urgent come now'. It went to his phone and always gave him a GPS of her exact location.

'Yes, Phil, there is a huge problem,' Lottie started without moving from her chair but looking at Liz who was both shocked by the arrival of the man and starry-eyed at him. Lottie had not missed the fact that he had mouthed silently if she was OK first before asking Lottie herself.

'Mrs Dean?' He had assessed the whole area, and straightening his jacket and breathing normally he really could not see an issue. On doing this he held Liz in his eyeline for longer than maybe he should have.

'See, there is the problem.' Lottie was having to contain her smile now and Liz joined in with the question.

'Lottie what problem?' She frowned and then it must have clicked what Lottie was referring to, and there was a short pause.

'Can I?' Her question went to the CPO who was fiddling with his tie now and he almost froze as if a shock was about to hit him from a punch in the stomach. He looked directly at Lottie who asked, 'Can she, whatever it is?' Reluctantly he nodded.

Liz reached for her bag and returned her hand to the table. 'We got engaged.' She just blurted it out as if the excitement was no longer able to stay within her. She showed the shining ring that sat on her finger.

Quickly standing and walking around the table to her friend she hugged and congratulated her, and then looked at Phil.

'Lighten up, man, this is awesome,' Lottie said, and for the first time got closer than she had ever to him and kissed his cheek. She pulled a chair up. 'Phil, please sit with us.' She had to insist again before he took the offer.

'Really, you two, why so secret? Liz, you should have told me.' Lottie was beaming. Liz was opening her mouth, but it was Phil who spoke.

'I was not sure how to tell you Mrs Dean, or Mr Dean. You see, I guess this means that I will have to stop working for you.' Liz instinctively put out her hand and Lottie was pleased that he took it. 'The contract of employment says that I have to be single and...' He was cut off mid-sentence.

'Phillip.' Only once had Lottie called him his full name. 'Really? What a load of rubbish.'

'Mr Dean made it very clear when I started and Pete...' He tried to carry on with an explanation.

'Leave them to me. Nothing has been set in stone. You are my CPO after all are you not?' The question was rhetorical as she never allowed him to time to answer. 'This is the most fabulous news. Keep that on that finger and don't you dare take it off for anyone.' She gave a little giggle. 'Oh, I'm so excited. When's the big day?'

The conversation had continued until they had parted, and Phil finally dropped Lottie off at the office.

Edward was on the phone but as she opened the glass door, he beckoned her in. She walked towards him, noting the child intercom on the desk. Charlie was asleep in the bedroom to the side of the office; the slight hum of his breathing was all you could hear. Taking your children to work was not an option for many men, but as Edward had explained days before, he would do what he wanted: he was CEO after all, and so the small baby had joined him through several business meetings and even sat through a business lunch in a busy expensive restaurant.

Lottie perched on the end of the desk and instantly his hand reached for her leg, rubbing it affectionately. Looking behind him, she noticed that it had stopped raining from earlier, although the clouds were a reminder that it was going to do it again before the night fell, which would soon not be long as the days were drawing in for the winter.

'Yes. Of course, I will arrange it all. Flights and times will be emailed across, but we will be there, and I'm looking forward to seeing you then.' Edward parted with the person on the end of the phone and then stood to his wife's side, kissing her head and she stood to receive the second kiss on her lips.

'Um, Mrs Dean? I notice by the array of bags it was a good shopping trip?' She smiled at him and nodded.

'Are you going away?' she asked, catching the end of his conversation.

'I hoped it would be a 'we' are going away. Shipping in Oz is doing well, and I want to go over for a while, but we can chat about that later. What have you bought?' His reply had momentary thrown her and she opened her mouth, but words did not come out.

'Earth to Lottie,' he said to get her attention. 'What's wrong?'

'Nothing, I was just, well I need to tell you, going away may be a...' She rubbed her mouth and smiled.

'What, Lottie?' He walked to her and took her in his arms. 'Is there a problem?'

'Not a problem, but Liz and Phil...' She quickly said, 'Before you hear it from anyone else, they got engaged!' She paused again. 'And I said we would throw them a party. I know all about how he is not allowed to, and you and Pete will kick off, so don't–' She was silenced by a finger being placed over her mouth swiftly followed by soft lips pressing down on her.

'Whatever, Lottie, I am pleased for them. Is that really the problem? Will that really stop us going away?'

Lottie looked up at him. The rumours were really true that he had changed so much. His reply was one that even three months ago she would not have expected.

'You don't mind? Will Pete have anything to say about it?'

'I am sure he will, but you know I am glad for anyone if they are as happy as me. I did mean what I said about putting you and Charlie first.' He kissed her head again and pulled her even closer. 'I could not wish for anything more.'

She giggled in his chest as the sweet sandalwood fragrance she loved so much passed her nose.

'You said that to me once before, remember, and I think you still owe me that penny!' She rubbed her hands up the length of his back, feeling strong arms around her. She felt safe, secure and the love that was radiating from him made her squeeze him.

'How can I forget, although the reason for the debt was one that I will happily pay again and again, and you know that this is all yours any way, remember you signed the paperwork.' He placed a kiss on her hair, and they stole the silent moment as if time had frozen.

She pulled back away from his grip and turned, but then pulled his arms back around her. She felt the ever-present reminder of his physical form pushing into her back. He rubbed his groin in her backside and she rubbed back in reply.

'Well, Mr Dean, it looks as if you will have to put your bank account to the test as you are in my debt for two pence now.' As she said the words, she placed his hands over her stomach and closed her eyes, listening to the sudden silence; the only thing she could hear was his heartbeat increasing. She felt herself being turned around, the heat of his breath present on her skin, his face almost white but the smile wide and his eyes shining.

'Lottie, are you saying...?' She smiled and his breath went once more.

'I guess I am and to answer your first question, that is the real problem with going away.' Still holding his eyes she could almost see a tear.

'Are you sure?' he started and she felt she had to spell it out.

'Yes,' she whispered, suddenly realising that she had kept the secret for a few weeks now. 'I wanted to wait a few weeks. I was not holding the information back, or worried for any reason. I just wanted to wait until it is two months.'

'Oh god Lottie, you are beautiful.' He kissed her.

'Sorry, I never meant to keep it from you.' He silenced her once more with his lips, followed by, 'I know, and I love you Mrs Dean.'

Epilogue

Four years later…

'Oh, Charlie look at you!' Lottie exclaimed, holding her son's hand and picking him up off the floor. 'Mrs B will have a nightmare. Look at your best trousers!'

'Oh, Mommy it will wash!' he said in his grown-up manner. 'Or Popper will buy me some more.'

'Charlie, don't be so flippant about money. It does not grow on trees.' She tried to remove the mud from the front of his jumper as well.

'Technically, Mommy it does. The plantation in South America is going well with the new rain forest and everything. Popper said that it was a good move to put the money in the trees as it will grow!'

Lottie laughed out loud. Her little man was for sure a chip off the old block. He spent hours in Edward's study and even went with him on the rare occasion when he had to attend board meetings in the city. She was sure he would be CEO before he was 10. She had cried when he came home in his first pre-school uniform. They had been able to get him into the local primary school not far from the village. Edward had been insistent this was where he wanted him to go. They had talked at length about a private school, but he was never going to let him go away, even when he was older.

'Hey, Mommy, there is Popper and Chelsie.' He looked quizzically at the oncoming twosome for a second and then continued, 'Look, Apollo, here boy. Quick run to them.' He let go of her grip and ran towards the dog who had changed direction to greet him.

Lottie did not want to run to them; she wanted to take the time to enjoy the sight of her family at rest in their garden. Even if she had wanted to, she was feeling unwell and the last thing she wanted was to bring up lunch.

'Momma!' the little girl shouted as she toddled in the opposite direction to her brother, arms outstretched, begging to be scooped up. Edward continued his journey towards Lottie, standing only an inch behind his daughter in case she tripped.

'All gone,' he referred to the afternoon guests as he approached his wife, kissing her cheek when they met up. She had picked up the bundle of lace and typical fairy-tale princess dress and was rocking her daughter in her arms.

'Popper?' the little voice asked now, stretching out her chubby arms from her mother to want her father's arms, and within a second, Chelsie got what she wanted and was giggling and playing with the collar on his shirt.

'See she only wants me for a second choice!' Lottie referred to the fact that the small girl was never far from him when he was around.

'Good job I have two arms then.' He put his arms around Lottie's shoulders and pulled her closer, planting another kiss on her cheek and then kissing his daughter who had grabbed his face, wanting one too.

'Mrs B has Charlotte and Gerald is just clearing the rest of the kitchen and then he'll come and take the kids back to the cottage, so we will have the place to ourselves.' Lottie was about to ask what he was suggesting when their attention was taken.

'Momma!' A scream from the other side of the garden made them all look round. A triumphant blue-eyed blond-haired boy lifted his hands up that were covered in mud for everyone to see, holding the stick he had thrown for Apollo. It had landed in the mud and dutifully returned to the other person in the game to be thrown again.

'Oh God, look at his jumper!'

'Relax, he will wash. Mrs B will be sure to scrub him and we can get him another jumper.' She put his hand over his mouth to stop the very words his son knew he would say to the complaints of the afternoon's fun. She smirked and gave a short laugh.

'What?' Edward said.

'Nothing.' She smiled and shook her head. He placed a kiss on her lips, and they turned and walked towards the house.

The water was warm as she lay back in the bath. Today had been a busy day; the first big event that they had hosted in their family home. The move to Kent had been discussed at length, but with the arrival of their daughters Edward was adamant that he was stepping back a bit and wanted to move away from the city. Lottie had not been so keen. She had resigned herself to the fact that she was not going to work in the centre anymore unless they really needed her advice and guidance and the offer for her to run the Dean Incorporated business did appeal to her, until the fifth month of her pregnancy. Ed and Lottie had been shocked that she was having twins, not known in her family but Edwards's mother had said that her grandmother was a twin and so it was in the family line. She had become very heavy early on accommodating Edward's children and was exhausted a lot of the time. She had been at work early in her third trimester and had a scare, which had seen her rushed into hospital for the night. With that the decision was taken out of her hands within a breath and no negotiations. Edward drew up the legal documents the next day to ensure they temporarily passed the day-to-day running over to the board and for him to remain CEO in the background with as little intervention as was required.

The house in Kent had been altered from when she first left it to be married. For them all to be able to call it their family home, Edward had persuaded her that they buy the land to the side and apply for planning to fully extend the property. A full move from the city would require them to create staff quarters, as well as extra bedrooms and guest accommodation. The land to the side had a small cottage and though Lottie knew the older couple who had settled there several years before, she felt guilty asking them to move. The attractive price tag that they had been offered ensured that the couple would have no more money worries for the rest of their lives, and within a month they had gone to a villa in Portugal. Mrs B had fallen in love with the cottage and after many months of negotiation Gerald had been granted a permanent place in the UK, so the stables had also been converted to give him a great apartment. A god send once the girls had come along because Edward did not want a nanny.

The plans took a few months to pass, but as soon as the builders had gone in it was little under a year to see the house totally transformed and then only a few weeks before the penthouse was closed, and they moved in. The only thing that was the same was how the house looked from the front; the rest of the building had been increased to almost three times the original size, with a new pool, double kitchens, and seven bedrooms all with bathrooms, dressing rooms and at least three windows or ceiling lights to get the maximum light and view of the countryside around. Although the room Lottie was in now was one of her favourites, with the large triple bath centre stage, and low windows so that the same view could be admired even as she laid reclined back, the best room was the music room. The whole room focused on the piano, which had been carefully transported from the penthouse once the house was free from workmen. The large wall of glass that sat south facing to the garden ensured that when it was open, any music would wash its way outside for all to hear. When they were closed it still gave the impression that they were outside; even when the weather was bad, the whole room came alive.

The large cream sofa placed at the back of the room was the only other piece of furniture in there. It had been designed for Edward to sit and relax without distraction to hear her play. It was a child-free zone. Lottie was insistent that little fingers needed to learn how to play, so another piano was put in the open study area.

This was not being used at the moment because, spoilt as ever, Charlie had been given a bespoke baby grand of his own for his last birthday, which sat in the side of the playroom. Although he was not reading music completely, he could pick up a tune by watching Lottie play a few times, and she was sure that the rest would come. Chelsie just bashed the keys, but ever the image of her father, when Lottie played she would sit fixed on her mother as if she could see the notes leaping from the piano into the air and remained silent until the piece was over.

'Wine?' Her husband's voice from the bathroom door broke into her thoughts.

'No, thank you,' she replied. He stepped further into the room.

'Back wash?' he asked, raising his eyebrows.

She shook her head, but quickly followed with 'Bathing partner?' He smiled.

Within a moment the white shirt that was already undone at the collar started to reveal the toned body underneath. The grey and pink tie he had worn all day had lasted until he had arrived home and Chelsie had pulled at it to wipe the jelly off her face earlier. Lottie had warned him that she could sit in the highchair on her own like her sister, but Chelsie and Edward knew the only way to stop the youngster from running around was if she sat on his knee at the table, and so the tie suffered the price of bowing to her every wish. She batted her eyes at him and like the jelly on his tie, he wobbled and caved in every time.

Lottie felt the ever-present tingle between her legs as her husband's chest was fully revealed to show the muscles in his arms, the defined ripple of his stomach and as she glanced in the large mirror his back muscles flexed as he moved closer, discarding the item to the floor. They had been to France for a long family holiday. It had started in Paris on a business meeting for Edward, but as always, his family were with him and so they made their way further up the country and stayed at the vineyard for three weeks. He had retained his tanned skin, even though they had been back for just over a month now. He ran every day, with the dog or on his own, and even with Chelsie in the running pram they had purchased. When it was warm, he would often return to the garden, remove his top and play with the children in the extensive space that had been given over to every type of outdoor play item currently on the market, keeping his bronzed colour.

The football goal posts she was sure were for him alone as he soon found that his son did not like to play with him. He always scored more goals and would never let the youngster win. Dean Junior did not like to lose and would storm off, refusing to play anymore. Lottie smiled, not just at the current view but the complete likeness of the two men in her life.

'Enjoying the view, Mrs Dean?' he asked as he made light work of his trousers and the white CK boxers that clung to his backside with elegance, but gave no hiding place for the growing, pulsating bulge he was acquiring in the front of them the closer to the water he got. He pushed them down his firm legs and she pulled herself up so that he could get in behind her.

With the increased mass in the bath the water washed over her upper body as he settled in. She felt his hardness behind her, and she closed her eyes as his arms encased her. Her head rested on his chest and he encased her left breast in his hand. They had spent hours in various bathtubs, in many different locations like this. Their own time, just for them. Many conversations, mundane, day-to-day, and important business decisions had been made in similar environments. Plans short and long-term were shared. Concerns and worries halved and laid to rest. Passions overflowed with lovemaking, arguments heated and then cooled in the same water. All the differences that had made them strong-willed individuals seemed to float around, never leaving them altogether, but these moments shared and empowered them as they joined forces, as if they were one.

'Good day all round then, Mrs Dean?' he asked, kissing the top of her head and with the free hand moving her already-damp hair out of the way of her neck to reveal the soft skin he prized so much.

'Yes, thank you, it was great to see everyone. Phil and Liz look great, I knew he would make a fantastic father.'

Phil and Liz had married after only a short engagement and she had only just given birth to their son four weeks before the party, but she was sure that they wanted to make the day out. Phil stayed in London to work for Dean Incorporated and still did some stand-in work for Pete, but he mainly stayed office-bound. Liz had soaked up the success of her fashion business, which was now bringing in a tidy sum of money and on display in over nine outlets in the capital.

Lottie paused. 'You happy?'

'Now everyone is away, the kids are tucked up with Mrs B in the cottage and you, my love, are here. I could not be happier, this is everything I need to be truly perfect,' he said, planting a kiss again, this time making his way to her ear for a nibble.

'Oh, Mr Dean, for the price of you owning me four pence I bet I can make you happier!' She had a smile on her face that he did not see until he turned her around. The water splashed over the bath but went totally unnoticed as it hit the marble flooring.

'Lottie, no!' he said, not in disbelief but joy.

'Edward, yes!' she replied, walking her fingers up his chest until they reached his lips.

'Oh my god, baby girl, when, how long?' he asked all at once.

'Let's just say, boy or girl, we could call them Paris!' He could not hold back the tear in his eye as liquid slid down his face and neck until it was consumed by the water around them. 'Let's hope it is not the same deal as last time, Mr Dean. Buy one get one free. Or at this rate, Dean Incorporated will be bankrupt by the time you are forty!'

'Mrs Dean, whatever deal I am in I will still be the richest man in the world, the richest man by far!' came the reply. 'Though we may need to steal some money to buy another small part of the village to extend the house again, if that is the case.' She splashed water in his face and he didn't stop the droplets from dripping down his skin. He moved towards her and sealed his mouth over hers.

'Mr Dean?' Pete interrupted them as they sat eating breakfast. Charlie was watching his father eat his toast and mimicking the actions he took. The past eight months had passed them by with a very normal family life. No money could change the screaming tantrums, the late nights, and the constant need to be parents. Edward was so sure he was going to be hands-on. He knew staff could step in if needed, and often they were, and as Lottie had got towards the end of her pregnancy he could see that she was tired. As beautiful as ever, after the birth she had bounced back and smiled every day to the outside world, pushing herself to the limit of her duties as a mother, and that of a very competent businesswoman. Whenever Edward thought of her, his heart would race, never understanding how it was possible to love them all more each day, but he was so sure he did.

The girls were still getting dressed. A military task, it seemed, with decisions on the clothes, hair, and final appearance. Lottie for sure would not be the one taking time to get dressed. Since the birth of their second son, she had still felt the need for flowing dresses and loose clothes. She had not found it hard to lose the baby weight, but she had somehow become very self-aware of her body. Though Edward told her every day she was the most enchanting creature he had the joy to love, she had somehow found the birth hard and a dark depression on some days came over her. Paris, as he was dutifully called, was currently sleeping silently in his cot. He had been a big baby when he was born four weeks ago and demanded his mother's attention mainly for food. Other than that, Edward was sure that Paris knew they had their hands full with his siblings and somehow just kept a low profile for any additional attention he needed, for now. He was a good, peaceful baby.

Edward took his attention back to the adult voice he had heard and looked up at the incoming member of his team, but it was his son who replied.

'Morning, Mr Peter!' He gave him a cheeky smile and Pete replied, daring to smile at the young man in front of him. 'Junior.'

Charlie looked back at Edward and the psychic understanding they seemed to have between each other in just a look indicated that the conversation which was about to come was for the grown men in the room, not for the younger ears.

'Sure, Popper, will do.' He pulled his little shoulders up and smiled a strawberry jam grin back.

Edward looked over to his son and wiped his mouth with the napkin.

'Charlie, carry on and eat your toast, and be good for Mrs B.'

The breakfast room door was closed, and a low noise of young female laughter came from the upper floor as they walked through. Edward moved out to the hallway where he looked at the closed electronic gates at the edge of the drive from the window. He looked back at Pete to carry on where he had left off.

'There is someone at the gate asking to see you, Mr Dean.' He showed no expression, but Edward knew this was not a normal visitor from his body language. They did not often have visitors to the house who had not been invited and so Edward cocked his head to the side as if there was more information about the person before he entered the grounds or the house.

If there was not more to the arrival of whoever it was, the gates would have been opened by a member of the team and they would have been shown into the house and into the reception room to wait.

'And?' Edward asked, looking for more information as to why they were here, skulking in the quiet to have this conversation.

'He said he is your father!'

And so, Let the Story End…